Burning Desires

Karen L. Rose

ISBN: 978-1-5356-1723-9

For Arleigh Sarah—Although we named you twenty years before you were born, we always knew that when you finally arrived, you would do great things. I am so proud of all you have achieved, but I am most grateful to you for never letting me forget that dreams do come true.

For Mark—We started our adventure back in high school, and your love and support have been my rock and my inspiration. Thank you, my love, for always believing in me.

Acknowledgements

Two English teachers sat together in a room and shared their love of reading and writing while grading a thousand essays. Thank you, Linda Furlong Dobinski, for starting this incredible journey with me. We shared our dreams, laughed at our escapades, and cried over our losses. You are an amazing woman and I am grateful we will always be friends.

A very special thank-you to Linda Levine. Your proofreading abilities are astounding, and I'm very appreciative of your incredible notes.

To my best friend, Robin Wilpon—you were the first to read my book and gave me wonderful encouragement. I know you are still waiting for the sequel. And to all my friends who have been so positive and supportive. I am truly blessed.

A tremendous thank-you to my family for their love and belief in me.

And to the many good people from Creede to Alamosa to Utah (specifically Pearl Baker for her encouragement)—thank you so much for your kindness and historical knowledge. Your stories have been greatly appreciated.

Contents

Acknowledgements....v
Prologue....1
Chapter 1....7
Chapter 2....20
Chapter 3....34
Chapter 4....53
Chapter 5....73
Chapter 6....84
Chapter 7....91
Chapter 8....97
Chapter 9....106
Chapter 10....113
Chapter 11....122
Chapter 12....129
Chapter 13....147
Chapter 14....174
Chapter 15....188
Chapter 16....206
Chapter 17....222
Chapter 18....246
Chapter 19....259
Chapter 20....274
Chapter 21....291
Chapter 22....305
Chapter 23....320
Chapter 24....328
Epilogue....342

Prologue

"For the mine is a tragic house,
It is the worst of prisons…"

FRANKLIN JUST DIDN'T LIKE THE feel of it. Normally, it was his job to drill the sixteen holes. He had the right touch. Harry Taylor had told him that. Even John Richards knew. But the boss had said just this morning, "Boys, we're gonna drive this tunnel clear over to Leadville if we have to. I know there's gold down there. Even Crazy Bob Womack's been hunting around here because he knows it, too. I want the whole Mother Lode down there, men."

Franklin worried. This new guy, name of Bobby J. Macmont, who hailed all the way from the Savage Mine in Nevada, was the new tamper today. He'd been working the Comstock Lode and just up and left. No one knew why. Men out here did all kinds of crazy things without no reason.

Franklin backed off. He leaned his worn body against the hard rock wall. The cold seeped through his blue cotton vest. He thought of his wife, Sarah, who was probably sitting right near the cave opening. Always did, that woman. And his daughter, Jolyn. She was a younger version of his wife with his sparkling blue eyes and rich auburn hair. Franklin sighed. He wanted to strike it rich for them. For them and his two sons out in Creede living with his brother. He'd promised Sarah this would be their last stake. No matter what, when this line ran dry they were heading for Creede and would make their living out there. Heard there were some good mines out in them parts, anyway.

The new man glanced over at Franklin. Franklin was helping him set up the dynamite sticks. It was perilous to be down in the tunnels at any time, but blowing out a new path was the most treacherous. Why, the last time Franklin was winzing over at Telluride the man next to him had slid and gotten his legs caught so badly they had to amputate them just to get him out.

The silence in the cave hung like the dew clinging to the rocks. Franklin nodded his head, tacitly giving Bobby the go-ahead.

And the new boy tamped in his first hole.

The men shifted their feet, bored and anxious and ready to drill. The waiting was the hard part, but they waited.

And the boy tamped in his second hole.

Franklin was tired and hoped the new kid would finish the job soon. Maybe this cocky boy wasn't so bad after all. He looked over at his friend, W. J. Curtis. W. J. had had a bad time of it over at Telluride and decided to head east to Clear Creek County. After this he claimed he was gonna go south to Cripple Creek, and then who knew? But that was the life of a miner.

The fourth hole was tamped in. A little roughly, Franklin thought. Easy, boy. Do her easy. Still a long way to go.

Franklin's eyes scanned the cool, cramped hole they called a dream. The men who lined the rough walls were a motley crew with hopes a mile high. Patience breathed audibly through their mouths and their dark eyes never left Bobby's hands.

And the sixth hole was tamped in.

Franklin whispered to W. J., "You got any extra caps in yer pocket jest in case this green boy forgot his?"

"No, sir. Not me. Not anymore."

W. J. smiled at Franklin in the glow of the carbide lamp. Franklin could spot the lump of wet, soggy weed as it lay buried in the dark cavern of his mouth.

"What's so funny?" asked Franklin.

"Well, sir, I heerd tell of a man over in Leadville. Seems he was carrying a few extra caps in his pocket. Well, one day this feller was so busy down at the gambling hall, drinking and playing and whatnot, well he jest was apaying no mind to what he was doing. Come time to refill his pipe, well, seems he emptied his cap instead and when that good ole boy lit up, hmmmmm, why, the rest is history. So, Franklin, no sir, I don't carry any extra caps in my pocket."

And the eighth hole was tamped in.

Minutes dragged on. Franklin's glazed eyes stared straight in front of him. He was tired of sweating, tired of being cramped, and tired of being tired.

"Hey, Franklin. Over here, man. I need you."

The other men watched as Franklin walked over to the new kid. The men had heard something they didn't like in that boy's voice—fear. All eyes were on Franklin.

"What's up, Bobby? Hit a snag?"

"Well, uh, I'm not real sure. This one just doesn't want to go in right."

Carefully, Franklin eased his worn body over near Bobby. Bobby quickly scanned the group of men, but his pleading eyes were lost on this group. Their lives depended on him, and forgiveness was not part of the plan.

Franklin took off his wide-brimmed hat and scratched his head. He slowly untied his dusty bandanna and wiped the sweat off his forehead and his neck, grimy with rock dust. He leaned very close to Bobby and whispered so that the others would not hear him.

"Just take yer time. These men have all the confidence in the world in you," he lied. "Take a deep breath and let it out slowly. Then double-check where your caps are and where your sticks are and begin again. Sometimes when you hit a deadlock like thissun, all you really have to do is slide down the tunnel a bit more to this side and get a fresh start. I'm with you, son. Go on."

Bobby's taut body relaxed with Franklin's soothing words and he replied gratefully, "Thanks, Franklin. I'll, uh…I can do it now."

And the ninth hole was tamped in.

Up above on this beautiful March morning, the cloudless Colorado sky shone a brilliant blue. White stretches of snow still graced the peaks of the mountains that loomed knowingly nearby.

Franklin yawned. He was tired, more so than usual. He grabbed his pickax and treaded to the farthest corner of the tunnel, being careful not to kick up too much dust with his boots. He eased his tall frame into a break in the wall and sat down, clutching his tool.

The kid tamping into the tenth hole was busy cursing his luck. He still had six more holes to tamp down and he was already worn out. He wasn't paying too much attention to the capping, and he should have had a break.

A cold chill slid down Franklin's arms and he bolted his head up. He stared at Bobby as he fumbled with the cap. Franklin tried to get up, but his legs had cramped up beneath him and he only fell forward on his knees.

"Bobby, wait! NO!" Franklin yelled, and suddenly all eyes widened and filled with fear.

The camp itself had no forewarning. There was a low thud as if thunder had ominously worked its way into this clear, cloudless day. The rest of the topside miners had time to look at each other in wonder as if to say, "Well, I do declare. Could that be a storm?"

Young Robert J. Macmont was tamping in his tenth hole when the cap accidentally exploded. The scorching whoosh rolled like a blazing wave of fire, strewing chunks of hard granite and bits of smashed timber out of its way. The rushing roiling gust of detonated dynamite rocketed the miners off the ground. Bodies and lumber and rock surged upward, crashing into the granitic ceiling, colliding together before descending into one lifeless heap. Limbs convulsed and torsos jerked as the dust settled. There was no time for screaming, no time for crying, no time for praying.

The dull roar rumbled up to the mouth of the tunnel, carrying in its destructive path severed body parts and other debris and spewing them out into the cold, clean mountain air.

Sarah, sitting quietly by the tunnel entrance, felt only a gentle quake below her feet before she was thrown one hundred feet in the air. Her head smacked into a solid rock wall, shattered, and she died instantly. The dead body of Harry Taylor, who was on his way out of the tunnel, was found alongside Sarah's. Mangled body fragments, boots, tools, strips of work clothes, and blood scattered the opening of the entranceway.

Those miners who were not blown away from the actual explosion died minutes later as the splintered timbers shattered and crumpled their tossed bodies. The sappers on top rushed to the scene but were unable to enter the underground passage because of the deadly gasses—the aftermath of an explosion.

Whatever miners survived the eruption and the crushing beams suffocated from these noxious gasses.

Jolyn Montgomery, working inside her parents' cabin, lifted her head and looked out the window. She didn't like the low reverberating rumble and knew something was about to happen. For a split second she thought she heard her mother's whisper as though her mother was standing behind her, and she spun around, almost falling. And then the deep ripple grew into a sonorous roar, and she raced out the door.

As the great boom resounded and pierced the peace of the camp, Jolyn lifted her head to the innocent sky and screamed violently, but no living soul heard her.

Chapter 1

Jolyn wiped the perspiration from her brow. She bent her head forward, her long auburn hair cascading across her slim back, and concentrated on the small stitches she was making.

"Now, Doc," she said soothingly, "these stitches in your arm need time to heal. I don't want you doing any sluicing until I tell you it's time."

"Yes, Miss Jolyn," Doc Weathering dutifully replied.

Jolyn tied the final knot of her stitching. She placed her tools in the leather pouch, the one her mother had made for her just before she… Jolyn did not want to think about that right now. She gazed upon the old miner in front of her. His wide-brimmed hat hung low, covering his glassy eyes. She had given him enough whiskey to numb the pain for the rest of the day. Drops of the copper-colored liquid still clung to the white stubble around his cracking lips. His greasy, long mustache had pieces of tobacco still clinging to it. Yellow teeth, tobacco-stained from years of chawing, sparkled in the morning sunlight. Doc was one of the lucky survivors. He had been within fifty feet of the tunnel entrance and had been injured when a pickax sliced the skin of his arm as it flew by.

Doc reached into his worn pockets and pulled out a frayed blue-and-white handkerchief. Arthritic fingers held the prized possession out to Jolyn.

"Miss Jolyn?"

"Yes, Doc. What can I do for you?" Jolyn was buried in her medicine bag, sorting out her bottles of quinine, hartshorn, and laudanum. She half turned her head to see Doc holding his dead wife's most valued article.

"For yer face," he offered.

Jolyn accepted the tattered cloth and slowly wiped the sweat from her smooth face.

Doc's wide smile exposed a few golden caps from better days. He was drunk. He didn't know which was better, guzzling all the whiskey Jolyn had made him swallow or sitting here so close to Jolyn. She was the sweetest young thing he had seen in a long time. There were few pleasures a man of his age could still have, a good drink of booze and a look at a pretty gal.

Jolyn gently folded the age-worn material and handed it back to Doc. He's such an old coot, she thought tenderly. He's a lucky old codger to have survived that blast the way he did.

Jolyn collected her bag, put on her large straw hat that had some early spring flowers stitched on the brim, and stood up. Automatically her soft blue eyes scanned the camp, searching for her mother.

Doc, seeing what Jolyn was doing, spat out some of his tobacco juice, chawed for a few seconds, and said, "I'm real sorry about your ma, Miss Jolyn. She sure was a special lady. And yer pa, too. Why, he was the one that told the boss to let me work here without putting up so much of a grubstake. A good man he was."

Jolyn sighed, fighting back the tears again. "Well, I'd best be getting back to the main cabin and see what else needs doing. Between the burying and the doctoring, I haven't had much time for mourning."

Doc was sympathetic, having gone through this in his life. "Sometimes," he said knowingly, "that's the best way. It helps you to keep on going, keep on living, even if it's to help the others."

Impulsively, Jolyn walked up to Doc and hugged him tightly. The old man, with his hands still dangling at his sides, was suddenly uncomfortable and tried to change the subject. "I hear your sweetheart has been the one doing most of the digging seeing's how almost all the men around were either killed or injured."

Jolyn stepped back, a small fire blazing in her blue eyes. "He is not my boyfriend. We are just good friends! That's all!"

Doc laughed. This was the Jolyn he knew, full of life. Grabbing her things, Jolyn turned around and sauntered off toward the center of the camp.

Jolyn examined the place she had called home for the last few months as she strolled through. It wasn't the worst camp she had seen in her life, and she had seen quite a few. There were a dozen or so temporary wooden shacks. One larger building stood in the middle, and the men used it for general meetings on Fridays, bloodthirsty poker games on Saturdays, and prayer meetings on Sundays. Most of the men ate their evening meal there and told their tales of love and gold, both lost and found. The whole camp was temporary, including the friendships. The Montgomerys were here to strike it rich and then to move on to Creede. Her father wanted to do it all by himself, but she recalled how her mother had fought him.

"Franklin Montgomery, I will not go to Creede without you. I will be by your side in good times and bad and that's all there is to that. Jolyn can stay with me. I will keep her up with her learning and she will be a great help at the camp."

Jolyn smiled. Her mother was a treasure. Stubborn and beautiful and smart. That was what everyone had always told her. And it was true. And if she were here right now she'd probably scold me for resting and thinking instead of helping the others. And there was much to be done.

Jolyn gently pushed back a lock of her hair that had found its way again onto her damp face. The dirt clung to her sweat and clothes and seemed to encompass the young woman. The gritty material rubbed along her teeth and crowded underneath her newly broken nails. She was too busy with burying the miners to take care of herself right now. They had built coffins out of pine and placed the deceased in a makeshift parlor that had been the general meeting hall. As the dead lay in repose, Jolyn moved as if under a spell.

She was completely exhausted. Her body ached, unaccustomed to this new type of work, leaving her stiff and sore. In her head, Jolyn repeatedly heard the explosion. It was a thundering roar that would not go away. Jolyn sighed uncontrollably.

Looking toward the shack near the tracks, she spied James. He was her friend, had been ever since they met on the first day the Montgomerys arrived. It all happened because her daddy wanted to live in the cabin farthest away from the camp. Franklin wanted to wake up in the morning and see the mountains that cradled the camp with pinecones and columbine instead of a bunch of smelly miners on their way to that day's dreams.

Jolyn's heart tugged as she saw her father's smile as he surveyed his mountain view. Trouble was, she remembered, James's father had claimed the same cabin and had earlier rights on it. Jolyn giggled as she recalled James's face when the two fathers met face to face. First Jolyn had introduced herself to James, and then for no reason at all he had declared, "I think, Father, that the Montgomerys should have the cabin. I personally prefer the one next to it, if that's fine with you."

His father had been so flabbergasted that he stumbled and muttered and then finally whispered yeah, turned around, and left. Ever since then she and James had been the best of friends. Rarely were there any girls her age at the camps. She had grown up with twin brothers who kept her knobby knees scraped and her tree-climbing legs agile, so friendship with James was nothing new to her.

Jolyn marched straight toward James. She needed to talk with him, be with him. Ever since the accident the two had become even closer. James had lost his father down in the mine, too.

Down by the tracks, coffins were being loaded into one of the boxcars. They would travel up to Denver, where they would be transported to family and then properly buried. The others would be interred here in the camp, especially those without any family.

Jolyn finally spotted James, tall and strong, with a shock of thick brown hair hanging over his eyes, as he sweated and strained with his work.

"Hi, James," she called.

James looked up. A warm smile split his dirt-streaked face.

"Howdy yerself."

"James," she began," are you almost done?" She knew she had interrupted him, but he seemed to enjoy the intrusion.

"It's just about lunchtime," she continued. "I thought you might want to come up to the cabin for lunch. That is, of course, if you have the time."

James smiled and stretched his back. He moaned and rubbed his shoulders. "Sure, Jolyn. I always have time for you."

Jolyn blushed. She knew James was just teasing her. He always did that, which was why everyone thought he was her boyfriend. But James had confided in her long ago that he had a girlfriend back in Utah. In fact, he planned to marry her just as soon as he had enough money.

Jolyn laughed as she called back, "And don't you be late, either, Mr. Curtis, or I'll be serving your lunch to the rabbits and woodchucks outside my window."

"So it's animal food you've got cooking for me now. Well, I'll be sure and find time to get to your place early. Wouldn't want those fat animals you keep feeding on the side to get any heavier. They might not be able to make it on their own, elsewise."

Jolyn smiled, tipped her flowered hat, and strolled away. She had been feeding most of the injured miners in the general meeting hall these past few days, but she always kept a special part of the day for James. And today was no different.

On the way back to her cabin she stopped and checked in with several of the men. They were all in the process of cleaning out their belongings; they were getting ready to move on. Breaking down this camp would take a few more days and then they all had their plans. Some were heading toward Leadville, others to Cripple Creek. Still others were going to go as far as California to try their luck. Nothing would hold them down, not a mining disaster, nothing.

Jolyn stared at her cabin as she approached it. The Montgomery shack was just that. Bits of wood and sweat with a few colorful curtains to camouflage the barren interior. Her mother had always tried to call it home, but Jolyn refused.

"It's just a shack, Ma. That's all it is. Just a pile of wood that's aching to fall down. When I have a house of my own, I know exactly what I'll have in it."

"Is that so?" her mother had asked, her twinkling eyes looking lovingly at her dreamy-eyed daughter. "And what will be in this grand place you call your home?"

Jolyn would not let her mother's gentle teasing deflate her picture. "I'll have white linen curtains on all my windows. Fresh flowers on my table every day. And nowhere will I ever tack on newspapers to my walls!" she cried as she looked at the newspaper that lined great portions of their walls.

"Well," continued her mother, "I do hope you marry rich, my child. Marry for happiness and for love, but try to add in rich!" Sarah had leaned her head back and laughed deep and hearty because she knew her daughter was just like her and would marry only for love. She enjoyed baiting her anyway. Sarah took her only daughter by the shoulders and whispered, "My dear Jo. I love you so much. I only pray good things for you. May happiness always be with you, my child. And if it's not, may you have the courage to go and seek it!"

"Oh, Ma." Jolyn had hugged her mother tightly, not knowing that that would be their last quiet talk and embrace. Two heads, both ablaze with russet locks, one tinged with gray streaks, leaned softly against each other and whispered privately, each nourishing the other with respect and love that only a mother and daughter could share.

Jolyn was still thinking about her mother when James strolled in. Her face was pale and her eyes misty as she stared at the mass of dough beneath her hands. She didn't hear James come in, nor did she hear him hang up his hat and clean up.

James sat down next to Jolyn quietly and gazed at her. He rolled down his worn blue work shirt. Normally he would have sneaked up behind her and tickled her or pulled her hair or something. She was like a kid sister to him. More. Sisters and brothers didn't always get along, and they did. He could tell her anything. His dreams, his girl, Nattie, even about his wish for his father to see him as a successful rancher and not some die-hard miner always digging for a dream. James waited a long time before he spoke.

"Jo? Are you all right, Jo?"

Jolyn sensed someone was calling her, but remained lost in her thoughts.

"Jolyn. Jolyn Montgomery, it's me, James."

Just then Jolyn snapped into focus. She took a deep breath. Fighting. She would not give in now. There would be time to mourn, but not yet. She sighed.

"Are you okay, Jo?" James asked softly.

"I'm fine, James." She smiled, but the happiness did not reach her eyes, and James knew.

"Sometimes, Jolyn, you just gotta let out yer feelings. I mean, hey, you keep them all bottled up inside and one day, well, one of these days, I swear you're just gonna bust."

"Honest, James, I'll be just fine. Now, you take a taste of my stew today and tell me that it is the absolute best and finest stew you have ever eaten!"

James was starved. He dug into the fare, and Jolyn didn't hear from him again until his plate was clean and he asked for a second helping.

"Jo?"

"Yes, James?"

"You know them tools your daddy's kept back in the cabin all winter?"

"Mm-hmm."

"Well…I was thinking if maybe I could borrow them. I swear I'll give them back to you sometime. It's just that I've been thinking about going back to Utah and starting up my ranch and all."

"You're leaving?" Jolyn's eyes widened with surprise.

"Well, not right away. There's still a bit more work to be done around here. At least another week or so. Well, then I thought I would head down cross southern Colorado and then over to Utah. I want to get to Nattie and see if her daddy will give us that piece of land he's been promising us. Then I could buy a few head of cattle and start my ranching."

Jolyn hesitated. She wasn't sure what she was going to do with her parents' belongings. Some of the clothes and tools she was going to give away to the miners and some of the personal items, well, she wanted to keep those for herself. But what would she do with all those things anyway?

James, having finished his dinner, stood up. He belched, laughed, and then, like a mischievous boy, whispered, "You got any of yer daddy's tobacco left?"

"Why, yes, he had some hidden from Ma in the back drawer. I'll go get some."

The two spent the next couple of hours relaxing and talking.

A rescue team had come in from Denver to help dig out the bodies and James was telling Jolyn some of the details.

"They found your daddy, Jo," James said haltingly. He wasn't sure if he wanted to tell Jolyn all the gory details.

"Are you sure it was him?" She knew that most of the miners they'd pulled up were not recognizable at all. It was only bits and pieces of clothing that sometimes identified the deceased.

"'Fraid so." James continued, "It seems like yer daddy had jest sat down in a corner. They found him all hunched up. And you know what else?"

Jolyn hesitated. She wasn't sure she wanted to know this part. She took a deep breath and let it out slowly. When she tried to answer James, her voice was barely a whisper.

"Go on, James. Tell me the rest."

James was too caught up in his reenactment to realize how Jolyn was reacting.

"Would you believe they found him still holding on to his pickax? Jest holding on to that tool as if in another minute he would stand up and say, 'Okay, boys, let's do some more digging.'"

Jolyn swallowed and then cleared her throat. She looked away for a moment and then back at James.

"Did you send off Mama and Daddy on the train today, James?"

"Yes, Jo. They'll get 'em down to Creede sure enough."

"You know I have an uncle and two brothers living there. They're working in some kind of store."

"Why don't you go on down there to be with them, Jo? They're your family."

"I don't know, James. I just don't know. I haven't seen any of them in almost a year now. You know we had always planned on going back there to live. And then Daddy would hear about another mine somewhere and off the three of us would go, lock, stock, and barrel. Mama was getting awful tired of it. She always threatened Daddy that she'd just take me and leave him alone. But she never did. She loved him too much. Do you think I'll ever love someone that much?"

James thought, chewed his finger for a minute, and then smoothed out a wrinkle in his forehead. "I think so, Jo. I love Nattie real hard. Why, I'd do anything fer her. That's why I want to borrow your daddy's tools. I need a head start on my ranching and his tools will come in mighty handy. I'll get in touch with you and ship them back to wherever you are. Maybe you want to come and live with Nattie and me for a while?"

"That's an idea, James. I'll have to think on that for a bit. Besides, you know Mrs. Fletcher?" James nodded his head and Jolyn continued, "She asked me if I could stay with her for a few days or so until her daughter could come. She's too old to be alone now that she lost her husband."

"Where's her daughter?"

"I think she said something about California. She told me she sent her a telegram and now she's waiting for her to come get her."

James stood up and stretched. "Well, you jest let me know what you decide. I'd best be going back. They need all the hands they can get. Will you be coming by later?"

"I'm not sure, James. Take care of yourself, you hear?"

James had already grabbed his hat, and bounded out the door and down the stairs, yelling his goodbyes into the air. Jolyn gathered up her dishes, stacked them in her pail, and headed toward the small creek behind the cabin.

This was her very private, very special place, thought Jolyn, as she made her way down toward her haven. The aspens were just beginning to bloom as she dodged in and out of their personal maze in the woods. Snow buttercups graced the foothills of the mountains that soared above the treetops, watchful and commanding. Small grouse flitted around her feet as she skittered among the soft pine.

The creek was swollen. Icy-cold water rushed over slippery rocks, cleaning away the varicolored lichens until they shone. On the edge of the heavy stream, nestled in clumps among the rocks, blossomed pasqueflowers, pale and dainty. A sweet, pine-scented breeze tickled Jolyn's senses.

Jolyn squatted. This was Sioux country. Sometimes Jolyn passed the time looking for arrowheads buried under the rocks. But not today. Jolyn had chores to finish and then she wanted to check on Doc once more.

She scrubbed her plates clean and set them on the ground to dry. Jolyn was tired. Scooping a handful of the frigid water, she splashed her face. She sat back and let the sun that split through the trees warm her young face.

It was peaceful and quiet. Only an occasional woodpecker tapping on a tree in the distance could be heard. Suddenly a crashing sound broke the silence. Startled, Jolyn whipped her head around and saw James running through the woods at great speed.

"Jolyn! Where are you? They need you! JO! Where are you?"

Jolyn jumped up, forgetting about her drying face and plates.

"Down here, James. By the creek. What's wrong?" she shouted.

James, spotting her through the woods, came running and hopping over fallen logs.

"You've got to come quick, Jo! There's been another accident. You've got to come down to the mine." James was out of breath and was having a hard time finishing his sentence.

James grabbed Jolyn by the hand to help her up the embankment and together they raced back to the camp. Before she reached the mine, Jolyn could hear the flurry of men shouting and screaming and running back and forth.

James pulled her along. "Make way, men. I got Jolyn here. Make a hole and make it wide, men. I got Jolyn here with me. Where is he? Where did you put that man?"

"He's over yonder, young Jim. Out under the big tree," an old miner volunteered.

Two men came rushing up to Jolyn.

"Miss Montgomery," one of them blurted out. "It all happened so quick. One minute we was in there collecting some things and the next minute we was out. Then suddenly, nary a second later, there come a whoosh and swish jest like the big explosion before and that man just crumpled in a heap."

The second man was speechless. His bearded mouth was wide open and his bloodshot eyes were stretched to their limit. He was nodding his head up and down so fast Jolyn thought he was going to get dizzy and faint.

"It's going to be all right, Mr. Douglas. Slow down, Mr. Jerome. I'm here now. Take me to the man." Jolyn spoke calmly and deliberately.

The injured man, one of the rescue team members, had tried moving some of the timbers that still buried some of the dead miners. Unfortunately, he had loosened some of the joints that held the ceiling taut and it had crashed on top of him.

Jolyn raced over to the man, taking off her leather pouch as she ran. Someone had brought over a bucket with water and a rag. She gently wiped the blood from his face. He was still conscious, still breathing, but barely.

Jolyn turned her head to the men behind her. "Mr. Douglas, what's his name?"

Ezekiel Douglas scratched his chin. "Why, I'm not sure. Oh, oh, now I remember. It's a city name. Tamermind. Louis Tamermind."

"Mr. Tamermind," Jolyn whispered. "Mr. Tamermind. Louis. This is Jolyn Montgomery. I'm here to help you. What hurts the most, Mr. Tamermind?"

Louis Tamermind struggled to find his voice. Blood covered his lips and bits of rock and dust clung to it. In a very weak voice he mumbled, "It's…my back…I think…it's broken."

Jolyn dampened the rag again and cleaned out his mouth as best she could. She was unaware of how the entire camp had now formed a semi-circle around her, watching her, praying for her and the injured man.

Jolyn had learned many things from her mother and her grandfather, but a broken back was beyond her skills. Delicately, methodically, she ripped his shirt in two and carefully peeled it off his body. Louis Tamermind groaned in pain and lost consciousness. Quickly Jolyn placed another cold rag on his forehead. His upper torso was twisted unnaturally, and she held her two hands over his chest and then paused as if thinking about her next move. She pulled away and fell to her knees. She grabbed her cotton slip and began ripping strips of the thin material. Satisfied, she stood up and leaned over the sleeping man. Taking great care, she slipped each strip of cotton under the man's body. Slowly she wrapped him, and he seemed to straighten out.

Jolyn looked up for James and, finding him, beckoned him to come over. "James, help me lift him onto that board over there." She didn't realize it, but Jolyn was pointing at a coffin cover. "He needs to lie flat."

Together the two bent down to hoist up Louis. Out of nowhere a dozen more hands bent down with theirs. Jolyn looked up to see six or eight of the miners, some of them injured themselves, bending down to help. Her eyes misted with gratitude and together they carried Mr. Tamermind to the board.

He looked awkward there on top of the coffin, out of place and yet not so. Someone, she wasn't sure who it was, passed her a flask, intending for the young woman to take a drink. Instead she doused her handkerchief and moistened the man's lips. The drink seemed to revive him.

With glassy eyes he looked up at Jolyn. "I can't feel my legs," he groaned, "I can't feel anything. What's… "

Jolyn looked straight into his dying eyes. "Relax, Mr. Tamermind. You've been hurt bad but we're doing the best we can for you." She pressed her hand against his cheek and smoothed his brow.

"Thanks, miss. You are the purtiest…gal I've…ever… Thank… you… " And then Louis Tamermind died.

For one fleeting second she felt a surge rush through her that took her breath away, and then it was gone. Hot tears suddenly poured down Jolyn's bloodstained cheek. She didn't bother to wipe them away. They slid down quietly, mixing with blood and grime, burning away her youth. She sobbed and swiped angrily at her face.

This was too much. It was not ending. The sorrow, the pain, the dying. Without any warning James was right beside her, holding her as she still held on to the dead man.

"Jolyn," James pleaded, "Jo, is there anything I can do for you?"

"Yes, James," Jolyn cried, "there is. Can you take me to Creede?"

Chapter 2

"JAMES," JOLYN CALLED EXCITEDLY AS she tripped along the uneven carpet of spongy leaves and protruding roots toward the main trail.

"James!" She reached the clearing where James patiently waited by the horses. "Look what I've found. Do you think we can save her?"

When Jolyn darted onto the trail, James glanced appreciatively over Jo's trim figure, so unlike his Nattie's. Her auburn curls, which danced in delicate disarray about her creamy face, were a vivid contrast to his Nattie's dark and steady profile. Jolyn's lightly tanned skin was flushed with excitement, and her deep-blue eyes sparkled like a mountain lake. She was beauty and light, and sometimes he wondered if he hadn't met Nattie first…

Even now he could recall that moment when Jolyn and her parents had first arrived nearly a year ago at the mining camp. She had lithely stepped down from her parents' overloaded wagon and had found herself surrounded by a sea of scraggly miners. Small and delicate, she had gazed at their wistful grizzled faces as they silently stood gripping their hats with worn and callused hands. Raising her chin a notch and squaring her shoulders, she had smiled shyly at the men, at him, and in that moment she had captured the heart of every lonesome miner there. She reminded them of all of the womenfolk lost or left behind, and somehow just being with her brought each one of them closer to that dusty memory.

So, after the mining explosion, when Jolyn had asked him to take her to Creede, he had grabbed the chance. He would drop Jolyn safely off at her uncle's, and then head southward toward Utah, where he could settle down with Nattie on a small horse farm. Being with Jolyn for the past week made him more eager than ever to see that dream come true.

"James!" Jolyn cast him an impatient glance. Her head was bent reverently over something she held in her cupped hands.

With a murmur to the horses, he dropped the reins and shuffled to her side. He peered through a veil of coppery tresses at the object she held gingerly in her slender hands. A red-breasted nuthatch, its blue wing dangling awkwardly at its side, lay nestled in her palm.

"Dang. Is she alive?" he whispered.

"Yes, but she's hurt. Do you think we can save her?"

"I don't know. She looks awful weak."

"I found her hidden alongside of a log. Her wing is broken, and she could barely move. I think she's starving. What do you suppose a little bird like this eats?"

Standing so close to her, James could not help but think of Nattie. Wisps of Jo's soft hair tickled his cheek, and her body gently swayed against him as she breathed. Her warmth radiated from her smooth skin, and memories of lying with Nattie in sun-kissed fields came rushing back.

"Well?" She looked at him inquiringly.

James looked at her flushed face. She was so innocent, even more innocent than his Nattie. She had no idea of the devastating effect she had on men. Well, for as long as the trip would take, he was determined to protect her from any harm.

"James!"

"Oh, sorry, Jolyn. Guess my mind was wanderin'. What did you say?"

She heaved an exaggerated sigh. Every now and then James's mind would start wandering, and she knew that he was thinking of Nattie again.

"I was wondering if you could find some food for her. Maybe if we could build up her strength, we might be able to save her."

"Sure, I know just where to look. You wait here. I'll be back as quick as a jackrabbit." James headed off in the direction from which Jolyn had just come.

Jolyn hunkered down and waited. James had been a godsend. Having traveled extensively with his father before they had settled in Clear Creek

County, James had become an experienced guide. His knowledge had carried them over quite a few rough spots during the past two weeks. Along the way he had taken the time to explain the trail signs and to teach her rudimentary survival skills. Even though she had moved often with her folks, she knew very little about mountain travel, and despite her handiness with a rifle and six-shooter, she doubted that she would have made it to Poncha Pass without him.

He had understood her need to be alone when memories of her parents had engulfed her, and yet he had also known when to tease her out of her melancholy moods. He would roll his laughing brown eyes, tell a silly tale, then twang on that foolish Jew's harp of his. James was a good friend.

She heard some thrashing in the undergrowth and nearly jumped out of her skin when James suddenly popped out. He dropped to his knees and peeled back the frayed corners of his folded handkerchief. In the center squirmed a dozen wood maggots.

"Worms?" Jolyn looked doubtfully at the wiggling mass.

"She'll love them." James nodded. "Since she's too weak to feed herself, you pry her mouth open, and I'll see if I can shove one of them into her beak."

With surprising efficiency, they achieved the required feat. The nuthatch feebly swallowed the worm and managed a second with a little more zeal. Together, Jolyn and James managed a makeshift splint for its wing out of twigs and string that James collected. Jolyn padded her left breast pocket with a clean handkerchief and guided the bird into the pocket. It snuggled with a weak "yank" into the cotton nest and closed its eyes.

"Thanks, James."

"My pleasure." James glanced upward at the sun that was tipping gently toward the west. "Let's head on out. I want to try and make it through the pass by nightfall."

With James leading, they guided their mounts along the winding trail. Aspen and white fir rose majestically upward, their multi-green leaves forming elusive patterns, like a giant stain-glassed window through which the sun's rays filtered against the earth's chestnut floor. The soft trilling notes of the Audubon's warbler, the hoarse whistle of the mountain chickadee, and the raucous cry of a Steller's jay joined in chorus. Occasionally, through the trees, they would catch a glimpse of the burnished craggy mountains in the distance. Dark-green spruce rose thin and spiked halfway up the mountainside, and sparse white patches of snow covered the crevasses above. Suspended in a pale shimmering sky, thin wisps of clouds wafted above the copper peaks. All too quickly, the mountains slipped from view, and the trees surrounded them once again. Like a healing balm, the peacefulness of the day soothed the raw wounds that the mining disaster had rent only a few weeks before.

After a few hours, Jolyn and James stopped to feed the nuthatch. The bird voraciously attacked five of the remaining maggots, and then, much to James's and Jolyn's delight, settled quite contentedly into Jolyn's pocket, its beak perched comfortably on the edge.

"Well," James chuckled as he remounted, "since I s'pose we'll be keepin' her till her wing is healed, what'll we call her?"

"I don't know. How about Nutty? It's not very original, but I think it suits her. What do you think?"

"Nutty. I think it's perfect." The nuthatch chose that moment to pipe a few lusty yanks. "You see, even she approves of it," he laughed.

Feeling carefree for the first time since the disaster, Jolyn joined in his merriment.

"Anyone hearing us would think that we had gone plumb crazy," he chuckled.

Jolyn nodded in agreement.

"It's been a coon's age since I've heard you laugh like that. It's right pleasin'."

Jolyn's laughter faded, and James could have kicked himself for his mistake. He paused and cleared his throat.

"It seems a shame, but I guess we'd better be pushin' on. We've got at least three more hours of good travelin' time. That ought to get us to Alamosa by tomorrow."

"Alamosa? By tomorrow? Oh, James, that means we'll make it to Creede before the week is out."

"Now, hold on a minute. I know that you're in a surefire hurry to see your brothers, but I had a mind to rest up a day or two before we headed on our final leg. We need to stock up on some supplies. I've got a few dollars put by, and I thought maybe we could rent a room and get cleaned up some. Maybe grab a steak at one of them hotel eatin' places."

Jolyn smiled at his thoughtfulness. Even though she wanted to get to Creede as soon as possible, the idea of a bath and a home-cooked meal sounded heavenly. Both of them had been riding hard for two weeks through spring storms and along muddy trails. Beans, hard biscuits, and jerky had become tiresome fare. Neither of them had changed their denims or cotton shirts since they had left Cripple Creek.

It would be wonderful, she thought, to put on a clean skirt and blouse over a clean body, and sleep on a clean, soft, well-stuffed mattress in a room with a ceiling overhead.

"You're right," she agreed. "You, me, the horses, we all need a rest. But no longer than two days, please? I was hoping to reach Uncle Hank's store before news of the explosion does. I know that they'll be worried."

"No more than two days, Jolyn," James promised. "Well, let's get movin'. Time's awastin'."

James and Jolyn built camp in a small clearing on the other side of a protective outcropping on the upper side of the trail. They had built a small fire to heat coffee and beans but planned to extinguish it as soon as darkness fell. Tucked under a narrow ledge of rock that jutted out from the rocks lay their bedrolls. On top of the ledge in Jolyn's floppy hat perched Nutty, alert to the activity of the two humans who had adopted her. James methodically bedded the horses down for the night, carefully grooming and checking them for any minor injuries. Jolyn dumped the beans, which had remained soaking all day in her watertight pouch, into a pan, added some wild mustard and molasses for flavoring, and placed the pan over the fire to heat. The coffee was already boiling, and she poured them both a cup. She walked over to where James was watering the horses.

"Coffee?"

He sighed gratefully and reached for the proffered cup. He slurped noisily.

She could barely distinguish his features in the waning light, but she saw him shiver slightly. Now that the sun had dipped out of sight, the night's chill quickly descended upon them.

"It's going to be a cold night, Jo. Unfortunately, we can only afford a small fire. With all the riffraff that's come to Colorado now that the silver mines are opening up, it gets real dangerous in the passes."

"I'll just have to keep my mind on that hot bath and warm bed you promised me in Alamosa," she called over her shoulder as she returned to the fire to rescue the beans, which sizzled angrily in the pan.

She pulled the cuff of her jacket down over her hand and quickly lifted the pan off the fire and onto a flat rock.

Without the loud hiss of the beans, they suddenly became aware of the muffled tread of approaching horses.

"The fire!" Jolyn groaned.

"It's too late," James whispered. "Get your rifle."

As James scooped up his gun and bolted into the woods, Jolyn darted toward their bedding and grabbed her father's Remington. She swiftly kicked dirt onto the fire before she slid into the bushes adjacent to the rocks. James had ducked out of sight behind the horses. Both listened intently. The oncoming horses had halted, and low, menacing voices carried upward from the nearly invisible trail below. From Jolyn's viewpoint she could discern five to six riders.

Men's voices lifted in anger.

"I tell you I saw a fire somewhere above those rocks," came a strident voice.

"So what if you did," spat a gravelly voice. "No one's gonna cause us no trouble. It's probably some lone miner on his way to find another grubstake. I bet he's sitting up their pissin' in his pants right now, hopin' we don't pay no social call."

"Yeah, but what if it isn't," the first voice sliced. "What if it's the law, or someone just itchin' to tell the law about five riders that passed through. I say we find out."

"And then what?" came a disgusted, more somber voice. "More killing? Leave it be. Why shoot a man for no good reason? Besides, you start shooting around in the dark and you're liable to blow a hole into one of us or yourself. C'mon, we're wasting time."

"I agree," Gravel-voice concurred. "I say we push on. First we got held down by that damn storm. Then Foster took sick. Thank God we left his dyin' ass behind. Then we was delayed crossing the valley. And now Shorty wants to go snipe-huntin'. Hell, we could be halfway to Leadville by now."

"Well, I don't agree," a rusty voice grated. "I say we take no chances. If anyone is up there, chances are they've been watching, and listening. And thanks to your big mouth, they now know where we're heading. We left no witnesses in Creede, and I say we leave no witnesses anywhere else."

Jolyn's hand tightened on her rifle. Creede? What had happened in Creede? She flattened herself further against the uneven ground and strained to hear the rest of the stifled conversation.

"What if it's Connor?" High-pitched said.

"It's not," a steely, passionless voice rippled outward in menacing circles.

"How can you be sure?" It was Rusty.

"You'd be dead."

His words covered them like a pall.

Somber-voice broke the stillness. "Well, Luke, you call the shots. Do we go or do we stay?"

Jolyn felt a hand press down on her shoulder and nearly jumped out of her skin. Her heart beat a crazy tattoo in her breast, and she took a shaky breath to steady herself.

"That was a damn foolish thing to do," she hissed. "I nearly screamed."

"Sorry," he whispered. "What are they sayin'?"

"They're trying to decide whether to check us out or to move on. James, they're dangerous men, I think we should leave our horses and hightail it out of here."

She glanced furtively toward the trail and gasped. The men had dismounted, and all but one, who was left standing with the horses, had disappeared.

"We've got to get out of here," she nearly sobbed with fright.

James nodded his agreement, and they both edged backward, aiming for the refuge of darkness further up the mountainside.

"Oh, no, we forgot about Nutty." Jolyn spoke unthinkingly.

They both glanced toward the slouch felt hat balanced on the ledge only feet from where they lay hiding.

"Look, if I don't make it, write a letter to Nattie. Tell her that I loved her, that I was going back to her." His warm brown eyes smiled recklessly into hers.

"No," Jolyn barely breathed. "Don't risk it. James?"

But James had already sidled into the clearing and snatched the hat from its perch.

"Idiot!" her mind shrieked.

Simultaneously she heard a gun roar like some vile obscenity. Rolling to her left, she whipped her rifle up to her shoulder and fired across the clearing.

"Run," she hollered. "I'll cover you."

Desperately, she thumbed back the hammer to full cock, swung the breech-lock back, inserted a new cartridge from her pocket into the chamber, flipped the breech-lock forward into place, and fired. Over and over, she repeated the process in an effort to form a barrage of bullets across the clearing. She was too busy to see whether or not James had made it to safety, but she could still hear his Colt, spitting lead near the rocks. If she only had a six-shooter, she might be able to pin these men down so James could get away safely. As she fired, she continued to shift to the left, slowly edging further up the hill in an effort to circle behind them. But it was becoming more and more difficult to tell where the shots were coming from. Bullets seemed to fly from all directions, and she listened with growing dread for James's answering fire.

Her rifle jammed. Panicked, she fumbled with the cartridge, her fingers wooden with fear. The cartridge popped out and rolled into the underbrush. With trembling hands, she reached into her shirt pocket for another. She slipped the cartridge in and slammed it home. With a relieved sigh, she fit the gun against her shoulder and looked down the sighting. Before her finger tightened on the trigger, she heard the click of a gun hammer drawn back and felt its icy metallic finger pressed against the nape of her neck. Frozen, she waited.

Why didn't the bloody bastard shoot?

And still she waited. The shooting had stopped. Nothing moved. No one made a sound. The acrid smoke of gunpowder singed her nostrils. She could feel more than hear her captor's breath, sawing at her back. Her arms burned from the weight of the Remington, and her fingers cramped painfully around the breech. Despite the chill, sweat trickled between her breasts and under her armpits.

Why didn't he shoot?

A callused hand roughly shoved her face into the ground. The barrel remained, cold and sinister, on her neck.

"Let go of the rifle."

She recognized the wintry voice. He was the leader.

He jabbed the gun painfully into her shoulder.

"I never ask twice."

She released her grip. Her captor gave two short whistles; then, seizing Jolyn by her hair, he jerked her to her feet and dragged her forward. She tried to turn her head toward the jutting rocks on the other side of the clearing, but her head was yanked savagely forward.

Oh, please, James, please. Don't be dead, she prayed.

"Well, lookee here," squealed High-pitched. "We done caught us a pigeon."

Three men stood casually in the dark clearing. Jolyn could barely make out their features. The one who had spoken was short, emaciated, and ferret-like. His eyes darted nervously from her face to her captors. To the left stood a large, stooped man. His craggy, pock-marked face was half-turned away from them as he stood reloading his Peacemaker, but he gave the distinct impression that he was keenly aware of everything that was happening. To his left and closing the circle stood a slim, pale young man with a strikingly handsome face. Cool and detached, he stared unblinkingly at the man who held her.

Her captor glared back.

"I thought I told you to stay with the horses."

"I thought you might need my help here." The young man shrugged.

"Riggs?"

"Dead."

All eyes turned on Jolyn. Torn and bedraggled, she appeared like some harmless rag doll dangling from a careless child's hand.

Something flickered perniciously in the young man's pale eyes, but it was quickly dampened. "I'll see to the horses. Don't take too long." He dismissed them in a glance and disappeared down the slope.

"And then there were three." Jolyn heard the jeer in her captor's voice, then felt herself released.

Before she could run, the men had formed a tight circle around her. She crouched, her eyes darting from face to face, looking for an opening, waiting for one of them to make his move, praying she could reach the knife tucked in her boot before they were on her. She felt a hand tug at her sleeve, and she slapped it away. Another brushed her leg, another her face, another her buttocks, another her breast, and another fondled her hair. They tugged, stroked, pinched, and jabbed until she was mindless with fear. Flailing wildly, she cringed away from their groping paws.

She had to think. Determinedly, she cleared her mind of what the men were doing. She had to act, and she had to do it now, before... She focused on the tormentor in front of her. Her terror-filled eyes stared into his gloating ones. He was the one, the leader, and he had kept her alive for this. For this. Not for the rape, not for the murder, but for this relentless cruelty. Howling, she charged directly at him, and struck him full-force with her body. She clawed viciously at his eyes and face, slammed the flat of her palm against his nose, and drove her knee toward his groin. He quickly caught her knee against his thigh and punched her in the jaw. He grabbed her staggering form, tossed her brutally to the ground, and towered above her.

"Stay back," he ground out between clenched teeth. The young man had returned from the horses. The two men silently retreated. Wiping the blood that poured from his nose against the back of his sleeve, he watched her intently. She would pay for this. Before he was through, she would cower at his feet and beg for him to kill her.

"Well, sweetheart," he exulted, "let's see how brave you really are."

Jolyn fought against the darkness that closed in around her. She was dimly aware that the man she had attacked now stood over her and was saying something to her, but his words were nothing more than garbled sounds carried away by the wind. She felt light slaps against her cheeks, and she feebly tried to push the hand away. Then an iron grip clamped down upon her jaw. Excruciating pain lashed through her face and stung her into awareness. She stared upward into deadly gray eyes.

Just for a moment, he wavered, her crystal-blue eyes reminding him so much of his gentle baby sister's, but then he saw the defiance that lurked not far beneath the surface. Enraged, he fell upon her, ripping her shirt and bodice, tearing at her belt buckle and pants. Jolyn was no match for his strength. He effortlessly batted her arms aside and backhanded her to the ground. He straightened, his knees now straddling her waist, and reached for his pant buttons.

Gasping and sobbing, Jolyn tried to wrench away. She was lost, lost. Then she remembered the knife. Swiftly, she lunged upward and reached around his left thigh. She slipped her hand into her boot and fumbled for the handle. It was there. It slid, hard and smooth, into her hand, and she swung it in an arc toward his back. Luke turned to pull her back down and caught the plunging knife against his cheek. It sank in at the temple and carved a jagged path to his jaw. Luke fell back with a shocked cry, his hand uselessly attempting to stem the flow of blood.

Jolyn stared blindly at the bloody knife still clutched in her hand. My God, what had she done? Horrified, she dropped the blade and slowly backed away.

"Get her," her attacker screamed.

Terrified, Jolyn flew into the night. She scrambled up the hill, desperately seeking a place to hide. Branches whipped against her face and arms as she madly dashed through the trees. On and on she stumbled, praying she could outdistance them. Her foot caught against a protruding root, and she crashed to the rocky ground. She lay stunned, her mind reeling.

Where were they? Had they followed her?

To her left, only feet away, she heard a branch snap. She pressed her scraped palm against her mouth and choked back a sob.

"Shorty?" The whisper came from ahead of her. She had nearly fallen into his arms.

"Yeah?" He had not moved.

"Do you see anything?"

"Nah, it's as dark as the grave."

"She's got to be close." Gravel-voice had moved farther to her right, but was still a few yards ahead.

"If we don't find the bitch, thar's goin' to be hell to pay." Shorty had moved closer.

Jolyn edged slowly backward, her eyes searching for a place to hide.

"Shh."

She stopped, pressing her face tightly against the ground. Thank God she was wearing dark clothing.

"Hear anything?" Shorty hissed.

"Jesus, I nearly blew your fucking head off." They had both moved to her right, still a few feet beyond where she lay.

She sidled noiselessly to her left and smacked against an outcropping. She froze, straining to hear an answering shout. Nothing. She felt along the rock and discovered that it framed some kind of an opening. How wide or how deep an opening she wasn't sure.

"Damn." Shorty's high-pitched whine seemed to come from directly above her. "Steavens, I think I see something."

She heard the booted feet come racing toward her. This was her only chance. Hoping their footsteps would cover the noise, she scrambled into the crevice.

Outside, the two men nearly collided.

"Well?"

"I swear I saw something."

"Well, whatever it was, it's not here now."

"Whadda we do now?"

"I say we pack it in. If Luke wants her, he can come and find her," Gravel-voice headed down the hill. "I didn't want any part of this from the beginning."

"Luke isn't gonna like this. What if we tell him… " Their voices faded into the night.

Jolyn sagged with relief. She could sense that the opening was much larger than she'd first suspected. Using the wall as a guide, she cautiously crept a few more yards into the cave. Exhausted, she sank to the gritty floor and wrapped her arms about her legs. She sat huddled, her body trembling, and pressed her head to her knees.

"Oh, James…James."

Chapter 3

CONNOR'S LARGE, POWERFUL FRAME SLUMPED wearily in the saddle. His steely gray eyes peered drearily into the murky light of hooded dusk. Doggedly, he coaxed Thunder, who slid tiredly in the mud, along the well-marked trail known as Poncha Pass.

For over two days he had followed the clumsy trail left by his father's murderers. Not only had they killed his father, but they had savagely cut down his father's partner, Hank Montgomery, and his twin nephews, Nick and Chris. Even now he could not erase the horror of that morning two days before when he had returned from a business trip in Alamosa to find his family slaughtered in his father's office at the back of the store, Richardson's Trading Post and Dry Goods Emporium.

The fragile rays of the morning sun had bathed the room in ungentle light, and Connor had stared disbelievingly at the carnage before him. Nick's bloodless face had formed a bizarre contrast to his brother's gory one, and Hank's face had been unrecognizable. At his feet, his father had lain, his face livid, his eyes unseeing, his chest a mangled pulp.

Fearfully, he had searched the room and had found Annabel, his tender-hearted sister, lying curled along the wall. Her face had been swollen and bruised where someone had backhanded her. Worse still, she had been a witness to this senseless killing. Annabel, whom he and his father had tried so hard to protect, had suffered irreparably at the hands of these murdering scum.

He knew his father, and he knew Hank. Neither man would have considered the money in the safe, nor the store itself, more valuable than his life and the lives of his family. And now, the serious Nick lay lifeless with a bullet through his chest, and the reckless Chris with a hole in his temple. Both his father and Hank had been blown away with a shotgun. Such waste…such a meaningless waste.

Connor, who hated to see anyone or anything suffer, had cradled Annie in his arms and had carried her to her room in their home above the store. He had held her until help had arrived and had only left her side when he was assured of her condition. As he had rocked his reviving sister in his arms, he had experienced the crime as she remembered bit by terrifying bit the incidents of that night. The wonderful celebration of the Richardson and Montgomery Trading Goods merger…the dancing and casual flirting with Nick and Chris…the late-night congratulatory drink…and the betrayal.

It had been Luke, she had said, Luke, their half-brother, who had led the men who had brutally cut down the unarmed men. It had been Luke who had personally taunted and then deliberately shot their father.

He had held her through it all, whispering soothing words to his troubled sister while all the time he had seethed with anger, wanting to lash out at the man who had caused so much pain. His brother would pay! he swore. As he lived and breathed, his brother would pay.

Thunder stumbled, and Connor lurched in the saddle. He tugged gently upon the reins and stopped. It was well into the evening. It was a cloudy moonless night, and a heavy, chilly air wrapped its damp tentacles around the night's inhabitants. He gazed impotently at the rising trail before him.

How far ahead were they? he wondered. For two days they had eluded him. Now, he felt so close, so close.

Thunder trembled beneath Connor's thighs; he would have to stop and give the horse a rest. He would have to make up for lost time tomorrow.

Connor swung a well-muscled leg over his horse's rump and stepped to the ground. He stretched his taut, sinewy muscles and glared determinedly up the dark trail.

Tomorrow, Luke. I'll find you tomorrow.

* * *

Freezing water dripped from the cave ceiling onto Jolyn's closed eyes. The icy wetness shocked her into full awareness and she quickly sat up.

For a few confusing moments Jolyn was dizzy and disoriented. Where am I? she thought, blinking her dazed blue eyes, waiting for them to adjust to the continual darkness. She huddled against the rock wall, shivering from the cold dampness of the tunnel. Her long, slender arms hugged her bent legs as she gently rocked back and forth. The trickling of the water was the only sound she heard. Her disheveled hair hung limply around her shoulders, caked with mud and filled with the scent of…who was that man, that animal? An involuntary shudder passed through her body, causing Jolyn to shake uncontrollably. She tried breathing more slowly.

Jolyn gazed into the darkness surrounding her. Up ahead, the faint light shone through the dusty air. On the walls, small slivers of turquoise glittered. I'm in an old mine, she realized. And then it all came back to her, rushing through her body like a torrential downpour. The campsite, James and the little bird, Nutty they'd called it, and those men, those awful men. Oh, my God, she cried to herself. Jolyn remembered what the leader had attempted to do to her. Unconsciously, her hands flew to her chest and clutched her ripped shirt. It wasn't a dream.

Unaware of what she was doing, Jolyn curled up tighter. Her head collapsed on her knees and she sobbed. Her body was tortured with grief and sorrow and shame. She gave in to her pain and let herself be washed clean with her tears. Then she stubbornly, almost violently, shook her head.

That's enough, Jolyn. Let's move on from here. I need to get back to James. God, I hope he's all right. Please, let him not be harmed. I need him.

Groping against the walls, Jolyn carefully guided herself along the tunnel's flanks. Sharp chunks of granite and ore scraped smooth layers of

Jolyn's skin. Jolyn winced from the pain but did not stop. She would not stop. The faint glow ahead signaled the entrance of her hidden sanctuary. Her eyes had become adjusted to the soft glow that seemed to hover around her. The ceiling was quite low, only a foot higher than her head. She could see another tunnelway that had been created and knew that these passageways crisscrossed in many different paths.

After she'd traveled twenty feet around a slow bend, the rays of the morning sunshine poured in, illuminating the dusty mine. Jolyn quickened her pace. Her foot slipped into a small hollow in the ground and she went sprawling. She hit the dirt with a soft thud. Sputtering grains of powdered rock and turquoise, Jolyn shook her head and tried to sit up. Brushing herself off, she turned around to see what had tripped her.

The hole wasn't very large and Jolyn was more annoyed with herself than anything else. She peered at the oddly shaped hole. Her slender hand touched the unnatural curvature, imagining what had been wrenched so abruptly from the earth's floor. A quivering sparkle caught her eyes. Her eyes widened, and her delicate mouth opened wide as they riveted upon a shimmering piece of treasure.

"Heaven on earth, I don't believe what I'm seeing!" Jolyn exclaimed aloud, and then cupped her hands around the gem and cradled it tenderly. It was smooth and cool to her touch. She softly pressed the stone against her cheek. The cold compress was soothing against her bruised face and she sighed.

Embedded in a very sharp piece of rock, the precious stone was as large and as round as a hen's egg. The blues and greens glistened in her hands. "Good God, what poor miner left you behind," she whispered to the sparkling jewel. "I do thank you, digger, for being so careless with so precious a gift!"

Jolyn struggled to squeeze her new possession into the large pockets of her baggy denim pants. The rough edges of the rock scratched and ripped at the worn pockets. Jolyn felt the hard granite push against her soft thighs. Feeling lucky, as if someone were watching over her, Jolyn made her way to the entrance of the cave, welcoming the sunlight ahead.

Before reaching the opening, Jolyn sat down on the floor. What if those men are out there waiting for me? The one I injured. I know he'll kill me if he finds me. James. I have to find James and see if he's all right. I have to.

Determined, yet cautious, Jolyn stood up and walked out of the cave. A small light-brown rabbit scrambled by her and she jumped back, startled. Alert and frightened, she began her trek to find James.

Stepping off the trail, Jolyn found a large fir tree and balanced her sore body against the trunk. She relieved herself quickly. These pants are not quite so useful for everything, she giggled to herself as she hurriedly tried to re-dress.

Back on the trail, Jolyn was focused on one thing: James. She had to get to him, and fast. What if…? No, she would not think that. She had only one plan: to get there.

The sound of splashing water interrupted her thoughts. About twenty yards from the trail, Jolyn spotted a small creek. Cautiously, she approached it. Clear, sparkling water raced over slippery rocks. A few silver-and-blue-striped fish swam lazily by. Jolyn bent over, cupped her hands together, and, scooping as much cold water as she could, splashed her face, reawakening all her senses. She longed to undress herself completely and jump in, but as her hands quickly flew to her torn shirt, she remembered she could not. Not now. She had to get to James as quickly as she could.

Once more she scooped up a handful of the icy liquid. This time parched lips slowly sipped the water. The cold wetness slid down her dry throat and eased the hunger in her stomach. Jolyn wiped her wet hands on her shirt. Feeling the shredded material, Jolyn looked down at her tattered remains. Automatically, she grabbed the edges of her shirt and tried to close them, but she was unsuccessful. She twisted the frayed ends of each half and tied a knot, which held the shirt together well enough.

As Jolyn stood, her eyes caught hold of something shimmering in the sunlight. She walked over toward the object and bent down.

"Why, it's an old miner's shovel." Jolyn picked up the small, broken tool. The worn-out handle splintered in her hands. It's useless, she moaned, but she held on to it anyway. I don't have my knife, she remembered painfully. I need something. This will have to do for now.

And so, with broken implement in hand, Jolyn trudged on.

The tall aspens swayed in the morning breeze. It was still cool in the early spring and Jolyn shivered under her tattered clothes. She brought her arms together as she hiked, hugging herself for extra warmth. The crunching of leaves and twigs under her heavy boots kept her moving almost rhythmically. Jolyn heard every sound around her, tuned in to what was natural. James had identified every sound to her before... before...and she concentrated on this, listening for...them.

Jolyn's intelligent eyes were not trained to detect animal tracks, let alone human tracks, or she would have been even warier of her situation. A lone wolf had crossed the path only a few hours before, leaving a heavy scent from its offal. Jolyn caught the wet, musky odor but failed to identify it. Her education, in the one-room schoolhouse back home, and her grandfather's and mother's teaching lent itself more toward doctoring than trailblazing. She knew she would be in good hands with James, but alone she was quite vulnerable. She quickened her pace, pushing herself to get to James.

The large gray rock face loomed in front of Jolyn. She had found the campsite. She stopped abruptly and crouched under the small bush next to her. She listened for any sounds, friendly or not. When she did not hear anything, Jolyn crept on all fours toward the camp. Her hands and knees collided with rock slivers and gravel. She grimaced in pain but clenched her teeth and crawled on. Her hair, stringy and clumped with brown silt, kept getting snagged under her legs as she plodded along. It seemed to take hours.

The closer she crept, the more frightened she became. Why was it so quiet? If James were alive, wouldn't she hear him? He would be tending the horses. Or fixing breakfast. Maybe he was out looking for her. Oh, God, I hope not, she thought, we may never find each other. Oh, James, please be here. I pray that those men, those bastards, did not take you. Or, worse, no, please… James, be here for me!

With each step, Jolyn's heart pounded harder and harder in her chest. She could hear her breathing, rapid and shallow, in the thin mountain air. Jolyn's skin suddenly turned clammy and broke out into small bumps. She bent forward and the crisp leaves beneath her cried out from her weight. Slowly, she crawled the last remaining feet into the clearing. Her eyes swept the site, or what was left of it. She swayed dizzily, and her stomach leaped.

The men had left. They had rifled through the supplies. Food bags were ruptured and their contents spilled out onto the ground, mixed into the earth by their constant stomping around. Their bedrolls, once so neatly tied up in bundles under the rock face, were sliced open from someone's wanton slashing. Shreds of cotton and material hung limply over the sides, wasted and spent. Cooking utensils had been smashed and lay crumpled amidst the destruction. And the horses! Gone! James's Jew harp, which had brought them both such pleasure throughout their journey, lay crumpled next to a dark heap.

Jolyn staggered to a standing position, trying not to sway from the dizziness that enveloped her. What was that dark-blue mound that lay so unnaturally on the edge of the site? She approached it nervously, cautiously. And then she knew.

"Oh, no," she whispered, "no, James, no. Don't let it be you. Dear God, if you're listening to me, please, have mercy on me."

Jolyn's feet would not move. She was frozen to the ground. A ringing throbbed in her ears and ice flowed through her veins. Her knees seemed to unlock, and her body folded underneath her.

Her knees smacked into the hard earth, jolting her. She would not pass out, she commanded her body. Not now, I cannot. I…can… not. Determined and deliberate, she crept toward the crumpled heap. Something small with blue feathers peeked out between the folds of James's scrunched old jacket. Jolyn let out a whimper, barely audible.

"Oh, Nutty…oh, you." Jolyn could not continue. Thin rivulets of the fatally wounded bird's blood had oozed between the folds of the jacket and dried. Jolyn tenderly picked up the dead carcass and sobbed, "James, where are you? Where have you gone? Where have they taken you?"

Jolyn's warm, sparkling sapphire eyes were now filled with determined hatred. She quickly scanned the campsite, looking for something, and when she found it, swooped on it. She had picked up the shovel that she had found by the creek. With her jaw firmly set, and her back rigid, Jolyn held her head up to the sky. There was a newly acquired derision in her voice as she cried out, "NO! I will not give in to this! I will find you, James, and together we will see this to the end!"

Jolyn squeezed her fingers around the shovel and commenced the interment. As she dug the small grave, she paid no mind to the way the dirt clung to her sweating body. The bloodstained outer shirt had long ago been stripped off, the next two layers of shirts also flung haphazardly on the ground, as Jolyn continued her digging, never stopping to take a rest or a drink. When the hole was deep enough, she positioned the bird as gently as she could. Standing tall, Jolyn shoveled the rich brown earth over the creature, her warm tears dropping delicately onto the dry mounds of soil.

"James," she promised, "I will not leave you with those murdering bastards. I don't know how I will do it, but I will. I am going to continue to Creede, somehow. I know I must get there. And when I do, I will get the help of my two brothers and my uncle and we will get those men. I swear to you, on my parents' grave, and with the memory of your father, that I will seek revenge and come for you. May God see you in good favor until we meet again."

Jolyn turned away, got dressed, picked up the saddlebag, her metal canteen, her mother's old medicine pouch, and James's woolen jacket, and headed for Creede.

* * *

Jolyn hiked the rest of the day. She did not stop to eat or drink. She blindly passed the early spring flowers. Warmed by the sun, the yellow sunflowers, white parsnip, and purple daisies were trampled and scattered in pieces; they would have to wait for another time to be enjoyed by this young woman. Another time when she was not filled with so much hate, so much pain.

"I'll make it to Alamosa. I can go that far," she projected. "Then when I get to Alamosa, I can get word to Uncle Hank that I'm there. He can send my brothers to come and get me. If I can only get down from these mountains soon, I'll be safe."

As the blood of Christ slowly ebbed down the mountainside, the deep purples of early night crept in. She wrapped herself in James's soft jacket. Snuggling with the memory of James, she walked on.

The Colorado sky directly above her was a deep aquamarine. Jolyn noticed the green fir trees and the small wildflowers ablaze with rich yellows, deep purples, and shocking crimsons. The scent of pines and earth and crisp air teased at her nostrils.

Treading over leaves and branches, Jolyn thought back to an Indian she had met a long time ago at Uncle Hank's post. He had taught her a few things about his customs, his heritage. He was old and proud, and she had truly admired his courage.

"Ah, Jolyn," Indian Joe had said to her, "the earth is alive. You must treat Her as the Mother to all living things. When you travel over the earth, you must not put pressure on Her. You must walk softly and not hurt Her with your being. Be one with our Mother and She will be good to you."

He would be proud of me, Jolyn thought. I can feel myself becoming part of the woods around me.

Had Jolyn been able to see the ominous-looking clouds coming in from the northwest that evening, she might have stopped hiking and tried to seek shelter. She hugged herself tightly with James's jacket, trying to keep what little body warmth she had from escaping. Jolyn inhaled James's odor on the coat and smiled tenderly, reminiscing about happier days.

If I could only have some of Mama's hot oatmeal right now I would never complain about the horrible taste again, she mused. Hot biscuits and gravy and steaming hot chocolate. Mmmm.

Jolyn was hiking so rapidly down the dark mountain and thinking so intensely about long-ago dinners, she did not see the small clearing ahead until she almost stepped into a pool of water. At the last second, she pulled her black boot back and gasped, sucking in the cold mountain air.

"Now, what is this? Oh, my! A real hot spring."

The spring was hidden within the woods and snuggled next to a large rock face that soared straight up in an attempt to pierce the blue ceiling above.

Jolyn bent down to let her hands touch the very top of the clear water. It was so warm, she pulled her hand back in shock. "I don't believe it," she cried. "It's for real. It's warmer than any bath I have ever had back home. Oh. Oooh, I have to try this."

And with that, Jolyn stripped her masculine garments right down to her torn pink camisole and stopped. She peeked around her, half expecting someone to be there.

With a gentle, unassuming grace, Jolyn set her long, lean legs in the nature-made warm waters. Still holding on to a large rock that resembled a pier, Jolyn lowered the rest of her body into the steamy pool. Her toes touched the silted bottom, and Jolyn let out a sigh of relief. For one brief moment she thought she would be sucked into the earth forever. The gentle warm water melted over her body, soothing her very soul.

Jolyn glided through the water over to the other side of the small pool, where the rock formation entered. There the rocks formed natural ledges, and Jolyn pulled herself up and sat down. She let her legs float in this warm bath, a gift from nature. Her young breasts, nipples taut, teased the surface of the pool, promising to dip under at a moment's notice. She splashed herself lavishly, soaking her auburn locks. She felt clean, all over, inside and out.

Feeling comfortable and secure, Jolyn glanced around her at the beautiful surroundings. Suddenly, the tepid water bubbled in the middle of the pond and Jolyn's heart pounded in fear.

As quickly as the underground stream had emerged, adding more of its bubbling brew, it disappeared, leaving a new layer of heated vapors. She threw her shaking body off the ledge and plunged under the water.

When she emerged she noticed that the light, translucent greens and blues of the water had taken on a darker hue. Glancing up, Jolyn saw the reason. The brilliant, solid-dark-blue sky that had been pierced with a bright full moon had transformed into a canopy of dark, menacing clouds that threatened to burst at any moment.

Oh, no, she thought, that could mean snow as well as rain at this time of year. Regretfully, she swam back to the other side of the pool and hoisted herself onto the rocks.

Jolyn quickly dried herself off with one of her shirts, and no sooner had she finished buttoning her outermost covering than the first few flakes drifted slowly down through the hanging branches. Realizing the danger of a late spring storm, she gathered up everything and hastened down the path.

The early evening grew late and Jolyn should have stopped and made camp. She wanted to reach the bottom of the mountain so desperately that even the icy pellets that were now slicing into her face like a million needles and blinding her vision did not cause her to stop. Jolyn, with her head bent down, did more tripping and sliding than walking.

Her stomach was growling, more punishment, she thought, for taking a few moments of leisure. She had wanted to wait until she reached the bottom of the mountain to light a fire and cook something for that evening's meal. Now, with this treacherous undergrowth slowing her pace, she wasn't sure when she would get down the mountain. The hunger was an annoyance, the snail pace was a frustration, and the warmth of the hot spring was now just a memory. She had not planned on a snowstorm and did not have her bedroll to give her the extra warmth she so desperately needed.

As she walked faster and faster amid perilous roots and fallen branches, Jolyn's journey turned into a race against time, against the elements. Had the weather been better, had Jolyn been walking slower, had she had her head up instead of facing the ground, she might have had a chance against the cliff she was trudging toward. Jolyn's right boot hit the granite rock, now caked with icy remnants, and she lost her footing. She plummeted ten feet down a sheer wall coated in ice-glass.

The force of gravity pulled her head down. The shimmering frost-covered auburn locks were no cushion as her head smacked into the mantle, and she immediately lost consciousness.

A frozen tree root that had burst out of the wall years ago ripped through Jolyn's outer clothes, slicing deep into her thigh. Unconscious, limp, and still falling, she collided into a clump of bramble bushes, which cushioned her lifeless body from breaking any bones.

Warm blood soaked her leggings and pooled onto the rocky ledge. It quickly coagulated and froze. Jolyn's hair, caked with ice and dusty rock particles, lay strewn over the bush as if hiding and protecting her quiet, unresponsive face. Her breathing was raspy and irregular, and her body quivered uncontrollably from the cold and wet. She would have cursed herself had she realized she was only one hundred yards away from the bottom of this monster she called a mountain. Straight down from the ledge rolled a rushing river that had flowed cold and unfeeling for millions of years.

The ice storm softened to all snow, gently covering the young woman. The pearly white snow crystals glistened on her jagged crimson wound.

Jolyn wasn't sure how long she had been unconscious, but the constant pressure of something cold and wet upon her closed eyes awakened her. Her head would not clear. She was dizzy, and her head throbbed. With her eyes still shut, Jolyn lifted her almost frozen arms and brushed off the snow. She sputtered and spit out the frozen precipitation.

Jolyn tried to sit up. Pain ripped through her. Sharp spasms tore down her leg, and she moaned. Jolyn gently touched her head and when she pulled her hand away it was covered with blood. Her stomach rolled over and pitched up mucus, watery and green. Jolyn wiped her mouth on her sleeve and sat up some more.

"Oh, God, what has happened to me?" Jolyn looked upward at the top of the cliff and realized what her carelessness had caused. The storm clouds had already blown through and once again the yellow-white moon pierced the cold night and lit the mountainside.

Jolyn was afraid to move. When she slowly turned her head to take in her surroundings, waves of dizziness and nausea whipped through her and the pain in her head almost caused her to black out again.

Jolyn tried to reposition her legs, but the gash filled with dry blood in her thigh reopened and blood drizzled down her leg.

"I need something to wrap around my leg or else I will bleed to death before I freeze to death." Once again she cursed the man who had assaulted her. "If only I had not dropped my knife after I sliced that hole in his face," she pondered. "How can I cut some strips of cloth?" She thought deeply. Another ache in her other thigh brought a slow smile to Jolyn's pale lips.

"My stone. My stone that I found in the mine."

Carefully and very slowly, Jolyn dug her stiff fingers into her pocket and tugged the sharp rock free. She held it lovingly, balancing it between her cold fingers, like her mother's tools she'd used to practice with at home.

Delicately, Jolyn tore the cold, soaked bottom of her pants off. Her firm jaw did not waver an inch at the intense pain that stabbed through her. Black dots clouded her vision and Jolyn clenched her eyes shut for a few seconds and then reopened them, forcing herself to go on. Her fingers were growing increasingly numb, and fearing loss of control with the cutting device, Jolyn eased her freezing fingers into her punctured skin. The temporary warmth brought back enough feeling for Jolyn to finish cutting the material.

Throwing the bloodstained strips of denim over the edge, Jolyn followed it as it dropped into the rushing river below. In the moonlight, Jolyn watched as red frothy water fused into swirls of pink and raced over smooth stones. Just beyond the water Jolyn saw the base of the mountain.

A moan escaped her taut lips and her shoulders sagged just a little bit more. With deliberate determination, Jolyn continued her doctoring. She skillfully cut a piece of her softest cotton material from one of her inner shirts.

She gently wrapped the bandage around her thigh. Not too tight, she instructed herself, just enough to create the pressure.

Scooping up a handful of wet snow from the bush, Jolyn wiped the excess blood from her leg. Huddling over her thigh, she rubbed it with her arms, drying it and building up the circulation at the same time. Satisfied with the results, Jolyn eased herself over to the wall and leaned back.

Jolyn needed warmth and food, but she tried not to think about it. She knew she was in a hopeless situation. She had to fight her growing weakness, her chilling body. Jolyn drew her knees up to her chest and wrapped her legs underneath her jacket for more warmth.

I won't give up, she thought. Jolyn gazed across the San Luis Valley. The majestic purple tops of the range swayed in a foggy haze. It was hard to make out the details around her. Jolyn focused on the roaring river below and for a fleeting moment had a strange compulsion to leap in. The cold had numbed her body and she wanted to let sleep envelop her and gently ease her to a warmer clime.

The sun, cold and harsh to Jolyn, was stretching across the mountain range silent and strong. Jolyn moaned. Her lips mouthed her thoughts.

I…need…help…I…

Jolyn's head slumped forward and her body followed. She lay curled in a tight huddle. Her teeth started chattering uncontrollably. Jolyn curled up even tighter and pressed her hands against her face, forcing her mouth to be still. Her head rolled to the side so that she was staring straight up into the merciless sky.

Dull, hazy blue eyes tried to focus on the top of the cliff, but the sparkling crystals played havoc with her eyes and she was confused. The Colorado dawn was upon her. Frosty stars still twinkled at the weakening woman, and the golden moon sliced farewell across the purple sky.

Vaguely, Jolyn thought she heard a horse neigh. I must be going crazy. I must be dying. I just want to go to sleep. Again Jolyn heard a sound. With her elbows, she dragged herself along the ground toward the edge.

The pain was excruciating, and Jolyn cried out. She stretched her stiff arms in front of her and grabbed the bush to help pull her out farther. A slight shadow fell over her arms and Jolyn blinked in utter disbelief, and then it was gone. Jolyn looked up, but the throbbing in her head jolted her forward like a rushing wave, and her head collapsed on her arms. Her eyes fluttered open to see the shadow once again on her arms growing larger and larger.

Using all her strength, Jolyn pushed on her hands and heaved herself up. She tilted her head back once more and gazed upward. Jolyn saw a vision of black astride a dark horse, standing on the cliff.

I'm not dreaming, she sighed. It's an angel. My angel of death has come.

"I'm…down…here…" she whispered, and then plunged into her own darkness.

Connor edged Thunder near the top of the cliff. He thought he had heard something, someone? This was no time of year to be playing out here in the mountains. He grimaced.

Thunder neighed again and stomped his front legs.

"Easy, boy, easy. It's going to be all right."

Aware of the danger, Thunder had stubbornly halted his large frame, refusing to go forward any farther. Connor, with the ease of a natural horseman, hoisted his leg over his steed and jumped down. He was cautious. One never knew what could be on the other side of a large tree, let alone over a cliff.

Slowly he approached the icy bluff. It was too slick to stand over it and peer down, so he awkwardly dropped to his knees.

Connor slid one leg over the edge, holding precariously onto a tree root that had worked its way out from the rock. His curious gray eyes peered over the edge and spied a natural ledge covered with a large patch of bushes.

Jolyn moaned softly.

Connor pulled himself back onto the slanting edge, and then sat frozen.

"What? What was that? Did I really hear something?"

Down below, Jolyn groaned.

"Whatever it is, it needs help," Connor said, half to himself and half to Thunder.

Cautiously, Connor stood up and walked to Thunder.

"Something's hurt down there, boy, and I've got to help it. And you've got to help. You understand, Thunder? Yeah, I know you do."

Connor eased his grass lariat, snugly coiled on the side of his new California saddle, into his gloved hands.

"This is gonna take the two of us, Thunder, and even then, it's not gonna be easy."

Connor clutched the reins and guided Thunder to a nearby tree. He positioned his steed on one side, all the time talking and whispering calmly to him.

Methodically, he unwrapped his coiled rope and twisted a few dallies around his horn, locking it with a half hitch.

"No, that ain't gonna do, Thunder," Connor realized, unhitching his knot. "I'd better go for a figure eight on this one. I don't know how heavy an animal it is down there."

Expertly, Connor finished tying his rope on his pommel and then wrapped the lariat around the large tree next to Thunder for extra support.

"Okay, boy, here I go. You stay there now, you hear?" Connor cocked his head to one side as if expecting an answer and, accepting the soft neighing from his animal companion as a "yes," turned away and headed for the ledge, rope in hand.

Connor stood at the top of the cliff, legs wide apart, with his rope coiled in both hands. Skillfully, his hands found the honda, and he slipped the rope through it, creating his catch rope. He squatted down on his haunches and eased the loop down over the icy edge. The soft plunking sound signaled the arrival of his rope. He turned back around, facing Thunder, and gave a tug at the cord. It was taut. He was ready.

Holding on to the rope, he slowly glided his massive frame over the edge. He slipped twice and cursed himself. Every time he mumbled he heard the form below him moan. He quickened his pace, racing against the encroaching night.

Finally, Connor felt solid ground below him. He let go of the rope, and when he turned around his steely eyes widened at the vision he saw at his feet.

There, curled into a ball, huddled a small figure covered in blood. One leg lay stripped of its pants, with only a blood-soaked cotton bandage covering some kind of wound. Caked blood dotted a face and clumped in russet hair.

"Oh my God! What have I found?"

Again Jolyn moaned and shivered, unaware of Connor's presence.

Connor quickly stripped off one glove and, kneeling down, placed his hand on Jolyn's forehead. The soft auburn hair tickled his rough palm, but Connor ignored those sensations as he focused on her bruise, which was already an ugly purplish-brown.

This tiny figure was a woman, and she was barely alive. Softly he said to her closed eyes, "You've taken quite a fall, young lady, and I hope you're okay."

Connor stood up and placed his worn leather glove back on his hand. He quickly marched over to the icy wall where his rope lay, poised for action.

Connor grabbed his lasso and, bringing it toward the curled and battered figure, he gently eased it over the quivering, huddled frame. He winced at the moans the young woman emitted, fearing the pain was too intense for such a fragile female.

He tightened the lasso around her waist, tiny even though it was surrounded by layers of clothing. Connor was focusing so hard on his job that he was unaware that the girl in his arms was trying desperately to awaken.

For a brief second, Jolyn's sea-blue eyes fluttered open. She gazed into two warm silver pools of liquid that were concentrating on something by her waist. Thick black hair flew into his eyes and his black hat was almost blown away by the wind.

Jolyn felt the strong arms of someone cradling, but not crushing, her. A warmth flowed through her and she felt safe. Her dark angel had descended to take her away.

Connor gently hoisted the young woman onto his shoulders, and, pressing his boots against the sheer rock wall, he began his climb. Taut muscles strained against Connor's flannel shirt and sweat, even on this frigid night, cascaded down his stubbled face. Connor's thighs bulged under the added weight of the girl and he prayed he would not slip back down.

Every foot higher was sheer agony for Jolyn, whose jostled body screamed in pain with every movement. Hazy blue eyes opened and closed, unaware of her whereabouts.

Slowly, cautiously, Connor ascended. He grunted and focused on the moss and rock in front of him.

Finally, Connor sensed he was approaching the top and pushed himself even harder to reach the peak. Finding the exposed root again, Connor used it as a lever, and with a final burst of energy he hoisted himself and his cargo gently over the edge.

Bending down, he picked up the girl, peeled off his lariat, and carried her over to his horse, where he tenderly placed her on some pine needles under the large fir tree.

"Easy, little one," a soothing voice whispered. "I've got you now."

Jolyn gazed upon the face of her savior. He was dressed all in gray and black and he smiled so sweetly. She had been saved by her vision in black and with that secure feeling, Jolyn submerged into a deep, pain-free darkness.

Chapter 4

JOLYN WOKE TO THE SOOTHING tones of a man's deep, resonant voice.

"Easy, boy, easy. You're going to be fine. Just a little more of this ointment for this rope burn, and I'll be through." The man's voice droned on.

With an effort, Jolyn opened her eyes. She stared upward into the clear cerulean sky and wondered if she had imagined the snowstorm from the previous night. For the moment her body lay quiescent. She was dimly aware of a dull ache in her temple, and her jaw felt like a bloated tree stump. Every muscle felt stiff, not sore, but she knew the moment she moved her battered body, she would know the limits of her body's pain. She wasn't quite ready to face that test.

Ever so slightly, she eased her head toward the comforting sound of her rescuer's mellifluous voice.

"That's it, Thunder, that's it. You'll be prancing in front of those mares in no time."

Standing in front of the horse, his back toward her, a tall, well-muscled man stooped over his horse's gray flank. The man's raven hair curled unevenly at the nape of his neck. Despite the briskness of the early morning air, he wore only a red-checkered flannel shirt. The sleeves were rolled to his elbows, exposing fine tufts of light hair that glinted against his deeply tanned, sinewy forearms. Worn, well-fitting Levi pants hugged his lean hips and long, firm legs. Jolyn had never seen such a sleek and powerful two-legged animal.

Her attention was caught and trapped by his wide, sensuous hands as they tenderly stroked the horse's back. Mesmerized, she watched as his strong tapered fingers dipped into the salve and rubbed it onto the raw wound. In ever-widening strokes, he smoothed the balm onto the flesh, all the while murmuring encouragement as the horse quivered beneath his expert touch. He continued to caress the horse, his palms gliding along its back and sliding smoothly down its flank, as his head was tilted, furtively watching his sleeping new companion.

Jolyn felt a strange tingling sensation that had nothing to do with the aches caused from her ordeals. Her half-opened eyes slid from his moving hand along his arm across his broad shoulders toward his dark head. Surprised, her eyes widened, and she stared into concerned, pensive eyes. A warm flush rose in her cheeks, and her heart beat crazily in her throat. How long had he been watching her watch him? Her heart racing, she openly studied his face. His forehead was broad and creased, etched with a dozen fine lines. Chiseled into his determined face were high cheekbones, an aquiline nose, and a square jaw. His straight eyebrows slashed above thick dark lashes and wide-set eyes edged with deep crinkles. Dark shadows played beneath his eyes, and his full lips looked drawn. He looked weary and tense. Her sapphire eyes locked onto his smoky ones. Something unexpected, almost tangible, hovered between them. His face grew rigid and she heard his sharp intake of breath. She was not breathing at all. Her heart hammering in her throat, and she felt herself drawn out of herself, pulled magnetically toward his vibrant masculinity. He turned away, and the tenuous thread pulled tautly between them snapped.

Reaching for a worn pouch, her pouch, the stranger strode across the few feet of ground between them and knelt carefully beside her. Dropping the bag on the ground, he gently slid his hand beneath her chin, his callused palm scuffing softly against her sensitive skin, and turned her face toward his. His eyes melded with hers, his lips parted. He leaned forward. For a fleeting moment she thought he was going to kiss her, and in that same moment, she knew that she was going to let him. She closed her eyes and waited breathlessly.

"How's my mountain maiden this morning?" His deep, mellow voice shimmered through her.

Her eyes flew open and darted away. So he hadn't intended to kiss her after all. She felt another rising flush. She wished he would stop stroking her cheek. As though he had read her mind, he dropped his hand to his side and leaned back on his haunches. She took a deep, steadying breath. Now that he wasn't so close, she would be able to think more clearly.

"Does my wood sprite have a voice, or must I be content with her lovely face and form?" he teased.

Jolyn's eyes narrowed with annoyance. Mountain maiden. Wood sprite. What kind of backwoods fool did he think she was? She jerked her body upward and then groaned as her body rebelled. She glared angrily at him, expecting a mocking grin, but saw only a tightening flex along his jawline.

"Not a fairy after all." Even though he was deeply concerned about the pain this fragile girl must be feeling, Connor tried to keep his voice light. "The first few movements are always the worst."

"Thanks," Jolyn moaned. "That makes me feel a great deal better."

He smiled at her attempt at humor despite the pain he knew she must be suffering. Though Connor tried not to show it, he was surprised at the womanly timber of her voice. Perhaps she was older than he had first thought, and he needn't feel so guilty about those less than innocent thoughts he had been entertaining only moments before. In any case, he needed to get her on her feet and on her way. He had already lost twelve precious hours, and he hoped that he had not lost Luke's trail as well.

"Well, in that case," he bantered, "let's see if we can get you onto your feet again. Perhaps if I offer my services, we can do so with the least amount of damage to your body and my nerves."

"That sounds reasonable." Jolyn's voice quavered. She wasn't quite sure which was going to be worse, the pain of her injuries or the feeling of his powerful hands on her body.

"Before we start, let me present you with a name so that you can hurl at my head any well-deserved curses as I help you up. I'm Connor." He smiled a warm earthy caress.

"And I'm Jolyn." She smiled a bright ethereal answer. "And I never swear."

He shook her hand solemnly. "Nice to meet you, Jolyn." His huge hand lingered on her small one. He seemed reluctant to pull his hand away from hers. A raucous jay startled them, and Connor dropped her hand as though he had been scalded.

"Well, don't put off tomorrow…" He gently slipped his arm beneath her shoulders. "Ready?"

She nodded. As carefully as possible, he lifted her to a sitting position.

"Damnation!" Jolyn could not hold back the stifled curse. Her head throbbed painfully, and every muscle was screaming in protest.

"Never swear, huh?"

Jolyn blinked back the threatening tears and squared her jaw. Curses. She'd show him curses. She'd be more than happy to strangle this sniveling jackdaw with curses. As she petulantly glared at him, she realized that most of the initial pangs had subsided. Had he deliberately provoked her for that very reason? Suspiciously, she scrutinized his face. He gazed back disarmingly.

"Well, I might as well get this over with," she muttered determinedly. "Ready when you are."

She gripped his shoulders and, holding with all her strength, she got to her feet. He held her dizzy form against him, and then, by degrees, he allowed her to support her own weight. She felt surprisingly steady. Except for an initial twinge in her thigh where the root had cut her, her legs felt strong. Her head still throbbed, but if she added a few herbs with her morning coffee, she'd be fine.

"Thank you!" She threw him a quick smile and stepped back. "Well, my legs are working." She glanced toward her medicine pouch, and Connor swiftly picked it up and handed it to her.

"It was all I could find," he murmured apologetically.

"There wasn't much else," she replied.

She painstakingly made her way toward the bushes, and Connor, worrying that she might fall, remained glued to her side.

"Thank you, Connor, but I'm feeling much stronger now." She blushed, embarrassed. "In fact, I prefer that you…that is…I think that it would be better if…"

Connor looked as uncomfortable as she felt. "I'll be by the fire. If you need help, just give me a holler." He ducked back toward the campsite.

When Jolyn returned, Connor had already saddled Thunder and packed most of the gear. A cup of coffee sat propped on the ground next to the ashes from the small morning fire. Evading her glance, Connor offered Jolyn the steaming cup, and, carefully avoiding his touch, she accepted it. He reached into his jacket pocket, pulled out a chaw of beef jerky, and held it out.

"It's the best I can do. I was travelling light."

Jolyn looked rather dubiously at the hard, stiff piece of meat. She was ravenous, but she wasn't quite sure with her swollen jaw and throbbing head how she would chew it.

"Thank you." She took the proffered meat.

Connor watched her as she attempted to gnaw off a portion of the resinous strip. After a few minutes, when she hadn't successfully taken a bite and still failed to appeal to him for help, Connor lost patience.

"Here, let me have that." Pulling out his knife, he sawed off a small bite-sized chunk and handed it to her.

"See if that helps. You might want to let it soak in your mouth before you try chewing it."

"Thanks." Jolyn grinned, not in the least put off by his peremptory behavior.

"You're welcome."

She watched as he hacked off more bite-size pieces.

"You know," he said without looking up, "you don't get bruises like the ones you've got on your face and neck from a fall off a ledge. Do you want to talk about it?"

"No," Jolyn spat out defensively.

Pensively, he dropped the chunks into her palm, and watched Jolyn as she added some dried leaves from her pouch to her coffee and sipped gingerly from the tin cup. He noticed that she had made an effort to repair some of the damage from her fall. She had a fresh bandage on her leg, and she wore her brushed but soiled jacket buttoned to her neck. She had finger-smoothed her auburn hair back from her face and tied it at her nape with a piece of twine.

Who was she? What was she doing out here alone? And how had she come by all those bruises? he wondered. He watched her large, expressive eyes, the color of a mountain lake, gaze sadly across the clearing. A purplish bruise spanned her right cheek, and a narrow cut on her temple swelled above it. Despite her injuries, her face was exquisite. With her slightly arched brows, straight, pert nose, full, wide lips, and delicate chin, she appeared like some delicate wildflower warmed by the Colorado sun.

A wave of protectiveness swept over him, and he quickly shook it off. Connor could not afford these feelings. He was already two days behind. He could only hope that the storm had slowed Luke and his gang down enough that he could find their trail again. First, he had to find a place to unload her. He couldn't very well leave her out here alone without food or protection, especially not in her condition.

"Look, Jolyn," Connor rasped, "is there someplace I can take you? Do you have family, friends, someplace? Someone waiting for you?"

Jolyn's hand trembled slightly around her cup. Who was this Connor, anyway? How much could she trust him? He had rescued her, yes, but she could see by his restlessness and the tightness about his mouth that he regretted the gesture. If she were to trust him, and he were to desert her—or worse, attack her like those men… She had lost so much. She had lost too much. She had learned in the past few days that she could make it on her own, and that was just what she intended to do. She couldn't afford to put faith in anyone but herself. She couldn't bear to lose any more than she already had.

"No. I mean I…I live out here. Just over that hill. Thank you for the offer, though, and thanks for all your help. I appreciate what you've done for me, and if you wouldn't mind leaving just a little water…" Her voice faltered.

"I'll take you," Connor declared.

"No. It would just upset my pa to see me riding in with some stranger. It would be much better if I returned alone. Really."

"I said I'd take you," insisted Connor. Grabbing the empty cup from Jolyn's nervous fingers, he lifted her effortlessly into his powerful arms and strode toward his horse. He set her sidewise on the saddle, shoved the cup into his saddlebags, and reached for the saddle horn.

"What are you doing?" she demanded, her anger overriding her fright. "I told you that I…"

"Look, Jo, get this through your head. I'm not leaving you out here alone. And if you think that I buy that cock-and-bull story about you living in the mountains with your daddy for one minute!" shouted Connor accusatorily. He took a deep breath and started over. "Listen. I don't blame you for not wanting to trust me, but I don't have time to argue with you. I'm pressed for time, and even though the easiest thing for me to do would be to leave you out here, I have no intention of doing so. So where will it be?"

Jo. He'd called her Jo. No one but her parents and James had ever called her Jo. Sentimental memories came crashing down upon her. She looked at Connor without suspicion and took a deep breath. She had to tell him, and she could not hold it back any longer.

"My parents were recently killed. I was on my way to Creede to see my brothers when I…" Jolyn squeezed her eyes shut and gripped the horn, fighting the memories that despairingly rushed in. "When I…I… ran into some trouble. Perhaps, if it's not too far out of your way, you could take me to Alamosa." Her voice hopelessly faded to a whisper.

Connor fought against taking her in his arms and comforting her. She was hurting, hurting mercilessly, but she was also fighting to hold on to every ounce of dignity, and he wasn't about to take that from her. At this point he would do anything for this courageous young woman. But Alamosa. Alamosa meant another day's delay. It meant explanations, explanations he hadn't the time or the heart for right now. He'd much rather leave her at Salida. It wouldn't be hard to pick up Luke's trail from there if Luke and his gang were, as Connor suspected, heading toward Leadville. But Alamosa would put her within a couple days of Creede and would place her under the protection of his good friend, Hawk. Connor didn't know what had happened to Jolyn on the trail, but she was scared and hurt and vulnerable. Somehow, he just couldn't leave her with strangers in Salida. She'd be no better off there than she was now.

"I can take you as far as Alamosa. I've got friends who can see you make it to Creede from there."

"Thank you," Jolyn mumbled gratefully into Connor's stern face. "You said that you were in a hurry. Will this take you too much out of your way? I mean, if it's important, I…"

Jolyn froze at the unchecked hatred that crossed Connor's face. For one chilling moment, she gazed into cold steel-gray eyes, eyes that reminded her of a deadly voice, of a macabre dance, and of a savage moment when metal bit into flesh. And then the expression, along with the memory, was gone.

"Yes," Connor's answer rumbled deeply from his chest, "it's important." Without waiting for a reply, Connor slipped his left foot into the stirrup and swung his sleek frame into the saddle. He shifted to allow more room for Jolyn, who now sat more on than off his lap. Her head rested against his chest and her left hand on his thigh. Not for the first time that morning, he felt a familiar warmth surge through his groin.

"Is your leg giving you any pain? Do you think you'll be able to ride?"

"No, and yes." She relaxed even further against him, her soft hair grazing his chin.

This is going to be a longer trip than I thought, he thought self-mockingly, grinning.

"Hang on, then," he warned, and they took off at a low gallop.

Jolyn, with her head resting on Connor's chest, listened to the steady thud of his heart. She could smell the pungent woodsmoke and faint tinge of shaving soap on his shirt. Even through her jacket, his warmth radiated into her and wrapped comforting tendrils about her chilled body. She felt the increasing heat of his thigh beneath her hand, and she slipped her hand onto her lap, her palm still burning. Slowly, she relaxed against him, content to feel his firm body rocking gently against hers. She had lost her parents, lost James to a gang of killers, nearly lost her life, and now she lay in this stranger's arms, feeling as comforted, as nurtured, as she had in the hot spring pool. She felt her mind drifting, and with a gentle sigh, she sank into the sanctuary of sleep.

A horse's shrill whinny pierced Jolyn's dreams, and the whir of a menacing rattle jolted her awake. The glaring whiteness of sun against sand blinded her. Before she could reach up with her trembling hand to cover her tortured eyes, she was thrown back against Connor's chest with jarring force. His arm tightened painfully about her ribs and still she slid skyward. She clutched at the horn, her fingers slipping as she tangled her fingers in the horse's mane, and still it was not enough. As the horse lunged forward, Jolyn slammed against its shoulder, the horn biting into her leg, Connor's arm slicing across her belly, his weight a crushing force. Then she was twisted, upward, outward, away from the punishing blows of leather and flesh. With a strangled cry, she was flung downward, her hair whipping across her eyes, her body rolling and crashed against the searing sand.

She lay on her right side, weighted, unmoving, like a sack of grain. Sand spattered across her face and shoulders as Thunder thrashed above her. Dimly, she was aware of another movement, of sand, sliding, not splashing, next to her outstretched hand. The distant buzz of clacking stones became a rushing roar. Rattler. Someone somewhere above her was shouting, but the snake's rasping rendered the words meaningless. Darkness, cold and unappealing, descended upon her, but Jolyn fought against it. She would not faint; she must not faint. A deafening roar exploded through the din. The air was suddenly mercifully silent.

By degrees, Jolyn became aware of her surroundings. She was lying half-buried in prickly sand. Something cool and sticky clung to the skin on her right arm, which lay stretched above her head. Gritty sand irritated her cheek and neck. Bitter, dry granules of sand choked her. Very close, she could hear the exhausted wheezing of a horse. She felt the thump of a man's feet strike the earth and heard the crunching sand beneath hurriedly approaching feet.

"Jolyn. Jo?"

She did not want to respond. His deep, sultry voice wove a silky cocoon about her, and she felt herself sinking deep within it. If only she could curl up in this wonderful safe place, where…

"Oh, no you don't."

She felt his callused skin scuff along her cheek as he pushed her tangled hair away from her delicate face. His strong fingers gently brushed the sand from her body. She felt a slight tingling sensation along the planes and curves where his fingers last touched. A growing lassitude swept through her body, and again she shut her eyes.

Connor gripped her arm and gently shook her. Her eyes blinked open at the disturbance.

"Can you move?" Connor asked worriedly.

Jolyn groaned. "Do I have to?"

Jolyn looked so miserable, so disgusted, so unhurt, that Connor couldn't swallow his relieved grin.

"Unless you have a better idea." His smile broadened.

Casting him a withering glance, she carefully unfolded her cramped and twisted limbs, grimacing occasionally, and eventually sat rather satisfactorily if a bit unsteadily on a small dirt mound, her legs stretched in front of her.

Connor reached concernedly for her right forearm, which was splattered with blood.

"You're hurt?" he gasped.

"No, it's the snake's." She glanced toward the upturned, still-writhing carcass and quickly turned away. A bullet had ripped through its head. Somehow Connor had managed a precise shot at a striking snake on a bucking horse through a screen of glaring sun and flying sand. She stared at him in open-mouthed amazement.

"An excellent shot," she managed. "You must be very good."

"I've known better. I didn't have time to think; I just reacted to the situation."

With dawning awareness, Jolyn realized that she was alone with a powerful, potentially dangerous man, a man she knew nothing about. He had rescued her from the ledge, had helped her this morning, and had even agreed to take her to Alamosa. But what was he doing out here alone? He was obviously travelling light. In fact, but for a bedroll and a limited food supply, he carried nothing but a repeating rifle, a six-shooter, and a saddlebag of ammunition. She eyed him with growing unease.

He recognized the small flicker of alarm in her deepening violet eyes. Damn. She was frightened of him. The last thing he wanted from her was her fear. What he really wanted was her trust. He wasn't quite sure when that had become important to him, but he wanted it. He wanted her to confide in him, to tell him where the bruises on her face and body had come from and what secrets she held locked so guardedly inside herself.

"I'm not a gunslinger, Jo," he declared boldly.

Her eyelashes fluttered downward, her thoughts hidden. Connor lifted her chin and stared straightforwardly into Jolyn's face.

"My name is Connor Richardson. I own a chain of trading posts that run from Alamosa to Creede. When I found you"—he hesitated—"I was on the trail of a gang of outlaws who…well, that's not important. What is important is that you believe that I mean you no harm. I have agreed to take you to Alamosa, and I intend to keep that promise."

Connor Richardson. Connor. The name resounded through her head. She remembered now. The men on the trail had feared that name. Even the leader had respected it. What had he said? If Connor had been there, they, his men, even himself, would have been dead. But Connor hadn't been there, and James… She studied Connor's face. His eyes were steady, the line of his jaw determined. His look was forthright, candid. Yes, she could trust this man. If he was their enemy, then he was her ally. But if she were to trust him enough to tell him about herself, about that night, she had to know one thing more. She rose to her knees and planted a hand tentatively against his shoulder.

"When you find these men, what will you do?" Her voice was deathly quiet.

He gazed steadily into her burning eyes, acutely aware of her hand on his arm. He nearly had her trust. It was like some rare tiny jewel suspended by a fragile thread, and he knew if he said the wrong thing, failed to give the answer she was waiting for, that thread would break. But not even for her could he deny the truth. Harsh and blunt, he answered her.

"I will kill them."

She understood, now, his preoccupation, his impatience, his drive. These men that he hunted must have committed some terrible crime. In Creede, she remembered now. A crime against someone who Connor was connected with and as senseless and as savage as James's death or his kidnapping—she was not sure of anything right now—of this she was certain. She also knew that if these men were to be stopped, Connor was the man to do it. She marveled at the strength in his carved face and well-honed body. Yes, he could do it, but not with her slowing him down.

"You should not be taking me to Alamosa," she snapped. "You should be heading north. You must go, now, before you lose them."

"How do you know this?"

"I…I saw them… In the pass. There were five of them."

"Are you sure? What did they look like? What did they say?"

"I… It was dark. Difficult to see. They were riding fast. But I know it was them. I'm sure of it."

He pondered her growing agitation. She was hiding something, he could see it in her eyes. She was greatly distraught, too. Her hands clutched and unclutched at his shirt, and her voice trembled like the frantic heart of a trapped hare.

"What is it, Jo? What are you hiding?"

"Hiding?" Her voice rang false. Yes, she thought, she was hiding. Hiding memories too recently buried for her to dig up their still rotting corpses. The anguish and pain of her parents' death and the uncertainty of James's whereabouts had been cleansed in the soothing waters of a hot spring, but the fear and rage she felt at the memory of her captors' unadulterated evil could not be so easily assuaged. Yes, she was hiding, but now the need to keep these memories buried no longer seemed so overpowering. She could trust Connor; he would understand.

"You're right," she whispered softly. "You know those men, the ones I told you about, the ones I saw in the pass, they didn't just ride by. They stopped. They spotted our campfire. They could have just kept riding. There was no reason for them to…to attack us like they did. We were no threat to them. But they did, anyway. I think they took James, and I'm not sure if he is still alive. All I have left of him is his woolen jacket."

Jolyn began to tremble, and Connor gently eased her onto his lap, wrapping his arms protectively about her. She shuddered and continued, "They would have killed me if I hadn't run away. It was the leader—one of the men called him Luke, who actually saved me. Oh, not deliberately, you understand, but he could have shot me. But he didn't. He and his men tried to…they were going to…"

"I understand," Connor stopped her. "You're safe now. No one's going to harm you again."

"Connor," Jolyn asked cautiously, "why are you after these men?"

Connor appeared not to hear her. "This James. He was your sweetheart?"

"No, he was my very good friend."

"I see." For some odd reason, Connor felt pleased at her answer. "Jo, I'll be returning through the pass after I've dropped you off in Alamosa. I'll see if anyone has heard anything, anything at all."

Jo gave him a swift hug. "Thanks, Connor, I guess I owe you."

Jo wanted to stay tucked in Connor's strong embrace, but she realized that she had delayed him long enough.

"Connor, I'm fine now." Astonished, she realized that she was. With Connor close by, she thought that she would always feel fine. But she was being foolish, and she tugged out of his arms and rose unsteadily to her feet.

Connor was immediately standing by her side. "All right, Miss Independence, this is one instance in which, fine or not, you get my help." He swept her in his arms and carried her to Thunder. She hid her smile in his neck.

"How close are we to Alamosa?" she asked.

Connor deposited her safely onto Thunder's waiting back and gazed southward across the mottled sands of the desert. Tall white cottonwoods, standing between dark-green junipers and rusty spiked willow brush, dotted the plain in a few scattered clusters. Beyond, through a wavery haze of heat, he could dimly make out a dark swatch. That was Alamosa.

"I'd say we've got a little over an hour's ride." He gazed toward the west, measuring the hot sun's descent to the white-capped mountains on the horizon. "And, providing we have no further hostile hosts, we should arrive there about suppertime." He glanced toward the snake. "Shall we make him dinner?"

She followed the direction of his head and crooked a devilish grin. "Roasted rattlesnake, my favorite."

Connor collected the snake, and while wrapping it in onion cloth to place in his saddlebag, glanced curiously at his slender, resilient companion. She had been through a great deal. He had found her trapped on a ledge in freezing weather. She had nearly been bitten by a rattlesnake. She had seen her friend kidnapped, was nearly raped and killed herself. And hadn't she said something about her parents being killed? Yet here she was, small and delicate and tough as nails. She was some kind of woman. Rather besottedly, he smiled up at her.

"Does Jolyn have a last name?" Having secured the snake in the bag, he swung effortlessly into the saddle, repositioning Jo onto his lap.

Much to Connor's distress, Jolyn innocently wriggled in his lap. As he felt the warm surge and familiar tightening in his loins, he shifted uncomfortably.

"Be still," he ordered.

Jolyn immediately complied. She stared fixedly at Thunder's left ear, trying nobly to conceal a satisfied grin. It seemed Connor was no less immune to her charms than she to his.

"Well? Are you holding out for a ransom? How much will it cost for the prize of your last name?"

"How much are you offering?" she teased.

"What will you take?" His voice had grown deeper, sensual.

"Well," she listed, "I have no need of money. I have adequate transportation. Dinner has already been arranged. It seems that you have little to offer me." Despite the glibness of her words, Jolyn's heart was pounding. Never had she flirted in such an outrageous manner.

"Perhaps, then, you will accept payment of a more personal nature." His reply had been whispered huskily behind her left ear. His breath tickled her hair and tingled down the curve of her neck, spreading goosebumps along her arms. His right hand had slid upward along her ribs below her breast, his fingers smoothed flat along her rib cage, his thumb lying daringly along its side. Fighting the emotions that were reducing her bones to mere jelly, she jerked straight.

"Your price is too high. I offer it to you free of price. It's Montgomery. Jolyn Montgomery," she announced breathlessly.

Connor reined Thunder savagely in. "What? What did you say?" He was shouting.

"I said it was Montgomery. And stop yelling!"

"I'm sorry." Connor fought for control. Lowering his voice, he asked, "And your relatives? Their names?"

"Uncle Hank. My brothers are Nick and Chris. Why? Do you know them?" Alarmed, she turned to face him, but he held her rigidly in front of him. Intractable, his arm felt like a steel rail.

Harsh and relentless, the silence between them swelled in crushing waves. He stiffened in the saddle, and his arm dropped away from her. An angry heat radiated from his tense body. And then, as though driven by some inner demon, he dug his heels into Thunder's flank and charged at full gallop, Jolyn clutching at his side, toward the growing dark splotch that was Alamosa.

* * *

They reached Alamosa at dusk. Jolyn, barely aware of the icy wind that whipped against her and whirled brush and sand against the trim wooden structures along Main Street, slumped wearily in the saddle. Her leg and head ached, and she longed to curl up somewhere, far away from the jolting, racking ride of a galloping horse. Thunder had halted, and before Jolyn had time to assimilate the lack of movement, she felt herself lifted down and held in Connor's impersonal, rock-hard embrace. Connor mounted an outside stairway and shoved his way through the latched doorway. She felt a blast of warmth against her frozen face as he hurled them both into a brightly lit sitting room.

"Hawk!" Connor bellowed. Hearing no immediate reply, he cursed impatiently, "Where the hell is he?"

He strode over to a tattered divan and eased Jolyn down into its comfortable folds. "Hawk?"

"Is it myself you'd be wantin', me boyo?" a boisterous voice roared from across the room.

Connor whirled about and glared at his fatuous friend.

"Hawk, I'm in no mood for your shenanigans. Where the hell have you been?"

Hawk, recognizing Connor's barely restrained anger, tempered his humor and with a wry look toward the bedroom, said with aplomb, "I was tending to the needs of a very demanding young lady. I hurried as fast as I could."

Connor cast a baleful eye over Hawk, clad only in a brief towel that was wrapped casually around his waist. "Jesus." He stepped back, shielding something on the couch. "Will you get some clothes on?"

Hawk, his curiosity piqued, sidled farther into the room and peered intently around Connor's shoulder. Lying half-propped on the settee was a wisp of a girl with auburn tresses, a shimmering halo about her fine-boned face. Thin and pale, dark smudges and a yellowish bruise marring her delicate features, she looked like some lost waif.

"Well, I'll be damned," murmured Hawk in awe.

Jolyn, through an exhausted haze, stared at what appeared to be a blond hairy bear. He towered across from her, his shaggy head swinging from side to side, his hulking arms flung wide.

"Connor?" Both men heard the rising panic in her voice.

"Here, Jo." His soothing voice, so close to her, covered her with its reassuring blanket.

"Where are we?"

"Alamosa."

Jolyn nearly bolted upright. Struggling against the rising waves of exhaustion, she managed to sit up and swing her legs to the carpeted floor. Elbows propped on her knees, she held her head clutched in her faintly trembling hands.

"When will you be leaving?" she mumbled.

"Tomorrow morning." His usually expressive voice was guarded.

She relaxed visibly. "You will be care…" She halted as she came eye to eye with Hawk.

"So there really is a blond bear," she blurted.

Hawk for the first time in his life blushed from the soles of his feet to the roots of his hair. Enjoying his friend's discomfiture, Connor introduced them.

"Jolyn, may I present Hawk. Hawk, Jolyn Montgomery." Connor watched amusedly at the shifting emotions that flitted across Hawk's amazed but chagrined face.

"Montgomery. You wouldn't by any chance be related to Hank?" Hawk questioned.

"Why, yes. Do you know him?" Her shining sapphire eyes gazed hopefully into his astonished green ones.

"Why, of course. Didn't Connor tell you? Why, we're…"

"Hawk." The sulky whisper hung cloyingly in the air like heavy musk. "Have you forgotten me?"

Glancing uncomfortably toward the sound that grated from his bedroom, Hawk turned a shade redder.

"Hold up, honey. I'll be there in a second."

The occupants of the outer room heard a rather undignified harumph, and the loud crashing of a pitcher or perhaps a chamber pot. Ignoring Connor's unabashed grin, he bowed stiffly to Jolyn.

"Your pardon, miss, but duty calls," he muttered, and awkwardly backed out of the room, banging against the doorjamb as he stumbled into the other chamber.

Jolyn whirled upon Connor, all her previous doubts rushing to the surface. "You know Uncle Hank," she said accusingly. "And if you know my uncle, then you surely know Nick and Chris as well. Why didn't you tell me?"

"I didn't tell you because…" He stopped abruptly. Wearily, he faced her hostile glare and searched his mind for a way to tell her. "Jolyn, would you care for some coffee?"

"Coffee?" She glared at him as though he had lost his mind. "Coffee?" A rush of weariness flooded her, and she leaned achingly against the divan. "Yes," she sighed, gratefully, "I'd love some."

Connor swung toward the stove and poured the strong, day-old brew into tin cups. As Jolyn half-listened to the clatter of pot against cup, she speculated over Connor's motives. She thought back to when he had first heard the Montgomery name. From that moment on, he had treated her like a leper. What was so terrible about the Montgomery name?

"Jolyn, here you go."

She took the proffered cup and cradled it gingerly in her palms.

He watched her take a sip and spoke quietly, his words a brutal contrast to his gentle tone. "Jolyn, I don't know how to tell you this. Creede is a very rough town. A very rough town. Well, there was a robbery there." He stared back, guilt and remorse wrenching through him.

"Those men on the trail?"

"Yes."

"How did it happen?"

"Luke and his gang robbed my father's store."

"And your father?"

"Dead. Also, some other men."

She reached a tentative hand toward his, and he gripped it in silence.

"Connor, I want to go with you."

He dropped her hand and lifted her face to meet his. Staring into her determined face, Connor did not have to ask her what she meant; she intended to join him in his search for Luke's gang, the very last thing Connor wanted.

"No." His answer brooked any refusal.

"Yes, Connor, please. I'm not begging you. I have to do this."

"No, Jolyn, and that's the end to it." He strode away from her and grabbed his bags.

She was at his side, grasping his arm in paltry effort to hold him there.

"Connor, I'm going after them. Do you understand me? With or without your help."

He wrestled with her clutching hands futilely. “Hawk! Get in here!” Surprisingly, Hawk was there in seconds. Fully dressed now, he gazed perplexed from one struggling form to the other.

“Take her!” Connor bellowed in frustration. When Hawk hesitated, Connor nearly shook the foundations with his anger. “Take her, damn you!”

Hawk wrapped Jolyn in a bear hug and pulled her away from Connor’s retreating figure.

“NO! NO!” she shrieked. “Connor, you can’t keep me here.” She twisted and turned in Hawk’s unrelenting grasp.

“Keep her here, Hawk, and take care of her. I… Treat her with respect. Do you understand? Treat her like you would Annabel. But don’t let her out of your sight.”

Connor, confused by the conflicting emotions that raged through him, looked longingly into Jolyn’s peaked face as his eyes tried to plead for forgiveness. “Jolyn, please understand, you’ll be safer here.”

“No. You have no right. Don’t you see? They took James. They may have killed him by now. They tried to kill me. I should be the one to go with you. Me. Damn you, Connor. Who has more right than me?”

“I do.”

The slamming of the door resounded through the room.

Chapter 5

JOLYN'S MOUTH FELL OPEN BUT no words came out. Her feet were glued to the floor as she watched Connor explode out the door.

Hawk stared at the beautiful creature in front of him, his hands wide apart as if he were waiting to catch her.

The room closed in on Jolyn, spinning around her, and suddenly as though everything in her world wanted to collapse, Jolyn fainted.

Hawk, with his arms ready, caught Jolyn. My God, he thought, what the hell is going on around here?

Just then, Lucinda, Hawk's young-lady friend, drifted into the room.

"And what in tarnation are you doing, Hawk?" she demanded.

Hawk, uncomfortable with his new conflict, stammered, "Uh... uh...this here is Miss Jolyn. She...uh... Connor just brought her in and by God she just fainted right out."

"Hawk," Lucinda said dryly, "do you expect me to believe that story?"

"Dammit, Lucy, would you just mind helping me get this here thing up them stairs. She just rode in with Connor I tell you and I don't think she's too strong to do much of anything right now."

Lucinda was not used to Hawk dismissing her in that tone and as if stung by a bee, she jerked her head toward Jolyn and quickly hurried over to the young woman.

"My," said Lucinda soothingly, "she sure is a pretty girl. Where do you think Connor found her? Wasn't he out on a business trip somewhere?"

Hawk ignored Lucinda. He did not want to be mean, but he had better follow what Connor ordered him to do. Gently he lifted Jolyn in his arms and headed up the stairs with Lucinda in tow.

Up in his room, Hawk's face flushed with embarrassment. His large bed was a mess, blankets and sheets all astray—testimony to his afternoon romp with Lucinda. It didn't seem right now to bring Jolyn up here. Behind him, Lucinda seemed uncomfortable also.

"Hawk, I, uh, have to go now. I'm sure my father will be wondering where I am, and I only told him I was coming over here to pick up some supplies. I'll tell you what I took later, and we can settle the bill then. You just take care of what you have to and, well, thanks. I'll be going now."

Without even waiting for a reply, Lucinda flew down the stairs, grabbed the few items she had come for, and raced out the door. Once outside, she took a deep breath, looked back for a moment wondering what had just happened, shook her head, and sauntered home.

Hawk never heard her leave. The quick closing of the door was his only signal that he was finally alone. Delicately, as though he were holding a soft butterfly, Hawk lowered Jolyn on his bed, her copper tresses sprawling on his white sheets like a slow-emerging fire. Jolyn moaned softly.

"Easy there, little one. It's just me, Hawk. I'm a friend. Now just rest your pretty little head awhile while I sit here and try to figure things out."

His eyes scanned his room and Hawk saw it as if for the first time. It was a bit chaotic, he thought. No, he admitted to himself, it was an awful mess. Next to the bed stood a large brown commode with a rectangular mirror covered with dust. On the bottom shelf lay strewn several different bottles of ointments. On the far wall an immense chest of drawers rested heavily on the wooden floor. It could have been a deep mahogany, but the layers of dust gave it an eerie light-brown color. Every drawer was partially opened with the contents carelessly spilling out. Piles of reds and brown lay curled on the floor. There were several frames on the top of the dresser, the serious faces blurred by the dust.

On the opposite wall sat a square brown table. There were two chairs that went with the table, but they seemed to have fallen down somewhere near the doorway. On top of the table were books, assorted papers, and several candles. A stack of cards had been hastily thrown down at some point and rested where fate let them fly.

"What a slob I am!" exclaimed Hawk to his room.

Jolyn stirred. "What? Hmmm. Where am I?" she groaned.

"Shh, little one. It's okay. It's me, Hawk. I…"

Now Jolyn bolted up. "Where is Connor? Where did he go? Did he leave me? Where?!"

Hawk gently grasped Jolyn's arms. Her deep-blue eyes were filled with anger and hatred and hurt, and Hawk was surprised to see such a young beautiful woman as this washed with so many emotions.

His soft amber eyes stared into hers as he tried to calm her down.

"Jolyn, it's really all right." Hawk spoke slowly as if to make his words more believable. "Connor has not left. He only went down the street to get a drink. He will be back. I promise you that."

"How can you promise me anything about that man?"

"He's my closest friend. He's an honest man. He wouldn't leave you here."

"I have business to tend to, Hawk. I thank you for your hospitality, but I really have to go now."

"No, Jolyn, you can't go anywhere."

"What do you mean I can't go?" Jolyn asked, fear choking her throat as the words struggled to be released.

"Well, fer one, I promised Connor that I'd watch you. And fer another, well, I don't know, but you just can't go. At least wait until Connor comes back."

Jolyn sighed. Why is everything so damned hard? she pondered. Her fear was swallowed and resignation took its place. Jolyn glanced around the room.

"Good God, do you live here?" she half-chuckled.

Now it was Hawk's turn to turn red. He mumbled and uncomfortably shifted his feet. "Yeah, I guess it could use a bit of cleaning up."

Jolyn laughed. That felt good. Hawk was a very nice man even if he did resemble something of a blond bear. It wasn't his fault that Connor had dumped her on him.

"So," said Jolyn. "What do we do now?"

Hawk's tense shoulders relaxed visibly as he hoped Jolyn's demanding words would drift into a more comfortable banter.

"Well, how about a bite to eat? It is dinnertime and the, uh, young lady that was here was going to be my dinner partner, but since she has, well, left, how about me and you going for something to eat?"

"You know, Hawk, after weeks of beef jerky, that is the absolute best offer I've had."

"Fine. Well then, let's go."

"Hawk, could I clean up? I mean, I've been riding for a long time and I really could use a little bit of water. I feel like my skin is just pure dirt."

"Oh, uh, sure. I'll just go on down the stairs here and wait for you to come down."

Hawk went down into the store. He never did like this part with women. He could never figure out what their needs were, and he'd just as soon ignore it all.

Connor, smelling of whiskey and smoke, burst into the store.

Hawk stared at him.

"Well, man, what the hell happened out there?"

Connor had wanted to tell it all but had not been able to. He needed his good friend to confide in, to help him, especially now, since he was sure he had lost Luke.

Slowly Connor's gray eyes glazed over as he remembered it all. Taking a deep breath, he scanned the room.

"Where's Jolyn?"

"She's upstairs washing up. Don't worry. She can't hear us."

"It was bad, Hawk. Real bad. It seems Luke came looking for me again. Only this time…" Connor stopped. The words did not want to come out. It was too painful. "Only this time he found my father, Hank, and his two boys. Luke and his men shot them all," Connor spat. "I'm only surprised he didn't shoot Annabel, too. He just left her there on the floor in shock."

Hawk stared incredulously. His mouth clamped shut and he did not know what to say. Connor continued.

"I was late coming in to Creede that night. Remember I had stayed with you to work on the books instead of heading back early like I had planned. Somehow Luke had it all figured out, only he didn't know I had changed at the last minute. By the time I got to Creede Luke had already left."

"Did anybody see him, Connor? Anybody at all? Surely somebody must have come a-running with all that noise?"

"That was part of Luke's plan, Hawk. You see, there was a big party in town that night. Everybody was there. And with all that ruckus going on, who's gonna pay attention to a little gun popping?"

"So what did you do next?"

"Damn, I didn't know what to do. I carried Annabel up to her room and put her to bed. Right before she fell asleep she muttered something about Denver. Luke and the boys and Denver. So I left her and started following him."

"Denver? What the hell would he do up there?"

"I hear he and his gang have been messing around with robbing trains. Besides, from there they can head right up to Wyoming and hit the Outlaws Trails. I was close behind him, Hawk. I could smell him. His tracks were so fresh they practically cried out to me. And then up in Poncha Pass, well, I stumbled upon Jolyn. She had fallen off a ledge. She was running from Luke. Seems Luke and his boys crossed paths with Jolyn and her friend. They must have kidnapped her friend for some no-good reason and if they had found Jolyn I know they would have used her and then probably killed her."

"So why didn't you take Jolyn with you up toward Denver? You could have left her there in safety with some friends."

"I know, but there's more to this story. Seems Jolyn was coming this way to her only family—Hank Montgomery and her two brothers, Chris and Nick."

Hawk swallowed hard. "No!" was all he could mutter.

Connor nodded his head. "Actually, I'm glad we did come back down this way. Over at the saloon there's talk about a bad storm up north. In fact, I'm even thinking that Luke will change his mind and head back south."

"Where would he go? He doesn't know you're here. He wouldn't come looking for you here, would he?"

"No, the bastard's too stupid to do that. He's probably figured that I'm still in Creede burying the dead. No, if I know Luke, he'll head right for Conejos, hole up there for a spell, and then work his way into New Mexico and then Mexico."

"Not the old cabin by the river?" Hawk's and Connor's fathers had built a cabin snuggled in the mountains by the Conejos River. Memories came flooding back to both men as they remembered so many good times together as boys.

Connor shook his head as if to forget the old happiness. "I'll leave first thing in the morning, Hawk. But you have to take care of Jolyn for me. I guess she might want to go to Creede to take care of her dead kin. Would you do that for me, friend?"

"It's already done, Conn."

"Well, where's dinner? I'm starved. And I bet Jolyn is hungry, too. So where do we head?"

Hawk laughed, his blond beard shaking up and down. "How about Alamosa's finest? Pepe's. I hear his chili will keep you hot for a whole week?"

Connor grinned. "I think that's exactly what I need."

Just then they heard a soft noise from the stairs. Both men looked up in time to see Jolyn standing in the doorway.

At first Connor couldn't believe his eyes. This was the same woman he'd saved from the ledge. The same woman he at first thought was a runaway child.

Jolyn's soft copper-colored hair had been brushed till it shone as it cascaded gently down her shoulders. Small flecks of gold mottled like diamonds waiting to be touched. Her face, cleansed from days on the trail, was silken. For an instant Connor's fingers itched to caress her, and instead he balled up both his hands into fists as if to fight away any emotions that were strangely emerging. Jolyn's sapphire eyes gazed at both men, unaware of the burning lust in their eyes.

"Did I hear something about dinner?"

Connor coughed, regained control, and unclenched his fists. There was a heat that had slowly spread through his body that had never happened before. Oh, sure, when he was with one of the girls from the saloon his desire had always risen quickly, but never had he experienced this sensation before. He walked over to Jolyn and the sweet fragrant smell of her hair tickled his nostrils. He didn't know what to do. He sneezed.

"Are you feeling all right, Connor?" Jolyn was hoping he wasn't getting sick. She had other plans, big plans. But as Connor got closer to her, she couldn't think of anything else. His deep dove-gray eyes reminded her of something, but she was not sure what. His thick dark hair lay in clumps on his head and she wanted to comb her fingers through the wild strands and feel the texture. Up close she noticed a tiny scar above his right eye. Her fingers tingled to touch the smooth, shiny line. She wondered what had caused the mark and who had hurt him. For a minute she felt the pain that he must have felt at that time. Gray eyes locked onto bold blue eyes.

"Miss Jolyn, would you care for some authentic Alamosa cooking?"

Jolyn laughed and the smooth carefree notes sent chills down Connor's back. At first he seemed annoyed at the effect this stranger was having on him.

Jolyn noticed the change in his mood almost immediately, as if a dark cloud had somehow crossed over his face.

"Is something wrong, Connor?"

Connor cleared his throat, unaware of how tuned in Jolyn was to his mood swing.

"No, I was just…uh, thinking of something."

Now it was Hawk turn to laugh, only his guffaw was loud and contagious. Jolyn smiled at him, confused over his laughter. Hawk had witnessed the entire tacit exchange between Jolyn and Connor and realized his good friend was finally smitten.

Connor in turn glared at Hawk.

"Hawk!" he roared. "Where the hell is this place? I'm starved!"

Still chuckling, Hawk answered as the three of them left the store, "Just down the road, my friend. Just down the road."

***

Alamosa was a bustling new town in the late 1880s. It was a main roadway to points north and west and for the many Mexicans it was a new beginning.

Main Street was filled with townspeople. Many new shops had recently opened and with the coming of the train through Alamosa, business was at a new high.

Pepe's was a favorite spot. Inside it was dark and noisy and the chili was bubbling with meat and juices and hot enough to make your eyes tear uncontrollably. Jolyn was not used to this spicy food and only attempted to eat as she gently pushed the foreign meat concoction around the plate.

Jolyn looked up at Connor. Her dark-blue eyes in the dim light said nothing, but just looking at him made her feel weak. What is it about this man? she thought. James never made me feel this way. No one has ever made me feel this way.

Connor casually glanced at Jolyn. He had the strongest desire to touch her hand and hold her softly. He wanted to feel her skin against his. He breathed deeply, hoping to catch a whiff of her scent. It just ruffled his nostrils and made him heady. Good God, he cursed to himself, how can I be angry with her when she makes me feel so out of control?

Jolyn spoke first. “Connor.”

Connor ignored her. He stuffed his mouth with more chili and washed it down with some cold beer, all the time pretending he hadn’t heard her.

“Connor.” This time Jolyn was not going to be disregarded. Jolyn stared at Connor. Was this the same man who had held her so gently and brought her to safety? Or was it all just deceit?

Hawk turned to Connor and stared in disbelief. What the hell was wrong with his best friend? He had seen how Connor had looked at Jolyn. What was he doing ignoring her like a she was not even in front of him, staring up at him for words of comfort or kindness or anything?

Jolyn was too hurt to continue. She looked down at the table, her eyes blurry from the tears that were forming. I won’t cry, she ordered herself. I may not have anyone in the world right now, but I will not give in to tears. I must be strong for myself.

Jolyn steadied herself before she spoke. She took a deep breath and let it out slowly.

“Connor.” She began very slowly. “I don’t blame you for being angry with me. I know you wanted to find Luke and settle your score with him. I realize I just got in your way. But it’s not fair to dump me with your friend. No, no, Hawk, don’t interrupt me. I know you’re just being a good friend to Connor. From the way he’s acting, Lord knows he needs every friend he can find. But at this point in my life, I have to realize that I am on my own. My parents are dead. Therefore, I must do what I think is important to me. I don’t know what happened to James, but I have to try to find him. I cannot leave him out there alone with those men.

"If you don't mind, Hawk, I'll stay the night with you, but in the morning, well, I'll be on my way. I do have some of my own matters to settle and they'd best be taken care of as soon as I can make it happen. I thank you gentlemen for your dinner and conversation." Jolyn's icy words settled on the table like a cold wind. She got up slowly, gathered herself, and left.

Hawk stared at Connor.

"What in tarnation has gotten into you, man? That is the prettiest, nicest thing to have ever come your way and you trash her aside like the used hay in the stables."

Connor took a long drink from his glass. He stared at the door, hoping against hope to see Jolyn return. Even if it was only to hear her yell at him again. Finally he turned to Hawk.

"I don't know what's come over me. That girl has a strange effect on me, ever since I found her. I can't seem to get her out of my head. But, Hawk, I must. If I'm going to find Luke I have to be clearheaded and ready to fight. I can't have thoughts of some beautiful young thing in my mind. And now it looks like this here James has been added to all of this.

"I had to be mean, Hawk. It was the only way. I had to make Jolyn think I didn't care for her so she won't be hurt when I leave her. And especially if I don't come back. Especially if Luke gets me first. Hawk. I'm not coming back without him. It's either him or me, but I'm not going to fail again. There's too much blood on my head to let that bastard go free. The marshals around here can't keep up with him, but I can and I will. I will find him and destroy him. And I'm not going to allow thoughts of Jolyn to soften my resolve. I cannot."

Connor's face relaxed for just one moment as he thought of Jolyn. He wanted to caress her face, to feel her soft body against his, to bury his face in her satiny hair, to forget about everything evil and just love her. How could he be feeling these things when he'd only just met her? He was confused by his strong feelings, yet he knew he loved her. He knew he loved her from the minute he had found her. And that made his resolve to kill Luke even stronger. Because he wanted to be with Jolyn and he did not want to have to worry about Luke anymore. He had done enough damage to the people he loved. And it was time to finish him. Suddenly Connor realized that just thinking of Jolyn made him lose control of his thoughts. I must concentrate only on Luke's whereabouts, he demanded of himself. Only then will I be able to find him and kill him.

Hawk, drinking slowly, watched his friend's face. At first it was hard and calculating. Then, suddenly, a dreamy expression clouded Connor's eyes and he was happy, and then, quick as a flash, the storm clouded over and the stern look of resolve took over once more. This is not going to be an easy battle, thought Hawk. My friend is deeply in love.

* * *

Back at the store, Jolyn carefully undressed. Fighting back her tears had been hard at Pepe's, but now that she was alone, she allowed herself the freedom to relax and to cry and to curl up in the soft bed.

So he thinks he's going to Conejos in the morning, Jolyn thought through her tears. Those two may have thought I was upstairs out of harm's way, but I did hear Connor say he was going to Conejos. Luke must be going there, too. And if Luke is going to be there, then, dear Connor, so will I. Just you wait, Connor Richardson. I will be right behind you all the way. And when your bullet reaches that bastard's heart, mine will be flying next to it, because I, too, have a purpose in life. I will not rest until I find my friend, even if I have to kill Luke also!

And with her future in her hands and her heavy head on the soft pillow, Jolyn fell fast asleep.

Chapter 6

The cool May wind blasted against Jolyn's window, awakening her with a jolt. "Oh no!" she gasped. "I've slept too long!" She bolted out of bed. She hoped against hope that Connor would still be there and that she could convince him to take her with him. She dressed hurriedly, knotted her hair so that she could wear a hat, and raced down the stairs.

"Well, good morning there," said Hawk in a jovial mood. "I hope you slept well. It's almost lunchtime!"

"What!" Jolyn was shocked. "How could you let me sleep so long!"

"Oh, I just figured a girl like you needed the rest. You've gone through an awful lot these past few weeks."

Jolyn stared at Hawk. She knew Connor must have left. And that had to have been hours ago. Hawk seemed to have read her mind.

"I'm sorry, Jolyn, but Connor left right before dawn. He had some business to attend to in a hurry. But don't you worry now, because ole Hawk here is gonna take good care of you. I got me a few things to do and then I'm gonna take you to Creede myself. Make sure you get there and be with you to help you along. How's that sound?"

Jolyn was only half listening to Hawk enthusiastically carry on about his plans for her.

"Oh, oh, sure, Hawk. That sounds very nice. I appreciate everything you've done for me. Really, I have. You are a sweet man to put yourself out this way for me, a stranger."

"A stranger? Nah. Anyone that's a friend of Connor's is a friend of mine."

Jolyn's eyes rapidly scanned the shelves behind Hawk. I'll need some supplies, she thought, if I'm ever going to catch up with him.

"...and so is that all right with you?"

"Hmmm? What? I'm sorry, Hawk. What did you say?"

"Good morning, Jolyn, you sure do take a while to wake up, now don't ya? I said I'm a-going to do a few things in town and then get us some train tickets to Creede and I'll be back. There's some rolls there you can have for breakfast, unless you want to come with me to the cafe for some real food. What do you say to that?"

Jolyn spoke cautiously and slowly. She could not afford to arouse any suspicion in Hawk.

"I'm still so sleepy, Hawk. Would you mind very much if I just stayed here and rested? I could watch the store for you if you'd like."

"Hey, now that's an idear. Okay, fine. I'll be back real soon. And, hey, if any customers come in, well you jest do the best you can and write me a list of the things they needed."

"Sure, Hawk. Now go on. Get out of here. I'll be fine. I promise."

And with that, Hawk broke into a tune and left the store, whistling all the way.

As soon as the door closed, Jolyn released a sigh of relief. Now to go to work, she commanded herself.

Speaking aloud to herself, Jolyn began organizing. "I don't know how long I'm going to be, so I'd better be prepared for everything." She took a pair of saddlebags off the shelf. On the counter was a pad and a pencil. Carefully she wrote out *saddlebags*. "I'm going to pay for everything I take, Hawk, only not right now since I don't have any money yet. But when I do, I promise to mail it to you." And then Jolyn rushed to the shelves.

"I'd better take some flour, sugar, some pinto beans, lard, matches, molasses. Some salt pork and hardtack would be good, too." While Jolyn was stuffing the articles into the bags, she noticed some clothes on the other side of the store. "Now, I guess I won't look so obvious if I'm wearing one of these," she whispered to herself as she picked up a Plainsman hat, a flannel shirt, and some pants. "In fact, maybe they won't even guess I'm a woman riding alone." Jolyn placed the hat on her head and gazed into the mirror. "Hmm, not bad. Not bad at all."

Jolyn was almost finished with her packing when she noticed it. A gun. She knew she needed one. She just didn't like having one. Slowly she walked over to the case where Hawk stored the guns. Each one had a name under it, but Jolyn didn't need to know. Two brothers, a father, and the life that she had grown to love had allowed her to know more about guns than most girls her age. She undid the glass case and her hands swooped in straight for the .45 Smith & Wesson. It was a Shofield revolver. Just like the one her father and she had practiced with growing up. She could hear him talking to her, nudging her along.

"Hold it sweet, my Jo. Now pull that trigger ever so gently, just like the teats on our old heifer. That's a girl."

Jolyn's eyes misted over for a minute. Then she shook her head as if to shake the memories away for another time. "I have work to do. I…"

Suddenly the door burst open and in strolled a blonde-haired woman who looked vaguely familiar to Jolyn. Before Jolyn could think of who she was, the red pouting lips opened wide and burst out a screech.

"YIIIIIII!!! And what do you think you're doing to Hawk's store?! A little stealing of the goods while my man is out working to earn a living? I knew you were a bitch the moment I laid eyes on you, you with all your pretty hair and soft-talking ways. I knew it. Now why don't you just put all those things back where you found them, and I'll pretend like I never even walked in on you!" Lucinda was so proud of herself as she finished her speech that she never noticed Jolyn loading the gun.

Jolyn raised the revolver straight at Lucinda. I have to be strong if I'm going to get out of this town, she thought. I'm not going to let some floozy stop me now. Hawk may think this blonde hussy is special, but I have my own ideas.

"Now you listen to me, whatever your name is. Hawk knows what I am doing. He gave me permission to pack a few things. I have here a list of every single item I have taken so that I can pay him back. He told me to meet him at the train station and that's where I'm heading right now. And if you still don't believe me, then believe that I know how to shoot the third petal of a blue columbine cleaner than you can wipe that red paint off your face!"

Lucinda gasped. "I…uh…oh!"

Jolyn was getting desperate. "I said to move out of my way and I mean it!" And with that she slowly pulled the hammer of the gun back and aimed it straight at Lucinda's eyes.

Lucinda was not used to this type of treatment. It was all too much for her. She was not as strong as she liked to pretend she was and she was no match for a revolver.

"Oh, you…" And with that Lucinda ran out of the store. Jolyn, her hands shaking, lowered the gun. "I'm sorry I had to do that to you, but I really have to be going."

Jolyn quickly picked up the saddlebags and the hat, and, with the gun tucked neatly under her riding skirt, walked defiantly out the door, closing it gently behind her. "I'm sorry, Hawk. I had to."

Main Street was filled with customers, passersby, and strangers all looking for their dreams. Jolyn blended in with the crowd, never once looking back. She wasn't exactly sure where she was going, but she had heard Connor and Hawk talking about a new horse Hawk had purchased. If Jolyn could borrow that horse, she could be on her way.

In the distance, past the general stores, past the cafes, past Rosalita's Silver Belle Saloon, was the livery. Beyond that she caught a glimpse of the Rio Grande as it lazily curled its way through Alamosa down south. On the northeastern horizon, rising above the clouds, loomed the majestic Mount Blanca. This was beautiful country, but Jolyn had no time for sentiment. Normally she would have loved to ride out to that beautiful towering sight, but not now. With her hat pulled low and the weight of the cold steel revolver against her thigh, Jolyn was determined.

Jack's Livery was set apart from the town. Jack had always felt that his horses needed the quiet of the country, but mainly it was Jack who liked being away from everyone. He was a serious little man who never joked and never laughed. His son, Arliss, had helped him run the stables ever since his wife had died from the sickness of '85.

Fortunately for Jolyn, Jack was busy with errands in town that morning. As Jolyn walked into the livery, a small boy, not quite ten, greeted her.

"Well, howdy, ma'am. Sure is a beautiful morning."

Jolyn smiled and Arliss's heart skipped a beat. He had never seen such an attractive woman up close before. He didn't even wait for her to answer, too afraid such a delicate female would realize where she was and leave.

"Hey! What's yer name? You new here? I'm Arliss. Arliss Johnson, and I take care of the horses."

Jolyn's smile spread into a hearty laugh. Here was this small ragamuffin of a boy talking so fast she could not keep up with him.

"Well, good morning, Arliss. You did say Arliss? I'm sorry but I'm in somewhat of a hurry this morning."

"Sure," responded Arliss, not really paying attention to Jolyn's remarks. He was too caught up with the excitement of his conversation.

"Yes, ma'am. Arliss. Named after my granddadday who fought in the war. Died from a wound he got somewhere over in a place called Geddeezburg. Yep. And I live right above this here place." Suddenly Arliss took a breath and realized he was monopolizing the talking.

"Gee, I'm sorry. What's yer name, lady? You know, yer awful purty." Arliss blushed, but he was too eager to make friends with such a pretty face.

"My name is Jolyn Montgomery, Arliss. But my friends call me Jo."

"Gosh, that's a nice name." Arliss started kicking at the sand beneath his feet, suddenly tongue-tied.

"Excuse me, Arliss, but do you perhaps know of a man named Hawk?"

"Oh, boy," Arliss answered eagerly. "Do I know Mr. Hawk! Why, everybody in this here town knows Mr. Hawk. Why, he is the biggest man in this entire town. I heered he's nice, but I'm too ascaird to find out. Not that I'm a scaredy, but no, oh no, not me. It's just, well, I sure heered some scary stories about him. And, and, and, well"—Arliss seemed afraid to finish his story—"and I heered he's got a friend who's an Indian chaser." Arliss took a deep breath, as if that long explanation had worn him out.

Jolyn narrowed her respectful blue eyes as she gazed into serious hazel ones. The boy needed a haircut desperately and his worn clothes were too small on his growing body.

"You have heard quite a bit, young man."

Now Jolyn tried to choose her words very carefully. "Well, you see, Arliss, Hawk is a good friend of mine. In fact, I will be staying with him for a while. He told me this very morning, well, he said, 'Jo, why don't you go on down to the livery and find my old friend Arliss. He's a good boy and he'll do just whatever it is you need a doing.'"

Arliss's eyes opened wide. "Ya mean he knowed who I was and all?"

Jo swallowed her laugh. "Why, yes, Arliss. He said you were a very kind and dear young boy and one of the best workers he has ever seen. In fact, he said he was right proud of the fact that you've been seeing to his very special horse."

"You mean, you mean Granite? Why, that's the purtiest, biggest horse I've seen in a long time, and I've been around," he bragged.

"Why, that's what I've heard," cooed Jolyn. "And when Hawk mentioned him last night, why, don't you know what he said, Arliss? Only that I should come right here in the morning, see you, and have you saddle him up for me to go for a ride. We're going to have a picnic over at the Dunes."

Arliss shuffled his feet a bit, not really sure what to do. He was the only one here this morning and if he woke up anyone just to answer a question he might get the leather strap again.

This woman was awfully nice to him and she knew Hawk and all. If he didn't let her have the horse and Hawk had to come down here and see why not, oh, boy, would Hawk let him have it.

Arliss had decided. He felt very grown up and he said with confidence, "Okay, Miss Jolyn. I'll have Granite ready for you in just a bit." And he turned away.

Jolyn sighed. Now if she could just get out of town before anyone noticed that she had stolen Hawk's horse, she might make it.

Granite was a huge horse. Bigger than any other horse she had ever ridden. Arliss had not really questioned Jolyn's baggage. He must have assumed she needed all of that for the picnic. But she was on her own now. She was heading south. In her pocket was a map of Conejos she had found on Hawk's bedroom wall. She knew Connor was heading there. If only she could find him in time. If only she could be there with him. She wanted to find James's kidnapper. She needed to be there with Connor when he found Luke.

And most important of all, she wanted to be with Connor.

Chapter 7

The Sangre de Cristo Mountains emerged behind Connor as he and his horse raced southward along the range. Menacing late-spring clouds threatened his journey, yet he galloped on with his thoughts focused on only one thing—finding Luke. The aspens, just starting to flower, swayed in the spring winds, but Connor saw none of this. His eyes were closed to the rugged beauty that raced past him. He had to find Luke. He had to beat Luke at his own game and then destroy him. Luke had hurt too many people now and his time was up.

His steed needed a break from the unyielding course that Connor was imposing on him. Connor slowed down by the stream and allowed Thunder a quick drink and a short rest. Giving Thunder a fast rubdown and a few comforting and encouraging words, Connor hoisted himself back on top, and while he didn't gallop anymore, he wanted to push south as quickly as he could.

Taking a long breath, Connor surveyed his surroundings. From ten miles out on the high plains, he saw the subtle changes in the land formation. The Sangre de Cristo Mountains that had formed millions of years ago in the Colorado and New Mexico region were both ominous and breathtaking to behold. From the red glow on the mountain peaks to the gentler slopes farther south, the range was a part of his life; he had spent so much of his youth out here. As boys, they had cursed and laughed and teased. The mountain, they cried, why, it looks as ugly as a monkey's face. And from then on it had become their very own. It was officially named Monkey Face Mountain.

And every day he and Luke and Hawk had hunted and fished and swam. The Conejos River, always cold and clean and beautiful, was their playground. It sliced through the valley and meandered its way around the bend of Monkey Face. Many a day had the three of them climbed that mountain and stared down at their cabin and the river.

Connor's face grew dark and thoughtful. His memories took on a new meaning, a deeper insight. No, he shouted to himself, as he recalled hiking up the mountain and Luke—it was always Luke's game—daring them to stand at the very edge. Ten thousand feet above the valley and Luke sneering, laughing. "Go on," he would press them, "you can't stand there and touch the sky because you're afraid to. You're afraid of what I might do." And Connor and Hawk would just smile and hunt for more snakes. But now it dawned on Connor. It careened into his mind as if a bolt of lightning had suddenly struck him. Luke was evil. He had always been evil.

Connor had been so deep in thought that he hadn't realized how far and how fast he had gone. There it was, just down the hill. The cabin. How long had it been since he had come down here? They had all grown up and, well, it had been a long time ago. Connor's father and Hawk's father, closest of friends, had worked hard together to build their dream. Hawk's father died in the winter of 1875 from pneumonia and Connor's father had unofficially adopted him right away.

Connor slid off his large horse and tethered him loosely to the post by the front porch. There were no signs of Luke, but it was obvious someone had been here. Hoof prints surrounded the cabin and fresh muddy boot marks zigzagged along the porch.

Connor clenched his fists and pounded the railing. "Damn, I've missed him again. God damn you, Luke! I will find you! And when I do, you will rue the day you were ever born!"

Discouraged but resolute, Connor strode into the cabin. The floor-to-ceiling fireplace welcomed him with a familiarity and a warmth that played with Connor's memories. He knelt by the fireplace, knowing before he even touched the warm ashes that he had only just missed his brother. He squeezed the soft flaky substance in his fists and cursed silently.

Gazing up, his eyes scanned the bearskins and the elk heads that lined the walls. Each one told a story, a faded memory that tugged at Connor, leaving an ache inside him. His gentle gray eyes stopped at the hand-painted picture hanging a bit lopsided on the wall. It was a painting of the cabin and a very young family surrounded by trees alongside the river. Hawk's mother had painted it that last year of her life. She had died right here in the cabin, during childbirth. She and the baby girl who had not survived were both buried beyond the cabin, nestled against the massive mountains that overlooked the river.

Connor shook his head from side to side as if to toss away the memories that fogged his mind. This was no time for sentiment, he scolded himself. He had to change his plans again. Had to decide where to follow Luke. Had Luke gone straight to New Mexico? Maybe Santa Fe? Maybe Albuquerque? Or had Luke fooled them all and gone up North? There was a hideout he was known to frequent up in Utah. Someplace he bragged that he and his friends could hide from everyone. Oh well. Connor was tired. He would spend the day here, rest up, and then gather his thoughts and move on.

Connor collected a couple of worn buckets and headed toward the river. Might as well cook me something, he thought. The spring wildflowers squeezed up through the slowly thawing ground as Connor trudged toward the Conejos River. The rushing ice-cold water raced under the small wooden bridge he and Hawk had rebuilt years ago.

Beyond the bridge was a silver mine that they had all thought would make them rich one day. She had a few good veins in her, but they could never find the mother lode, and finally they just boarded her up. Some of the locals loved to tell the stories of the ghosts that walked the cave, but Connor would just smile at their fantasies.

Squatting on his haunches, Connor let himself dream and remember. His nostalgic eyes scanned the looming mountain above him and for some strange reason he could only think of her. Her soft skin, her eyes, the color of the gentle columbine flowers that graced the river's edge.

What did he see in her? What did he want from her? He had no time to get involved with a woman right now. He was too busy tracking Luke and a woman would just get in the way. She would just confuse his mind and ravage his soul. No, this would not be a good time for him to get involved with anyone, and yet he had an aching in his loins that he could not shake off so easily with his logical thoughts.

Suddenly he heard a horse neighing in the distance. Could Luke be back? Could he have only just gone out for some supplies? Leaving the buckets of water, Connor quickly scrambled back to the cabin. He loosened his horse's reins and guided the large stallion to the rear of the cabin.

"Hush, boy," he whispered, "be good for me now. Don't make a sound." Connor rubbed Thunder's large mane, all the time murmuring in his ears. He tied him up and then, hugging the walls of the cabin, snuck back inside.

Again he heard a horse from afar, this time much louder and much closer. The horse was not galloping, but it wasn't a slow stroll, either. Good, he thought. Whoever it is is not expecting me to be here.

Inside the cabin, Connor grabbed the long rifle off the wall and, remembering the drawer with the slugs, swiftly loaded the weapon. Louder and louder, and nearer, until now he could hear the horse's hoofbeats clearly. That's no small horse, he said to himself in amazement. Connor, rifle in hand, crouched behind the door. He could not look out the window without being seen, so he decided to wait it out until whoever it was entered the cabin.

The smacking of the horse's hooves against the ground pounded in his ears along with his heart. This is it. It has to be Luke. He must have dumped the rest of his gang for a while and come back here to hide out. This is finally my chance. Oh, you bastard of a brother. I only hope I have the courage not to kill you with my bare hands. I pray I have the patience to bring you back with me and see you hanged by the law. I swear, even if I have to be the one to wrap the noose around your evil neck, I will see you hanged for good.

Suddenly the noise stopped. Even the birds were stilled. Everything was silent. Connor focused on his breathing, afraid that his shallow breaths could be heard through the thick wooden door. His hands gripped the rifle more tightly, the sweat now pouring down his wrist onto his knees. His eyes sharpened, and he felt as though he could see right through the door. He saw Luke. He saw himself grabbing Luke's large frame, wrestling him down, cocking the rifle, aiming it at his matching steel-gray evil eyes.

Footsteps. Slow. Cautious. They did not sound like the feet of a large person. Connor raised his eyebrow. Could it just be a friendly neighbor come by to say howdy? Could it be another one of Luke's gang just on his way back from somewhere? Too many thoughts were racing through Connor's brain as he struggled to concentrate on the approaching stranger.

The door handle slowly turned. Connor almost dropped the rifle from his soaked hands. The wooden door screamed in protest as it was being shoved open. Connor wasted no time. With a piercing shout that shook the windows of the cabin, Connor leaped up. With one hand clutching the rifle and the other hand free, he grabbed the intruder and threw him to the ground. Strange, thought Connor, as the body crumpled underneath him as though it were an empty sack.

Connor could not make out Luke's body, tangled in a dark shroud. Straddling the body with his hips, Connor hoisted his rifle high above his head and, holding on to the butt of the gun, screamed, "I've got you, Luke. Give it up, you bastard! You are mine now! None of your friends are here. It's just you and me." Poised over the body, his hands shaking, Connor slowly squeezed the rifle and was about to smash his brother on the side of his head when suddenly an exhausted but raspy cry escaped through the muffled layers of clothing.

"NO!"

"What!" shouted Connor. "What the hell is going on here?" And with that he grabbed the black shroud and ripped it off.

"It's you!" he cried. "What?! What?! What the hell are you doing here, Jolyn?"

Chapter 8

JOLYN SAT UP, SHAKING UNCONTROLLABLY. She had not expected to be jumped and thrown to the ground as soon as she arrived.

"Connor, I'm…I'm sorry but I had to…"

Connor was purple with rage. "You had to what?!"

Jolyn brushed herself off and tried to stand up, but her leg was so bruised that she only fell back down again. She looked up at Connor, who completely ignored her pain.

"Tell me, Jolyn. What the hell brought you out here? How did you even know where I was? How did you get a horse? More importantly, why? Why, Jolyn? Why is it always you that seems to pull me farther and farther away from what I have to do?"

Jolyn just stared at him. How could she explain that the only things that meant anything to her—her parents, her friend James—were gone? Gone forever. And there was nothing else that mattered. Yes, she had family to go to. But it was family she had not seen in many years. Brothers who had grown up without her. They did not know her. It really would be like moving in with strangers. She felt nothing. But finding this man who had taken James, well, that gave her purpose. A reason for living. A reason for caring. Nothing else would do for now. She looked into those cold eyes, eyes that were filled with hate, and yet eyes that pierced her very soul. Small shivers raced down her spine and for a quick second she wished this man would hold her, hold her tightly and tell her all would be fine. All would be well with the world. But those rock-hard gray eyes held no warmth and Jolyn felt very much alone. How could she answer him with her feelings when it was obvious this man knew nothing of love, let alone friendship? She took a deep breath and held her head up high.

"Connor, I had to follow you because I have to find this man that you are after. Luke may be your brother, but he is my enemy, too. I want to see him dead as much as you do."

"Then let me find him and take care of this, Jolyn. What good will it do me to trail him when every time I turn around you are on my back? You are keeping me farther away from finding Luke."

Jolyn tried to move again and this time Connor did not ignore her, but instead bent over to pick her up.

Jolyn recoiled. "Don't touch me. I am not the little child you seem to think I am. I may have been weak and hurt out on the ledge, but I am fully capable of taking care of myself, Connor. And like it or not, I will be behind you, since you do not think it possible that a mere woman could ride beside you in hunting down Luke. I am sure it is worthless to tell you that I am well trained with a rifle and can ride for days, unlike many of the women you obviously are comparing me with."

Connor's icy glaze melted as his lips turned up into a small smile. This woman is very special, he thought. I knew it from the beginning, and damn that Luke, he's even in the way of my having a normal relationship with a woman.

Jolyn noticed the change in Connor's expression, but took it as another form of his mockery. Slowly she got herself up and hobbled to the couch by the fireplace, where she sat down, forcing herself not to wince at the pain in her leg.

"I think I twisted my leg when you greeted me at the door," she said coldly, "and if you do not mind I think I need to attend to it. Would you possibly have any cold water around?"

Connor, standing up, stared at this woman in amazement. His gaze was frozen as he watched her unashamedly pull down her large pants she was wearing. His fingers longed to touch her gently, caress her firm legs, and soothingly tell her how sorry he was for his brusque ways. A large welt, already turning deep shades of purple, had formed above her knee and he was mesmerized, watching her hands. She seemed skilled at what she was doing. What else did he not know about this incredible woman he had only known a few days? What mysteries lay beneath that crown of copper that reflected the sunshine even in this dusty old cabin?

Jolyn interrupted his thoughts. "Connor. I asked you if you had any cold water. Please, I think the sooner I can put something on this, the sooner the bruise will heal."

Connor cleared his throat. "Yeah, sure. I'll be right back." Quickly he left the cabin, realizing that the buckets of water that he had filled were still by the river.

As soon as Connor was gone, Jolyn sighed, tears sluicing down her dusty cheek from the pain. Tenderly she touched her leg and knew that she could not let on how much Connor had hurt her when he threw her down on the floor. With Connor gone, she relaxed her head against the couch. She breathed deeply, knowing that she could not show him her weakness, could not show him her tears. How could she convince him she was capable of following him if she was going to allow a small bruise to bother her? Thank goodness she had her pouch with her. Her mother had taught her many things, but most importantly doctoring. The pouch belonged to her grandfather, a doctor. He had always wanted his daughter to carry on his work, teaching her all that he knew, but Jolyn's mother had not wanted to do that. She had fallen in love and had only wanted to raise a family. But at the very least she had taught Jolyn everything her father had taught her, and now Jolyn never went anywhere without her granddaddy's worn leather pouch.

She opened it slowly, as if some great secret would come rushing out before its time. There were many packets of powders and ointments that she had used many times in the past years. Living at the camps with her parents had given her numerous opportunities to try out her mother's teachings. She pulled out a tiny blue packet and rubbed it gently on her leg. It felt cool to the touch and she knew that with cold water her bruise would heal fine.

Connor opened the door very quietly. Jolyn was so busy with her leg that she did not hear him. He stood there, a bucket in each hand, and could not explain the feelings that were stirring in his body. Her dense, dark-cinnamon hair cascaded over her shoulders, covering her face in a reddish-bronze cloak. He wanted to grab those locks with his fists and caress the silky thickness. Watching her rub some ointment on her leg made his knees grow weak with desire. Her soft fingers patted the growing bruise on her leg, the injury he had caused her, and yet all he could think about was what those long, delicate fingers would be like touching him.

Connor moaned, surprising himself because he had not realized he had uttered a noise. Jolyn turned. Her face was blank, as though she were waiting to see Connor's reaction. Connor wanted to apologize for being so gruff, for being so tense, but those soothing words would not surface. Instead he quietly positioned the buckets next to her.

"Here's some cold water."

"Thank you," Jolyn answered icily.

Connor grunted. He wanted to ask her how badly her leg hurt. He wanted to tell her he'd thought he was tackling Luke, but again, this was not the time for casual conversation. He had to rethink his position and deal with losing Luke's trail—again.

Connor cleared his throat. "Jolyn, how did you know to come here?" If Jolyn had known so easily, then perhaps Luke had also known, and that could be the reason Connor had found an empty cabin.

Jolyn squeezed the excess water from her wet handkerchief and placed it tenderly on her bruise. Her creased forehead relaxed for a moment as the pain subsided. Jolyn knew she had to tell the truth. She was not one to make up stories and she would not do so now. Bold cerulean eyes met cold leaden eyes and she shuddered from the anger that was behind the stare. She took a deep breath.

"I overheard you and Hawk talking last night."

"What do you mean you overheard us?" Connor asked. How much had this woman heard, and how would it now affect his chances?

Jolyn was very calm as she detailed the events that had taken place unbeknownst to Connor, hoping that her straight answers would not invoke another battle between the two.

"I was upstairs cleaning myself before dinner," she explained. "I was about to come down the stairs when I heard you and Hawk. Then I heard Luke's name. I decided to stay at the top of the stairs and gain whatever information I could. I know that wasn't fair, wasn't right. I had to listen, Connor, whether you like it or not. I don't always do things to please people; I do what's necessary even if that means hurting you…I mean others."

Connor clenched his jaw, his face turning crimson in anger. He had to know. He had to know exactly how much she heard and knew. "Tell me, Jolyn. Tell me absolutely everything you overheard. It's important that I know all you heard."

Jolyn spoke slowly. "By the time I heard Luke's name, all I remember is that you mentioned someplace called Conejos. You said that he might have headed down that way. Oh, yes, and especially because the weather was so bad up north. I wanted to rush down and tell you that I wanted to come with you, but I knew what your answer would have been. I decided I would follow you somehow. I thought if I could stay back a ways you would not see me until you came upon Luke. That's when I wanted to be right next to you. I want to catch him as much as you do."

Connor still did not feel good about this. Was she holding something back? There had to be more. "But you did not follow me here. Otherwise you would have arrived much sooner. How could you possibly have known where I was?"

Jolyn smiled. "Somebody must be helping me. As I sat on Hawk's bed thinking about how I would be able to find you, I saw a map above his bed. Conejos was on the map. I just memorized the way to go and followed you early this morning."

"What else, Jolyn? There has to be more. What else did you hear that you're not telling me?"

"There is nothing else, Connor. I do not lie, and I am not lying now. Just Luke and a few choice words you used to describe his animal nature and the chance that he might go to Conejos. What are you so worried about? What are you keeping from me that perhaps I should know about this villain? He kidnapped my best friend. He has probably killed him by now. And he would have raped me had I not escaped. Or had that part eluded your mind?"

Now it was Jolyn's turn to grow angry. Yes, she had followed him willingly, but this was no way to treat her. She spat out, "I have every right to be here, Connor. He is just as hateful to me as he is to you and I want to see him hanged!"

Connor's gigantic frame flew across the room and grabbed Jolyn by the shoulders so abruptly she froze. "He is a dangerous man, Jo. He is a murderer. What do you think he would have done to you had he found you? Yes, he would have violated you. And then he would have watched in joy as his gang raped you one by one. And then, when they were all finished with you, you would have begged him to kill you, but that would have been too merciful. No, Luke would not have been so kind, so thoughtful. He would have left you there for the wolves and for the cold. And as he rode out, he would have relished hearing you scream his name out, cursing him. Yes, Luke is a cold-blooded killer, and he enjoys every moment of it."

Connor's angry tirade rushed out so quickly and so forcibly that he never realized he had gripped Jolyn so tightly. His knuckles were white from the force and yet Jolyn had never flinched. Slowly he unfurled his fingers. Jolyn rubbed her arms mechanically. Connor reached out, but she swiftly slapped his hands away.

Her voice was filled with venom and Connor was surprised to find that it hurt him. "I do not need your help. I did not follow you here for your help. I want to catch this bastard as much as you do and maybe even more. You may not want me right behind you, Connor Richardson, but I will be there. A step away, a mile away, a day away. But I will find him with you."

Connor strained, wanting to tell her more, but would not. Not now. Hopefully not ever. She did not need to know who Luke really was. It would only hurt her, and he did not want that, although he wasn't sure why. It was just a feeling. A feeling he could not rid himself of, and for a moment he was filled with confusion and indecision.

Connor, taking deep breaths as though he was trying to calm himself, inquired more gently, "Jolyn, where did you get that horse? Surely you did not buy one, and I do not think you have it in you to just steal a man's horse. Or am I wrong?"

Jolyn's anger switched to pride. "I have my ways. I am a very resourceful person."

"I am sure you are," agreed Connor, "but a man's horse is very special to him. Did someone loan it to you?"

Jolyn shook her head. "Actually, it is a bit more complicated than that." Jolyn took a deep breath. "I took Hawk's horse."

Connor's eyes flew wide open. "You what?!"

Jolyn continued, "I went to the stables and explained to Arliss, the stable boy, that Hawk promised to let me ride and so would Arliss saddle him for me. Arliss seemed rather afraid of Hawk, but I explained it was all in good faith, and Arliss was more afraid of Hawk yelling at him for not believing me, so I was on that horse in a matter of minutes."

There was an eerie silence, and then suddenly Connor threw his head back and released the loudest wild laugh, causing a frightened Jolyn to shrink back on the couch. Connor lost all control, his shoulders shook, and his eyes filled with tears from laughing so hard.

"Oh…no… Jolyn," he gasped in between guffaws, "that was not just Hawk's horse you took. Oh, no, that was his absolute most prized possession in the world! And Granite used to be mine! Hawk won him from me in a card game one night." Connor stopped talking to catch his breath from laughing. "I always swore to that son of a bitch that I would steal it back when he wasn't looking, and sure enough you did that for me. Ha ha, he'll never, ever believe that you did that, or that you did it without my knowledge. Ooowheee, Jolyn you just made this horrible day a little bit brighter."

Jolyn tipped her head sideways in a cold shudder. "Well, Mr. Richardson, I certainly am glad I was able to bring some mirth back into your dreary hard-driven life. If there is anything else I can do to ensure you a better day, please let me know."

"Well, come to think of it," Connor replied, wiping his eyes, "you can do me the honor of returning that great horse and leaving me alone once again."

With that Connor scooped Jolyn in his arms, ignoring the cold cloth on her leg, which immediately fell off, and with a few long strides, carried her out to the large stallion. He hoisted her up, dumped her unceremoniously onto the saddle, and handed her the reins.

"Do what you want with the damn horse. I've had my day just knowing how Hawk will react. But you cannot stay here, Jolyn. It isn't safe for you here or anywhere where I am going. I don't care how much hatred and anger you feel toward Luke. You will get your revenge when you hear that I captured him and that the law saw fit to hang the bastard. And that will have to do for you. I'm sorry you won't see it my way, but you have no choice. This is no place for a woman," Connor said slowly, and then more quietly, "and a fine woman you are. If you stay here much longer I'm afraid what I might end up doing with you myself. I need to concentrate, and as much as I love your company, the smell of your shiny hair, the touch of your soft skin, I cannot have you here with me. I work alone. So back to Alamosa you go, and give my apologies to Hawk."

Jolyn was stunned. This was not how it was supposed to turn out. This was not going according to her plans. She was just about to reply when something cold and wet softly fell on her face. She looked up. Another snowflake floated through the air and landed on her cheek, where it quickly melted and transformed into a teardrop that raced down her silky face.

At first Connor thought that he had finally hurt her so much she had tricked herself into tears for effect. But when Jolyn glanced skyward, so did he.

"God damn you, you fiery witch! You've even got the damn heavens on your side!"

This time of year a snowstorm could be a very treacherous act of nature. Colorado was known for its famous late-spring storms and Connor knew deep in his heart that there was no way he could send Jolyn back to Alamosa without fearing for her life.

His anger was hot and palpable in the chilling air and even Jolyn feared to express any thoughts. Roughly he pulled Jolyn down, ignoring the whoosh of air she involuntarily released in pain as he tossed her down, leaving her staggering on her feet. Turning his back on her, Connor grabbed Granite's reins and walked the large steed to the small lean-to that was in the back of the cabin. There he made sure his tired stallions were tethered and that there was food for both. He wasn't sure how long this storm would last, but he knew he could not take any chances.

Jolyn strolled quietly back to the cabin, looked up to the heavens, and smiled to herself. Silently she thanked all those she knew were looking out for her. Then, with a newfound strength, her shoulders held high, she marched into the cabin, bracing herself for she knew not what.

Chapter 9

JOLYN SQUATTED IN FRONT OF the fireplace, scooping out the last remains of Luke's hastily made fire. Connor had been gone for over an hour. He'd mumbled something about food, grabbed the rifle over the fireplace, and left. She knew he wasn't happy, but she also knew he would not be so cruel as to send her off in such a storm. If she had a good, blazing fire before he returned, then perhaps that might improve his mood.

Jolyn could not stop thinking about Connor. Sure, she and James had been good friends, and there were even times when she had wanted their relationship to blossom. Yes, James had a girlfriend back in his hometown, but lonely nights tend to persuade the most loyal of men. She'd never loved James. She had always told him that. He was the brother she missed, but still, at times she'd pondered what it might have been like. And now, she wondered in fear, where was he? Was he hurt? Why did they take him? Had they gotten tired of dragging him with them and just killed him out of pure meanness?

But with Connor it was different. When he spoke to her she felt flushed all over and then suddenly she was cold. Sometimes if he looked at her a certain way her knees buckled. That had never happened before. She wasn't sure what to make of it. When he had grabbed her and carried her outside to her horse, she hadn't struggled. Instead she'd found herself accidentally nuzzling his neck to smell him. He had smelled earthy and musky, and what was happening to her? She liked the way he had thrown her in his arms, forcing her face to press against his rough cheek. The scent of his tobacco and his masculine odor mixed together made her heady. Suddenly she remembered. That was the same essence she recalled smelling when she was half conscious on the ledge. It had stuck with her and it made her feel warm and secure.

She laughed out loud. What would Connor, or, for that matter, anyone, say if she ever told them how she felt? But how did she really feel? Was it truly the search for Luke that pushed her into following Connor over territory she knew absolutely nothing about? Or was it Connor? And if it was Connor, well, what? What did she expect from all this? He did not know her. She was just someone he'd picked up half dead on a trail—someone who only caused him more grief and frustration.

He did not need some female following him all over the country because of a little revenge. Maybe he did not want her because he also did not like her company. Did he love another? How much did she know about Connor anyway? His past? Anything at all?

Just then, with Jolyn so deep in thought, Connor returned, slamming the door and jolting Jolyn so that she fell back on the floor, ashes flying off the scooper and landing on her face.

"Having trouble with the fireplace?" Connor asked, his smile a sarcastic smirk.

Jolyn, embarrassed, quickly got back up, brushing the ashes off her lap. "Thank you for being so concerned," she replied coldly. The way this man treated her, how could she even think he was worth dreaming about?

Instantly Connor was sorry he had spoken so roughly. Every time he was alone he thought about Jolyn and the minute he was with her the wrong words fell out of his mouth.

"I, uh"—Connor wanted to speak carefully this time—"I snared a rabbit. I can cook it if you want. I thought that maybe you'd want to do something with it. I'm not really that good with it anyways."

Jolyn relaxed a bit. She put out her hand and carefully took the rabbit. "The fire is still small. If you want to take over with that, well, I'll work with the meat." Jolyn was content to have something constructive to do, anything rather than going back and forth in verbal combat with Connor.

There was a silent agreement. Connor finished stoking the fire while Jolyn skinned and cleaned the rabbit. The cupboards were empty, so there wasn't anything to add to the meal except some salt, but that would be fine. She brought the seasoned carcass to Connor, who placed it on a spit in the fireplace. Together they sat in front of the mammoth rock structure and gazed at the animal roasting slowly.

Jolyn finally broke the silence. "It really is a beautiful fireplace."

Connor grunted.

Jolyn did not want to give up just yet. She was uncomfortable, but she'd be damned if she let him force her into silence. "You must have paid someone an awful lot of money to build this cabin. Course I don't know much about building a house, but this one does look sturdy."

Connor could not take anymore.

"I built the house," he spat, despite not wanting to share his story. "Me and Hawk and my brother and our daddies." The last part was said very softly.

"Your mother must have been very proud of you. All of you. Why don't you come here more often? Or do you, since I really don't know what you do with your time when you're not hunting down murderers and such."

Connor sat staring at the fire, mesmerized. He wanted to answer her. He wanted to tell Jolyn all about himself and how things really were with him, but something held him back. He was almost afraid to show the true Connor. What if she didn't like the real Connor?

"Connor?" Jolyn interrupted. "I'm sorry if I'm stirring up sad memories."

Connor cleared his throat. "No, it's all right. It's just, well, it really has been a very long time since I've been here and thought about this other part of my life.

"Hawk's family and mine were very close. We built this place together hoping to spend many good years together. And we did. Until some bad things started to happen. Hawk's mama died during childbirth and so did the baby. My mother died giving birth to my sister. My sister,

Annabel, lived, but it was hard on all of us. My father was so broken up that the rest of us just tried to make it as best we could. We had to get someone to take care of Annabel until she was old enough to just be independent and didn't need no mothering. So then Hawk's daddy and mine decided to go into business together and they left this place. They headed toward Creede where everything was booming. They set up a general store and began expanding. But then Hawk's daddy died from pneumonia. Hawk and me got more involved and we've been doing that ever since."

Jolyn was stunned to hear him talk so much. She didn't want him to stop. Hesitantly she asked him, "And how long have you been hunting Luke?"

Suddenly Connor's mood shifted. He grabbed the rabbit from the fireplace and dumped it on a wooden plate. He cut it up into pieces to cool, all the time avoiding Jolyn's gaze. He jumped up from the floor and darted into the back room only to reappear with a couple of bottles.

"I'm glad I always kept these hidden." He handed Jolyn a bottle. "Eat up. It looks good."

The warm glow of the fire did nothing to soften the mood in the room. Connor had opened up a little only to shut down again. Jolyn felt she could cut the air in the room with her knife along with her piece of meat, but she said nothing. She did not look at Connor while she ate, but whatever was in the bottle did her insides good. She felt warm and full and even cozy.

Jolyn cleared up their dinner remains and then stared at the cabin as if seeing it for the first time. It had taken on a new ambience with the hot crackling fire, the falling snow outside, and Connor sitting comfortably in one of the huge chairs, smoking his tobacco, his face serene.

The snowstorm outside had only gotten stronger and the wind even fiercer. Jolyn shuddered to think what it would have been like to ride home in this.

Connor looked up. "How's your leg?"

Jolyn answered quickly, “Fine.”

Connor wanted to say more, but hesitated and then finally blurted out, “I’m sorry I was so rough with you this afternoon. I guess I’m very frustrated at having been foiled again by Luke. It’s taking all my determination to stay here instead of following him.”

Jolyn looked at him hard. “You would follow him even in this storm?”

“I’d follow him to hell and back just to get him. He’s done a lot of damage to many innocent people and it’s time he was captured.”

“Why aren’t the authorities after him, Connor? Why is it just you? Why don’t you have a whole band of men with you?”

Connor thought for a moment. “It does sound wrong, doesn’t it? But to tell you the truth, there are men after him. Unfortunately, Luke isn’t the only criminal around these parts, and what makes it really hard to bear is that compared to some of the other outlaws, his crimes aren’t the worst. When it all adds up, yes, the sheriff and his men are looking for Luke, but not full-time and not all over the country. Just when they hear a lead or when they think he’s in their part of town, well then, that’s when they all get on their horses and head out. But I can’t wait for Luke to be unlucky and get caught. I’ve got to make things happen or he will keep eluding them and me the rest of his days, and I can’t bear to think what that would be like. And now that he has taken someone—your James—well, this is a new angle for him and I’m not sure what he plans to do next.”

“Connor.”

“Hmm.”

“First of all, James is not mine! We are best friends. And I’m sorry I keep messing you up. I’m sorry you ever found me on that cliff, because if it weren’t for me you would have captured Luke by now. He’d probably be hanging right this minute and you’d be celebrating with Hawk and your other friends instead of having to play nursemaid to me out here in the mountains.”

Connor looked into the most beautiful cobalt eyes he had ever seen in his life. They were misty, as though Jolyn were about to cry but would not allow herself such weakness. He wanted to touch her silken face with his hands and feel her creamy cheeks. He wanted to hold her in his arms and tell her everything would be fine. He wanted to...but instead he heard himself saying almost too distantly, "Don't worry about it. It's fine. I'll get him. It just wasn't meant to be now. But I'll get him. His luck can't hold out forever."

Jolyn hugged her knees for comfort. She felt all alone, even though she was next to Connor. She had wanted him to hold her in his arms and to feel his warmth surrounding her, but his cool replies only forced more distance between them.

"Well," she said quickly, "I guess I'd better get ready for bed. I will be heading for Alamosa in the morning."

Connor cleared his throat uncomfortably. "Yes, uh, that sounds like a good idea. Normally I'd suggest you sleep in Hawk's room, but since we're not prepared for this cold, I think it best we both sleep out here by the fire. That is, of course, if you don't mind."

Jolyn answered a bit too hastily, "Fine."

Connor left the room for a few moments and came back loaded down with several blankets and pillows. "Here," he said as he threw a bundle toward her, "these should do you nicely."

Jolyn almost fell back as she caught the huge stack of down blankets.

"Umph. Thanks, Connor. Your hospitality is overwhelming."

She was too busy setting up her blankets to notice the wide grin on Connor's face. He liked teasing her and seeing her get all fired up over his actions. When did he ever tease someone besides Annabel? And that was when they were just kids.

On this cold, snowy night in May, a roaring fire in front of them and an enormous brown bear rug underneath them, Jolyn and Connor made themselves as comfortable as they could be in the small cabin by the river.

Jolyn thought she would be nervous and not fall asleep right away, knowing how close she was to Connor, but the minute her head touched the soft pillow, she was sound asleep.

Connor was not so lucky. Staring at her so close only made him realize how much he wanted to hold her and how many times he had had an opportunity to but backed off. He wasn't sure why he would act aloof with her every time she was getting close or making him open up. There was something special about this girl. Besides being the most beautiful woman he had ever seen, besides being the smartest female he had ever dealt with, besides being so God damned stubborn about things, he found himself falling in love with her and he was scared.

Knowing she was sound asleep, Connor rechecked the fire to make sure it would last the night. Cautiously, so as not to awaken her, Connor moved his blankets closer to Jolyn.

Softly he whispered, "Oh, my dear Jolyn. How lucky for you I have not ravaged that exquisite body of yours. I long to touch you and when the time is right, I will. I long to kiss those sweet, full lips of yours and hold you in my arms. I've never said that to any woman, awake or asleep, and I don't know when I will say them again. I want you, Jolyn. I want you more than I want to see Luke dead. And that scares the hell out of me because I cannot stop my quest. So if I am rude or cold toward you, that is my reason why. If I allow myself to fall in love with you, sweet woman, I will never be able to leave your side. Goodnight, my love, and may you one day soon be my true love."

The tempest outside stormed on as the two quietly and peacefully slept.

Chapter 10

JOLYN WOKE SLOWLY, THE ACRID smell of the leftover burning wood from the fireplace irritating her nostrils. She was so warm and so comfortable she did not want to move, let alone get out of the warmest blanket she had ever slept in. She couldn't remember feeling so good in a very long time. Like a waking cat, she stretched her long, graceful legs and arms and then accidently bumped into something hard.

Oh my God, she almost cried out as she realized she was sleeping not just next to Connor but practically underneath him. Connor, who had been several feet away from her when they'd both lain down together, was now so closely entwined with her body that she could not fully reach out her arms without pushing him away.

He was in such a deep sleep that Jolyn was now afraid to move lest she wake him and then start the day with him in a foul mood. She curled back under her blankets and studied this man who was so wrapped up around her. His deep, dark hair was tousled, and it hung in huge chunks over his forehead. Gently, very gently, so as not to disturb him, Jolyn lifted a thick lock and twirled it back on top. Connor breathed deeply and Jolyn thought for sure she had awakened him.

With one slender finger Jolyn traced his cheekbone. Her feathery touch would not rouse him, and she had been wanting to caress him for a very long time. His face was so strong, so full of character, as if he had been carved from stone. His stubble was hard and prickly, and was a deep dark brown with hints of maroon intermixed into it. Long, thick lashes delicately grazed his upper cheeks. Full lips, somewhat chapped from being out in the wind and the cold, caused Jolyn's heart to beat a little faster. She longed to touch those lips with her own. Instead she outlined them with her fingertips, wincing at the thought of the cracked spots. She made a mental note to give him some of her special ointment. That was, of course, if he would even let her give it to him.

Suddenly his breathing pattern changed and before Jolyn could pull her finger away, Connor's eyes flew open. Soft and dove-gray, they looked upon her tenderly. Jolyn, lying prone on the floor, was grateful she was not standing up because she did not think she could. Her knees were weak and a warmth, the likes of which she had never known before, spread from her loins all the way up to her cheeks, so hot they felt as though she were on fire. Could Connor tell? she wondered.

Awkwardly and slowly, she removed her arm from underneath his neck and slipped away from him. Sitting up, she tried explaining.

"Um, I think you somehow tangled up with me last night and I didn't want to wake you."

Connor grinned. "And my lips? Were they tangled up too?"

Jolyn lost all sense of humor. "No, they were not tangled up, too. I was just, well, I was touching them to see the degree of chappedness that you were exhibiting and thinking over my list of several different ointments that I have that could possibly alleviate some of your dryness."

"Oh. That sounds very official to me."

"Yes, and just as I was coming to some sort of conclusion you decided, and I might add somewhat prematurely, to wake up before I could reach a final decision."

"Oh, I am sorry, Jolyn. Do you think perhaps you need to touch them some more? They are feeling a mite sore." Connor's smile reached his eyes, changing the soft dove to a mocking silver that sliced through Jolyn.

She had had enough of his teasing. "I'm very well now, thank you. I do have something that will ease your pain if you can spare the time to put some on. In fact, I'll go get it right away." And with that Jolyn jumped up and staggered over to her bag. She hadn't realized how stiff her legs were from the riding, the bruising. Jolyn knew she was a strong woman, but everything she had just been through had taken its toll on her body and she felt rigid and clumsy.

While she was rifling through her bags, Connor got up and ambled to the front door. He attempted to open it but realized that the late-spring storm had dumped over ten inches of snow during the night and the snowed-in cabin was not going to be left at all today. Another day of waiting, another day of not fulfilling his quest. Damn!

And with that he flung his body around, cursing quietly just as Jolyn had raced over to show him her ointments. They both collided and fell back onto the floor. This was too much even for Jolyn and despite the frustration and the clipped conversations, the two of them released their bubble of outrage and burst into a fit of laughter. The tension in the air lifted as both of them grabbed hands and hoisted each other up.

"Here, Connor," giggled Jolyn, her face relaxed and smiling, "this stuff really does work. I'll have those chapped lips good as new in no time at all."

"Well," Connor quipped, "what good are smooth lips in the middle of a snow storm if I have nothing to do with them but eat some old leftovers?"

"Hmm," replied Jolyn, not giving in to his playful banter, "I guess I'll just have to find some good use for them when they are indeed healed."

Now it was Connor's turn to enjoy a burst of warmth as it spread throughout his body. He could feel his manhood swell and, not wanting to frighten Jolyn, he quickly turned away and strode to the fireplace.

"Okay," he said a bit too loudly for just the two of them, "let's get this here fire going again, because it looks like you and I are going to be here for a spell."

Jolyn was nonplussed. What was going on with this man? First he's tender and sweet, then he's gruff, then he completely ignores any type of flirtation I attempt. Men! I do not understand them!

* * *

Breakfast was a quick warm-up of something brown in a can. Jolyn wasn't quite sure what it was, maybe some kind of meat and beans. She and Connor had come to an acceptance of each other. They were not arguing or fighting, but they weren't laughing, either. It wasn't comfortable company, but it was better than the constant quarreling.

After the silent meal the two spent several hours cleaning up the cabin from years of disuse plus a few days where Luke and his men had carelessly shoved and tossed various items. The cleaning helped pass the time as the storm outside had left them paralyzed from moving on. Connor was content in knowing he had left enough feed for the two horses and planned on making his way out there soon enough. In the meantime, the two of them worked well together and Jolyn, singing softly, spied Connor smiling at her tunes.

Morning passed quickly and soon it was lunchtime. Jolyn pulled out some of the supplies she had taken from the trading post and managed to create a fulfilling fare. The atmosphere seemed casual as Connor relaxed and shared more stories about his past. Jolyn especially enjoyed hearing about the good times Connor had with his father along with Hawk and Hawk's father. She noticed he never mentioned the rest of his family, and since things were going so well, Jolyn never questioned it. As long as he wasn't talking about Luke he was in a good mood and she liked that. She liked him. In fact, as the day waned, Jolyn found herself growing more and more attached to him and blessing the storm and their situation.

* * *

Late in the afternoon, Connor and Jolyn shoveled their way over to where the horses were penned. It wasn't easy work, but Jolyn enjoyed getting out and breathing in the cold, crisp air. The horses had managed well with the storm and were both content as their riders took the time to give them a long and satisfying grooming session. The sun was sliding over the mountains and a chill seemed to wrap its icy fingers around Jolyn.

Even with the temperature dropping the early sunset was breathtaking. Sunset over the Conejos River was truly a reflection of beauty. The golds and crimsons played havoc with the snowy crystals on the ground as the purple rays sliced through the budding aspens. Jolyn and Connor left the horses to their feed and plodded back to the cabin. They sat on the porch and Connor found an old quilt to cover them as they watched in quiet wonder as nature wove her spell.

"I think I could live here forever," breathed Jolyn. "It is so absolutely beautiful. I don't miss the old miners and their stench and their dreams and their faded memories."

"Was it always so rough on you, Jo?" asked Connor.

Jolyn looked at him quickly. She felt something stir inside her when he called her Jo. This new closeness she felt made her eyes suddenly welled up.

Connor was concerned. "Is something wrong? Did I say something to upset you?"

Jolyn shook her head and took a deep breath. "No, Connor. I'm okay. It's just that, well, I like hearing you call me Jo and it, well, it was nice."

Jolyn gazed up at the dimming mountains and thought for a while.

"Being with my parents was the nicest part of all my travels. The camps are not a fun place to live in. Everyone is so intent on finding that mother lode that there is little time for anything else. It's a rush to see what each person brings up that day from the mines, and then again it's terrifying because once someone goes down you are never quite sure if they're ever going to come back up.

"Oh, we have parties and dances and church. We are a civilized group, after all, but still, it's a town put together on hopes and dreams, and once they're used up the town dies and scampers away in shame only to rebuild somewhere else. Even my own parents constantly talked about the day we would all be together again. My dad never wanted to leave Chris and Nick with Uncle Hank. Oh, they would be fine with him, but Dad hated separating the family. I can't tell you the nights we spent talking about the house we would build together and how we would spend our money. Now I have to go to Creede and tell my two brothers that not only is our dream dead, but so are our parents. I haven't seen them in over two years. I can't imagine how on earth I'm going to be able to tell them the news. And if I don't find James, somehow I need to find his girl and tell her. Tell her that her dream has been squashed. They were going to get married and raise a family and…" Jolyn's breath caught and she could not go on. She could not envision James being murdered or being used for other means on the trail. Was he being tortured? Icy despair rushed in and enveloped her, turning her inward, and she shivered underneath the quilt.

Connor stiffened. His eyebrows tightened together the more he listened to Jolyn. He could not believe what he was hearing. He had to be sure. He could not let Jolyn go on believing something that was no longer a truth. He braced himself as he began a speech that he was afraid to make, knowing this information would surely overpower what little resolve she had left in her.

"Jo," he said softly. "I think I have something to tell you that is going to be very difficult for you."

Jolyn turned to face Connor. The sun had slipped silently beyond the mountains and the pale stars had taken their rightful place in the sky. A sharp frost filled the air and Jolyn shuddered. Quickly Connor placed his arm around her and pulled her closer to him, tightening the quilt around the two of them.

"Jo. Remember how I told you my father had set up business in Creede with Hawk's father?"

Jolyn nodded, her face filled with innocent wonder.

"Well," he continued, "Creede can be a very dangerous place. People are coming and going every day in that town. It's a real boomtown, with businesses popping up every day as well as falling apart every day. Seems like people thought Creede was going to be the next major city in Colorado or something like that. Well, one day about four or five years back, Hawk's daddy was on his way to the bank with the mortgage payment and that day's earnings. He passed his favorite saloon, Kirmeavy's, and he couldn't resist going in. He wasn't a big drinker, but he was so proud of being able to pay that last mortgage payment that he wanted to celebrate. By the time he got to talking and drinking with his pals he also got a little bit drunk. That's when he started bragging about what he had in his pockets. Sure enough, by the time he finally left Kirmeavy's, the banks had closed and it was dark.

"In the saloon that afternoon were a couple of ole gunslingers who heard the whole story. When Tom, Hawk's dad, finally left, these men followed him. They pulled him into a dark alley, robbed him and beat him near to death. He was so physically weak that he never recovered and then he developed the pneumonia that finally killed him. And worse part, they never found the bastards who did it."

"Oh, Connor," cried Jolyn, "I'm so sorry for Hawk and his father. How awful!"

Connor cleared his throat and continued. "That's not all to the story, Jolyn. My father of course was very upset, but he also had to realize his situation. He had another friend in town with whom he had gotten very close. Since my father was now a little short of cash, this friend told him he would help him out and perhaps they could become partners."

"That's so nice," whispered Jolyn. "What a nice man."

"Yeah, I thought you'd think so. In fact"—Connor slowed himself down to make sure he would say his words carefully—"you know this gentleman, too. His name was Hank. Henry. Henry Montgomery."

Jolyn gasped. The sudden realization came crashing down. "My uncle! Oh, no! And you're telling me this because…because Henry was the other man you spoke of. They killed Uncle Hank. Oh, Connor! Chris and Nick? Are they…?" She could not say the words, but she had to. She had to force herself to. "Were they, Connor? Were they killed also?"

"I'm sorry, Jo. Yes. I'm so sorry."

Jolyn could not talk. Her head fell heavily to her chest. This was too much. First her parents, and now the rest of her family. She was all alone, but the reality of this was beyond her. Connor could not stop her from shaking uncontrollably and he quickly scooped her up off the chair and carried her inside and with steady hands lowered her onto the couch next to the fire.

The tears would not fall. It was too much of a shock and Connor could not stop her shaking. The fire was blazing and yet Jolyn's skin was ice. She did not see Connor. Her eyes were glazed as if all life had been sucked out of them. Connor reached for another blanket and threw it on the bearskin rug next to the fireplace and then carried Jolyn over and gently eased her onto the thick warmth. He had to get her as close to the flames as possible. He was afraid. Really afraid. He had never had to deal with someone like this before. Maybe it was because he felt so much for this woman that he was so frightened. Afraid that she was in immense pain from her losses and because he felt her agony. He pushed all of that out of his mind and concentrated on making her warm. He lay her head softly on some pillows and then rubbed her all over. She was frigid. Her body temperature had dropped and her lips were turning blue. "Oh, God," he prayed out loud, not caring if Jolyn even heard him, "don't die on me. Oh, Jo, I can't make it without you. I want you. In the time we've been together I've been such a fool. I say the wrong things and I get so angry at you. I'm so sorry. Only please don't die."

Connor did not realize that while he was talking and rubbing Jolyn so vigorously he had been crying. Maybe it was for the death of his own father, or maybe it was for the fear that Jolyn might die; he did not know or care. He just knew that Jolyn had to get warm.

Connor could feel her body temperature rise ever so slowly. But he did not stop. He was possessed. He could not rest until she was completely safe. He could not lose her.

Jolyn closed her eyes tightly. She was still numb. She felt Connor massaging her, but it did not seem to help. She was trembling and could not stop. Taking a slow, deep breath, she willed her body to relax, and only then did she feel warm drops of liquid trickle down her cheeks. She opened her eyes slowly only to see Connor's worried face wet with tears. Her heart ached deeply for him, and at that moment a pain so deep inside her grew and throbbed and she knew something between them had bound them forever. She reached up to him and gently drew his head onto hers.

Together they embraced and cried, holding each other until, exhausted, they fell asleep wrapped in each other's arms.

Chapter 11

The bright Colorado sun poured in through the windowpanes, slowly stirring Connor and Jolyn from their deep sleep. The fire was long out, and a strong chill had fallen heavily in the room. Connor lazily opened his eyes and gazed at Jolyn, his body warming to the closeness of them. With one hand he gently touched Jolyn's shoulder, his rugged fingers tracing her as he glided his hand downward.

Jolyn moaned and stretched and opened her eyes. At first she wasn't sure what was happening, where she was, or why she was so close to Connor. Then a spreading redness from the roots of her hair down to her toes cried out her embarrassment. Uncomfortable in her surroundings, she pulled away, but Connor would not allow her. He held her tightly.

"Jo. My beautiful Jo. I have loved you ever since I found you."

Jolyn stared up at Connor in shock. Could this really be Connor talking? Was this the man who had roughed her without pause and thrown her on her horse? Was this the same man with whom she had also fallen in love but to whom she was too afraid to admit her own true feelings?

"Oh, Connor. I…I…"

"Shhh, my darling. You are like the Conejos River out beyond the cabin—wild and beautiful and filled with a sweetness from which I can never stop drinking. I want more of you. I need more of you."

Jolyn watched as Connor's robust lips hovered above hers. As his head descended, her eyelids fluttered shut. She felt a delicate whisper cross her own warm lips, a gentle pressure, and then it was gone. She opened her eyes and gazed into his melting, soft, dusky eyes. She watched as he lowered his face toward hers once again, as his lips hungrily captured her own. His tongue explored her mouth unhurriedly, and Jolyn felt an electric tingling race through her. She gasped. Then, curling her fingers about the nape of his neck, she pulled him eagerly back to her waiting swollen lips. He kissed her again, now more deeply, his breath mingling with hers. His fingers stroked her cheeks, her thick hair, her long, graceful neck, and slid sensually down her back and up again to encircle her warm shoulders. He pressed a myriad of light kisses across her eyelids and face, down along the back of her ear and into the hollow of her neck. Jo shivered in response.

"Jo, you are so beautiful," he whispered huskily. "I want you. I want all of you."

Jolyn trembled at his deep, masculine voice. She knew she should stop him before…before… She wasn't sure why, only that she had never experienced these sensations.

Connor pulled her sultry body even closer. Jolyn felt the firmness of his chest press into her breasts. Her nipples ached, and a subtle throbbing erupted from her loins. Her body burned with its first awakening. Again Connor kissed her, and this time she surrendered to him, wildly matching his passion with her own. Jolyn was lost. Strong hands cupped her breasts, gently massaging them to their fullness as his thumbs lightly stroked her hardened peaks. Fiery sensations shimmered outward in ever-widening circles. Jolyn shivered again and grew weak. With glazed, unfocused eyes Jolyn stared innocently into Connor's flushed face.

Connor, breathing heavily now, was almost out of control with his own raging emotions. His hands threw back the quilts of last night's cold as he sought to free her from her clothes. He murmured soft words of passion to her as he deliberately peeled off her layers. Finally, Jolyn was completely and utterly exposed to Connor. His feverish eyes burned into her body in total awe, unashamedly and boldly staring at her, memorizing every satiny inch of her body.

"Oh, Jo." Connor could not find the words to describe his feelings at that very moment. He undressed himself quickly and knelt over her. His lips took hers and the fullness of the heat from his naked body covered hers and melted the two together. Flushed and fevered, she waited taut and trembling.

Jolyn's velvety-smooth skin sang beneath his touch and her hungry responses to his kisses fanned his burning desires. Connor's mouth was in the hollow of her neck, his tongue searching, his teeth nibbling a molten path to her breasts. Finding her hardened nipples, he suckled the sweet nectar. Jolyn arched upward. Unknowingly, she dug her nails into his shoulders and instinctively pressed her loins against his hips, undulating as he swelled with a scorching craving that would not be cooled.

Connor could wait no longer. He was a man possessed by this goddess. Gently he eased his large frame over Jolyn's and softly spread her creamy thighs open. With his tongue he glided downward over her soft and flat stomach, drawing little circles. He rested his head on her thigh, deeply inhaling her womanly scent.

Jolyn was panting. Having never experienced these sensations before, she was not sure what to do or how to respond, only that her own body was responding to Connor's every touch, his soft puffs of breath on her, his torrid tongue, and his exploring fingers; she lost all control. Suddenly deep within her loins there was an eruption of fire as she realized Connor was kissing her! Small butterfly strokes tickled and singed at the same time and Jolyn moaned uncontrollably. Connor now pressed his tongue deep within her and Jolyn closed her eyes, fearful that she might faint from the weakness she was feeling. Her hips heaved, and she unknowingly pressed her mound higher and higher to allow Connor more depth.

"Ohhh, Connor. I never…I have never been with…"

"Quiet, little one. I know. I understand. I want you, Jolyn. With all my heart and soul, I want you."

Connor rose to his knees, his manhood so large, Jolyn gasped. He positioned himself so that he might enter her lovingly and gently. Jolyn's heaving breasts rose partially from fear and partially from the increased excitement. She wanted him. She'd desired him from the moment she saw him and had not understood those emotions until right now.

"Connor, I love you." Her hands stretched out to him and pulled him down into her and she was a wild animal filled with passion and desire surrounded in a wild haze.

"Hey! Connor! Are you in there? Jolyn?! Where are you two?"

Connor disentangled himself awkwardly and sprung up to his knees. "What the hell?! What? I never heard horses!"

Jolyn quickly covered herself with the quilts and ran to the couch. Who could that be? she thought, her face flushed with lovemaking and the knowledge that someone had almost walked in on them.

Connor easily threw on his jeans and flannel shirt and ran out to the porch. From the couch Jolyn could hear the conversation.

"God damn, you son of a bitch, what the hell do you think you're doing out here?"

"Connor! Good God, man. I didn't know what happened to you and then I heard Jolyn took off. And with my horse. My Granite! And then the storm. Shit, man, are you going to invite me in or are you going to turn me away?"

Connor, realizing his situation, exploded into intoxicated laughter. At first Hawk was afraid. Had Connor done something to the girl? Had he killed her in a rage? Had Connor found Luke? Hawk was too scared to question Connor. He got off his horse, tethered him cautiously to the post, and hesitantly walked slowly through the snow toward Connor. At first glance Connor looked like a wild man, his eyes bright with fever, his arms akimbo, shouting and carrying on.

"Connor, are you all right? Is everything okay?" Hawk slowly followed Connor into the cabin.

Inside Hawk's eyes flew immediately to Jolyn.

Cautiously he asked her, "Miss Jolyn, are you fine?" Her face was so crimson he thought perhaps she was stricken with fever. And then it hit Hawk, like a boulder crashing down the mountain. He had interrupted their most intimate interlude and he felt like a fool. Not knowing what to do, he laughed until his shoulders shook and his hands rested on his knees, otherwise he would have fallen right on the floor. Connor saw that there was little else he could do but give in to this awkward moment. He looked at Hawk, turned and looked at Jolyn, and snorted.

Jolyn was the only nonplussed person there. How could these two men stand there, amused by it all, while she just sat there completely naked under the quilt and totally embarrassed?

"Excuse me," she spat icily, "but if you two have nothing further to say I would appreciate some water from the river and some wood for the fireplace so that I might at least warm up some food. That is, of course, if you are both done with your merriment."

Both men gawked at Jolyn, then at each other. With rolled eyes that only barely suppressed their guffaws, they shrugged their shoulders and left the cabin. Quickly Jolyn jumped off the couch, threw off the quilt, and grabbed her clothes. Shivering, she dressed as fast as she could, not wanting to be in an uncomfortable situation when the two chuckling men returned.

* * *

The three of them at their food slowly and quietly, as each was deep in thought. Questions needed to be answered but no one wanted to commence the conversation. Finally Hawk spoke.

"Hmmm. Uh, excuse me, Jolyn, but just exactly how did you manage to weasel young Arliss out of my most prized possession?"

Jolyn blushed and stammered, "I really am sorry, Hawk. Please do not blame little Arliss. He really is such a sweet child. I, well, I said that you had told me it was okay to take the horse and he was too afraid of you to disagree."

"So," Hawk said, half to himself, "the boy wasn't lying after all. I guess I didn't need to whup him so much."

"Hawk," cried Jolyn, "you didn't lay a hand on that innocent boy, did you?"

"Well, Jolyn, you have to understand. The boy has no mother. His father tends to forget about him. If I didn't discipline him every now and then, why, the boy would just turn wild. Everyone in town seems to be a little bit of his parents. We all watch over Arliss."

"That still doesn't give you the right to hurt him. What he needs is a little more loving and a lot less hurting."

"Mebbe. Pass those grits. They sure are good."

Now it was Connor's turn. "Hawk. Did you hear anything? Anything at all? We've been holed up here with the storm."

"Nah. Not a word. There's a new picture of him down at the sheriff's office, but other than that, nothing. So," Hawk asked while stifling a guffaw, "tell me, you two. Cooped up in this here cabin for two days like a bunch of chickens with nothing to do. What did you do? Did you come up with a new plan? Were you able to take care of the horses? This place looks like you shined it up a bit."

Jolyn looked down at her plate as she felt her cheeks grow warm with awkwardness.

Connor saved her. "What in tarnation do you think we done here, Hawk? Hell, when was the last time you been down here to see what's become of this cabin. There was so much cleaning and fixing to do, I don't know where the time went!"

Hawk smiled and nodded at Connor as if to say your secret is good with me, brother.

Then Hawk's tone turned serious. "Were you close enough to smell him, Connor? It just seems like you're a footstep and a holler behind him all the time."

Connor's face flared with rage as he propelled himself up so hard his chair went flying backward. "God damn it, Hawk, I am always on his trail so close I can feel his sweat on me as it flies offa him in fear. And every time, every blessed time, I can feel him within my grasp, something, God damn it all, something always happens." And with that, Connor's long strides had him storming out of the cabin with only the smacking of the screen door resounding through the room.

Jolyn's pleading eyes looked over at Hawk. She had so many questions but was too worried to ask Hawk for fear of what he would tell her.

"You have to understand, Jolyn. Luke means an awful lot to Connor. He just has to find him."

"But he's just a criminal, Hawk. Just another bad man in this world of injustice. I want to get him, too. He kidnapped my friend. James must be dead by now, or hurt, or who knows what they have done with him. His gang killed my uncle; they killed my brothers. I know I was just being stupid following Connor out here, and now I admit it. Actually, well, I think I was just following Connor. And why can't Connor see it that way also? Why can't he give it up and let the authorities get Luke? Why is Connor so intent on being the one to capture him?"

"Why, didn't you know, Jolyn? Luke's not just any old criminal. Why, no, young miss. Luke Richardson is Connor's brother."

Chapter 12

QUIETLY, EACH BURIED WITH THEIR own thoughts, the three made their way back to Alamosa. It was slower returning because of the snow-covered trail, but each was anxious to leave Conejos.

Connor realized that Luke's trail was so cold now. As soon as they got back to Alamosa Connor would pack his things and take the wagon. Normally he liked to ride the new train to Creede, but he knew Hawk would have a load of supplies he wanted him to bring to the other store. He had other plans for Jolyn, but how could he tell her? How could he let her know that she needed to stay in Alamosa while he checked on things in Creede? Then perhaps when he figured out what to do with the trading post he might ask her to come be with him. What was he thinking? Why would she want to be with him? He was conflicted, and his face contorted in agony over decisions he'd never thought he would have to make in his life.

Jolyn was nervous. What should she expect now? Her journey was almost over and it was not going to be the reunion she had envisioned. No brothers, no uncle, the unknown whereabouts of James. She wasn't sure what to make of Connor since this morning. Had their feelings changed already? A dark cloud seemed to hover over him as they travelled and only loomed larger as they came into town. Jolyn knew she had to go to Creede at any cost to see what had happened to her brothers and her uncle. Had they been buried properly? How could she help? After all, without her parents she had no reason to travel to any other mining towns, and she was tired of the lack of stability. She wanted a place she could call home. She wanted to settle down and build roots.

Hawk just felt bad. He wanted Luke caught as much as Connor did. Hawk and Connor were more like brothers. The two of them shared everything. If it hadn't been for Connor and Connor's dad, Hawk knew he would have followed along with Luke and a life of crime. He was thankful Connor's father was compassionate and accepting, for Hawk had nowhere to go. It was due to Connor's dad that Hawk had turned out to be a decent human being.

And what of Jolyn? He felt sorry for her. She was something very special to Connor. Hawk could tell. If it hadn't been for Luke shadowing Connor's every thought, Hawk felt Jolyn could be the one shining light in his life.

As soon as they rode into Alamosa, Jolyn desperately needed to clear things with Arliss. She was wrong to have put the boy in such a precarious predicament and she wanted to apologize.

At the livery she found Arliss sweeping up the floors.

"Excuse me, Arliss," she interrupted. "I want to talk to you."

Arliss looked up and then his face turned to fear. He did not want to deal with this tricky woman again knowing a whipping by Hawk would surely follow.

Hesitantly he answered, "Uh, what do you want, ma'am?"

"Oh, Arliss, please don't call me ma'am. My name is Jolyn. And I want to apologize for lying to you the other day. I'm very sorry that I got you into so much trouble." She wanted to scoop up this young waif and hug him, but he was too distant, moving backward with each of her words.

"Yes, ma'am. Miss Jolyn. Whatever you say."

Just then Hawk strolled into the stables with his horse. As he did, little Arliss's brown eyes filled with fear and trepidation while he pressed his back against the wall.

Hawk tried not to be gruff, seeing the boy through Jolyn's eyes. "It's okay, boy. I ain't gonna whup ya. Miss Jolyn here told me the whole story. Seems like you was telling the truth. I am mighty sorry I hit you, boy. I guess I'm agonna have to believe you more often. Now, you finish up your work here and then you come on down to the store and I'll have

Miss Jolyn give you some of that red licorice I know you like so much." And, satisfied with himself, Hawk turned around and lumbered out of the stable.

"Gosh, he's a good man," sighed Arliss. "I always knowed that. It's jest that he does scare me a mite, him being so big and strong and all."

Jolyn laughed, and then she reached out to hug Arliss. He didn't fight it. He actually liked the feel of this woman hugging him. It reminded him of, well, he didn't like to think of the past.

"Miss."

Jolyn interrupted. "You call me Jolyn."

"Okay, Miss Jolyn. I really do appreciate you telling Mr. Hawk what happened. Most folk wouldn't do sech a thing."

"You know, Arliss, there's an awful lot of people who don't seem to be doing anything right these days. And if there is anything I can do for you, well, you just tell me. And if I'm not around here, you tell Hawk for me. Is that a deal?"

Arliss beamed with pride. "You bet, Miss Jolyn. You jest bet."

And with that, Jolyn leaned over to Arliss and placed a quick kiss on his young cheek. She left Arliss standing there with his fingers touching the very spot she had kissed.

It was almost noon before Connor had filled the wagon with the supplies for the store in Creede. He told Jolyn to meet him at the Pepe's Restaurant for lunch. Hawk found Jolyn and Connor at Pepe's and together the three sat and ate in silence. For Jolyn, the silence was deafening.

It would take Connor all afternoon by wagon to get to Creede, but he didn't mind. The three of them walked slowly to where Connor had set up the wagon filled with supplies. This was the hard part and he knew it would not go well. He looked at Hawk and nodded.

Jolyn looked at Connor and then at Hawk. What was going on now? she thought. She did not like the way the two glanced at each with furtive, hooded eyes. Her intuition was mounting and she was breathing rapidly.

"What's happening? What aren't you telling me?"

"Jolyn," whispered Connor softly, "I have to go to Creede alone. I need you to stay back for a while, so I can take care of things. I can't have you with me. I need to settle a score and you are in the way. Hawk is going to take care of you while I'm away and I…well, we were both hoping you might stay here and help us in the store."

Jolyn's eyes widened and her mouth opened to shout, but nothing came out at first. And then she shoved Hawk aside and pounded her fists on Connor's chest. "You will not leave me here! I demand to go with you! I must go! It's my family who was murdered, too! I won't stay here!!"

Connor grabbed her wrists so tightly he thought he'd broken them. "I promise to come back, Jo. I want to come back and bring you to Creede, but I have no choice. I have too much to do and I do not…" He couldn't finish. He wanted her with him with such intensity, but he knew he had to accomplish his quest alone. Again, he looked at Hawk.

Hawk's massive arms pulled Jolyn in a stronghold that she could not escape.

"Let me go! Leave me, Hawk! I want to go with him! I have to go with him! LET ME GO, DAMN YOU!"

Jolyn twisted and kicked the big, burly man, but it was useless. He was too big and too strong for her and he was not going to let go.

The sounds of Connor's footsteps echoed in Jolyn's ears as she watched this man mount his wagon and exit from her life. She would never forgive him for this; she would never forget him, either.

Hawk slowly released his bear hug and Jolyn stood there staring into the distance. She would not follow him this time. She would go to Creede on her own and would not feel that she had to sneak in the cloak of night.

She turned to look at Hawk, her fire extinguished but not resolve. "Okay, Hawk. For now and until I say I'm done, I guess I'm in your care, but I won't be taking any handouts. I will do whatever it is you need me to do for you. I can work hard, I can sweep and cook and take care of…"

"Whoa there, little wildflower. I know Connor is a mite headstrong, but I know the man feels he has a job to do and was too afraid you'd get in the way. I think I'm going to like having you here for a while, but let's take it a bit slow."

With the mention of Connor's name, Jolyn froze. He was gone. Really gone. And now whom was she left with in her life? Her uncle dead. Her brothers both dead. And poor James. Where did they take him? This was all too much. She had been so focused on finding Connor and finding Luke with him that she had not taken the time to really process the gravity of all her losses. What was left for her? Whom would she live with from now on and what would she do? The hopelessness flooded through her veins and Jolyn swayed unknowingly.

Hawk stared at Jolyn. He knew her mind was reeling with everything that had just taken place and he was worried. My God, he swore to himself. What would he do in her situation—orphaned and all alone at such a young age? She was strong, but how long till she… And then Hawk grasped what was happening to Jolyn. She was swaying—no, she was wavering and teetering on the edge. Quickly he reached for her and swooped her into burly arms. In a few long strides he stormed into the trading post and bounded up the stairs. Gently he lowered her onto an old soft divan outside his bedroom, feeling suddenly embarrassed at the conditions of his living quarters. With Jolyn still unconscious, Hawk rushed to a small unused sink and found a worn washcloth. He dipped the cloth into a pitcher of water, squeezed out the excess, and tenderly placed it on Jolyn's forehead.

He crouched on his haunches, silently muttering a prayer he remembered from his childhood, hoping this might be the time to say something, anything. He gazed upon Jolyn's face and noticed for the first time the number of cuts and bruises that marred her otherwise flawless features. She was incredibly beautiful, and Hawk felt a tug at his heart for her.

Hawk was not sure how much time passed before he noticed a slight movement in her eyes. Slowly, the sad blue-gray eyes opened and bore deep into Hawk's liquid brown eyes.

"What happened? Where am I?"

"Hush, little bird. It's okay now. You were feeling a mite faint just a while ago. I think it's all catching up with you now. The journey, the bad news, Connor leaving you with me, everything. I think you need some time to rest. You need time to heal."

Jolyn reached out to touch Hawk on his thick hands. Her hands seemed to meld into Hawk and at that moment Jolyn allowed herself to fall into a deep, dreamless sleep.

Hawk was afraid to leave Jolyn, and so with her hands still holding on to his, he stayed right by her side.

"It's a good thing you're asleep, Miss Jolyn, because it's awful hard for a man to stay away from such a vision as yourself for too long. I'm not sure Connor knew what he was doing when he left you in my care, but I will try to do my best by him."

The door to the upstairs flung open so hard Hawk almost fell on his backside. He spun around to gawk at a pert yellow-haired woman whose rich green eyes were ablaze with anger.

"And who is that whore?" the fiery-eyed woman spat.

Hawk slowly disentangled Jolyn's delicate hands from his, rose, and turned to face another emotional scene. This had been one hell of a day, he mused, and it wasn't over yet.

"Up so soon, Lucinda?"

"I almost forgot. Daddy had something he wanted me to do for him. Now, are you going to tell me who this creature is or not?"

Hawk slid his strong, thick hand into Lucinda's soft, somewhat pudgy one and guided her down the stairs.

"Connor left Jolyn in my care, Lucinda. She has lost her parents and her family; her best friend was kidnapped while they were traveling. She has nowhere to go and no one to be with now. I'm asking you, as a friend, a close friend. You be nice to her. If that preacher daddy of yours has taught you anything, it's be kind to others. And I'm asking, no, I'm a-telling you to do right with Jolyn."

"Why, Hawk, sweet. How could I have known? Anyone could have made that mistake. I apologize. You accept apologies, don't you?" Lucinda sighed as Hawk pulled her in closer, crushing her with his massive arms. He was all hers. And no one would ever take him away from her. She fingered his reddish-brown beard lovingly and gazed deeply into his gold-speckled copper eyes.

Hawk felt his body responding as Lucinda pressed her eager breasts against his chest and he moaned as his masculinity betrayed him; his burgeoning manhood answered Lucinda's eager caressing hands.

"Now, Hawk, I told you I was on a mission. Daddy sent me over to buy some more nails for the pews he is fixing."

Hawk, feeling quite agitated by her interruptions, adjusted his pants by the waist and turned away from Lucinda. Oh, God, he cursed. What a she-cat that woman was with him. All blonde and full and…

"Hawk, Daddy is waiting, you know," Lucinda cooed sweetly, feeling immense satisfaction with her ability to turn this large bear into a clumsy fool.

* * *

Connor was worn out. The spring snow had melted under the strong Colorado sun as the three made the silent trek from Conejos back to Alamosa. Connor left Jolyn in Hawk's good hands there and was now making a painstakingly slow ride to Creede. In a creaking, rumbling wagon packed with supplies, Connor had followed the newly lain railroad tracks that led almost all the way from Alamosa to Creede. As he maneuvered his steed into the single main thoroughfare of Creede, he realized that this might be the last time he would need to carry goods by wagon to Richardson's Trading Post and Dry Goods Emporium.

It was dusk, and the usually bustling town appeared empty. Aromatic scents of freshly baked bread and savory beef stew wafted through the street, and the distant clank of dishes and soft discourse and laughter hovered in the evening air. This was how he remembered it. Nostalgia tugged at his heart, yearning for those bygone days.

He pulled up in front of the store and tied the reins to the hitching post. He hesitated for a moment, wondering, doubting, hoping that there would be someone here to greet him. Had Annabel recovered? Had she managed to keep the store running without his assistance for the past weeks? Would she hate him for not finding her father's murderer, or did she hate him for having left her so soon after Sam's death? Enough! He was home, and that was all that mattered.

With a leap from his wooden seat, Connor dashed up the outside stairs and flung open the kitchen door. He careened to a halt, amazed at the picture before him. Memories flooded his mind as he surveyed the scene before him.

The room was as he remembered it. Two well-stuffed chairs and one rocker formed a half-circle around a pot-bellied stove. A tall cupboard whose shelves were lined with fine china and crystal, a grandfather's clock, and a rolltop desk lined the various walls. Freshly starched blue gingham curtains framed the two windows. In the center of the room, a brightly lit kerosene lamp, sitting on a neatly set table, cast a warm glow over the room. Annabel, dressed in a scarlet smock, her dark curls tied back with a red bow, sat demurely at the table, her arm suspended midway toward a bowl of greens. Across from her, frozen in a wary crouch, half-stood Chris Montgomery.

"Annabel? Chris?" Connor's head swiveled from one to the other. "What? How?"

"Connor!" Annabel cried joyously. She pushed her chair back and flung herself into her bewildered brother's arms.

"Annabel! My Bel!" He crushed her to him in a surge of happiness. He was home. Home. For one fleeting moment, he envisioned Jo sitting at the table, welcoming him as happily, but not in quite as sisterly a fashion, as Annabel did now, and then the startling image was gone.

"Welcome home, Connor." Chris's strong hand warmly clasped his own. "We've been worried. I thought Annabel would go mad with the waiting. How have you been?"

"Me? My God, Chris, I never expected to see you again. I thought you were dead? What? How? Lord, Chris, but it's good to see you!"

Chris grinned unabashedly. "Come in. Sit down. Have you eaten? Annabel, when you've finished mauling that ugly brother of yours, fetch an extra plate." Chris grabbed a chair from beside the fireplace and set it at the table. Annabel, with one more tight hug, slipped out of his arms and arranged another place setting.

Connor gazed curiously from one to the other. Like kids, Chris and Annabel grinned at each other and then back at Connor.

"Well?" Chris waved an arm toward the seat. Connor looked at the tantalizing dishes, then hastily shed his trappings and sat down in the proffered chair.

"Well, Connor," Chris explained as he passed a dish of potatoes toward Connor. "As to the what and how of it. I was no less surprised than you to find myself alive. I woke up with a doozy of a headache just as Barney Milford and Chet Parker were dragging me feet first into the street. Well, I must have groaned, because the next thing I knew they'd dropped my legs and taken off down the street. From what they told me later, I was one bloody mess, and I guess I nearly scared them out of their wits. Anyway, as I lay there looking up at the clouds moving across the sky, I tried to figure out what had happened. The last thing I remembered was seeing Nick plastered against your dad's office wall.

After that, nothing. I never heard or saw another thing. I'm sorry, Connor, I wish I could tell you more."

"Are you kidding, Chris? I'm just glad to find you alive. When I think that I just left you lying there… "

"Nonsense, Connor. You didn't know. You were suffering a shock. Naturally you assumed—in fact, everyone assumed—that we were all dead."

"How are you feeling now?"

"Physically, couldn't be better. The headaches disappeared about two weeks ago, and I haven't had an ache or pain since. As soon as this hair grows back, you won't even see the scar. As for the rest, well, Annabel has been a great help."

"Chris, Annabel, I'm sorry I wasn't here for you. I wanted to stay, see to the burying, but at the time, I had to go after them. I had to see justice done. For a while there, on the trail, I came so close. Then I got delayed at the pass. Later, I almost surprised them outside Leadville, but then I lost them in the Rockies and then I…" Connor stopped. He could not continue.

Annabel reached across the table and squeezed Connor's hand. "I understood, Connor. I wanted you to go, too. If there was a chance that you could get the men who killed Father, I wanted you to take it."

"That's right, Connor," Chris agreed. "You did the right thing. I only wish I could have joined you. Losing Uncle Hank was hard, but Nick. Nick. He should have been the one to make it."

"Chris Montgomery, you stop that foolishness. You survived because you were meant to survive. And if you hadn't, just where do you think I'd be?" Annabel chided.

Chris's eyes locked with hers and something vibrant flashed between them.

Connor cleared his throat and applied himself to the delicious dishes before him. Soon they were all munching companionably on the meal.

"Tastes wonderful, Annie. Your cooking certainly has improved since I've been away. I kind of miss the old charcoal flavoring," Connor teased.

Annabel blushed. "I didn't cook it," she confessed. "Chris did. He's been helping me with…things." She glanced shyly at Chris.

"Of course you did," Chris defended her. "She cooked everything but the roast." His hand slipped easily into hers and he pressed it gently before letting go.

Connor frowned at the familiarity. "Just what exactly has been going on since I've been away?" Connor asked a little stiffly.

"Oh, Connor, now, don't be a boor," Annabel scolded. "Chris has been a perfect gentleman even though I have tried my best to get him into my bed."

"You what?" Connor rose halfway out of his seat. "Young ladies of your age should not speak that way. And if I hear you talking that way again, I'll take you over my knee and whale the daylights out of you. Do you understand?" He then pointed a furious finger at Chris's placid face. "And as for you…"

"Connor," Annabel interrupted sweetly, "be a dear and stop shouting. If you would just listen for a moment, I can explain."

"Explain? If there is any explaining to do, I'll do it, young lady. And I am not shouting!"

Connor plopped down, blasting them both with an angry glare. Seemingly unaffected, Chris smirked idiotically back at him, and Annabel, a saucy grin covering her face, did not appear at all chastised.

"You know, Connor, I have been lecturing Bel on that point for weeks now," Chris said cheerily. "With little success I might add. I was unable, of course, to use the threat—whaling the daylights out of her, wasn't it? Although I'm not quite sure how effective that would be… The shouting was a nice touch though. A nice change from my pleading, don't you think?"

Connor stared back at Chris as if Chris had lost his mind.

"Connor," Annabel said blithely. "We're engaged! We've only been waiting for you to return so that we could set a date. Chris has insisted that we have your approval first. And I had begun to think that you would never make it back. So I thought if we could… I mean, if I, well, if something happened and I, well, you know. Then we wouldn't have to wait until you…"

"Enough. Have pity, Bel," Chris moaned. He clasped his head in his hands and shook his head slowly. He raised his head and stared frankly into Connor's eyes as understanding dawned.

"Connor, I swear I haven't laid a hand on her. I'd cut off my right arm before I'd disgrace her in that way. I swear to you I had every intention of approaching you with…"

"Say no more, Chris. It's not necessary. I can see where the land lies." He gave Annabel's nose a tweak, then turned once again toward Chris. "My friend, I congratulate you on your fortitude—and on your upcoming marriage."

"Oh!" Annabel cried happily.

"And as for you, minx," Connor said ferociously, "there will be no more attempts at seducing your prospective husband until the vows have been spoken. Is that clear?"

"Yes, Connor." Annabel's reply lacked the proper remorse.

"I believe you will have to continue to watch her, Chris," Connor said despairingly.

"Yes," Chris sighed heavily, "I believe you're right."

"Chris, I have some news for you as well. I haven't mentioned it yet because, first of all, I was not expecting to find you among the living, and, well, because I can't tell you the good news without including more distressing news about your family."

"If it's about the Clear Creek mining disaster, I received news of my parents' death a little over a month ago. The company sent the bodies to Creede to be buried here. I couldn't believe it. If it hadn't been for Annabel, I think I would have lost my mind. At least they died while they were both near each other. My sister's name was not on the casualty list, but no one has seen her since the disaster. Since many of the bodies were unidentifiable, I can only assume that one of them must have been

Jolyn's." Chris's voice tightened, and he stared resolutely into the dregs of his coffee cup.

"She's alive, Chris," Connor whispered slowly.

"What?" Chris unconsciously gripped the cup he was holding. He wasn't sure if he had heard Connor correctly.

"Jolyn's alive," Connor repeated, adding more volume. "I saw her only last night." Saw her, he thought. Yes. Saw her. Smelled her. Felt her. Made love to her. His body burned in memory.

"And she was all right?" Chris peered anxiously at Connor.

"Yes. She's fine, Chris, very fine. A little thinner maybe, but healthy, and tough as nails. I asked her to stay in Alamosa for a short while so I could work on some things here with the store."

"That's her all right." Chris smiled with both pride and relief. "But how did she end up in Alamosa of all places?"

"I guess you'll have to ask her. I'm not clear on all the details," Connor remarked evasively.

"What am I thinking? Who cares how she got to Alamosa? At least she's alive. And well. Did you hear that, Bel, Jolyn's alive!" Chris leaped to his feet, scooped Annabel willy-nilly into his arms, and whirled her about the room. Abruptly, he halted in mid-sweep. "We've got to send her a telegram. Let her know I'm here. Better yet, I could leave tonight. I'd be in Alamosa by dawn. Blast. I've got a real-estate deal at ten tomorrow morning. It's too big. It'd be much too late to cancel. I've got it. I'll send her a telegram and have her come here. If I sent the telegram tonight, she'd get it tomorrow morning and could be here by tomorrow evening. That's it. Connor, do you think she could catch a safe ride here by tomorrow evening?"

"By tomorrow evening?" Connor paused dramatically. "Oh, no. I think if she's half as excited as you, she will probably arrange to shove the train conductor aside and lead the train herself!"

Chris rolled his eyes. "I'm serious, Connor. Maybe I should wait until after the meeting and leave then. That would get me into Alamosa by late evening."

"Chris, if you're serious about this, and I can see that you are, then I think the best thing for you to do is..."

"Enough, Connor. We're wasting time. I've got to get to the telegraph office right away." Chris gave Annabel a quick peck on her forehead.

"Got to go, Bel. I'll swing by the store sometime tomorrow."

He snatched his coat from the peg by the door.

"Bye, love. Good to see you, Connor. The store and the citizens of Creede have sorely missed you. Not that Annabel hasn't tried her best." He threw an apologetic glance toward Annabel, and then muttered as he swept out the door, "Maybe if I wired money to the telegrapher in Alamosa, he might send word to Jolyn tonight. That way she could..." The door slammed behind him.

"Maybe I was wrong. You two will probably make the perfect match."

"Well!" Annabel harrumphed at Chris's precipitous departure and Connor's light-hearted comment. She stood, her arms akimbo, where Chris had dumped her, trying to look her haughtiest, but Connor couldn't miss the telltale quirk of her lips as she tried to conceal her impish grin.

"Well?" Connor queried.

"Oh, Connor, I'm so happy that you're home," she cried, and threw herself into Connor's waiting arms.

* * *

It had been a tough few days and Connor needed some time alone. He had helped his sister with the cleanup, and then he and Bel had talked for a long time before she could not keep her eyes open and said her good nights, and how happy she was, and more, but he lost track of what she was saying. Despite his long day, he had been unable to settle down, let alone go to sleep. He knew why, and it had nothing to do with Luke or the business or the excitement of coming home. It was Jo. Every time he closed his eyes, he could see her lying beneath him, her soft auburn locks spread about her rosy face, her sapphire eyes passion-darkened to royal blue, her lips reddened and full.

And so he came to Kirmeavy's. He wanted to spend some time at the saloon and have a drink and think. So much had happened and he wasn't sure what he needed to do next. He knew he had to settle some things at the trading post, but Luke was forever on his mind. And Jolyn. Mainly Jolyn. Thoughts of her kept sweeping in and out of Connor like the wind in Wolf Creek Pass, leaving him breathless.

So Connor sat and drank and thought and drank. He was milking his third, or was it fourth, glass of red-eye at a table in a solitary corner of Kirmeavy's. Sponsilier's Theatre was featuring Annie Weigel in *Bronco Kate*, and nearly the whole town had turned out for it. Here, except for a few regulars, the place was empty and that was what he wanted. Tomorrow he'd be ready to greet old friends and listen to their memories of his father and their gripes about needed supplies and the latest news. But not tonight.

"Need some company, cowboy?" a husky voice whispered against his neck.

Nearly overpowered by the cloying scent of cheap perfume, Connor glanced toward the girl who leaned provocatively against his left arm. She was blonde, blowsy, and fleshy—everything Jolyn wasn't.

"Have a seat?" he offered. "Would you care for a drink?"

"I'll have what you're havin'." She licked her lips invitingly, and slipped forward in her chair, pressing her plentiful breasts against the table.

Connor's eyes gazed at the ample flesh exposed temptingly before him and then slid upward toward her heavily made-up face. She was older than most of Sandy's girls, and she was new, maybe not to the business, but certainly to him since he was home last. She was attractive and certainly had plenty enough to go around. Usually such a show would have sparked at least some interest, but Connor was left untouched.

"Two more whiskeys here, Pete," Connor called, then produced a smile for his companion. "What's your name?"

"Emmaline. My friends call me Lina."

"You're new here, aren't you?"

"That's right. I've been here nearly two weeks now. A drifter lost me in a bet to the house." She shrugged. "They treat me better here. I'd move on if didn't suit." She walked her fingers up his arm and caressed the neck of his shirt. "And what about you, cowboy? Haven't seen your handsome face here before."

"Well, Lina, that's because I didn't know Sandy was hiding such a beautiful woman as you." Connor gulped down his drink. Maybe this was the answer. After all, he hadn't had a woman in nearly three months, not counting the very close encounter with Jolyn. And maybe that was why he couldn't keep his mind off of Jo.

"A beautiful woman gets a hankerin' for the company of a good-lookin' man. How'd you like to share a little time with little ole me?" Her hand had slithered down his chest and now rested high on his muscular thigh. She gazed at his broad shoulders, handsome features, and arresting eyes. This would be the easiest ten dollars she had made in a long time.

"Sure, honey, just lead the way." Connor grabbed an open whiskey bottle from the bar and followed Lina up the stairs, watching her ample hips twitch side to side.

No sooner had Lina pulled Connor into her room than Connor tugged at her and swept her into him. He wrapped his muscular arms about her waist and his lips descended upon hers. His lean fingers deftly unfastened the back of her dress, and soon his hands cupped her pendulous breasts. A wave of heavy perfume mixed with sweat assaulted him.

Connor's hands dropped away, and he stepped back. He took a swig from the bottle and set it on the messy dresser.

"Get undressed," he said indifferently, and swayed toward the unmade bed. As he went, he slid off his vest and shirt, then sat down on the bed to shed the rest. When he'd finished, Lina was already before him. Kneeling, she slid her painted fingernails along his inner thighs, a slight smile on her rouged lips.

"I can perform any service you desire. You have only to ask." Her head moved forward toward his half-aroused manhood, but he caught her up and leaned back, pulling them both lengthwise onto the bed.

For a few minutes he just lay there, disgusted.

He wondered why he couldn't just relax and enjoy what the whore had to offer? He'd never had trouble performing before, and now he'd just rejected an intimacy that he'd enjoyed as part of the ritual. Maybe he'd drunk too much. No, he'd drunk much more than this before and had pleasured more than one woman well into the morning hours. Damn. It couldn't be Jo; it just couldn't be. Even the thought of her brought a response from Connor's body.

Frustrated, he turned to the woman in his arms. He turned her onto her back and pressed her into the mattress. He buried his head in her hair and then kissed her savagely. He squeezed her breasts roughly, then rose above her and plunged with one quick thrust into her. He shut his eyes tightly and saw before him Jo's pale firm body and passion-filled face.

"Jo. Jo," he whispered, and then, stunned, he stilled his movements. Contritely, he stared down into Lina's face, and immediately pulled away.

"I'm sorry, Lina. I guess I'm just not in the mood." His hands shook as he moved about the room, gathering his clothes and putting them back on.

"What's the matter? I was enjoyin' it. C'mon back. I've got ways that'll make a man forget any woman."

"There is no woman," Connor snapped. He slipped on his boots and reached stiffly into his pocket. "I'm leaving you twenty dollars. I know that's twice Sandy's rate, but you're a nice girl. Thanks for a great evening." Without looking back, Connor left the room.

Emmaline shrugged into her robe and sauntered over to the connecting door. She tapped twice, then turned back into the room and reached for the bottle Connor had left behind on her dresser. She found two glasses and filled them generously. Behind her she heard the tap of booted heels stroll into the room.

"Good work." A voice as cold as death rippled through the room. A gloved hand reached for the filled glass. "Now, what can you tell me?"

Chapter 13

"HAWK, ARE YOU SURE?" JOLYN asked excitedly.

Jolyn grabbed him and swung him around, giggling like a young schoolgirl. Hawk grumbled, grabbed her at the waist, and sat her down on the chair.

"Whaddya mean? Of course I'm sure. Take as long as you like. Good God, Arliss will probably drive me plumb crazy asking about you all the time. No, you go right ahead. Imagine. All this time you thinking you had no family left and now you finding out about this brother of yours. Aw, heck, as soon as Chris wired the news to me I couldn't wait to tell you!"

Jolyn's happiness was infectious. Hawk couldn't stop smiling himself.

Jolyn had initially and begrudgingly agreed to work with Hawk at the trading post, but she loved working with people and the trading post was so much safer than the mining towns. It was only her first day and already Jolyn was feeling comfortable. She was still smiling to herself, reliving the unbelievable news about her brother Chris. It was a double-edged sword, because as soon as the bubbles of joy arose, they were pushed down as she remembered Nick had not made it. How can there be such joy and sorrow at the same time? she questioned to no one in a silent prayer.

Hawk's voice sliced through her personal reflections. Jolyn's dazed eyes focused and she turned to Hawk.

"I'm sorry, Hawk. What did you say? The barrels of what?"

"C'mon, Jolyn...I have to leave. Okay, I get it. You are just overcome with the joyful news. But let me get back to my business so I still have a business. Now, you know what to do with those barrels of molasses when they come in, right?"

"Uh-uh, sure."

"And Mr. Teeger has been waiting for some of those new nails we had on order, so be sure to let him know when they come in, unless, of course, I come back first." And with that Hawk grabbed a pair of quilled hide gauntlets he wanted to show this new cowboy who'd just ridden into town and was staying over at Rosalita's place.

Jolyn hesitated. After her parents were killed she thought she would stay with her brothers. Then when she found out they were both killed by Luke and his gang she felt she had no choices in her life. Now she had more than she wanted to handle. Should she move to Creede to be close to Chris? What about Alamosa? What about Connor? Where was he going to be? What about Connor?!

Exasperated, Jolyn picked up her carpetbag and headed toward the door.

"Whoa, young lady!"

Jolyn almost knocked herself out by walking straight into Hawk, her bag left swinging with her body. There stood Hawk, feet spread wide apart, hands on his hips, and a look of scorn that would have frozen Arliss right to the ground.

"Now that's a fine how-do-you for yer! One minute it's oh, how can I help you Hawk, and let me do this for you Hawk, and let me sew that shirt up for you Hawk, and get this! Walking out the door without so much as a grunt goodbye. Well, is that what I've come to be for you! A regular doormat, am I!"

Jolyn blushed from the tips of her toes to the roots of her red hair. How could she do that to her new friend who has been so helpful and kind? My God, whenever she thought of Connor all her rational thoughts went flying out the window.

Jolyn dropped her bag, ran to Hawk, and hugged him tightly, giving him a squeeze that almost knocked the air out of him. Then, finding the one spot of exposed skin on his cheek, Jolyn planted a large kiss.

Hawk grinned from ear to ear.

"Now, that's more like it!"

Jolyn stared up at him. "Hawk, you mean everything to me. You are like the brothers I had lost, and now, well, now I'm richer with one more brother. And I thank you for that. And I will come back and help you here in the post, I will, but I have to go to Creede. I must see Chris. How can I stay here and not learn how he survived, and what happened to Nick? Oh, poor Nick? How did he die? Was he in so much pain? I want to be the one to tell Chris about Ma and Pa and how they were so strong until the explosion and how I ended up here and what happened to James… and, oh, I must be rambling like crazy. But don't you understand, Hawk? I have to go, and I have to go now."

And with that long farewell, Jolyn pushed past Hawk into the warm fall sun and ran all the way down Main Street to catch up with Clem, who was driving a freighter. He had come into the store earlier today to pick up some supplies. He was loading up to travel to Creede and then up north to Grand Junction and maybe, just maybe, he wouldn't mind having a companion with him on the way to Creede.

Clem wasn't exactly thrilled to tolerate a female riding with him. It was, after all, a man's job to ride alone and he wasn't much of a talker, especially to womenfolk. But Miss Jolyn had helped him get his supplies and when he fell a bit short with his cash, well, Miss Jolyn just said he could owe it to Hawk next time he came around. That was good enough for Clem to seal a friendship, so he told Jolyn she could hop on the burlap sacks since there was no room for her to sit.

Jolyn was grateful that she could get to Creede even if it was going to be a long, uncomfortable ride. Chuckling to herself, she knew she wasn't about to talk her way into taking Hawk's stallion and get away with it this time. So she relaxed for once and witnessed the incredibly beautiful changing countryside. Jolyn was just getting used to the arid, dry winds of Alamosa—always blowing, always blowing. And the striking view of Mount Blanca, ever present, ever awesome. The flat plain of the sand-covered San Luis Valley was surrounded by the majestic San Juan

Mountains. As if by a master artist, the terrain transformed, and the aspens climbed higher and the rich green leaves trembled in the breezes as though they were waving to her as she rode by. The lush green tree lines were overflowing with fields of rosy and yellow paintbrush, white bistort, and buttercups. The blue columbine quivered in the gentle breezes, a swallowtail butterfly caressed the parry primrose, and the blue sky overhead smiled at them all. And then, without permission, thoughts of Connor swooped in and overwhelmed her. And Connor's moods seemed to change like the countryside around her.

They made one quick stop for a brief lunch, allowing Jolyn to wander off the trail to relieve herself. She was much more alert and aware of herself in the wilds now. She had grown in many ways in the past few months. She smiled inwardly, a smile that was laced with sadness.

Clem was traveling carefully. One never knew who was on the trail and with a female sitting on top of his freight, he'd better be extra cautious. He'd heard about the killing in Creede and talk was those men were still rucking it up and doing who knows what to who knows who. And because he was going a mite slow, sunset was casting long, eerie shadows. He did not want his horses to catch a whiff of something evil and go amok turning over his goods. He tried to push his animals a bit harder, hoping not to overtax them. He could barely see Miss Jolyn on top of the sacks, but every now and then he heard some sounds coming from her. He guessed she was okay. He hoped she was okay. You just never knew with womenfolk.

The encroaching night dipped the temperature to a chill that caught her breath and Jolyn hugged James's blue woolen jacket tightly around her. Her thoughts shifted to Connor. She found herself snorting out loud as her anger ruffled her thoughts at his leaving her once again, and then, like a pendulum swinging her thoughts back to those scorching desirous moments, she recalled with a tender smile the sweet whisper of his breath on her cheek and scorching lips against hers. She remembered the way his strapping body molded with hers, and had they not been interrupted by Hawk... Jolyn reached up and touched her flushed cheeks and said a silent prayer of thanks that she was on top of the freight where Clem could not see her as she sat hugging her knees.

Clem wanted to get to Creede before nightfall, so he continued pushing his team even harder. Jolyn dozed off, dreaming, always seeing a large broad man in dark above her on a cliff.

A gentle nudging awoke Jolyn. It was Clem.

"Miss Jolyn. Miss Jolyn. We're here. We're in Creede. C'mon, Miss Jolyn. I got to get this here team over to the stables for some water and grain."

"Hmm. Hmm? Wha? OH. Oh, I'm sorry, Clem."

Jolyn sat up straighter and stared at the sights in front of her, dimly aware of the town in the darkness.

"We're here? Oh, Clem, we're here. And I'm going to see Chris!"

And with that realization Jolyn grabbed her carpetbag and quickly jumped down from the burlap sacks. She turned around to thank Clem.

Clem nodded curtly and headed toward the livery. He was tired and was looking forward to a good night's rest.

Jolyn watched him leave, his trail dust lingering in the shadows of the gas lamps. Still holding the carpetbag, Jolyn slowly turned around to face a row of storefronts, multi-colored in appearance and each one as different as the next.

In front of her large black letters read *Richardson's Trading Post.* And then in smaller letters underneath it read, *You need it, we got it. If we don't got it, we'll get it.*

Jolyn's mouth turned upward in a tender smile. So this is where it all began for Connor. I wonder.

Jolyn did not have much time to wonder before a very attractive young woman emerged from the store door. She sucked in her breath as she saw in the lamplight that this woman looked exactly like Connor, only in female form. She had the same rich dark hair, only hers was worn loose and very elegantly graced her rounded shoulders. Her skin was porcelain white and smooth. Her dove-gray eyes warmly gazed into Jolyn's searching eyes. Annabel laughed, her whole body shaking.

"Hello. You must be Jolyn. Jolyn Montgomery. I'm Annabel Richardson. And by the way you're staring at me figuring out who I am, I can tell you've met Connor."

Jolyn blushed.

"Hello," Jolyn sputtered. "I apologize for staring at you, but you really do look…I mean there really is a family resemblance and I didn't know…"

Annabel finished it for her. "And you didn't know Connor had a sister." She laughed, genuinely. "Connor doesn't talk much about his family. He is rather private. But now it's my turn to apologize to you. The reason I'm laughing so hard is because you look so much like your brothers, especially Chris. And I figured the reason you were staring at me was the same reason I was staring at you and I just couldn't help myself. Oh, Jolyn, it's so good to meet you."

Jolyn put down her bag. Joy filled her heart and she reached out and hugged Annabel. She stepped back, smiling, her face flushed with happiness.

"How do you do, Miss Annabel Richardson. You're right, Connor has never told me about you. In fact, he's told me very little about his family. Actually, it was Hawk who told me that Luke is his brother. Luke is the cause of a great deal of grief we both share in common."

At the mention of Luke, a dark cloud fell upon Annabel's face and her body turned rigid.

"I want you to know, Jolyn, that there are still a few men out there on the trail besides Connor hunting for my"—she spat out the words—"my other brother, our half-brother. But now, let's move on to a brighter note. There's a very tired man inside the store working incredibly hard on some accounts that he still can't figure out, and he told me to keep an eye out for his baby sister. You don't really fit that bill, but I'm figuring

Chris hasn't seen you in quite some time. Anyway, I know you don't want to keep each other waiting, so let's head into the store."

With that, Jolyn picked up her carpetbag, her feet barely touching the wooden planks beneath her, and followed Annabel. The store was an exact duplicate of the one back in Alamosa. Inside, Annabel took Jolyn's bag and jacket from her and pointed to the back of the store.

"I know you both have been waiting and dreaming of this moment for a long while. I'll be upstairs warming up some dinner for you."

Jolyn hesitated. For a moment she did not know what to do. Was she really scared to see her own brother? Jolyn, her legs too paralyzed to move, stood erect, trying to take a deep breath. He was alive. After living so long with the misconception that he was dead, she was afraid that something would go wrong. Was it really Chris in the other room? She took one step, another, and then another until she was in the doorway. She had come upon the back room so quietly that Chris had not heard her and sat hunched over with his head bent low, pouring over his books. One hand was curled in his thick brown hair. Chills ran up Jolyn's spine as she recognized the resemblance to her father. The other hand was poised motionless over the paper, a half-chewed pencil in hand. Chris's flannel shirt was unbuttoned, and he was not wearing any long underwear. Jolyn saw a hint of a scar that stretched from his chest up past the shoulder, under the shirt. He had been shot and survived. We're survivors, he and I. And we are both going to make it.

A flicker, a shadow, in Chris's kerosene lamp caused him to look up, and his mouth fell open. He bolted up so hastily that his stool clattered to the floor behind him. Like a sleepwalker, Chris walked out from behind the desk. Neither one spoke a word. They were both too busy staring.

Jolyn broke the silence first.

"Chris, it's really you. Oh, God… I…"

Chris ran to her and smothered her in his arms. Hot tears raced down his cheeks, mixing with Jolyn's.

"Jolyn. Oh, God, Jolyn, I can't believe it. I thought you had died along with Mom and Dad. The papers I read were so unclear…so confusing, just a list of the miners and their families that were there, and when I saw your names and didn't hear from you, well, I…I'm sorry, I assumed the worst." Guilt ripped through Chris, his body twitching with the consuming pain.

Jolyn grabbed Chris at the shoulders and for a split second saw him wince a bit as if in pain. Quickly she dropped her hands to hold his as her clear blue eyes probed his.

"Chris. I'm just as much to blame. When I left the camp I was hoping to come straight to Creede to tell you in person what had happened to Mom and Dad. But a few things happened to me along the way and, well, Connor found me and brought me to Alamosa and there I met his friend Hawk. Connor told me Luke had shot all of you and that there were no survivors. I listened to him and believed him. I shouldn't have. I should have come here to check on my own. Please, please forgive me for that." Jolyn lowered her head and fresh tears cascaded down her already tear-streaked face.

"Oh, no, Jolyn. It's not your fault. From what I understand, everyone thought we were dead. Annabel, well, she found me still breathing and she nursed me back to health. Connor did not know. He had already left town in search of Luke. He couldn't have known. Don't blame him. And please, don't blame yourself. Let's just be glad we found each other again. And this time we'll never lose each other again."

Chris reached for Jolyn's chin and, placing his palm underneath it, brought her face up. Jolyn gazed into her brother's warm eyes and knew everything would be fine between them. They had each other and that was good enough for Jolyn. Who needed anyone else? Her smile broke through and she reached up and grabbed her brother and hugged him tightly. I'll never lose you again, she vowed silently.

A soft voice awakened the two from their own deep thoughts and they turned to see Annabel, grinning so widely her teeth sparkled in the dim light.

"Well, I see you two have become reacquainted."

Chris beamed when he looked upon Annabel and the spark that bolted across the room was not lost on Jolyn. For a moment she felt a twinge of jealousy. She had finally found her brother and now she was going to lose him to this woman. And Connor's sister, no less!

But Jolyn's worst fears were quickly washed aside as Annabel astutely observed Jolyn's fallen expression and continued, "Why, Chris, you inconsiderate lout. Your sister has been travelling all day and you haven't invited her upstairs for a drink of something wet and cold, let alone a plate of some of my outstanding stew!"

Dumbfounded, Chris stood with his mouth gaping open.

"Jolyn," Annabel coaxed, "c'mon upstairs with me and let me see you to some dinner. If that oaf of a brother of yours wakes up from his shock, he should follow us shortly."

Jolyn smiled and, taking Chris by the hand, pulled him along up the stairs.

Annabel scooted up alongside Jolyn and, slipping her arm through Jolyn's, whispered, "You know what? We both have something very much in common. We're both in love with that brother of yours! And to keep him in line, I do hope you'll stay with us and help me out."

Chris winked at Jolyn and added, "Oh, by the way, how's your cooking been these days?"

Jolyn wrinkled her forehead in question and cocked her head. "Hmm? What do you mean?"

Annabel interrupted. "What that ungracious slob is implying is my inability to cook as well as your mother."

Jolyn convulsed in a fit of laughter. "Well, you do know," Jolyn giggled, her voice filled with merriment, "my mother could whip up a feast out of a rock and boiling water. And, yes, she did teach me a few things. I'll tell you what, Annabel, you tell me a few things about your brother and I'll give you enough secrets to keep my brother fat and jolly for the rest of his life!"

Annabel beamed. "Jolyn, you've got yourself a deal. Now, let's go try out my stew and hope your brother didn't go too crazy with some of his seasonings this time. He swears his mother taught him about mixing herbs, and yet sometimes, I do believe dinner will taste just like dinner at the Orleans Club!"

Jolyn did not need to hear any more. She knew her brother was in good hands and she would be, too, if she needed it. Annabel might look like Connor, but the similarities stopped there. Her warmth and bubbling hospitality soothed Jolyn's aching heart like one of her own hot poultices.

Together, laughing and teasing, the three walked up the stairs to relax and have a family dinner together.

Alone that night in an extra bed next to Annabel's room, Jolyn stared at the plaster ceiling above. Connor hadn't made an appearance that night. He'd known she was coming to town. He really must think I'm just not good enough for him. Or else he has someone. Come to think of it, he never did tell me if he was involved or not. No wonder he left so hastily. He must have been in a hurry to get back to the one he really loves. I was just filling in for a while. Jolyn's troubled thoughts continued and she fell asleep tossing and turning. She woke up only once, screaming at a dark vision that hovered above her.

The sun was barely up the next day when Jolyn was jolted awake by a noise downstairs. Suddenly, heavy boots thudded up the stairs and flung open the door to Annabel's room.

"Get yourself up, you lazy bag of bones! The day's a-wasting and I've been waiting for breakfast for hours already!"

Jolyn thought she heard Annabel cursing back at this man, but who was it? It was hard to tell the voice clearly, but she knew she did not recognize Chris's voice.

The man's voice died down to a whisper and Jolyn strained to hear the conversation. She sat up in bed, pulling her comforter all around her and cocking her head, her auburn curls cascading down her taut shoulders. Suddenly there was complete silence and then raucous laughter. What was going on in there? Who was that with Annabel? Jolyn didn't have to wait much longer. The heavy pounding of the boots resounded again as they hastily left Annabel's room and turned sharply toward hers. Jolyn huddled into an even smaller ball as her door banged open with a loud crack, and there in all his glory stood Connor.

Jolyn opened her mouth and stared straight at him. Of all the nerve! "Why, you! You…I…"

In three large strides Connor swept across the small bedroom and now stood unyielding as he loomed above Jolyn. He was dressed in his usual blue denims with a crisp red flannel shirt opened to expose enough of his dark curly chest hairs. Around his neck was a blue bandanna, tied loosely. His rich dark hair peeked out from beneath his soft brown Stetson. Enormous sturdy hands rested on his hips and he casually placed one of his booted feet up on the chair next to the bed.

Connor nodded his head, tipped his hat, and very nonchalantly said, "Morning, Jo. You sure are a sight for sore eyes."

Jolyn, amazed at his insouciant attitude, could only murmur, "Morning? That's it? A simple good morning?"

"Well, what did you want? They only put out the red carpet in this town when Calamity's around. That is, of course, unless you want to compete with her."

The mirth in his eyes was a disguise for the real desire that hid behind them. Seeing Jolyn in bed like this was too much for Connor. He wanted to rip his clothes off right there and then and jump in bed with this copper-headed vision. God, she was all woman. Her hair, so soft and long. The russet locks were the color of the Pawnee Buttes at sunset and he longed to swoop her up and dive right into those curly tendrils. His gaze shifted to her eyes, the soft blue of the Colorado columbine. He yearned for her, desired her, had wanted her from the very beginning, and he'd only forced himself to leave her in Alamosa, afraid of what he might do. Afraid she would ensnare him in her womanly wiles and never let him go. He had too many things to pursue and a woman was not in his plans. A woman would slow him down, take him on a different path, and he would never find peace.

"Connor." Her icy tone broke his thoughts. "Connor, why did you leave me and not even say goodbye? Was it something I did? Something I said?"

Jolyn wanted answers. She had spent lonely nights having this conversation with herself and now she finally had the chance to have a real response. She was afraid to hear what he had to say for fear that when it came it would be the end of any future with him, and when it came, she was even more disappointed with his words.

"Jolyn. I…I had business to attend to." Connor paused for a moment and wiped his mouth with the back of his hand, waiting. The silence filled the room with a heaviness. There was no more explanation coming, so Connor tried to halt any more talk of his nighttime whereabouts.

Instead, Connor tried to lighten the mood, jovially quipping "So, are you ready for breakfast or have you already tasted some of my sister's famous stew? Around here we fondly named it 'Eat it and leave it right where you et it!'"

Jolyn knew there was more but Connor was not going to give her any satisfaction right now. She was hurt and angry, but she didn't want to be anymore. Her emotions had been so mercurial as of late that she needed to find some stability, some form of comfort, even if that meant not from Connor. She hoped she would get real answers someday. Maybe from Annabel. Connor wasn't about to confide in her right now. But maybe, someday.

Jolyn tried to make the best of her new situation. Again, another place for her to readjust. She would make it work. That was who she was, and her inner strength would carry her forward. So she smiled and split the tension in the air. She witnessed Connor's taut shoulders relax and immediately knew that he felt something for her, but she would be damned if she could figure him out.

Connor could not stand to see Jolyn angry, but he couldn't possibly explain how he felt. Not now, anyway. Perhaps soon. He realized he was still standing over her, staring, almost gawking.

"Excuse me, Connor. Would you mind turning the other way?" Jolyn said bluntly.

Now it was Connor's turn to blush as he realized Jolyn was asking him to stop gaping at her long enough for her to get out of bed.

"Hmrrrrupmhph. Yeah, sure. Listen, you get dressed and I'll meet you in the kitchen. I made a pot of coffee. Even my horses won't drink any of Annabel's coffee; God help the man she marries! Oh, yeah, and by the way, wear your riding clothes today. I'd like to take you somewhere after we eat, or, rather, swallow some of that stuff my sister calls hearty fare." Connor tipped his hat again, this time adding a wink that sent shivers down Jolyn's spine, and departed her room as quickly as he had entered it.

Jolyn sprang out of her bed, hastily throwing the thick comforter in place. She opened her carpetbag and wildly threw out the dresses and camisoles and leggings, digging deeper until she found what she was looking for at the very bottom. Her favorite denims, soft and faded blue from her repeated washings. She wore them every time she went on picnics with her family or long hikes with James. At the thought of her parents and even James, Jolyn's demeanor crashed as she silently whispered a prayer. "Ma and Pa, I think of you every day and now that I know Nick is with you, I pray that the three of you watch over Chris and me and the new lives we are trying to make." She thought of James and wondered again where he was now. "James," she promised aloud, "I won't give up on finding you. Please be safe, my friend." And with that she slipped her denims on, unaware of the way they snugly complemented her curves.

Her boots were of the finest leather and she chose a flattering red gingham shirt to complement the one Connor was wearing. Not that he will notice, she mused, but this is fun.

She giggled to herself and her cheeks grew a natural warm red from her cheerfulness. Completely dressed, she tied her long hair back with a leather fastener and donned a brand-new rich-brown Stetson that she'd picked out in Hawk's store with a promise that she would pay him back some day. Satisfied, she took a deep breath and headed toward the kitchen.

Connor had made himself a large breakfast, ignoring Annabel's leftover stew. Jolyn noticed that he had set a place for her too and had dolloped out quite a large helping for her.

Connor looked up. In one swift swoop he beheld all her beauty. Connor ached in his loins as Jolyn walked past him and he tried to quell his thoughts. The scent of lavender tickled his nostrils and he breathed even more deeply to savor the sweet perfume. Awkwardly he put the large pan back on the stove and sat down, grunting and clearing his throat.

Although Jolyn was too deep in her own anxious thoughts to notice Connor's quiet admiration, all the silent communication was not lost on Annabel's keen observance of the two.

Breakfast was eaten quickly and quietly, Connor concentrating on the food in front of him as if it were a map he had to memorize. Jolyn barely picked at the heavy fare, notably nervous to Annabel. Annabel tried to make light conversation but the two undeclared lovers in front of her were wound tighter than a rattler about to strike.

"Where're you two off to, Connor?" Annabel inquired.

"I've got something to show Jolyn." His terseness sliced the air more sharply than the knife he used to cut his meat on the plate.

"Oh?" continued Annabel. She was undaunted by his curt behavior and it did not curb her curiosity in the least.

Jolyn stared first at Connor and then at Annabel. When they sat side by side the family resemblance was indeed remarkable. The same color eyes, the thick dark hair, even the stubborn jutting chin. Annabel's sauciness was no less spicy no matter how much Connor tried to quench it with his solitude. Jolyn trod lightly between the strange loving combination of a wild cougar and a hungry grizzly.

"Well, wherever you two are today, do you think you'll be back later tonight? Remember, Brady's is having a special show tonight. Even Robert Ford and Bat are closing down early so they can go over to watch the magician and the show. I heard it's the best production ever. It even beats Calamity Jane showing off her aim. And Chris said…"

Connor cut in. "We'll be back in time. You got anything I can pack in my bags for a quick lunch? I don't think I'll be near town around lunchtime."

Annabel sniffed. "Fine, if you don't want to tell me where you're both off to, then fine, forget it. And, yes, I can pack you both a lunch. Anything else I can do for you, brother?"

Connor stared at his snippy sister. She was really a cute thing, he thought, even if she was a bit too talkative for him sometimes.

"Yes, little sister," he said lovingly, "last night's dinner was not bad, but tonight try adding some meat to the stew!"

"Why, you!!!!" Annabel grabbed her fork and flung it at Connor, barely missing his left cheekbone as he ducked out of the way.

Jolyn was frozen in her chair at all the commotion and it wasn't until she saw Annabel's wide grin that she realized the two were just enjoying each other, in their own way.

Connor pushed himself away from the table, stood up, and gave Annabel a quick hug.

"Love ya, Bel. Gotta go now."

He turned to Jolyn and said, "Meet you downstairs in a few moments. Bring the lunch Annie's packing. I'll see to the horses." And with a thud and a bang he was gone.

"Whewwww. Do you two always banter like that?"

Annabel laughed. "No, not always. It's been a while. Connor hasn't been like that since after Daddy…well, not for a long while now. C'mon, help me make that lunch for you two and I'll clear away breakfast later."

With saddlebags filled, the two gave a quick wave to Annabel and were off. Jolyn loved riding in pants and felt comfortable and at home on the horse Connor had saddled for her this morning.

Connor headed his horse southwest. Jolyn did not know this part of the country and her senses absorbed it all in. The quaking aspens towered on the San Juans, promising to scrape the clear blue sky with bits of young leafy greens. Every now and then a lone bristlecone pine teased the eager chipmunks with hints of hidden treasures.

Snow buttercups graced the timberline and down below mountain wood lilies hid in the meadows. A crushing roar announced a startled elk. The broad-tailed hummingbirds quietly nested in the lichens and moss of the rocks.

Jolyn loved it all. She could sense that Connor was deeply moved by it as well because he was constantly surveying all that surrounded him.

He enjoyed teaching Jolyn all that he knew. She might know doctoring and might possibly learn the trading business, he thought, but I know this country. The two of them, engulfed by the beauty encircling them, trotted, galloped, and casually walked their magnificent animals along a rolling path.

In just a couple of hours, the ten-mile journey ended as a large lake loomed in view. "They call it Santa Maria," he informed her. "And she is to be our hostess for lunch."

This was a new side to Connor. Then again, she did not really know him; she had only seen him passionate and resolute. She liked knowing that there were many more facets to him yet to be discovered. She dismounted her mare and let her graze. Connor likewise slid off Thunder, grabbed the leather bags in one hand, took Jolyn's hand in the other, and strolled to a copse of low trees near the water.

The sun was directly overhead. Jolyn took the saddlebags from Connor, reached in, and pulled out a blanket to lay on the ground. Jolyn was starved. Breakfast might have been only a few hours ago, but she had only played with her food. Jolyn and Connor took turns sorting the packages that were carefully wrapped. Annabel had fixed them a delicious feast of fried steak, biscuits, potato pasties, and chunks of melon to wash it all down. They both ate greedily, and the small spread was gone in no time. Almost on cue, they both sat back and sighed with pleasure as their satiated stomachs moaned.

Jolyn looked at Connor and giggled. The melon juice had dripped down his mouth and clung to the short stubble of his unshaven face. Connor glared back, unsure of what was so amusing, and nervously swiped at his face. Feeling the slimy residue on his face, he understood.

"So you like laughing at me?" he queried.

Feeling playful, Connor jumped up and swooped Jolyn up in his arms.

"PUT ME DOWN, CONNOR. PUT ME DOWN!!" Jolyn screamed.

"Not on your life!" Connor roared as he headed toward the lake.

"Oh, goodness gracious, no! Connor Richardson, don't you dare! Don't you even consider what you are about to…CONNOR!!!!"

Connor was enjoying the feel of Jolyn squirming in his arms. She felt good. Damn good, and he did not want to lose this feeling with her. But now, for the moment, he was having the best time he had ever had with a woman—anyone, in fact.

Connor's long strides had the two of them at the edge of the lake in no time. Jolyn was still struggling in his arms, but the more she fought him, the tighter he held her. He enjoyed this teasing. He had never done this with anyone else but Annabel, and that was different. She was his sister and Jolyn was his…what?

He knew what he wanted her to be, and hoped that maybe someday she would be his, forever.

The edge of the lake formed small ripples of foam as Connor trudged in. He only went as deep as he could before the waterline would enter the tops of his boots. Jolyn froze in his arms. She didn't know what he was going to do. Would he drop her in? Would he throw her under? What?

Laughing from deep in his belly, Connor leaned over and dunked Jolyn's head in. He quickly pulled her out sputtering and swearing.

"What was that I heard?" he roared. "I think maybe you forgot something." And with that he graciously dipped her head in again.

This time when he pulled her up he gently lowered her to her feet. Jolyn whipped her wet locks over her head, soaking Connor.

"Why, of all the unmitigated gall, Connor Richardson! Why, what!"

Connor laughed, and it was so pure and natural that Jolyn found herself giggling with him.

"The next time," Connor said between roars, "the next time you want to laugh at my messy face, think about the steak grease that adorned that lovely sweet chin of yours!"

With that remark, Jolyn's hand flew to her own face, wet from the lake, but was still able to feel the grease underneath it all. Crimson flooded her cheeks and she glared at Connor. He was still smiling, but this time she joined him. There the both of them stood, ankle deep in the lake and laughing at each other like the best of friends.

Connor pulled off his blue bandanna and handed it to Jolyn. She wiped her face free of the grease and the cold water and handed the wet crumpled kerchief back to Connor, who repeated the same ablutions. He put the damp cloth back around his neck. He took Jolyn's hand in his own and they made their way back slowly to their blanket, enjoying each other's company, quiet. The beautiful spread was now a strewn litter of leftovers, which the two of them packed up and tucked in the saddlebags. They took their time strolling back to the horses, mounted them, and headed toward home.

Jolyn glanced back at the pristine lake and softly murmured, "Connor, this was lovely, but why did you bring me out here?"

Connor was quiet for a while. Then his voice quivered a bit as he began.

"Jolyn. That lake was just a sidestep to where we're really going. I wanted you to remember the good part of the day and not so much where I plan on taking you now."

Jolyn didn't question him anymore. They trotted on side by side, both in silence, each deep in thought.

Creede was in plain view when Connor nudged Jolyn's mare onto a different path. Jolyn was quiet as she rode, waiting for Connor to unveil his next destination.

The scene arose as though in slow motion, and Jolyn immediately grasped the enormity of the location. They were on the western edge of town, at a graveyard. Connor nimbly dismounted Thunder and walked over to Jolyn to help her glide down. Quietly they both guided their horses to a nearby tree, where they tethered the tired animals.

Hand in hand, Connor escorted Jolyn to a section that was enclosed by an ornate iron fence. Connor opened the gate and almost timidly nudged Jolyn inside.

"Jo, I'll wait at the gate. I've just been here a little while ago. You go on in. Go ahead. I'm right here, Jo."

Jolyn hesitated for a moment, her feet like lead underneath her. There were three graves, three markers. The first one read: *Sam Richardson, born April 27,1836, died March 18, 1891, a good man, a proud man, R.I.P.* A picture of the mountains had been carved in the wood as if to protect all that lay underneath it. Jolyn said a quiet prayer. Her uncle's grave was next.

She read the epitaph through misty eyes, her hands gingerly touching the wooden grave marker. She noticed flowers had been planted all around and a slow curving smile broke through her tears. The next marker was the hardest of them all to read. Nick was very special to her. While she was close to Chris, Nick was the more serious of the two, and he shared a special place in her heart. Her hands lingered on the marker, her fingers tracing the beautifully carved letters of his name. Hot tears slid down her swollen cheeks as memories of her brother flashed through her mind.

"Oh, Nick, I'm so sorry about what happened. Connor will get him. I know he will. And then your soul can rest. Dear Nick, I love you."

Jolyn turned away and before she was about to exit the small gate her eyes fell upon two small markers to the side. She glanced at Connor, her eyes questioning him.

Softly he said, "Chris did that. As soon as he found out." Jolyn walked over to the two wooden markers that memorialized her parents. Their names entwined with each other's and the epitaph simply read: *In life they loved together, so shall they love in heaven.*

Jolyn sank to her knees and sobbed. Connor's heart ached to see her suffer so much, even though he knew she would be grateful later for having been here. Connor opened the gate and walked swiftly over to her, and, bending down, he cradled her in his arms.

Feeling the powerful arms around her, Jolyn sobbed even harder, crying for all she had lost and for all she would never have again. She felt Connor's warm breath against her neck and the gentle pressure of his lips as he caressed her hair. She inhaled his musky scent and felt secure in his muscular arms. Warmth radiated through her and her muscles relaxed. Jolyn lifted her face to Connor and her soft lips found his. His warmth melted her as he gently parted her lips and kissed her fully and deeply. Her nipples grew hard and pressed against the soft cotton fabric of her shirt, aching, wanting.

Connor wanted her now too, but not here, not in a place of sorrow and sadness. He lifted Jolyn in his strong arms and carried her where the horses were foraging in the grass and tenderly settled her in her saddle. Her soft indigo eyes were awash with love as she longed for him. Connor mounted his steed and, guiding Thunder closer to Jolyn, he reached for her hand.

"Thank you, Connor, for bringing me here…I…"

"Shhhh. It's okay, Jo. Let's head back."

Still holding hands, they allowed the two horses to slowly amble their way back to town.

That night, Brady's was once again the talk of the town. Jolyn was staying with Annabel, and although she wanted to share some of the events of the day with her, Jolyn knew exhaustion was overcoming her, and allowed herself, albeit unwillingly, to give in to her body's needs and lay down for a long and necessary nap. By the time Jolyn started stretching and waking, it was almost dusk outside. Annabel drew a warm perfumed-scented bath for her and Jolyn slid down and moaned at the simple glorious feel of pampering. The bath water was almost chilled before Jolyn gave a recalcitrant lunge and hoisted herself out of the tub. Feeling restored, Jolyn enjoyed donning one of her favorite turquoise gowns for the gala event that Annabel was busily describing to Jolyn. Annabel had primped and fretted too over what she would wear and finally settled on a light-blue gown covered with silver sequins. Together the two young women, happy and lighthearted, were as colorful and pretty as two peacocks on a Saturday night.

Connor and Chris had begrudgingly given in to their own grooming for the evening. They each had bathed and shaved, swearing through it all, and looked handsome and devilish and ready to party. A splash of their best colognes further added to their splendor.

What a party it was! Creede did not always sport such famous actors! Tonight Creede and Brady's were proud to have on hand an actress fresh from the East Coast.

The four well-dressed young people entered Brady's amidst cheers of welcome and hearty handshakes. Bat Masterson greeted Connor with a promise to talk business later on and Calamity Jane had ridden into town that morning just to see Mae West herself.

Chris and Connor had front-row tables and the two young ladies gossiped and chatted like old friends.

The evening was a great success, Brady himself puffed up and too proud to do anything but smile and nod his head up and down all night.

It was well after two in the morning when the wonderful festivities finally came to an end.

Chris and Annabel, their arms entwined, strolled past the closed shops as Connor and Jolyn followed. Out in the crisp early-morning air, Connor cleared his throat, still raspy from Brady's smoke-filled theater.

"Annabel and Chris," Connor called out, "good night, you two. I want to walk a little bit and move this beer out of my gut."

Chris and Annabel smiled at each other and then at Connor and Jolyn. Chris replied first.

"Sure, take it easy, Connor, but listen, we have to meet tomorrow. I have a few things to discuss with you."

"No problem, Chris. I'll come by your office first thing in the morning."

"Ah, if it's okay with you, Connor, don't be in such a hurry to come by." Chris shifted uncomfortably, and Connor just laughed.

"Okay, partner. See ya close to lunchtime."

The two couples said their good nights and parted.

Jolyn watched as Chris and Annabel slowly sauntered away, hand in hand with their bodies in perfect rhythm as they swayed. A twinge of jealousy passed through Jolyn and she pushed it as far away as possible.

Connor, too, was deep in his own thoughts. He turned to Jolyn and whispered softly, "Would you mind staying and walking with me a bit? I never could go right to sleep after so much drinking."

Jolyn's deep-blue eyes twinkled in the moonlight. She gazed into his soft gray eyes and nodded her head so slightly Connor was almost unclear of her response. Gently he placed her hand in the crook of his elbow and the two forms, silhouetted by the moon, seemed to glide over the wooden planks of Main Street.

Connor headed north toward the far end of town. He hadn't been up by the old silver mine in quite some time. Miners were still working it, but the mother lode had been found some time ago and the stubborn old fools were just there on a dream. Next to the old mine was a small meandering creek that ran the length of the town in its own foolhardy search for the Rio Grande.

The May night was cool and crisp. The stars were so plentiful and so bright you were almost afraid to reach up for fear of burning your hands on one who might have strayed too close. The moon, full and golden, was almost brighter than the morning sun. Connor glanced over at Jolyn, her face bathed in the warm glow of the heavenly body. He felt himself grow warm just from the nearness of her being. Her hair rippled as she walked, and the shimmering auburn curls seemed to have a life of their own as they bobbed up and down, catching moonbeams.

The wooden planks suddenly ended as the two found themselves at the edge of the town. The San Juans loomed like a great dark curtain in front of them as the town slept quietly, nestled in the comfort of the resting mountains.

Connor pointed to an old bristlecone pine tree that stood alone, in view tonight only because of the bright moon.

"My father used to tell me that tree was the oldest living thing on this earth. I didn't believe him at that time, but since then I found out he was right. That tree was here before the Indians settled these parts and I reckon it'll be here long after we're gone."

Jolyn listened to every word he said. There was a side to Connor she had only begun to learn about. It had poked out a little bit while they were travelling to Alamosa, but here, under nature's own dark blanket, Connor shed all the other sides to his personality. This was the real Connor, she knew. The one that was caring and loving, not harsh and violent and so cold. As she listened to him she unconsciously leaned her body into his, letting him hold her extra weight. She was tired. The evening was so full, she did not think she could do any more but listen to the deep soothing tones of Connor's voice. Connor sensed her growing weariness and guided her closer to the pine. The soft grass under the bristlecone, nurtured by the neighboring creek, was a welcome resting place.

Connor sat down and leaned his back against the pine tree as if to absorb some of its power, its history, its glory. Jolyn nestled against Connor's stomach and Connor wrapped his firm arms around her. He lay soundlessly, absorbing her lavender scent and the clean fresh scent of her hair.

Jolyn leaned her head back on Connor's chest and sighed. He was so strong yet so gentle, and she felt so good in his arms. Connor tightened his hold on Jolyn as he stared across at the creek, mesmerized by the continual trilling of water.

Jolyn purred. Her body, warmed by the closeness of Connor's, relaxed and she closed her eyes. She listened to the gentle beating of his heart. A soft whispering breeze glided over the two of them, massaging them with the cool night. The gentle pressure of Connor's burning hand upon her chest aroused her.

He tenderly caressed the open section of her dress and the touch of his fiery fingers shot heated sparks through her. Her nipples hardened, and she longed for Connor to touch them. Jolyn blushed with her thoughts. Connor's hands slowly, oh so slowly, travelled down her heaving chest until he cupped her firm breasts. Jolyn moaned and breathed more rapidly. Oh, God, his hands were so tender and so soothing. Smooth fingers teased her stiff nipples and a slow warmth spread from her loins.

Jolyn turned her face toward him and reached for his lips with her fingertips. They were burning. Her fingers traced their lines and the heat from his lips raced through her. Connor turned Jolyn over to face him and his hands explored her curving back. Jolyn's graceful fingers stroked his face, her every touch burning into Connor's desires, heating him and building the fires he knew would never be quenched until…until.

Connor's feathery fingers embraced Jolyn's face, his warm silver eyes gazing into deep-blue ones misted over with heated desire. Connor wanted her. He leaned closer and his lips softly tasted her, his warm breath tickling her soft face. Jolyn closed her eyes and groaned. Her supple lips, full and wanting, parted as she searched for his and they kissed. It was rich and all-consuming.

Jolyn swayed dizzily. The kiss swept her to new heights. A longing deep within her grew with intensity and her loins ached.

"Ohhh," she groaned. "Oh, Connor. I..."

"Shhh, my love. You are so beautiful, Jolyn. My Jo. Would you be my Jo?"

"Oh, Connor, yes. Yes."

Connor's scorching lips sought hers once again and she melted in his desires. His kisses covered her face, memorizing her beauty with his lips, inhaling her scent with his nostrils as his hands tangled and knotted her thick hair. His tumescence, hard and unyielding, was throbbing against his own clothes. Jolyn felt the pressure of his body, the hardness in his loins, and still she wanted more. She could not stop now, did not want to stop now. Connor, in one swift motion, lifted Jolyn to her feet and embraced her. His body molded with hers and he pressed his burgeoning manhood against her. Jolyn staggered, her knees buckling under her giddy body as Connor grabbed her more strongly and held her up. Liquid pools of silver swam into misty-blue ones as Connor bore wildly into her eyes, going beyond her own sight. Slowly, leisurely, he unbuttoned her gown, her supple breasts pressing against her strained camisole, longing to be free. Her gown slid gracefully to the ground and Connor slipped her camisole over her head, her rounded breasts falling free and unencumbered. Connor dipped his head toward them.

"Oh, Jolyn, you are so beautiful."

His hands cupped one soft breast and then another. His hot breath upon her pale bosom sent shivers through her spine and her nipples hardened again. Connor's searing tongue sought them out and as he suckled them his burning hands grasped her rounded bottom, squeezing her gently.

"Ohhh, Connor. I can't go on. I feel so..."

Connor finished her sentence by closing her mouth with his as he swooped her up in his arms and gently laid her down on the soft green blanket from nature. Hot, blazing fingers explored Jolyn's body as she quivered and moaned with his feathery touches. Connor's hands were light and soft to the touch, but as he reached her thighs his grasp became more demanding, more wanting.

Jolyn gazed up and beheld the sky above swarming with stars. Her hands grabbed hold of Connor's hair, so thick to her touch. She wanted all of him and she would not stop now, could not stop now.

Connor eagerly parted her legs, letting his fiery hands fondle her long, full thighs. Apprehensively at first, his hands lightly touched her mound, her soft hair yielding to his touch. Her legs trembled, and he breathed in her scent.

"Oh, Jo. I want you. I need you." Connor quickly stood and unbuckled his pants, stripping himself completely of all his clothes.

Jolyn shuddered in anticipation as Connor gently lowered his searing body upon hers. His manhood throbbed against Jolyn's soft thighs and she groaned again.

Connor's lips stifled another whimper as his burning lips sought out Jolyn's. Jolyn's hands roamed Connor's back, his taut muscles rippling under her velvety touch. Her fingers glided to his muscular thighs and she explored, touching, squeezing, massaging. She wanted to know the feel, the texture of his pulsing manhood. Delicate fingers traced the long lines of his hot, swollen shaft and Connor moaned uncontrollably. This time it was Jolyn's turn to quell the groans as she sought out Connor's full lips and kissed him deeply, longing for more of him.

Her hands pressed against his back, urging him on, demanding more of him. Connor's hand skillfully guided his pulsating member between her thighs. His heat melted all barriers and Jolyn gasped out loud as Connor moved deep within her. A sharp sensation ripped through Jolyn and her eyes widened with the filling discovery. Pain quickly dissolved as the burning shaft filled every fiber of her soul.

Her hips undulated with the rhythm of Connor's and she arched her back. Connor, lost in his passions, lunged himself more deeply within her, his desires so strong, dizziness forcing his eyes closed.

The ground beneath Jolyn swayed with their rhythm and their damp bodies, bathed in sweat, glistened under the moonlight.

Connor's smoky eyes met blue-gray ones bursting with love, and he consumed Jolyn, scorching her wherever his searing lips touched her. Their tempo grew faster, their torrid desire more urgent, until both lost track of themselves, so lost in their passion for each other. Faster and faster, Jolyn's breasts tingled and her heated body rippled with the night's breezes as her loins found a pleasure she'd never known possible. Harder and more powerful, their bodies pressed and swelled until finally, finally Jolyn never knew her mouth had opened as she screamed, the mountains the only ears to bear witness to her that night. Together they soared beyond the mountains, up to the stars, and there, with the heat of the burning stars, forged their love forever in the heavens.

Chapter 14

"Don't move," Connor whispered against the silky wisps of hair that fell along the curve of Jolyn's neck.

"Mmm. I don't think I could even if the worst blizzard ever known should strike Creede at this very moment," she sighed languidly.

He felt her shiver slightly as the chill air filtered down from the shadowed pines above them, and chuckled.

"How about a good northerly breeze?"

Jo lifted her leg in an attempt to give Connor a solid kick in his shin, but he caught her thigh and pulled her body across him, shifting onto his back as he did so. Lying naked across Connor, Jo was fully exposed to the night air.

"Why, you, no good, double-crossing…" Jolyn uttered, and slapped playfully against his broad chest.

Still rumbling with laughter, Connor swiftly yanked his soft wool cloak over them and wrapped his solid arms around her. Jo, feeling the advantage of a warm human mattress beneath her instead of the dampness from the ground plus a cozy blanket that effectively shut out the chill from above her, quickly ceased squirming and curled like a kitten into his muscled but yielding body.

"You were saying?" His deep voice sent shivers of a different kind down her spine. His hands were feathers stroking her back and buttocks, rekindling the fiery feelings that she thought had been quenched.

"Something about blizzards, I think," she purred.

Enjoying the freedom of movement that her new position afforded her, Jolyn eagerly explored Connor's body. Her right hand smoothed a path from his belly upward. Her long fingers spread along his lightly furred chest, then curled around the soft tufts and tugged gently.

"Hey, you witch, that's attached." But Connor made no move to stop her.

"Yes, I can see that," Jolyn murmured as she smiled in the dark.

Sensing that Connor was enjoying her explorations as much as she was, Jolyn grazed down his side with her nails. She paused as her fingertips brushed a slight puckering on his hip.

"An old knife wound," Connor answered before the question had left her lips.

The warmth of the skin beneath her palm where her hand now rested seemed to burn a hole in her hand.

"An ambush during one of your routes?" she declared distractedly.

"No. Nothing so noble."

Connor's hands had slid to the backs of her legs and were caressing them languidly.

"Tell me," Jo whispered as she pressed light kisses along his neck.

"Well," Connor continued huskily, his hands slipping up to rest in the small of her back. "It was Hawk's fault. We were drinking over at Bob Ford's Saloon. Lottie and the girls were…ouch!"

"Go on," Jolyn breathed sweetly against his neck and continued to nibble, more gently now, along the hollow of his neck.

"Are you sure that you wouldn't like to talk about something a little more interesting, like…?" Connor teased her mouth with his own and softly chewed her lower lip.

"No." Jo caught her breath, then pulled away. "I'll behave myself if you will. Now, go on."

Connor was tempted to pull her back down, but he thought it would be much simpler to get his story out of the way, so that he could once again apply himself fully to the matter at hand.

"Okay. I give up." Connor grunted and leaned back against the damp grass, tucking his hands behind his head as he did so. For a moment Jolyn nearly pulled his arms back around her but rested her elbows upon his shoulders instead.

"It was Hawk, as usual, who started the trouble."

Jolyn snorted in disbelief.

"Are you going to let me tell this or not?"

"Please, I'm all ears."

"Well, Hawk and I were playing five-card stud with a couple of drifters. After a few hours of nearly losing his shirt, Hawk accused one of them of dealing from the bottom of the deck, which, for the record, he was. Now, anyone with a lick of sense knows when you're in a strange bar, and you don't know your players, you take your losses and keep your mouth shut, but not Hawk. Before I knew it, two of the crook's cronies jumped Hawk, and as luck would have it, the card shark came after me with a knife. Hawk, being more or less prepared for an attack, managed to knock their heads together; meanwhile, I'm trying to avoid being carved up for dinner. Just as I manage to grab his knife arm, Hawk hits me over the head with a bottle. When I came to, Hawk has barely a scratch on him, and I'm being stitched by the local dentist. All Hawk could say was 'Where'd you learn how to duck?'" Connor started to chuckle. "It took the dentist and his assistant, his oldest son, and their housekeeper to hold me down. I think that's about as close as I've ever come to laying Hawk out…with one exception."

"Mmm." Remembering the exception, Jo reddened slightly, then peered disbelievingly down into Connor's shadowed face. "How is it that I get the feeling Hawk might tell this story a little differently?"

"Mmm. I guess you'll have to ask Hawk. But how you could possibly doubt my word when…" Connor's hands slipped from behind his neck and slid down her shoulders to her waist, his thumbs gently kneading her ribcage. "There's more, you know."

"To the story?"

"No, more…"

Connor slowly guided Jolyn's hand along his hip and across his thigh to the inside of his knee, where she felt a four-inch gouge running along the kneecap. In this position, her breasts and stomach were pressed flat against him, and she felt a hardness against her stomach that hadn't been there minutes before. A heat from his body began to radiate through her; she felt a slow burning from deep within her abdomen. Her heart hammered in her breast and she could barely catch her breath.

"And this one?" she panted.

"An Indian arrow."

Her hand, as though it had a life of its own, left his and slid upward toward his burgeoning between his thighs, but before she could explore further, his hand enveloped hers, raised her hand to his mouth, and pressed the inside of her wrist against his lips.

"I think that's enough, temptress, for now," he groaned.

"Connor, do you think we could..."

Connor pulled her head down and captured her mouth with his own. Fire surged through them and licked a molten path wherever their lustful hands and mouths pressed against the other. Feverishly, they stroked one another. White-hot flames licked fiercely everywhere they touched until both were caught in one glorious conflagration. Connor lifted her hips toward his.

Suddenly, a blood-curdling shriek rent the air. Connor and Jolyn froze, each now gripping the other.

"Connor." Jolyn's voice shook with fear. "What is it?"

They listened. The night had grown deathly silent.

"Sounded like some animal. Probably a hare. An owl must have caught her. I don't think there is any sound so chilling as the cry of a dying animal." Connor's whisper echoed loudly in the stillness.

Both now clutched each other in a subtly different way. Gone were the passion and fire and fear of moments before. Now their embrace was a consolation. Neither could help but reflect on the deaths that had so recently touched their lives. Nor could they separate those deaths from the very man who had caused them. Luke.

Luke. Had Jo said the name aloud?

Connor stiffened.

"Come, Jo. It's almost morning. We'd better be getting back. I have a feeling I'm going to get a long lecture from that sister of mine as it is."

Connor had already slipped from beneath her and was quickly getting dressed.

"Yes, I suppose we should be getting back," Jolyn repeated in a daze.

A barrier as massive as the San Juan Mountains that rose above them seemed ominous.

"Connor?"

"Get dressed." His was a stranger's voice.

"Connor, we must talk about…things. I feel as though if we leave this place now without having said…that we won't ever be able to say them."

"I'll meet you down at the stream. Hurry. We're late enough as it is."

She dressed clumsily. When she finished she tripped blindly to where Connor waited by the inky waters.

"Let's go."

Connor gripped her arm firmly and nearly dragged her along the path toward the sleeping town below.

Angry and hurt, Jolyn tried to pull away. Strangers, that was all they were. She had just spent a day sharing her sorrow and her joy with a stranger. She meant nothing to him. Nothing. While she, she was falling in love with him, was in love with him.

Jolyn halted abruptly in her tracks.

"Dammit, Jo. It's nearly dawn. Will you get a move on?"

Jolyn yanked her arm from his grasp.

"Is that all you can say to me?" Jolyn's head rose a notch in that defensive way of hers and glared fiercely up at him.

"What do you want from me, Jo? Today was a nice day, all right, a great day. We had a good time; I had a good time, but if I don't get you back down there before the whole town wakes up, there's gonna be hell to pay."

"Good time? Is that what that tryst was all about? A good time?"

"For God's sake, Jo. It's late. We can talk about this later when you've had more time to think, to put all of this in the proper perspective. Right now, I'm more worried about your reputation."

"My reputation? Don't you mean yours? You're scared, aren't you? Scared that you'll get caught sneaking into town with me and get stuck marrying me."

"No, Jo, that's only part of it. You see, I've sworn an oath that I mean to keep, and I can't allow you or anyone to get in the way of that promise."

"Well, don't worry, Connor Richardson. I have no intention of getting in your way. In fact, I'll be sure to steer clear of you from now on."

"Jo, this isn't coming out right. That's not what I meant. Please listen to me."

Jo brushed past Connor and marched down the few remaining patches of path. Her back ramrod straight, her fists clenched, she gave no clue to the tears that streamed uncontrollably down her face. As she reached the alleyway that led back to Cliff Street, she slowed her pace. As angry as she was, she still had no desire to be caught unescorted among the unkempt drifters who inhabited the streets at all hours of the day and night. When she reached the walkway, she felt Connor at her side. Together, they walked silently for several blocks to her room on Creede Avenue. Without a backward glance, she dashed up the back steps, unaware of the lonely tattoo her heels beat along the planks.

Connor watched her as she fiercely scrubbed at her tears with the heels of her hands and slipped unnoticed into the house. With a dark scowl, he turned and entered the store below.

Jolyn tiptoed into the small room that bordered Annabel's and quickly stripped off her clothes, leaving them in a rumpled heap on the floor. Exhausted, she slipped between the cool covers and stared hopelessly at the rafters above. Hot tears still cascaded down her cheeks, dampening the feather pillow she hugged tightly against her. She felt as though she were back at the graves, but this time she was mourning the loss of something that wasn't dead.

* * *

Jolyn woke late the next morning, feeling groggy and out of sorts. She struggled out of the covers and staggered to the washstand. She poured a healthy dose of water into the bowl and plunged her face into its icy contents. She stood up, the water dribbling down her neck and shoulders, and stared into the oval mirror above the stand.

She looked the same. Her hair sprang in all directions, except where it lay dampened against her forehead. Her eyes lacked a little of their usual sparkle. Her cheeks appeared slightly shadowed, yet she looked the same. She frowned at her image. How could someone feel so changed and still look no different? She had not planned to fall in love with him. In fact, she had even fought it. But since the moment she had met him, she had been unable to shut him out of her thoughts, her very senses. And now, when she had finally surrendered to those feelings, Connor had shut her out. Again. Twice in Alamosa and now here. Well, it wasn't going to happen a fourth time.

Jolyn snatched the towel from the rack and swiped at her face and shoulders. She hastily slipped on her pale-green shirt and dark riding skirt, grabbed her carpetbag, and jammed her clothes and various items that she had brought with her into it. She carelessly brushed her hair back and braided it. She flung her jacket and hat over the bag, glanced about the room to make sure that she had missed nothing, then marched off to purchase a one-way train ticket to Alamosa. At the train station, Jolyn was able to purchase a ticket on the noon train. That left her two hours to say her goodbyes to Chris and Annabel and get any purchasing orders that Hawk might need for the store. She had promised Hawk she would help him and even if she was not feeling up to it, she would keep her end of the bargain.

Jolyn returned less hurriedly to the house and found Annabel pounding something that might have passed for bread dough had it been less lumpy and more yielding. Annabel glanced up with a rueful smile.

"Do you think it can be saved?"

Jolyn looked doubtfully at the muddy blob.

"I suppose you could set it aside and see if it rose a bit more," Jo suggested helpfully.

"But it's been rising since last evening!"

"Oh, well, in that case, perhaps you had best let it die a natural death, and I can help you start another batch. If we do it now, there would still be time for you to bake it before dinner."

"Oh, Jolyn, that would be wonderful. I know with just a little bit of help, I could get the hang of this." Annabel had already disposed of the dough and was wildly pulling out flour and leavening for a fresh batch. "You're sure you don't mind?"

"Not at all. As long as it doesn't take longer than a half hour. I still need to check with Chris about any orders I can place for him when I return to Alamosa."

"But you'll have plenty of time for that." Annabel had already managed to douse her hair, pert nose, and calico apron with a dusting of flour. "Chris and I don't plan to let you go until after the wedding. We talked about it, and we figured that you could have anything you needed made in town and still help me with all these madcap preparations."

"Here." Jolyn rescued the mixing bowl in mid-air that Annabel was carelessly tossing about. "Let me help you with this."

Jolyn bent over the table and began measuring the proper amounts of flour, leavening, and water into the bowl. "I'm afraid I must leave sooner than that. I have a few important commitments that I made before I left that I just can't break. In fact, that's what I came here to tell you. I'm leaving today."

"Today? But Jo, I thought we were going to look over materials today, and Chris has already bought tickets for this Saturday to see another show."

"Yes, well, I guess I forgot to tell you with all the excitement and everything..."

Annabel now sat in the chair across from Jolyn, gazing perplexedly at Jolyn's flushed face as she furiously mixed the dough with her fingers. Even though Annabel had known her for such a short time, she knew that it was unlike Jo to be less than honest.

"It's Connor, isn't it?"

"Connor? Of course not. What could Connor possibly have to do with my leaving?"

"Jo, I'm not blind. I see how it is between you two. When you're in the same room together, I feel like I'm in the middle of a lightning storm. And"—Annabel toyed with the pocket of her apron—"I know how late you came in this morning. If there is anything I can do, if there is any way I can help..."

Jolyn gave the finished dough one last pat and stepped toward the sink. She paused and stared blindly down at her sticky hands.

"I have to get away, Annabel. Let's leave it at that."

"But he loves you, Jo. I know that he does. Why, he's never even looked at another woman the way he looks at you. And before you arrived, he was a different Connor—distracted, always moody. You've got to give it a chance."

"I have given him a chance. More than one. But I swear that I'm not going to give him another. Every time I think that we are getting close, closer than any two people can get, he shuts me out. And every time that he does, I feel as though I've been stabbed, stabbed in the heart. Well, I've had enough. I'm going home."

"You're right, of course. Connor can be self-centered and bad-tempered, but never unfeeling, Jolyn. Connor would never set out deliberately to hurt anyone, especially someone he cares for the way I can tell he cares for you. I know that there is no excuse for the way Connor has behaved, but ever since the…the robbery, Connor just hasn't been the same. I don't think that he'll ever forgive himself for not being here to stop what happened, and I think that somehow he's made up his mind that until he finds the murderers he doesn't deserve to carry on with his own life."

"If this is true, then what better reason for my leaving?" Jo cleansed her hands and took a seat across from Annabel. "If Connor has to do this thing, and he's not about to let anyone help him do it, then why stick around? I'm no quitter, Bel, but I'm smart enough to know when the odds against me are too high. I lost this race before it ever started."

"That's not true. Connor's already half crazy with loving you and without your help, Connor won't stand a chance."

"I think you underestimate Connor. I'm sorry, Bel. I've been through too much in the last few months, and I don't think I can stand to be hurt any more. I need time alone to think, and that's just exactly what I intend to do."

"Please, Jo, don't go. This is Connor's one chance to forget about Luke. If you go now, it'll just keep eating away at him until he goes after him again, and this time he might not come back alive."

Distorted images of Luke's leering face assailed Jolyn and she shuddered.

"Maybe if I explained to you how Luke fits into all this, you could understand Connor a little better." Annabel's voice trembled slightly. She looked down at the floor, exhaled a slow, long sigh, and then continued. "I have not spoken about Luke's past to anyone, not even Chris. You see, Luke was the oldest, and he wasn't Papa's son. Mama was raped years before Connor, but when she met Papa he fell in love with her and married her and accepted Luke as his own. Papa told me years later that Mama kept Luke close to her, protecting him, guarding him. Maybe she felt guilty. I don't know. And Luke, five years older and much bigger, would attack Connor when no one was watching. He would destroy Connor's playthings, kill Connor's pet mice, and steal Connor's valuables. Luke was just filled with jealousy and hatred. Then a few years later Mama died after giving birth to me. She had the fever and never recovered. Luke had no one else to protect him and he grew up hating everyone and everything.

Annabel shifted uncomfortably in her chair. Jolyn reached across the table and clasped Annabel's trembling hands.

"You don't have to go on. I can understand why Connor hates Luke so much."

"No, you don't understand at all. Connor never hated Luke. He always understood that Mama felt sorry for Luke. No matter how many times Luke hurt Connor, Connor would forgive him, try to be his friend. Luke and Hawk and Connor hung out together many times but it was clear that Luke wanted nothing to do with either of them. I was just the little girl who wanted to be with the big boys, but never was part of it. Papa tried to make Luke help Connor and Hawk with the trading route runs, but Luke just hung around town, disappearing for a few weeks at a time, then reappearing without explanation."

"Then, when Connor found out what Luke had done… He found the bodies, you know, only two hours after it happened." Annabel had become deathly pale, and her voice had died to barely a whisper.

"Bel, are you all right?" Jolyn rubbed Annabel's hands, trying to bring some life back into them.

"Yes, I'm fine. Just for a moment I was remembering…you see, I was there, too. I didn't think I would ever forget. I thought that I would never be happy again. But Chris didn't die, and our love has brought back hope into my life. Is it so selfish of me to want the same for Connor?"

"No, of course not. But Bel, I don't think Connor feels what you think he feels. I'm not even sure what I feel anymore. I must go. Please don't feel like I'm deserting you. I'll be back in a month for the wedding, and maybe then I'll have worked things out."

"Just promise me one thing." Midnight-blue eyes stared into sapphire ones. "Don't give up on that brother of mine yet."

Jolyn shook her head exasperatedly and smiled at Annabel's expectant face. "All right, my friend, I won't. Well, I guess I'd best check out with Chris before I leave. Good luck with all your preparations. I'll be seeing you very soon. I hope Chris appreciates what a wonderful prize he's getting."

"Oh, he does. I remind him daily." Both women laughed. Jolyn found her things where she had left them, slipped on the jacket, plopped on her hat, and snatched up the bag.

"Well, I'm ready. I'm going to miss you, Bel. I couldn't wish for a better sister-in-law."

"I couldn't have said it better!" Annabel gave Jolyn a swift hug and pressed her cheek against Jo's. "Goodbye for now, and don't worry; I'll take care of both our men while you're gone."

Jolyn skipped down the stairs, her heart lighter. Maybe, just maybe, things would work out.

"Chris. Chris!"

"Chris stepped out on an errand, Jo. Is there something you need?" Connor's deep voice sounded cool and impersonal.

As she turned the corner, she could see him sitting behind his desk, sleeves rolled, shirt unbuttoned, his lean face lightly stubbled. For a moment she thought her heart had stopped beating.

How could he sit there so impervious when she could barely stand? she thought angrily. Well, two could play at this game.

She advanced coolly into the room and stopped a few feet from the desk.

"Yes. As a matter of fact, you can. I'll be leaving today on the noon train." Did his fingers tighten about the quill he was holding or was it her imagination? "And I wanted to pick up the list of items that Hawk asked me to bring back on the next shipment."

"I didn't realize that you would be leaving so soon. I thought…"

"Yes," Jo interrupted. "You see, I made some commitments before I left, but as I explained to Annabel, I'll be back for the wedding."

"I see. Well, Jo, I'd like to talk about...about last night. I didn't intend things to go so far, and I wanted to explain why..."

"You don't have to go any further. I understand. Things sometimes get out of hand. I can assure you that it meant no more to me than it did to you. A good time. Wasn't that what you called it? I've had time now to review what happened from the proper perspective, and I realize that I was just being foolish. Do you think that you can find those purchase orders? I've only a few more minutes before my train leaves."

"Jo, I didn't mean that to sound the way it did."

Was that pity in his voice? Hadn't Annabel said Connor was never unfeeling? Well, she didn't want his pity.

"Connor, if you can't find the papers, I suppose you'll have to send them with the next mail coach. I'm going to miss my train."

Jo felt as though she might scream. One more minute and she would be in his arms, making an idiot of herself, again.

"Papers? Oh, yes, here they are."

Connor bundled them up and began to straighten them. Jolyn snatched them from his hands, whirled about, and raced for the door.

"Jo, wait! I..."

But Jolyn had already slammed out the door.

"All aboooord. Laaast caaall. All aboooorrd!"

Jolyn dashed madly through the bustling crowd.

"Just made it, miss."

The attendant had barely finished giving her a hand up when the train began to hiss. With its bell clanging loudly, the train jerked slowly forward, its wheels clacking along the iron rail.

Jolyn staggered to a seat and sagged against the plush cushion. Through her mind a myriad of thoughts flickered like the scenery now flashing by her. Alamosa...Alamosa, the train wheels clacked. She was returning to what? She had only been in Alamosa a brief time. Would she ever find a place she could call her own? Yes, she would see Hawk again, and Arliss. She would be among people who cared about her, who appreciated her. And maybe, she would settle down in Alamosa. Work for Hawk at the trading post. Make new friends. Lasting ones. Not like…Connor. Connor. She would do just fine without him.

Chapter 15

Late August in Alamosa was a mixture of golds and browns and blues. The aspens shivered and glowed under the sharp blue skies and the fields of potatoes rested in muted browns. Tumbleweed blew everywhere, and the winds were hot and dry.

Yet the townspeople of Alamosa were happy and gay. This was the beginning of a new era, a new future. Trains were coming and going to Creede on a regular basis, and the townspeople were joyous. They would be able to visit their relatives in the neighboring town. Miners had found some new possibilities in Creede so that many of the locals were once again pulling up roots to go and seek their fortunes.

It was a wondrous occasion on that day in Alamosa. Jolyn waited eagerly on the edge of the platform with Arliss, Lucinda, and Hawk. Jolyn was trying to calm the excited and exuberant Arliss.

"Now, Arliss, honey, you really do have to calm down," Jolyn said in her most soothing tones even though she herself was about to burst.

"Oh, Jolyn," interrupted Lucinda, "let the boy alone. He has never done anything this exciting in his whole life. Probably won't do nothing this great after this ride neither. Let the boy have his fun while he can. Just keep him away from me!"

Lucinda turned to Hawk and muttered a little bit too loudly, "Never did see what she sees in that boy, all dirty and scabby. Remind me of that boy when I get a craving for children of my own. I'll think more'n twice about it then."

Jolyn chose to ignore Lucinda's comments. She did not need to get into another argument now that she was about to leave. Hawk had enough trouble convincing Lucinda that he and Jolyn were strictly friends. If it wasn't for Hawk's persistence and loyalty toward Jolyn, she probably would have been without a job.

"Miss Jolyn?" Arliss tugged at Jolyn's red silk dress.

"Yes, Arliss, what is it?"

"Wh...wh...when's it gonna get here?"

Jolyn's pale beige gloves smoothed her surah silk dress. Her mind was wandering, and she was having difficulty concentrating. "Hmm?" she murmured.

"Miss Jo. I asked you when the train's gonna arrive?"

"Oh, soon, Arliss, soon."

"But Miss Jo...I...just gotta know..."

"Arliss, honey, it will get here soon enough. I promise you."

Arliss, unsatisfied with the answer, dug his hands deep into his pockets and kicked at the ground, causing a small little cloud of dust to form around him.

Lucinda stared at Jolyn's dreamy eyes. She wondered what Jolyn was thinking. Unconsciously she scanned Jolyn's new dress with jealousy and hatred. The fitted bodice accented Jolyn's curving waist and the pleated skirt with its over-draped ruffles lifted gracefully in the ever-present winds of Alamosa. Jolyn tightened the red bow on her feathered bonnet, its color adding a lovely contrast to her auburn hair. Lucinda hissed to herself and turned away.

Arliss was splendid too, in his brand new sailor suit Hawk had purchased for him for this special event. The knee-length trousers ran into his long ribbed navy-blue stockings and his button shoes pinched his toes. Every few minutes he tugged at his sailor hat, blue ribbon flying in the winds.

Finally he looked at Jolyn and burst out, "Oh, when, Miss Jo, when is it coming? Is it gonna be ole number 841? Whaddya think, Miss Jo, whaddya think? Huh?"

Jolyn looked at Arliss and smiled. He had already grown over an inch since she'd met him.

"Arliss," Jo said, "you know it will be old 841 and it won't get here until 8:15. We have almost thirty minutes till then. Why don't you go back to the store and pick out some licorice for you and me for our trip?"

"Oh, boy, yes, ma'am." His sparkling eyes glistened in the morning sun and Jolyn wished she could sparkle with happiness like that.

"Sure, Arliss. Just remember to go round the back door since Hawk locked everything up before we left. You be careful now!"

Arliss was off in a flash, leaving Jolyn staring at both Hawk and Lucinda. There was an discomfort that settled on them like itchy wool leggings. Hawk shuffled his feet, his boots scraping the wooden planks, their muffled clunking dying in the breeze. Lucinda turned her back to the two of them and stared at the empty tracks.

Hawk looked at Lucinda first and then at Jolyn. He loved Lucinda even though at times she could be an annoyance. Jolyn was his friend and he realized that was all she would ever be. It was a little uneasy being here with both these women and Hawk tried his best to make small talk.

"So, Jolyn, how is Chris doing in Creede?"

"Fine, Hawk. Just as fine as when you asked me this morning."

"Good. That's good. And how is Annabel? I hear she's just plumb tickled to have a sister-in-law."

"She's fine, too, Hawk, just as fine as Chris is."

"And Connor," Hawk floundered. "You haven't mentioned him. How's he doing?"

"Honestly," chirped in Lucinda, "you two are the most boring people to listen to."

"Now, Jolyn, what I really want to know," she continued, ignoring Hawk and his awkwardness, "is what kind of dress will she be wearing? Will it be the latest style from Denver, do you think? I hear that in Denver they have the most beautiful gowns and…"

For once Jolyn was relieved at Lucinda's constant interruptions. She was only half listening to Lucinda when she spied a figure slowly trudging along the street. Jolyn looked at him and then turned back to listen to

Lucinda, who was still talking. Something inside Jolyn clicked and she snapped her head in the direction of the man in the street. Lucinda, annoyed at Jolyn's rude behavior, stopped talking and turned around to see what had caused Jolyn to be so dumbstruck.

Jolyn stared. She couldn't help it. She hadn't seen this man in a long time. A bright smile lit across her face.

"What on earth are you staring at?" shrilled Lucinda, peering over Jo's shoulder.

Hawk had been ignoring the two women and their chatter until now when he spun around to see what they were staring at, but he only saw an old man hobbling along the street.

"Oh," interrupted Hawk, "must be some fool miner on his way to Creede. Lots of miners are heading over there. I even heard they found a mine with purple stones in it. They want to call it some kind of ameeathist mine or something like that."

Jolyn did not stay to hear Hawk's comments. She snatched up her skirt and raced to the elderly gentleman who was plodding toward them. He shuffled as if in pain, his worn hat hung low over his eyes, and his loose clothes whipped his thin frame in the cool breeze. The sun seemed to bounce off his golden glasses and the reflecting rays illuminated his stubby leathered face.

"Doc!" Jolyn screamed his name. "Doc Weathering, is that really you? It's me, Jolyn. Jolyn Montgomery!" she cried breathlessly. "Doc! It's…me…Jolyn… How…are…you…Doc?"

Doc stared at the beautiful figure in front of him. His glassy eyes absorbed the vision from head to toe and then, hesitantly, as if he might be wrong, he whispered, "Miss Jolyn. Miss Jolyn, is that you?"

Doc removed his glasses with one swollen arthritic hand and with the other he pulled out a thin greasy handkerchief. Slowly, methodically, he wiped his glasses and then replaced them on his nose, carefully placing the wire rims over his ears. One hand still clutched the filthy checkered cotton handkerchief as the other twitched and jerked toward Jolyn.

Jolyn reached for his hand gently, the gnarled fingers resting lightly in her grasp. She noted quickly that the handkerchief that had meant so much to him before now only served a menial purpose.

"Yes, Doc, it's me. How are you? How's that arm been doing? What on earth brings you here to Alamosa?"

Jolyn gazed warmly into misty hazel eyes that had seen too many years of pain and too many bottles of liquor.

"Well, Miss Jolyn, I'll tell you, it ain't been too easy on a feller like me, but I can't complain. I'm a-doing jest fine I am, and I made it down here to Alamosa to catch this here train cause I heered there's some mighty full mines in this next town called Creede."

"Oh, that's wonderful, Doc! Why, I'm on my way to Creede, too!"

"And now it's my turn, missy. How are you doing? I'm right sorry about your folks. They was fine people, they were. So tell me, how did you end up in Alamosa? I thought you were looking for kinfolk out near Creede somewheres. Now, don't tell me that feller who done took you got you so darn blessed lost you ended up here?"

Jolyn fought back tears as the thought of her dear James came flooding in.

"No, Doc, James did not get me lost." Jolyn smiled, her eyes glassy. "In fact, he was doing a very fine job of it until…until…well, we had… we were ambushed, Doc, and James was taken prisoner. I don't know where he is or if he is even still alive. Those men who took him"—Jolyn sobbed, then breathed in deeply, aware of how the pain of her past still hurt—"those men are evil killers. If they still have James with them, I don't know what they are keeping him for.

"Anyway, I met up with someone who helped me to Alamosa and I've been working here ever since. I guess I've been working at the town trading post for several months. Right now I'm on my way to Creede for a wedding. My brother's wedding, as a matter of fact." Jolyn smiled with pride as she talked about Chris.

"Well, that is exciting news. And I'm a-going to Creede to see what all the talk is about this little town and her mines."

Jolyn laughed deep and hearty, her spirits soaring with the high clouds overhead. She eased one arm through the crook of Doc's as they headed for the depot together.

The train was due to arrive in Alamosa in just a few moments. Arliss had returned with his pockets bulging and his cheeks fatter than a stuffed squirrel's. Hawk pretended to be angry with the boy, but only ended up laughing at the sight of Arliss and his goods.

The depot was quite full now. Many strangers had traversed the hills from New Mexico to pick up the train. Word had spread to Taos and Los Alamos that Creede was overflowing with silver and gold and amethyst. The men that filled the Alamosa depot were a rugged lot. They carried their lives and their dreams on their backs. If these gems were being found in the San Juans, then why not chance it? Jolyn did not have too much time to ponder her thoughts as she heard the long shrill whistle of the coming train. The white puffs of steam billowed out of the front engine, rising upward to tickle the blue San Luis Valley skies. Jolyn frequently heard her townspeople say, "Rare is the day that the sun does not shine in the San Luis Valley."

Jolyn introduced Doc to Hawk and Lucinda and Arliss. Arliss and Doc seemed to share the same enthusiasm about the approaching train as both of them strained on tiptoes to see the massive iron horse heading their way.

"Look! Look, Miss Jolyn! It is old number 841. Just like I told ya! I knew it! I just knew it! And I bet Harry Shaunessy is pushing her right along. He told me, you know, that if ever I could get on board with him, he'd let me watch him. Oh, Miss Jolyn, do you think he meant it? Do you think he'll really let me in the engine room with him? Mr. Hawk, sir, what do you think?"

Jolyn glanced up at Hawk, who was grinning like a bear dipped in honey. She loved seeing Hawk smile like that. She worried about him sometimes. And lately, especially when Arliss was around, she noticed how he would let his guard down and smile and joke around with the boy. Lucinda might make him happy, she thought, but Hawk needed more. He needed a family and she hoped Lucinda would give him that.

"That boy can talk faster than I can eat chocolate cherries." Lucinda glared scornfully at Arliss. "I just don't know," she continued, "what you all see in that ratty little boy. They're all the same to me. Give 'em snakes and candy when they're boys and meat and women when they're men. They don't change none."

"You know, Lucinda," Jolyn responded with a slight smirk, "as long as I was the one cooking the meat, I wouldn't mind if we ate rattlesnakes every night."

Lucinda stared hard at Jolyn, completely unaware of Jolyn's message. Lucinda turned around, mumbled something to herself, and grabbed her carpetbags.

Hawk, laughing over some joke he and Arliss were sharing, coughed and choked. Lucinda, bags in tow, hurled herself in front of him on her way to the train, stepping on his boots hard and growling to herself.

"Now what is she so damn fired up about?" he questioned Jolyn.

Jolyn smiled sheepishly.

"I'm not really sure, Hawk, but I think it has something to do with hating to eat snake!"

Hawk shrugged his shoulders, picked up his bags, and hurried to find Lucinda.

Jolyn chuckled, her eyes twinkling with mischief, as she picked up her bags. She instructed Arliss to get his belongings and they headed toward the train.

Doc was right behind her. He grinned, showing fewer teeth than he had had last time, and then winked. "I'm glad to see ya still got some of that fire in ya, Miss Jolyn. Ain't nobody but you could tell another woman off and her not even know she been blasted!"

Jolyn winked at Doc and boarded the train. The front engine overpowered their small depot. The words *Rio Grande* were written in large gold letters on the sides. Six golden cars were attached, already filling up with the anxious passengers.

Once inside, Jolyn could not believe her eyes. It was absolutely more beautiful than the last time she rode the train. Their car was decorated in red velvet chairs and tapestry carpet. Gaslights adorned the walls and the red flowered curtains hung from every window.

Jolyn and Arliss and Doc sat on one side while Hawk and Lucinda sat opposite, a table between them. Lucinda was pouting, Doc was smiling, Arliss was ecstatic, and Jolyn and Hawk were impatient to go.

The train's whistle blew while those unfortunate people who would not be taking this trip to Creede stood on the platform waving their arms, blowing kisses, and shouting goodbyes. The heavy train lurched forward, hissed twice, whistled once more, and then somehow gracefully pulled away from the station.

"Well," Jolyn exclaimed, clapping her hands, "we're on our way. Oh, Arliss, you're going to have such a good time. Annabel, my new sister-in-law, will be putting you up with some neighbors who have children your age. Oh, I think you're going to have a great time!"

"Miss Jo, I'm so excited, I don't know what to do!" And then Arliss eagerly pressed his face against the window and watched as the scenery sped by.

"So, Mr. Weathering," Hawk said, "you're off to Creede to do some mining?"

"Oh, please young feller, call me Doc," Doc replied. "I ain't gone by nothing else long's I can remember. And, yes, I plan on doing some digging. Well, what can you tell me of this here new town called Creede?"

Jolyn glanced over at Lucinda as the two men settled into a very deep conversation.

"Lucinda?"

"Huh?"

"Lucinda, would you like to walk back to the car where they have some drinks? I'm a bit parched and I don't think we'll be too involved with this conversation. Besides, you do look a mite pale. Everything fine with you?"

Lucinda touched her face with her hand. "I do feel a mite peaked. Maybe a drink will help me after all. I think this rocking motion is a bit too much for me."

The two ladies stood; the two men rose. Jolyn waved them back down again and their conversation never missed a beat. Arliss was too fascinated with the changing scenery to even notice the women leaving.

As the two stepped carefully along the aisle, Jolyn observed Lucinda almost stagger. Jolyn swiftly and nonchalantly slid her hand through Lucinda's.

"Thanks," mumbled Lucinda.

Up close Jolyn noticed that Lucinda was perspiring around her forehead as stray tendrils of golden hair curled wetly around her face. An attendant opened the doors to the next car and Jolyn guided Lucinda to a vacant spot. Sitting Lucinda down, Jolyn made her way to the bar and ordered two lemonades. With drinks in hand and a few crackers she'd spotted on the side of the bar, Jolyn scrutinized Lucinda on her way back.

Something is definitely wrong, she surmised, and I think I might know the cause.

"Lucinda? Here's a drink. Also, I think you might feel a bit better if you try eating some of these crackers."

Jolyn studied Lucinda's expressions very closely. She watched as Lucinda's pale face transformed from a very green shade into a very pale gray.

"Luce," Jo whispered, "what's wrong? Is there something I can do?"

Lucinda opened her mouth to speak and then shut it very quickly. She shook her head as if trying to say no. Then she grabbed Jolyn's hands, but it was too late.

Lucinda leaned over the side of the chair and emptied her stomach. Jolyn reacted immediately. She jumped up from her seat and in two swift strides she scooped up a large golden spittoon near the bar and positioned it next to Lucinda. Then, returning to the bar, Jolyn snatched a large pitcher of water and cotton napkins and raced back to their table. Several of the drinking patrons witnessed what was happening. A few belched loudly and continued with their drinking. Still another few groaned and cursed their luck and quickly departed.

Dipping one of the napkins into the pitcher of water, Jolyn leaned over Lucinda and gently wiped her face. Lucinda tried to sit up, and Jolyn helped her. She gave Lucinda another wet napkin. Lucinda rubbed her cheeks with the cloth and, leaning her elbows on the table, rested her face in her hands.

At first Lucinda just stared straight ahead. Then, suddenly, as if she had been holding back a long time, she wept.

Her damp hair lay limp on her quivering shoulders. Jolyn moved her chair around the table and curled her arms around Lucinda, soothing the girl.

"Lucinda. Lucinda, look at me. Lucinda, come on now. I'm here with you. Wipe your face and look at me." Like a little obedient girl, Lucinda blew her nose and with her napkin she wiped her eyes. She lifted her face toward Jolyn.

"Lucinda. Do you know what's wrong?"

Lucinda shook her head no and almost started crying again.

"Have you been feeling this way for a while now? Have you thrown up before? Think, Lucinda."

"I...I really haven't felt good in a long time. And...I...I vomited three times this week."

Jolyn shook her head and stared at Lucinda.

"Jo, do you think I'm dying?"

"Well, I should hope not. Lucinda. Listen to me. Can you tell me when you had your last, well, your woman's time?"

Lucinda blinked her green eyes several times, as if to help her think.

"I always have it around when Hawk pays his mortgage on the store. But he's paid the rent two times without my time coming. Oh, Jolyn, what's wrong with me? Do I need to see a doctor? I mean, I'm sorry, you've been like the doctor in town, I know, but what do you think it is? I just haven't been the same. And I know I've been so nasty to Hawk lately."

Jolyn smiled to herself. Lately, huh? I can't imagine what you're like when you're really sick!

"Lucinda, honey, I don't know how to break this to you, but, well, let me tell you flat out. Lucinda, you're going to have a baby!"

"WHAT!!!"

The few remaining patrons cast startled eyes toward the two women who sat head to head by a spittoon. It was a scene they would tell and retell to their friends later on, but for now, the travelers went back to their drinking.

Jolyn took Lucinda's hands in an attempt to calm her.

"I'm sure of it, Lucinda. You have all the signs."

"Oh, Jolyn, I can't be. I won't be. I don't want to be."

Lucinda's eyes swelled with tears and her lips quivered.

"Lucinda, I thought you'd be happy. I'm sure Hawk will be excited. Why, you know how much he loves Arliss. He'll probably rush out and build you a baby's bed right away. What could be worse than that?"

"Oh, Jo, you don't understand. I don't want this baby. Not now. Not ever. My mother died in childbirth. Having me. And my father's blamed me ever since. I know it. And I always knew that if I ever had a child I would die the same way my mother did. I don't want to die, Jo. And I don't want to have this baby!"

Just then Hawk walked through the doorway.

"Say, what happened to you two?" Hawk asked as he suddenly noticed the spittoon next to the ladies. "What's the matter? Are you sick,

Luce? Tell me, darling, what's wrong?" Hawk's worried eyes gazed into Lucinda's scared green ones.

"It's nothing, Hawk," Jolyn said convincingly. "Lucinda and her breakfast and the ride just didn't agree with each other. She'll be fine in a few moments. I'm going back to Arliss and Doc. Hawk, make sure she eats these crackers. It will settle her stomach for a while."

Jolyn glanced down at Lucinda as she was leaving. Lucinda was grateful for Jo's silence and her eyes were filled with thanks.

Jolyn squeezed Lucinda's shoulders and whispered, "We'll talk later. Eat those crackers for now."

Jolyn's mind filled with troubling thoughts as she careened down the aisle to her seat. Her eyes gazed upon Doc and Arliss. They were sitting knee to knee and by the intense look in Arliss's face, Jolyn could tell Doc was filling him with all kinds of tales. She smiled.

"Hmmph. Well, excuse me, boys, but I guess you didn't mind my absence a bit." Jolyn stuck out her lip and pouted, but she wasn't fooling them.

"Oh, Miss Jolyn, you wouldn't believe all the stories Doc has been telling me. All about the Injuns and..."

"Indians, young man."

"Yes, ma'am. And how these Inj...I mean In...dee...ins came up on Doc one night and almost scalped him and then later when he was..."

"Fine, Arliss," Jolyn interrupted. "But I think you should let Doc rest a bit for now."

Arliss looked at Doc and wrinkled up his lips and nose. "All right," he conceded. "But can we talk some more later on, huh, Doc, huh?"

"Sure, little feller, sure. I'll tell you all about how me and this here Injun, ah, excuse me, Miss Jolyn, shared a tent and hunted buffalo together. But for now, I think mebbe I oughtta get some shut-eye." And with that, Doc let his worn hat fall onto his face as he leaned back and sighed deeply.

"Well," said Jolyn, "I sure can't compete with Doc's stories, but I can at least teach you about the country you're riding through."

"Oh, gosh, I completely forgot to look out the winda for so long, Miss Jo. He's such a swell man, that Doc is. How long till we're there?"

"Oh, just a little bit more to go now. Look at those mountains, Arliss. They are so beautiful, aren't they?"

"Not half as beautiful as you, Miss Jo."

Tears swelled in Jolyn's eyes as she squeezed Arliss tightly.

"Thank you, my little man. Thank you very much."

The three of them sitting there portrayed quite a story. Doc busy snoring and dreaming of pans of gold, and a young woman cradling a young boy in her arms.

* * *

The train trudged on. The lush green aspens bowed and waved as the Galloping Goose made her journey on man's steel roadway that was once nature's highway. The San Juans threatened to crumble and crush the rocketing rush of steel, but the engine roared on, its whistle blasting its own defiant place in the world. Sure-footed mountain goats on top of the rocky cliffs stared. The countryside lifted and swayed, and the Rio Grande kept flowing on. At one point, the steep mountainside loomed within inches of the steely sides of the train while a great cliff dared to pull them down and under forever. The engineers kept a keen eye on their destination and safely guided their steel prince through virgin territory.

The group was once again seated together. Laughter and loud talking filtered down from the other cars and mixed with the singing and music from yet another car. Gambling was always present somewhere on the train; it was the highlight for most of the men as they traveled.

Jo watched her assorted party under lowered lids. Arliss had finally fallen asleep along with Doc. Hawk and Lucinda were silent as they gazed out the window, deep in their own thoughts.

The train stopped at each small town. Men and women, miners and wanderers, all with their own stories and dreams, boarded the train to Creede. As they passed Monte Vista, Hawk suddenly renewed his interest in the trip and talked about the New Hotel Blanca that had finally opened. He droned on and on about the newest furnishings the hotel had to offer.

The town of Del Norte flew by, as did Granger and then Wagon Wheel Gap. As the train approached each town, Jolyn's heart beat faster and faster. Why am I doing this? she thought. I'm going to Creede to see Chris, not Connor. For all I know, Connor won't even be there. He'll probably be in the neighboring town of Bachelor checking out their stores.

But still, her body reacted with each passing mile, her mind clicking off the beats of her heart with the clanging of metal on the rails. Trying to forget, Jolyn focused on Lucinda. She was looking a little better, but very tired. Lucinda's hands were folded together, and Jolyn could tell by their whitened color that she was squeezing them very tightly.

Soon, Arliss, awake and antsy, was bored with the scenery and tried imitating Doc by slipping his hat over his face. His feeble attempts at snoring would have been more amusing had Jolyn been in a better mood, but the morning was waning and so was her patience.

The people aboard the train sensed that Creede was imminent and so had begun gathering up their belongings. Doc began to stretch and mutter aloud, his own style of awakening. No sooner had he started rustling about than Arliss began shaking his sleeves and questioning him about his earlier adventures.

Jolyn's throat was dry. Cold shivers raced down her arms and her legs threatened to crumble should she try and stand up. She repositioned her hat, tucking in loose auburn tendrils. Digging into her dress pocket, she retrieved an old lace handkerchief and began wiping her forehead. She was perspiring. Her gloved hands, somewhat damp from her unusual clamminess, were cloying and uncomfortable. She felt embarrassed as her body's reactions seemed to shout out to everyone how tense she really was.

The train's high speed slowed down dramatically and Jolyn's stomach lurched. It threatened to follow the same action as Lucinda's had done earlier and Jolyn swallowed slowly, trying to calm herself.

Creede, or Jimtown as it was commonly called, did not have a depot as of yet. Instead, old boxcars substituted as rest areas for the time being, and yet for all the hoopla that surrounded the platform, one would think they were arriving at Denver with free gold.

Arliss could no longer contain himself. He had left his seat and was running up and down the aisles shouting, "We're here! We're really here! Hey, everybody, we made it to Creede and no Injuns stopped us!!"

Jolyn was too absorbed with her own troubling thoughts to be admonishing the young boy and Arliss, sensing his freedom, carried on with his ramblings.

Hawk, still concerned with Lucinda and her health, was busy helping her gather her belongings. Doc travelled light and therefore sat quite content, watching everyone around him falling apart at the seams.

The train whistled once, again, and then, with a heave and sigh, shut down. Outside, the townspeople of Creede were screaming and laughing and crying. The town would never be the same with the coming of the Rio Grande and they knew it.

The passengers departed carefully, watching their steps and searching for familiar faces in the large crowd. Doc and Jolyn and Arliss, all holding on to each other, stepped off their cars onto the platform. Following them were Hawk and Lucinda. It was too hard to talk with one another with the shouting from the crowd, so Hawk urged the group off the platform and away behind the permanently stationed boxcars.

There they stood, transfixed and somewhat in awe of the event. Everywhere they looked, people were celebrating. Whiskey was passed around freely and cigars were thrown with no real destination. The excitement in the air was thick and infectious as smiles and cheers filled the small town.

Jolyn scanned the crowd. Would Chris be here to meet them, or would it be Annabel? She hoped, no, prayed it would be…but no, that was asking too much. Blue eyes blinked away tears and Jolyn jutted her chin forward.

"Miss Jolyn?" Doc approached her gently. He could tell something was wrong, but he was too private a person to be barging in on someone else's affairs.

Jolyn raised her head slowly and gazed into Doc's warm brown eyes.

"Miss Jolyn, I'll be taking my leave now. I'm going to the closest bar in town and after a few drinks I guess I'll get started at setting myself up here. I do hope we can see each other sometime just to chat."

Jolyn clutched Doc's hands together with her own. The smooth leathery feel of his swollen hands reminded Jolyn of her past, her lost family, her old life. She embraced him warmly and whispered in his ear, "Doc, you take good care of yourself, you hear me? I do not want to hear bad things about you in this town. And if you need something, anything, anything at all, well, you damn well better get it from me. Good luck, Doc. I hope Creede is your dream come true."

"Miss Jo"—his hoarse voice cracked—"I got a notion this here town is gonna be lucky for the both of us. You jest wait and see. And Miss Jo, if that feller that is causing them tears in your beautiful eyes gives you any trouble at all, why, you jest send him to me. I got a few good jabs left in me yet."

"Oh, Doc, thanks. Thank you so much. Goodbye."

Doc tipped his hat, but Jolyn rushed in and gave him a bear hug. Doc blushed and winked at Jolyn. Then he shook Arliss's hand and whispered something in his ear that made Arliss laugh and jump up at the same time. Arliss replied yes frantically to Doc and then waved his goodbyes. Jolyn turned toward Hawk when suddenly she heard her name being hollered across the platform.

"Jolyn! Jolyn! We're over here! On the other side. Wait! We're coming over!!"

Jolyn's heart skipped a beat. We? She recognized Annabel's high lilting voice over the throng, but who with her? Did she bring him? Would he come here with her? Please, oh, please, I want so badly to…

Lucinda interrupted her thoughts.

"Jo? Who was that? Do you know her? She looks so familiar. I can't place it, though."

Hawk came to Jolyn's rescue.

"That's Annabel. Annabel Richardson. She's Connor's sister."

"Oh!" cried out Lucinda. "I knew I recognized something about her."

Annabel was making her way across the platform and through the crowds with a gentleman in tow. His dark suede hat sat low over his face and Jolyn could not make out who it was. Jolyn's mouth hung open, dry and trembling. She placed one shaking hand on the shoulder of Arliss to steady herself. Hawk moved in closer, sensing Jolyn's tenseness, ready to do—what? He wasn't sure, really.

The pair seemed to move closer and closer and then they were pushed backward and sideways as the crowd was partying and singing and drinking. Someone passed a bottle to Annabel's partner and just before he leaned his head back to sip the brown brew, he turned his face back toward the train in a toast, keeping Jolyn from identifying him. Cold tremors spurted down her legs and she felt weak. She could smell his musky warm breath on her neck and she longed to feel his arms wrapped around her, embracing her, loving her.

Jolyn's haunted memories came flooding back as she remembered every second she had ever spent with Connor. The scenes came rushing through her mind like a lightning bolt seeking its home. The electricity jolted her, and she swaggered a bit.

"Jo?" Hawk quickly rushed to her side. "Are you all right? Do you want to sit down somewhere?"

"No, no, I'm fine. Thanks, Hawk. I just need some fresh air. The crowd here is so stifling. I…"

"Hello, Jo. How are you?"

Jolyn lifted her scared eyes and her stomach rolled over. Her hands went numb and all muscle control left her legs as she was lifted high in the air.

"Good God almighty, it's so good to see you again!" cried Chris as he hoisted his sister up on his shoulders.

Jolyn never heard a word of the conversations. The loud ringing in her ears launched a debilitating headache as the group slowly made their way downtown to settle in for the day.

Chapter 16

"Jo, help me with these buttons." Annabel cast a desperate look over her shoulder. "Why did I insist on having the tiniest-sized buttons? I'll never be ready in time!"

As Jo brushed Bel's fingers aside, she glanced ruefully at the Little Ben sitting on the mantel. It was almost two o'clock, and the wedding was planned for three.

"Annabel, you have over an hour yet," she soothed. "And all the preparations have been finished for hours. Now please stop worrying."

As Jo finished fastening the pearl buttons, she turned Annabel gently around to face her and smiled at Bel's worried but radiant face. Affectionately, she surveyed the excited bride. Annabel's satin gown clung gently to her shoulders and bodice and swirled gracefully from her waistline. The sleeves were long and fit tightly around her arms. An intricate network of lace rose above the modest V of her satin gown to the base of her neck. Her veil, which lay spread on her bed, was patterned with the same lace. Her silky dark tresses still hung to her hips. She appeared more like a fairy than a mortal woman.

Jo's warm smile broadened. "You're beautiful, Bel. I think for once in his life, my brother will be rendered speechless. But you're still missing something."

"I know, my hair. Would you just look at this mess? Will you help me pin it up, Jo?" Annabel looked nervously at the clock. "Oh, I just know I won't be ready in time."

"In a second, Bel. Think. Aren't you forgetting something else?"

"Jo! Will you stop teasing and help?" Annabel grabbed a small mass of hair and tried to sweep it upward but only managed to entangle it further.

"Annabel Richardson. This is serious," Jo declared, a mock frown forming on her face. "Do you mean to tell me that you would endanger the future of your marriage by ignoring the wedding traditions of something borrowed, something blue?"

Annabel started to raise an objection but halted when she saw the shimmering blue cornflower necklace dangling from Jo's hand.

"Turn around." Jo hid her grin.

Annabel whirled and faced the mirror. She watched mesmerized as Jolyn fastened the necklace about her neck. She stared, stunned at the breathtaking effect. The gems lay glimmering against the soft creamy lace and accentuated the rosy hue beneath the lace and the deeper blue of her own eyes.

"Oh, Jo, it's exquisite. But how…"

"It belonged to my mother. She had left it behind with the boys with several other personal effects. Both Chris and I felt you should have it. Now you have something both borrowed and blue."

Annabel still stood gazing into the mirror, awestruck. It was a wonderful present.

"Oh, Jo, thank you, but this was your mother's. I can't accept this."

"You can, and you will. Now, hadn't you better sit down so I can pin up this hair of yours? What happened to the fussbudget a minute ago who was so worried about being on time?"

Jo couldn't resist a grin when Annabel immediately plopped down on the chair. Jo efficiently gathered Annabel's wayward locks and swept them into a loose chignon at the nape of her neck. Small curling wisps still framed Bel's fragile face while the rest of her hair was pulled smoothly back. Jo secured the headpiece at the crown and pulled the veil forward.

"Is that really me?" Annabel whispered.

"That's you!" Jo cleared her throat, then hugged Annabel affectionately. She glanced again at the clock and grinned. "Two thirty. You are going to have to sit there and not move one muscle for the next twenty minutes."

She watched amusedly as Annabel's expression transformed from rapture to dismay. Before Annabel could raise an objection, Jo exited with a parting excuse.

"I'll be back as soon as I've repaired my hair."

Jo stared unseeingly into the mirror, distractedly pinned back a few wayward curls, and sighed. All the gown fittings, table decorations, last-minute preparations had saved her this past week. Every night she had fallen into an exhausted sleep, her thoughts held at bay, but whenever she had a few spare moments, her mind drifted to thoughts of Connor. He had not met her at the train, nor had he, in the week past, spoken any more than polite pleasantries over dinner or business arrangements in the store. And she…she had merely followed his lead. She had answered his questions as politely and as concisely as he had asked them. "Yes, Connor, I believe the backlog problem on the Shannon order could be resolved if we contacted the Leadville store. No, Connor, the situation with Bramer's has not been resolved. Perhaps a court order might prove necessary. How do you do, Connor? Good evening, Connor." Connor. What was she going to do when just thinking his name brought a wildfire of emotions storming through her?

"Jo? Are you finished? It's about time to leave."

"Yes, Bel." Jolyn took a last look in the mirror, then stuck out her tongue at her reflection. "Take that, Connor!"

"What?" Annabel's stood at Jo's bedroom doorway.

"Oh, nothing," Jo laughed, "just talking to myself."

Jolyn stood up and shook her gown free. She wore a turquoise satin gown that matched the style of Annabel's without the lace adornments. Her lightly tanned shoulders rose starkly above the V neckline. Her hair was gathered at the crown and hung in soft curls down her back. A polished turquoise stone, taken from the stone she had found in the miner's abandoned shaft, hung in the hollow of her neck. Where Annabel looked like an angelic sprite Jolyn appeared elegantly regal.

"Why, Jo, you are so…so splendid."

"Thanks to you and your wonderful seamstress I shall be the best-dressed maid-of-honor there, and you," declared Jo as she slipped her hand into Bel's and pulled her toward the outside staircase, "shall be the most beautiful."

Despite Chris and Annabel's attempts at keeping the wedding quiet, word had spread via the mix of saloons, bathhouses, and even from the gossip at the trading post. Everyone wanted to see some of the Montgomery and Richardson wedding. A motley crowd of nearly five hundred milled along Creede Avenue hoping for a glimpse of the bride. Apart from the usual bustle of new arrivals and busy townspeople, curious miners and interested acquaintances had formed a hundred-yard gauntlet from the Richardson's Trading Post to the courthouse. At the bottom of the steps, Connor waited impatiently for the two approaching women. The three of them would be lucky if they made it to the courthouse in one piece.

Connor looked magnificent in his dark woolen suit, which fit snugly on his powerful frame. He was an imposing barrier for anyone who chose to approach uninvited the two lovely women now floating down the steps toward them. Since Connor towered above most of the men in the crowd, a hush spread among the waiting group, and hands slipped unconsciously to discard their battered hats in respectful salute. All eyes remained glued on the breathtaking beauty of the bride and maid who now stood amidst the dull unpainted buildings and grayish-brown muddy planks. All except one. He remained half-hidden, his steely eyes locked menacingly on the tall, dark man who awaited Annabel and Jolyn. He tilted his head downward to avoid looking into anyone's eyes. Anyone who just might recognize him.

Ignoring the crowd's stare as best as possible, Annabel tucked her hand beneath Connor's proffered elbow and bent forward so that he could hear her nervous whisper. "Ready to give the bride away, Con?"

He smiled down at his sister and covered her cold, thinly gloved hand with his. "You're not frightened, are you, little one?"

"Just a bit," she admitted. "Oh, but not of Chris," she hastened to add. "Just all this…" She waved vaguely toward the now restless crowd. "Where did they all come from?"

Connor chuckled. "It's not often that the most eligible bachelor and the most beautiful woman living in Creede get married, you know. How about giving them a little smile? Most of them have been standing in the same spot for the past two hours."

Annabel smiled shyly at the line of miners on her right and a rousing cheer went up among them.

"I believe there will be even more celebrating than usual in Creede tonight, if that's possible." Connor grinned.

"Here, Bel, don't forget this," Jolyn murmured as she thrust Annabel's bridal bouquet into her free hand.

Connor, who had managed to avoid looking directly at Jolyn, now did so, and rocked backward with a blow that felt tangible as he gazed upon this vision in blue. Jolyn's hair shone with burnished highlights. Her face was flushed from the warm summer air, and her lips were full and moist. Her chest rose shallowly and the material rimming her breasts trembled slightly at the cleavage. The gown molded her tiny waist, her slightly flaring hips, and her long, slender legs. Jo. Connor burned with a need so overpowering that he could scarcely catch his breath. All week he had deliberately avoided her, reduced his conversations with her to the bare necessities, and then in one swift, unsuspecting moment, all his intentions were swept aside and replaced by an all-consuming hunger. His hand involuntarily tightened on Annabel's hand.

"Ouch, Connor, you're hurting me."

Connor shook his head as if to release the scorching ache in his heart. He looked at Annabel, gave her a sorry smile, and immediately relaxed his grip.

Somewhere in the crowd, the grubby, half-bearded stranger with the cold gray eyes pressed himself closer, attempting to see what had captivated Connor's attention. Despite his attempts the outsider was blocked from doing so, and, frustrated, he pushed farther through the crowd toward the courthouse.

"Sorry, Bel." Connor glanced down apologetically. If he could avoid looking at Jo, he just might make it, he thought. "And I thought it was only the groom who was supposed to be nervous." He managed a smile.

"Connor, what are you doing?" Annabel snapped. "You know that Jo is supposed to lead us to the courthouse, and in this dangerous crowd, what are you thinking?"

Damn if Annabel wasn't right. This sure wasn't making the encounter with Jolyn any easier. He nodded briefly in Jo's direction.

"Sorry, Miss Montgomery. Didn't mean to forget you." His voice sounded steady enough. Now, if he could avoid touching her as she passed...

Jolyn's hips brushed his thigh as she squeezed by the line of miners who had jimmied their bodies forward. Connor clenched his fist to keep himself from pulling her against him.

"That's quite all right, Mr. Richardson. I expected nothing less from you," said Jolyn primly, her face flushed from their brief physical contact. "I'm quite ready now. Shall we go?"

Connor had to shake himself. As long as he didn't look at the gentle swaying of her hips, as long as he didn't breathe too deeply of the fresh fragrance that wafted back to him, as long as... One of the sots in the crowd crowed a halloo of delight as the two women passed. Connor gritted his teeth and focused on the courthouse doors, which swung outward in a welcoming gesture toward the approaching party.

The man in gray slithered eagerly forward. That woman in blue was important to Connor, the man thought. He could sense it. She also was somehow connected to him as well, thought the stranger. He was certain of it. Whoever this woman was, she just might hold the key to Connor's destruction. If he could only manage a glimpse... Triumphantly, he reached the head of the line, just in time to see the wedding group step into the building. Angrily, he swung away, elbowing and jabbing everyone and anyone in his path. He might have missed her this time, but he would find out exactly who this woman was…damned if he wouldn't.

Despite the sonorous tones of Mr. Lindstrom, the marriage ceremony swept by swiftly. Chris and Annabel, their hands clasped, their voices steady, and their eyes filled with love, exchanged vows. Connor and Jolyn, who stood side by side behind them, were dimly aware of the words spoken. When Chris turned toward Connor to receive the wedding ring, Jolyn's eyes locked with his, and both were caught in a maelstrom of emotions. Shaken to her core, Jolyn faced the altar and fought back the tears that threatened to erupt.

When Chris and Annabel turned and raced joyfully down the aisle, Connor, with an unsteady hand, guided Jo as they followed the wedded couple. The crowd pressed in about them, shouting congratulations to the newlyweds, and Connor and Jo were caught in the crush. Jolyn, already a jumble of nerves, fiercely gripped Connor's hand and glanced pleadingly up at him.

Noticing her desperate look, Connor lifted her into his arms and carried her out of the church and away from the boisterous townspeople. When he reached the corner, he darted into the alleyway and was halted by some empty barrels that lined the street. Jolyn, embarrassed by her show of weakness, pushed futilely against his rock-like chest. Connor continued to hold her pressed against him, his head bent closely over hers.

"Thank you, Mr. Richardson." Jolyn's voice sounded brittle even to her ears. "I can manage now."

When Connor made no motion to release her, she began to squirm in his arms. She could not stand this closeness one more moment. Even now she could feel every nerve screaming surrender. She doubted that even if he did release her she would be capable of standing alone.

"Connor, please put me down, I…"

Connor released her legs, and Jolyn slid full length against his firm, well-muscled body. She was now standing, but somehow she seemed more entangled than before. Her soft curves fitted snugly against his, and his hands, now free, slid from her shoulder down her back, cupped her buttocks, and pulled her more tightly against his growing heat. His mouth descended upon her own, and with a small groan, she welcomed his invasion. Their breaths mingled and became one. Reluctantly, they drew their heads back, then stared wonderingly at each other.

"Nooooo," Jolyn moaned.

Connor, unable to face the denial in Jolyn's eyes, crushed her face against his neck.

"Listen to me, Jo. I care about you, care what happens to you. I don't mean to hurt you. It's just that I need you so. I've tried to stay away, but you're like a fever in my blood. If you'll just give me a little more time to work some things out, maybe we…maybe then…I could make some sort of commitment." Connor faltered as he felt Jolyn's body stiffen.

"Mr. Richardson! First you will unhand me. Then you will allow me to compose myself. Then you will escort me to the parlor where the bride and groom and the guests are certainly waiting."

Connor released his grip and watched her take a few steps back. He reached forward to tuck her few stray hairs back in place. His errant hand was immediately slapped away, and her eyes snapped her disapproval.

Chagrined, Connor smoothed back his own hair, straightened his wide tie. He surveyed the nearly empty street, took a few hesitant steps, and turned back to Jolyn. She had managed to secure her hair once again and looked, except for the fuller reddened lips and blush on her cheeks, as unruffled as she had before the wedding.

"You're not going to make this easy for me, are you?" Connor said exasperatedly.

"I cannot see how I have the power to make anything easy or hard for you, Mr. Richardson. If you will excuse my brief lapse in behavior, or should I say a lapse in memory, I will consider this incident over. As to any commitments on your part, you have made your views quite clear on that subject. I hope that you don't think that I'm the kind of namby-pamby woman who expects a man to marry her just because of a silly one-night fling? If so, I wish to inform you that marriage is the last ..."

Connor gripped Jolyn's shoulders and nearly shook her in frustration. "Yes, I do expect you to be the kind of self-respecting woman who would expect precisely that. And I want to be the man to give it to you."

For a moment Connor looked as stunned as she did at his declaration, but then, after a brief moment, he seemed to settle rather satisfactorily on the idea, and a grin slowly spread across his face.

Jolyn frowned doubtfully at his cheerful expression. He certainly didn't look as though he objected to the idea, and the idea, most certainly, was his. She had never raised the issue, not aloud, anyway, and not in his presence. Sure, he had shied away from any mention of commitment before, but hadn't his reasons always been linked to Luke? Wasn't this very moment precisely what she had dreamed about? So why wasn't she leaping at the chance?

Connor, sensing her indecision, eased his hand through the crook of her arm and escorted her toward the bustling street.

"There's no rush, Jo. Let's just give it some time. There is, however, one very important promise you can make me."

"Oh? What's that?"

"Promise me you'll stop calling me Mr. Richardson?"

Jolyn relaxed and hid a smile. "Only if you'll stop calling me Miss Montgomery with that pompous tone of yours."

"Pompous? Why, if you're not the most irritating..." Connor caught a glimpse of a familiar gleam in her eyes and quickly changed tactics. "Agreed. Now, shall we find that brother of yours and sister of mine and congratulate them?"

"Agreed." Together, Connor's arm tucked snugly beneath hers, they marched by canvas and slab buildings toward Sponsilier's Theatre, which stood flat-faced and accommodating on the corner of Creede Avenue.

Laughter poured from the theatre's doors and faded into the noisy crowded streets. A warm-hearted cheer from the good-natured guests arose as Connor and Jolyn entered. Jolyn blushed furiously, and Connor bowed decorously. Both quickly stepped aside to avoid being knocked over by a whirling couple and gazed in awe at the pandemonium before them.

Sponsilier's shook with rollicking, foot-stomping merriment. The men, looking out of place in their dark suits and wide ties, scouted out dance partners, milled about the beer kegs, or chatted boisterously with fellow miners. The handful of women, adorned in high-necked lace-trimmed gowns, were swept energetically around the spacious room. Flushed and breathless, they dodged flying elbows and leaden feet.

No sooner had Jolyn spotted Chris, who was scowling darkly at one of the flying couples, then she felt someone snatch her hand and whisk her away into a merry polka. She caught a brief glimpse of Connor's fatalistic shrug before she was borne wildly into the melee. She glanced at her partner's grinning, ruddy face and smiled in return. There was neither time nor breath for conversation, and no sooner had they completed one turn about the dance floor than Jo was grabbed and swept away by another miner—this one being a score older and as many pounds lighter.

Connor watched as Jolyn flew from one miner's arms to another's, and he retreated good-naturedly toward the beer stand where Hawk had now joined Chris. After Connor had helped himself to a frothy mug of beer freshly arrived from Zang's depot, he fought his way to Hawk's side.

"Why are you both looking so gloomy?"

"Women," Hawk snorted. "Chris can't get Annabel away from the dance floor, and I can't get Lucinda near it. I swear that woman gets more contrary by the hour."

"Dammit. There she is flirting with the Tortoni boy. Why, I've a mind to drag her little behind out of here—wedding party or no wedding party," Chris growled.

"Will you listen to yourselves? What happened to my fellow devil-may-care partners? Don't tell me that you're going to let a couple of harebrained females ruin the evening? This is a celebration, so let's celebrate."

"Watch it, Connor, one of those harebrained females, as you call them, is my wife," Chris snarled, his fists clenched.

"Uh-ho, so that's the way of it. Well, if you're so determined to play the outraged groom, get out there and start doing something about it. Don't pick a fight with me; I'm just the brother-in-law," Connor advised. "And you." Connor shot Hawk a disgusted look. "If you want to dance, then get out there and dance. Lucinda will come around soon enough."

Without so much as a grunt between them, the two men charged forward. Chris captured Annabel in mid-whirl and spun her masterfully away from her surprised partner. Hawk barged through the small group of men waiting for Jolyn and snatched her out of the hands of the next eager miner. Jolyn, pleased to find herself in the arms of her friend, laughed gaily as he carried her off. Connor's fist tightened jealously on the handle of his mug. Served him right for opening his big mouth. He felt a soft feminine hand slide down his back and he instinctively turned toward the touch, a half-smile forming on his lips.

"Emmaline." Connor did not hide his surprise. "I didn't realize you were invited. That is, I didn't expect to find you here."

"Well, I didn't expect to be here neither, but Zang's boy invited me along. I didn't do nothing wrong, did I?" Emmaline's eyes grew wider and she pressed closer to Connor's side.

"No, of course not." Connor unsuccessfully attempted to extract himself from her cloying arms.

"Well, as long as we're both here together, why don't we go ahead and maybe dance a step or two. I ain't danced a single dance all afternoon what someone didn't stomp on my sinseetive feet. I bet you wouldn't step on a lady's toes, you being so gentlemanly-like." Emmaline batted her eyelashes and gazed provocatively up into Connor's disbelieving face.

Just at that moment Jolyn whispered something into Hawk's ear, causing Hawk to bellow with laughter as the two passed Connor. Connor ruffled at the comfortable intimacy he could sense the two shared, knowing full well Hawk and Jolyn were just friends. After all, the two had been working together in Alamosa while Connor was in Creede. Still, it unnerved Connor and, forgetting Emmaline's presence, he took a threatening step forward.

"I've seen her with Hawk before, lots of times," Emmaline whined. "Who is she?"

"Jolyn," whispered Connor, mesmerized by her graceful stature as she swept around the polished floor on Hawk's burly arm. He suddenly snapped into awareness and turned abruptly toward Emmaline, who still clung to his side. "Her name is Jolyn Montgomery. She is Chris's sister. And I doubt that you could have seen them often together, if at all, since Jolyn arrived little more than a week ago for the wedding."

"Oh, I must have been mistaken, but I could have sworn that I saw them only two nights ago at Kirmeavy's. I guess it must have been someone else."

If Emmaline was hoping for some jealous reaction from Connor with her lie, she failed to get one. Realizing that she wasn't going to get any further with Connor, who continued to sip from his beer while ignoring her completely, Emmaline caught the eye of the nearest miner and was soon swept away in a rousing waltz.

An exhausted Jo begged Hawk to deliver her to the refreshment stand in an effort to hide from her determined admirers and the frenzied activity. Hawk did as Jo asked and was rewarded with a swift appreciative hug from her. Hawk nodded curtly to Lucinda, who sat behind the table with Arliss, who was happily stuffing his mouth with refreshments and homemade pies. Hawk was hoping Lucinda would get up and be with him, but when she turned from his gaze, Hawk swaggered off for a sorely needed swig of beer.

Jolyn noticed the angry pout on Lucinda's face and decided to tread warily. "Hello, Lucinda. How are you feeling? You look wonderful." Jolyn's compliment was sincere. Lucinda, her blonde hair pulled neatly away from her round face and her full curves gowned in a shimmering rose watered silk, appeared quite captivating.

"Thank you, Jolyn. That's kind of you, sweeter than I deserve."

"Nonsense." Jolyn ladled a glass of punch into a waiting miner's glass and served him a plate of pie. "Yes, we certainly have had our differences, but when it comes to roving men like Hawk and Connor, we women have to stick together."

"I haven't told him, Jolyn. I don't know how. What if he just laughs in my face? Oh, I'm just so miserable."

"Lucinda, don't you dare cry. Shhh, he's coming this way. Do you feel well enough to dance?"

"I guess so. I haven't felt at all queasy since this morning."

"Good. Now listen to me. When he gets over here, you…"

"Excuse me. I do hate to break up your jawing, but could a girl get a drink around here?"

Jolyn turned toward the owner of the brassy voice and gawked at the poorly painted female who stood before her.

"Punch? You are serving it, ain't ya?"

"Yes, of course, please pardon me." Jolyn reached for an empty cup and concentrated on ladling the pink liquid into it.

"I'm in a bit of a hurry, don't you know, as my lover gets impatient when I'm gone too long."

"That's nice," Jolyn replied, at a loss for words. "Would you and he like some pie?"

"Oh, none for me, thanks." Emmaline stroked her bodice and arched her shoulders back, her large, pendulous breasts nearly escaping the low-cut gown. "Have to watch the figure, don't you know. Con just loves my…well, I'd better hurry. Thanks ever so much for the punch."

Jolyn's eyes narrowed as she watched the flashy blonde sashay directly toward Connor. When the woman reached Connor, Jolyn watched as she placed a hand possessively against his chest, and saw Connor quickly cover her hand with his own.

She whirled toward Lucinda, who was rising to greet Hawk. "I'll kill him. I'll lure him into the storeroom and drop a vat of molasses on his two-timing head."

"She's lying, Jolyn. That's why they call her 'Lyin' Emmaline' behind her back! I heard the gossip just sitting here! Can't you see? Look, he's already turned her away."

"He knows her, though, and that's enough. To think that I, for one moment, could have fallen for that hulking lout!"

"Good evening, ladies." Hawk's loud welcome caused both women to turn.

"Good evening, Hawk," said Lucinda demurely. "Would you care for some punch or pie?"

"No, thank you, Lucie, but I would certainly enjoy your company on the dance floor if you're feeling up to it."

"I suppose one dance wouldn't hurt," Lucinda replied coyly. She winked slyly at Jolyn and placed her hand in Hawk's waiting one.

"Do you think the guests can manage without anyone here to serve the punch?" Connor's resonant voice sent shivers down her spine.

"I fear that would be quite out of the question," said Jolyn, a little stiffly. How had he managed to appear without her seeing him?

"In that case I offer my services. If I can't serve to dance with you, I'll dance to serve with you." Connor performed a two-step and arrived by her side.

"Stuff!" Jolyn muttered.

"What? Did you say something?"

"No, nothing, Mr. Richardson. It's just that…"

"Ah, ah, ah." Connor wagged a disapproving index figure beneath her nose. Jolyn longed to bite it.

"I mean—Connor, you're making this rather difficult. It just appears unseemly that we should be standing so closely together where everyone is watching."

"This, of course, is far more unseemly than arriving at your brother's celebration a half hour later than the rest of the invited guests."

"Oh, you!"

"Connor! Jo!" Annabel's eyes sparkled with excitement as she and Chris rushed over to share some news. "Stop arguing for a minute and listen." Chris joined Annabel at the table and wrapped his arm about her waist, hugging her to him.

"We're sneaking out. Neither of us can stand another moment apart. We just wanted to say goodbye before we headed out!" Annabel bubbled.

"I don't suppose you'll tell us where you'll be heading?" Connor asked.

"No, and we're not going to. It's just going to be the two of us for the next week. We'll return after that to open shop," Chris said smugly.

"God bless, Bel." Jolyn gave Annabel a hard hug and then faced Chris. "And you take proper care of her." She kissed Chris on his cheek.

Connor reached over the table for a parting handshake. "Be careful, Chris. I've heard rumors."

"I'll be cautious. C'mon, Bel, we'd better duck on out of here before our guests catch on to what we're doing."

Jolyn and Connor watched as the two maneuvered through the crowd and then dashed unseen out a side exit.

"May I have this dance?" Connor whispered huskily against Jolyn's cheek.

"Yes." Jolyn smiled too brightly into Connor's warm, embracing eyes.

Connor held her at arm's length and held her brimming eyes with his own. "They'll be good for one another."

"I know."

"Shall we dance?"

"Yes, and the refreshments be damned."

Connor threw his head back and laughed. He clasped her to him and guided her expertly about the room. The beautiful strains of the Strauss waltz shimmered in the air, and Connor and Jo soared on winged feet. Swirl, dip, glide. Whirl, bend, slide. They danced as one, their bodies undulating together. Jolyn's head dropped back, and she gazed dazedly into Connor's passion-filled eyes. Slowly, even as they still swirled, Connor's head dipped toward her.

Out of nowhere, Jolyn felt herself roughly pulled away. "I believe this next dance is mine," announced Hawk in his deep voice. "And you, Connor, if you wish to save a scrap of Jolyn's reputation, had better take yourself off. I'll see Jolyn home. She's got to get up early and help me in the store before I head back to Alamosa."

Connor, glancing around at all the curious stares, realized the wisdom of Hawk's words. "You're right. We do not need townspeople spreading rumors, do we?" He looked longingly and apologetically into Jolyn's eyes. Then he turned back to Hawk and said somewhat threateningly, "I place her in your capable hands. You will guard her well?"

"With my life," Hawk replied. Lucinda coughed as she moved possessively to his side.

"Goodnight then." Connor pressed his lips against Jolyn's ear and whispered, "Sweet dreams, Jo."

Happier than she had been all day, Jolyn watched as Connor walked away. Only once since they had met had he said the words that she longed to hear. That was a long time ago, and in a place where maybe it was easy to say the words. But she felt it in the way he held her, in the way he said her name, in the way he looked at her. Surely it was there. But she longed to hear the words again. Now, as she turned to leave, Hawk with Lucinda by her side, she no longer felt Connor's hypnotic presence; she was no longer sure if his love for her would survive his hatred for Luke.

Chapter 17

THE WEDDING FESTIVITIES OVER, IT was time to start the day helping at the trading post. Jolyn had promised Chris she would stay until he and Annabel returned. Then she would travel back to Alamosa to work with Hawk. With Lucinda pregnant, Jolyn felt she needed to stay close by her and help her during this time. In fact, Jolyn was hoping that while she minded the store, Lucinda would be sharing her news with Hawk.

Still, whenever her mind wandered, her thoughts immediately turned to James. Where was he? Could she convince Deputy Sheriff Light in town to talk to other marshals? Would they think her just a silly female for thinking James was even alive? Perhaps she would write to the other marshals up in Denver?

Jolyn's mind was filled with thoughts of James and she did not hear someone enter the store. Jolyn looked up to see the woman she recognized from last night's festivity. She was the rude lady who was hanging all over Connor. What was her name? Lucinda was rhyming something last night. Lying, she remembered. Oh, yes, Emmaline.

Jolyn stared into Emmaline's bloodshot eyes and realized this woman must have drunk quite a bit of liquor last night. Jolyn held her head high and, with a sweet smile, proclaimed in a rather loud voice, "Well, good morning, Miss Emmaline! Did you enjoy yourself last night? Is there something I can do for you this morning?" Jolyn stifled a giggle when she noticed Emmaline wince at the booming voice that must have felt like icicles cracking on her face.

Emmaline, however, was a hardened woman. She took a slow, deep breath, exhaled, and declared, "Do I know you?"

Jolyn had listened and learned from the miners over the past few years. Their tales of the women they loved and lost gave Jolyn fodder; she could sweet talk a woman right out of her pretended self. Emmaline was like the women the miners cried about when they were left alone, and while she felt anger toward this woman she also felt sorry for her as well.

"My name is Jolyn. We spoke last night at the wedding festivities. Miss Emmaline, you look a little pale. Can I get you something to help you feel better? Perhaps some head remedies I could fix for you?"

"Why, no, Miss Jolyn," Emmaline cooed. She was not about to let this new hussy think she was hurting from her drinking last night. In fact, she thought, I'm not even sure I remember who shared my bed last night, but I do remember he was wild and wicked! On second thought, though, my head is pounding and maybe this temptress could mix me up something.

"You know, my head is suffering a bit…you know, from all that dancing last night I am feeling a mite peaked. If you don't mind fixing me something that might help, that would be so sweet of you." Emmaline appeared friendly, but Jolyn could see through the false façade and remained guarded.

Emmaline, feeling more confident, continued to look for some gossip she could squeeze out and spread around town. "I thank you for your kindness, though. Where did you say you were from? I thought I heerd you were mining with your daddy. Were you really down in those dark, cold caves with all those filthy, dirty miners?" Emmaline enjoyed riling this new woman in town even though she did not know her. She only knew Connor liked her and that was enough reason to hate this woman. Jolyn was everything Emmaline despised. She had beauty, intelligence, grace—all the traits Emmaline desired for herself.

Jolyn's frosty blue eyes locked onto Emmaline's before she turned around to locate the necessary ingredients to cure a long night of drinking hard liquor. Emmaline watched Jolyn with envy and jealousy and her confidence waned.

Jolyn returned to the counter but by now she was only feeling pity for Emmaline. The long night had hardened Emmaline's once-pretty features. Bits of rouge and eye powder remained caked in the creases and were no longer flattering.

Emmaline reached out to take the medicinal liquid Jolyn had mixed for her and her tone softened. "Thank you, Miss Jolyn. I do appreciate what you put together for me. And now that I remember some of the men talking last night about the camp you came from, I am mighty sorry about your mama and daddy."

Jolyn's eyes softened at the mention of her parents and she felt that perhaps Emmaline was being kind after all.

"Well, I'll be saying good day then, Miss Jolyn. You be sure to tell the owner of this establishment, Mr. Connor, that he is a lucky man. You'll tell him that now, won't you?"

Jolyn nodded and smiled as Emmaline turned around to leave. "Oh," Emmaline remembered, "tell Mr. Connor to put this purchase on my account, unless of course he wants to barter with me like we done before!" And with a cackle, Emmaline scampered out the door.

Jolyn laughed out loud and snapped for her own pleasure, "Why, sure, Miss Emmaline, I'll tell Connor tonight when I see him for dinner. Or later on during the evening as we discuss our future plans together."

Jolyn was unaware that Connor had sidled through the back door. He walked quietly up to Jolyn. He wanted desperately to cradle his strong arms around her. He longed to breathe in her scent, sweet lavender that made him heady and full of longing. He yearned to bury his face into her auburn hair and touch the richness of her tresses, but he stopped himself from such pleasures.

Jolyn, unaware of his ardor, turned toward him as he walked in the room and smiled. She gazed into silvery soft eyes and then, somewhat embarrassed, lowered her eyes.

Connor spoke first. "Good morning, Jo."

"Morning, Connor," Jo returned kindly. A wave of emotions washed over her. She shuddered.

Connor seemed concerned. "Are you feeling okay, Jo?"

"Yes, I am," Jolyn replied, forcing herself to remain calm. "I guess I'm still a little tired from last night."

"I know what you mean. That was one great party, wasn't it?" Connor seemed ill at ease and he nervously poked at the barrels on the floor as if giving himself a purpose for being in the store and, especially, next to Jolyn.

"Is there something you want me to do today?" Jolyn asked. "I am all caught up with the books and it seems as if the rest of the town is sleeping off the effects of the party also."

Connor released a rich, deep, hearty laugh. His gray eyes sparkled with delight and suddenly he realized he was tired of playing games with this woman.

"Jo." Jolyn looked up. She had been avoiding his gaze, and then his laughter had sent warm shivers up her spine. The nearness of his masculine frame was overpowering. She could feel the heat from his body and could smell his musky scent. Jolyn leaned against her broom, afraid she might actually swoon.

Connor walked over to the front door and flipped the card announcing that the store was open for business to the *sorry, we are closed* side. He didn't want any distractions, any interruptions, this time.

Jolyn watched Connor, a shocked expression on her face. She was not sure what was on Connor's mind.

His long legs brought him over to Jo's side before she could think any further. He grasped her trembling shoulders with his large hands and searched her face with his warm eyes.

"Jo," he began, "I'm sorry about last night. I..."

"No, Connor," Jolyn interrupted.

Connor barked, "Don't stop me, woman! I want you to hear this." Connor's face softened and he began again, this time much more gently.

"Last night I wanted to be with you, Jo. Hell, every night I want to be with you. And then 'it' stops me from feeling, from thinking...from everything."

Jolyn was puzzled, but she did not want to interrupt him again.

"I got an awful lot on my mind, Jolyn Montgomery, and one of those things is you. Seeing my sister married off last night made me feel proud and happy. I wanted to share that with someone. I wanted to share that with you. I tried, but damn, everyone was so anxious to dance with you, well, I never got a chance to tell you how much I care for you. Hell, I never got a chance to tell you how much I love you."

Jolyn's eyes swelled with tears. He did love her. He truly loved her. She dropped her head against his chest and her long fiery hair draped over his arms. Connor leaned down and tangled his hands through her thick locks, possessing each strand.

Tenderly, Connor cradled Jolyn's face in his hands, and, tilting her up toward him, kissed her. Jolyn swayed and Connor grabbed her and held her tight. Her body flushed with his touches and she felt light, almost floating.

Connor's kiss was more urgent now and he eased Jolyn's lips apart, wanting more and more of her. Jolyn yielded, her back arching and her eyes closing; she wanted him more than ever.

Connor reached down and scooped Jolyn up in his arms. His long strides carried the two of them up the stairs to his bedroom.

Upstairs, he laid Jolyn gently on his thick comforter. Jolyn sighed. He was hers. She did not have to worry about Emmaline or anyone else. He loved her. His kisses told her that. His mouth explored her face and neck. With each move, each gesture, Jolyn's body reacted. She radiated heat and a lust she'd never known she possessed. Her toes tingled, and a fire grew in the center of her being. She clutched him tightly, felt his manhood, hot and full.

Slowly Jolyn unbuttoned her pinafore as Connor helped unbutton her dress. With only her camisole and slip, Jolyn fell upon the bed, admiring the man in front of her, watching his every move. She shivered, partly from the cool air and partly from watching Connor undress. Naked, he stood before her, unashamed and very much in love.

Jolyn sighed. Connor eased onto the bed and carefully lifted her camisole over her head, savoring her female scent. With feathery fingers he peeled off her slip and in an embrace they lay facing each other, unclothed, their faces flushed, their blood racing and pulsing.

Jolyn moved first, her long, slender arms brushing against his hard muscular ones. Long fingers caressed his thick torso and Jolyn stared unashamedly at his masculine organ pulsating with life and desire for her. Jolyn leaned forward and pressed her hot cheek against the soft downy fur of his chest. One hand gently twisted the silky dark hair while the other rubbed his already hard nipple.

"Ohhh, Jolyn, my love."

"Connor." Jolyn scanned his face as she asked her question.

"What is it, my Jo?"

"Connor, is it true you and Emmaline have been sharing merchandise for pleasure?"

Connor leaned back abruptly, the soft gray eyes turning steely and cold.

"What on God's earth made you even ask such a question? Has she been in here? What lies has she told you? What?"

"Connor—I—she… Yes, she was in here. In here right before you came in, and after I fixed her a quick remedy for her head, well, she asked me to remind you that she was available for you to, as she put it, barter for the cost of the medicine."

Jolyn lowered her head, regretful for telling him and ashamed of the tears that were welling in her eyes.

Connor grabbed Jolyn roughly in his arms and stared deep into her tear-filled eyes.

"I want you, my love. You can show your sharp claws, my beautiful feline, but don't feel you have to scratch anyone, least of all Emmaline. You have nothing to fear with me, my Jo, for you are all the woman I ever wanted and then some."

His burning kisses sealed all fears away. Jolyn relaxed with each kiss, yet deep in the back of her mind she knew she was not through with Emmaline. That woman was no good, and Jolyn twitched with feelings of foreboding and evil. A cold shudder sent icy shivers down her spine.

Connor mistook the quivering, and, thinking it was due to his warm, wet kisses, he paused.

"Are you cold, Jo?" he asked, worried.

Concern shadowed his face and Jolyn smiled sweetly, her heart tugging at feelings that this man aroused in her. She giggled, her white teeth sparkling in her soft pink mouth and her long auburn hair flying in her face.

"No, my love, not anymore."

Connor was confused, but quickly shifted with the mood. He grabbed Jolyn around the waist and wrestled her down to the floor. Her hips gyrated against his as she grappled with him, her skin glowing with perspiration in the candlelight.

Unaware of Connor's deft skill, Jolyn gasped as he maneuvered himself in such a position that enabled him to cradle her in his arms, his manhood protruding against her soft mound. With thighs intertwined, both sat on the cold floor breathing rapidly from their physical play. They were nose to nose, chest to chest, and Connor, never moving his eyes from those of Jolyn's, guided his throbbing organ in between her yielding satiny thighs. Jolyn inhaled the cool air deeply when his large manhood entered her. She melted under his touch and shuddered as his scorching lust reached the depths of her soul.

Jolyn thrust her hips forward, creating a slow, sensuous rhythm. On the floor the two rocked back and forth, arms clutching one another.

Jolyn sighed and sighed again. Connor bent down and, finding her hot, soft lips, kissed her even more deeply than before. Their hips moved faster and faster and faster and their grasp became tighter and tighter, their sweat cascading down their sides.

Gently, without separating, Connor lowered Jolyn's back on the floor. He gazed down at his copper-haired vixen who had captured his heart and his soul.

"I love you, Jo. Now and for always."

"Oh, Connor. I love you so. I will be yours, now and for always."

Entwined, the lovers sealed their vows with a kiss as their bodies exploded with sparks of pleasure and joy.

* * *

Another couple lay naked on a torn and stained mattress in a cheap, drafty hotel. Her hands wrapped around his neck, lips pecking at his rough, unshaven cheek, when she was suddenly and coldly pushed aside.

"I thought I told you to find out more information for me," Luke spat at Emmaline. "Don't come in here throwing yourself at me when I asked you to find out who this Jolyn bitch was and what she means to Connor. Now, woman, what did you find out for me, or do I have to beat it out of you?"

Emmaline's swollen lips ached as she pushed back some greasy strands of her hair.

"No, I didn't find out everything you asked me to, Luke, but then again you haven't paid me all the money you've been promising me, now, have you?"

Emmaline backed away. She knew she had to be careful. He had already beaten her once the other night. This morning when she tried talking to Jolyn she knew she looked miserable, her head pounding from too much liquor. Jolyn had given her something for that alcohol-induced headache, but her head still ached from where Luke had smacked her in anger. Hit her in the back of the head so no bruises would show, but the pain was real. Even still, there was something promising, something in the future with this man. She was hoping he would take her away from this small town. He teased her about some hideaway he and his boys traveled to whenever they needed time away. He bragged about some kid he left there for safekeeping. She might ask him more about that place later when he wasn't so annoyed with her.

Luke slowly chewed on his piece of tobacco and then spit at the spittoon next to the bed. Pieces of chaw hit the side of the golden receptacle and slid down.

"I want to know what this woman means to Connor." He sliced his words slowly. "I got to know how important she is to him. Now, what can you tell me?"

Emmaline knew she had him. She was playing a game, and even though the stakes were high, she was playing smart. Give him a little, and then back up a bit. A little more and then back up even more. All these men are alike, she thought. Cold-hearted bastards the lot of them; transparent as the river that flows through this God-forsaken hellhole of a town. I'm gonna squeeze this bastard for all the money he's got and when he takes me away that will be my chance to spit in his eye and take off for a new town, maybe Denver, maybe make it all the way to San Francisco. She heard there were many opportunities out there and she could make a new start. No one would know her there. No one would know her past and the baggage she carried. It was definitely giving her reason to do whatever she had to with this man, this outlaw.

Luke squinted at the woman. She wasn't bad-looking, he thought. A bit rough on the outside, but a good piece to take to bed. His look softened as he realized he might get more from her if he pretended to be nicer with her.

"Emmaline, let's you and me go on downstairs and get something to eat and we can discuss our arrangement a bit more. Besides, I'm waiting to meet a few friends down there. There's talk of something going down in a few days and then everyone is going to meet at Robber's Roost. C'mon, grab your shawl and let's go."

Emmaline stared at this man with his split personality. One minute he was ice on rocks and the next he was the fire in the rose. She liked a man who was a challenge. It made everything in the end that much more fun. She grabbed her shawl and, rushing to keep up with him, skipped out the door and down to the bar. Robber's Roost, she thought. That was the name of that hideaway. She tucked that little bit of information inside her to be used at another time when it would be to her advantage. Her mama had taught her right.

Down below the gaslights were bright and the small band was loud. Men were drinking even thought it was just shy of noon and women were trying to line up business for later in the evening. Kirmeavey's Saloon was known for its fast women, weak beer, and fatal poker games. Luke had been playing last night while the wedding party was in full swing, and he'd left after winning a great deal of money. He ambled in this early afternoon with Emmaline on his side and a big grin splitting his unruly bearded face.

"Howdy, boys," he smirked as he sauntered past the poker table where the gambling never stopped.

Harry Larkin, a loser from way back, glared up as Luke strolled by. He had lost quite a bit of money last night—most of it to Luke. He grabbed hold of Luke's arm and swung him around.

"Want to give me some of my money back, you lyin' son of a bitch?" Harry bellowed.

Luke was unconcerned and nonchalant.

"Twern't yours to begin with, Harry, and you know that. If I was you, I'd take that small mountain you're holding on to and cash it in for something better like a fine warm woman for tonight. Poker just isn't your game."

With that Luke laughed long and hard and continued walking over to the bar with Emmaline. The other men joined in the laughter. Harry had been a sad sight that night at the poker table.

But Harry had had enough of losing. He knew Luke had cheated him out of his winnings and he was too drunk to care about the consequences any longer. He stood up, his chair falling over backward. The rest of the men watched Harry, but, having seen too many of these fights before, ignored him and continued playing.

Luke didn't hear him approaching. He was too busy grabbing Emmaline and joking with the bartender to even sense the danger.

"Luke, you bastard, I've had all I'm a-gonna take from the likes of you!" screamed the staggering drunken man. He pulled out his small Winchester and aimed straight at the back of Luke's heart.

Luke whirled around, his eyes bulging in surprise. He threw Emmaline aside and she collapsed onto the floor. In the same fluid motion Luke whipped out his Colt .45, jumped off the stool, crouched on the floor, and cocked back the lever.

"Watch out, Harry. I'm in no mood for your drunken brawls again. I told you back in Leadville I never was near your money. You was robbed, plain and simple, but it wasn't from my gang. Now put your gun back in its holster and I'll pretend this spat never even happened. Get the hell out of here, Harry, and I mean it, now." Luke's cold-steel eyes never left his intoxicated enemy. His body was rigid, his gun hand steady, and his thoughts murderous.

Harry reeled, his gun now aiming at several other gamblers, drinkers, and patrons. Like a drill planned nightly the surrounding crowd all fell to their knees.

"I told you back in Leadville, Luke Richardson, that I'd get even with you. My best friend was shot by one of your men when they ambushed me and my group on our way home. I swore I'd get even and by God I hope you rot in hell with the rest of 'em."

Emmaline stifled a scream. My God, her mind raced. Luke Richardson. Luke Richardson. Connor. Connor Richardson. Those two are brothers! But what is Luke after? Why does he want me to spy on his own flesh and blood? Holy Mother of the Mines! Why do I get involved with these things!

Emmaline felt a hard kick in her ribs as Luke shoved her aside. "Get out of my way, woman," spat Luke. "I ain't your man, Harry," Luke warned. "Now leave me the hell alone, or you're gonna find yourself kissing this dirty rotten stinky floor with your last lousy breath."

Harry, a little sobered from the action, was finding out he wasn't as brave as he thought he was. Sweat beaded on the fat man's pale forehead and his swollen cheeks shook from fear. His chubby, short fingers cupped the cold steel gun that trembled with his false bravery. The hard metal trigger slipped slightly against his moist fingers and paused. His mouth filled with cotton, and he licked his lips, the chapped roughness brushing against his hot tongue.

Luke's eyes saw all this. He knew Harry was a nobody, a nothing. He'd wait till Harry put away his gun and then he'd kill him.

But Harry, nervous and scared, wasn't about to give up. Not just yet anyway. He scanned the room, noticing for the first time how everyone was lying on the floor, not moving a muscle, and all because of him. It gave him a rush, a feeling he had never had before. Harry felt his blood racing through his overweight little body and experienced for the first time in his life the real feeling of power.

"I'm Harry T. Larken and I'll threaten any man that's done harm to my family or friends, and, mister, you just bought your last drink."

Harry raised his gun, took careful aim, and squeezed the trigger.

Unfortunately for Harry, Luke was much more experienced. He shot Harry a full second before Harry's chubby little finger could even finish squeezing. The impact of Luke's Colt .45 threw Harry completely off his feet, but not before his small gun exploded with a vengeance. Luke had miscalculated Harry's aim and the hot bullet sliced through his arm and lodged itself deep within the flesh, painfully pressing against the bone, but not penetrating it.

Harry writhed for a moment, the only sound coming from his corpulent body the dry clink of the poker chips hitting the dusty floor as they dropped one by one out of his pocket.

The men from the table rushed over to his body, but sadly enough they only fought over his few chips. When his pockets had been stripped clean they returned to their game, hardly noticing the now empty chair.

"Shit, Emmaline, don't lie there like a dead bitch. Come over here and help me out with this God damn arm."

Emmaline struggled to get up. Her head was pounding and now she was completely flummoxed with the new knowledge of who Luke was and Harry now dead on the floor. She liked Harry. He had spent a few nights with her in the past and he paid well. Not a mean man, not a great lover, but gentle in the bedroom and generous with his money. Still swerving to get over to Luke, Emmaline ripped a long stretch of her cotton slip and, squatting beside Luke, she wrapped it around his arm. Hot blood seeped through the material, staining it a bright crimson in seconds.

"I'll need to take you to a doctor, Luke," Emmaline declared calmly. "That arm looks bad. I don't think I can treat it myself." Emmaline swallowed hard, forcing the bile that rose in her throat back down again.

She did not like ripped arms and blood and guns. All she wanted was a man with money who would give her a good time. She wasn't sure what she had gotten herself into with Luke but it was too late to deal with it now.

Luke held on to Emmaline's arm, ignoring the stares of the locals in the bar. For one brief second he squinted his eyes and scanned the room, looking, perhaps, for anyone else who might want to continue Harry's revenge, but, finding no one, and hanging onto Emmaline as he straightened himself up, he staggered out of the room leaving a dead man on the floor while the others scurrying to find help.

Luke and Emmaline returned to the small hotel room, where Emmaline continue to unwrap and clean the wound again and again as Luke slipped in and out of consciousness. Dipping a washcloth in the cool water on the commode and gently dabbing his forehead, she whispered softly, "I don't rightly know who you are, Luke Richardson, or why you hate your brother so much. I guess after today's little event there must be a few people out there who seem to dislike you. Does your brother hate you, too? Or are you just trying to get him before he can get you?"

Emmaline kept her vigil up all afternoon while Luke drifted in and out of a troubled sleep where he kept seeing his father and Connor dressed all in white with blood on their hands.

* * *

Connor dipped his cut fingers in the warm water that Jolyn had just heated for him.

"Ow, that hurts," he cried as skilled fingers examined his bloodied ones.

"Now, Connor, I promise you this won't hurt at all, you big baby. If you hadn't been so amorous and physical at the same time you wouldn't have broken the mirror on the dresser," Jolyn cajoled, holding back laughter.

"Now, how was I to know that was where you had left your looking glass? I was just sweeping you up out of pure joy and excitement and…"

"Fine. Fine. That's enough. Now, let me finish wrapping your hand. The next time you decide to clean up broken glass, ask me for help. You do not sweep up the fragments with your fingers, no matter how tough you think you are. We have brooms for these things, you know!"

Connor gazed up at this woman. Her warm presence was more therapy than any medicine in the world.

Completely wrapped and doctored, the two lovers snuggled back in bed together, wrapped in their comforter and their love. "Oh, Connor, why can't it always be like this? It is so perfect. You being here with me in this bed. I just want this moment to last forever. Oh, Connor, I love you so much." Jolyn squeezed even closer, their naked bodies tangled and joined.

"Don't worry, my sweet. Nothing could ever change this. I love you so much. I will never let you go. Never."

And together they slept. Peacefully. Their hearts beating as one.

The afternoon raced by and the Richardson men sought solace with their women.

The yellow light from the cold looming moon broke through the window. Connor sat up suddenly in bed, the cold air rushing over his taut body, his dark hair standing on end.

Jolyn was disturbed by this unexpected start and tried snuggling against Connor's body.

"Come on back to bed," she whispered. "Soon it will be time to have dinner. We have made love and slept the day away. Besides, I don't want to hear from Hawk, who will be angry with me for not being in the store all day! And poor Arliss hanging around them just driving them plumb crazy!"

But Connor had felt something, some presence, some disturbance, and he couldn't shake the nagging feeling that something was wrong.

The sharp banging on the front door brought the two lovers fully awake. Connor quickly jumped out of the bed and slipped on his pants and flannel shirt and raced down the stairs.

Jolyn, scared, a bit more cautious, slowly slipped out from beneath the covers and slipped on her clothes from earlier that morning. She heard muffled voices but could not hear what was being discussed. The stairs creaked and moaned under the pressure of Connor's boots as he bolted up the stairs.

"Jo, there's some guy down the stairs named Doc Weathering. He says he knows you. Says there's been some kind of trouble of sorts and he needs your help."

"It's fine, Connor. I know Doc. Someone must be hurt and people always go to Doc for help. They assume because his name is Doc that he must be a medical doctor. I'll go help him out. It shouldn't take me long." Jolyn finished buttoning the rest of her clothes, her mind busy racing.

My God, she thought, I haven't put my herbs and medicines together for quite some time. I'm sure Connor has quite a supply downstairs. Let me see. I'll probably need some…

Connor stared at this woman. He had not witnessed this side of her. He was in the room and so was Jolyn, but from the looks of her face, all scrunched up, she was a million miles away. He stared, his widened eyes riveted and fascinated with her. Jolyn finished donning her clothes without paying any attention to herself, her hands moving as if she were mentally calculating some list.

"Excuse me, Connor. I'm going to need some things downstairs and I won't have time to write it all down for the record. Would you follow me and just keep a list of everything I take so we can write it up later when I come back?"

Connor nodded his head in reply and was about to ask a question, but Jolyn never waited for his reply. She had already darted down the stairs and her lavender scent barely stayed with him as she flew by him.

Down the stairs and in the store, Jolyn found Doc pacing back and forth, nervously awaiting her arrival.

"Doc, it's good to see you again. What's wrong? Who's hurt and how bad is it?"

Doc stared admiringly at this strong woman. She was everything he'd always thought a woman should be: beautiful, smart, and short on gossip.

"A woman by the name of Emmaline came to see me late this afternoon. Seems her man was shot at Kirmeavy's around noon and the boys told her to come get me seeing's how they knew me from the bar. She didn't come right away thinking she could take care of the wound, but he's bad, real bad. This woman, Emmaline it is, said her man doesn't want no trouble from the law, so he's afraid to go to the local doctor in town. He's been shot, Miss Jolyn. I heerd it's pretty bad. He's run a fever and he's been unconscious most of the afternoon since he got hit."

"Thanks, Doc. Let me get a few things together and I'll be right behind you. You say the woman's name is Miss Emmaline?"

"Yes, ma'am. One of Sandy's girls."

Jolyn gave no sign of recognition. She grabbed a black leather bag and began filling it with her supplies. Connor had finally regained his senses to come back down the stairs and, following Jolyn's earlier instructions, began writing down all the items she was quickly selecting and storing in her bag.

Connor could not keep pace with Jolyn. Castor oil, bandages, needles, thread, opium, whiskey (two bottles), coagulants, alcohol, salves of several different colors. Finally she was through. She snapped the bag shut.

"All right, Doc, I'm ready. Let's go. Connor, I don't know how long I will be. It may take all evening so don't worry about me." She didn't wait for a reply. Her auburn hair glittered in the moonlight as she hastened out the door with ole Doc in tow.

* * *

Luke groaned in his unconscious state. A raging fever was burning and sweat sluiced down his face.

Emmaline was scared and confused. When she'd begun having trouble keeping Luke awake, she'd run over to the saloon to check with the men to see if they knew anyone who could help. The last thing Luke had said to her before he drifted off into a feverish sleep was not to let any doctor touch him. The men at the saloon said they thought this new guy in town might be a doctor seeing how his name was Doc, and being a stranger in town he probably wouldn't know Luke. Emmaline had found out where this stranger was staying and had run over to ask him for help.

Luke's delirious comments still floated in Emmaline's head as she recalled him babbling, "I'm not…I'm not real popular in this town, Emmaline. There's some folk who would love to see me suffer in pain. You got to take the bullet out yourself. I can't risk the chance of someone slicing my arm to shreds because I done him wrong a few years back. Promise me that, woman, or I swear if I live through this thing and you cheated me…I'll kill you. Do you hear me?… Do you…" And that was all he said before falling back on the pillow and floating into his own Hell.

Emmaline touched his arm. She knew nothing about medicine or gunshot wounds or even a fever. His arm was swollen, and the dried blood had turned a deep brown color. Her stomach heaved and she breathed deeply. Gently she placed her finger on the wound. Luke moaned. There is no way I'm gonna do this, she whispered to herself. Ain't no way on heaven or earth is this man gonna make me touch that arm. I'd just as soon let him kill me when he wakes up. And with that she left the room and went down to the saloon. It was there that the men told her about Doc.

She raced over to the place he was staying at in lower Creede and practically begged him to come and fix Luke. He seemed hesitant at first, and then suddenly his eyes had widened and he'd told her to go back to her room. He told her that he would get a good friend to help him. When Emmaline started crying, Doc assured her not to worry because he would bring this person over to the room right away.

Sniffling back tears and feeling somewhat relieved, Emmaline sprinted all the way back, so afraid that Luke was already dead. Emmaline could barely catch her breath as she stood over Luke, staring at his face to see if he was still breathing. Suddenly he let out a moan. The tightness in Emmaline's chest subsided and she pulled up the chair to sit next to Luke. If only I could work out a way to conceal his identity, Emmaline thought. This friend of Doc's must not be able to identify Luke.

It took Emmaline several minutes to nudge Luke aside and then at least ten more to turn him over on his stomach, but she did it. He moaned and cursed but he didn't wake up. Emmaline took up the wet toweling and covered his head completely with the cloth.

Just then there was a knock at the door.

"Who is it?" Emmaline asked as softly as she could.

"It's me, Doc Weathering. I brought the friend I told you about."

"Oh, all right. Just a minute. Let me unlock the door." Emmaline fumbled with the lock, nervous and fearful of what would happen next. Before she opened the door she glanced back at Luke. The towel was sliding down his face, but only a shock of black hair poked through. This might actually work, she thought, and opened the door.

Staring face to face with Jolyn, Emmaline gasped.

"What are you doing here?" Emmaline demanded.

"I'm the friend Doc spoke of to you earlier. Now, if you want me to take a look at your lover there on the bed, you'd better let me in, or else I can turn around and go back home where my bed is still warm and my companion still eager for me."

"Uh, no, please, please come in, Jolyn. I'm sorry I was so rude to you. My friend, he's hurt real bad. He's been shot. In the arm." Emmaline was so upset that this stranger named Doc had brought Jolyn. Of all the people in this town. But there was no time to think about meeting up with Jolyn at the trading post and how she'd tried to trick her earlier that morning. Emmaline reported, "I tried to wrap it, but I'm afraid I ain't no good at these things. He's got a fever and I can't wake him up and I…I…I thought he was dead!" Emmaline was exhausted from running to the saloon and then trying to find Doc and then running back to check on Luke. And now trying to tell Jolyn what had happened. It was all too much. Emmaline was woozy but this was not the time to fall apart. She took a deep breath and let Jolyn and Doc enter their cramped hotel room.

Jolyn entered cautiously and quickly surveyed the scene. She was not sure what she was going to find in this broken-down hotel room. She shed her woolen wrap and pulled up a chair next to the body and lifted up the bandages. She turned around to see Emmaline in the farthest corner of the room, sitting in a chair like a child being punished.

"Why is his face covered with the towel?" Jolyn was gently removing the cloth when Emmaline suddenly screamed out.

"NO! I mean, please no! I'm kinda embarrassed about this, you see, and I don't want no one to know who I've been with up here. Please, Miss Jolyn," she pleaded.

Jolyn shrugged indifferently. What did she care who Emmaline was sleeping with?

"Fine, Emmaline, fine. But you'd better come over here closer to me, because when I leave here you will be the one taking care of him and I want to make sure you know what to do. Understood?"

Emmaline nodded and dutifully carried her chair over next to Jolyn.

Jolyn paced herself. This was not too difficult a wound.

The bullet had hit the bone, but had not entered it, so removing it would not be an intricate task. Methodically, skillfully, Jolyn cleansed the area, opened it, and searched for the damaging piece of lead. The man moaned and once his head jerked in pain. His towel slipped off a bit and Jolyn caught a glimpse of very strong cheekbones, but Emmaline quickly jumped up and recovered his face.

"Aha, there it is," she announced, finding the bullet and clamping onto the small ball. She pulled it out and dropped it in a cup. Doc quickly retrieved the cup and placed it on the washstand.

Time passed slowly. Doc did not want to leave Jolyn alone, so he made himself comfortable burrowed in a large overstuffed chair in the corner. Jolyn worked quietly with Doc's snores an occasional break in the silence. Jolyn's extensive experience with bullet wounds from the raucous miners had her skillfully stitching the stranger. With clean gauze she wrapped his arm and gently rested it on top of a pillow. Wiping her hands on her own towels, Jolyn turned to Emmaline.

"He's going to make it, Emmaline. Whoever he is. Now, here are the steps you need to do to ensure his recovery."

Several hours later Jolyn wearily walked into the store. It was late. She was tired and hungry, having exchanged her lunch for an intimate interlude with Connor. She heard laughter in the back room and, curious, she headed straight there.

To her surprise, there stood Hawk and Lucinda and Arliss.

"Well, this is certainly a treat!" Weary eyes lit up as she gazed lovingly upon the few people she loved so much.

"It certainly is," replied Hawk.

Lucinda giggled, looking much better than she had these past few weeks.

"All right, all right, I give up," sighed Jolyn. Exhausted and feeling left out of the private joke, she let annoyance creep in for a moment.

"Jolyn," continued Hawk, his grin getting bigger all the time, "well, I…we…that is, Lucinda and me are…I mean, I asked…"

"Oh, Hawk, you are terrible," interrupted Lucinda. She turned to Jolyn, grabbed both her hands, and announced, "Hawk has asked me to marry him and I accepted. We're to be married at the end of the month."

"Oh, Lucinda, I am so happy for the both of you," Jolyn cried. Jolyn grabbed Arliss to her and the four of them stood in the middle of the room hugging one another. Jolyn was genuinely delighted for the two of them. Hawk had been very special to her and if Lucinda was going to make him a happy man, then Jolyn was ecstatic. She gave Lucinda a puzzled look, as though she wanted to ask her something. Lucinda knew immediately what question Jolyn was thinking and a slight shaking of her head gave Jolyn the answer. So Lucinda had not told Hawk she was pregnant. Yet. Well, that would come in good time. The marriage proposal was excitement enough for one afternoon.

Jolyn looked around at the three people in front of her who had become her family and smiled. Her heart was filled with joy until suddenly a slight touch of remorse smacked Jolyn hard in the chest and she wasn't quite sure why. She shook her head as if trying to shake off a bug and still something was nagging at her, leaving her with a foreboding air of despair that she could not quite diagnose.

Maybe it was the man she'd taken care of earlier. She didn't like the arrangement, what with his face being covered, Emmaline so tense and nervous. Something bothered her about the man, but she couldn't pinpoint it. She squeezed her eyes shut for a moment, trying to analyze what she was feeling, but could not envision anything except the queasy feeling enveloping her.

She left Hawk, Lucinda, and Arliss still celebrating and pulling out some drinks and cake to make it very official. Jolyn crossed the shop floor and found herself sitting on the outside bench staring into space. She heard Connor's voice as though her head were in a tunnel. Jolyn, her elbows on her knees and her hands cradling her head, felt very much alone.

Connor had been waiting for Jolyn to return from helping someone, but he hadn't expected to see her in such a distressed state. He was disturbed by the faraway look in Jolyn's eyes. "Jo? Jo, is everything okay?"

Jolyn took a long time before she looked up into the thoughtful gray eyes, and chills raced through her body, causing a momentary shudder.

"I…I…I must be tired, I guess, from lack of food and rest and working so hard this evening. I'll be fine. Say, did you hear about Hawk and Lucinda?" Jolyn tried to redirect Connor's concern. "How about a little celebration for the two lucky people in there. C'mon, Connor," Jolyn pleaded almost too urgently, "we certainly can throw a party here in honor of their big announcement! And I could use some dinner!" Jolyn forced a cheery smile, but the chills lingered on.

Later that evening Jolyn hesitated before getting in bed with Connor.

"Sweetheart, is there something wrong? Is there something I did today that is making you so distant?"

"No, Connor. I just don't know what's wrong with me."

Unexplained tears trickled down her cheeks and Connor felt his heart tug at him. Gently he covered her naked body with his arms and buried his face in her breasts.

"Oh, Connor, I love you so much."

"Jo, you are everything to me." Slowly he began to caress her body with his soft warm kisses. He started at the top of her head, inhaling her sweet lavender fragrance. He kissed her eyes and her nose and every stray tear. Searching blindly he found her mouth, open and warm and ready for him. Jolyn loved his strong mouth. Gently he urged her to kiss even more deeply, more openly. His hot tongue searched and explored as the two felt a need and a desire that would not be easily quenched. Connor continued kissing her face slowly, languidly, and found the soft hollow in her neck. Jolyn moaned and realized she was moving her hips intuitively to Connor's intimate advances.

His burning tongue traveled downward, searing a line down her chest as he encircled each breast unhurriedly. Jolyn breathed deeply, her taut nipples stretching and hardening. Connor cuddled each breast with his hands, massaging and kneading her satin orbs. He teased her nipples, already hardened, as he enjoyed hearing the groans that rose from deep within her throat. Connor explored her body. He could never have enough of her. Each portion of her that he kissed left a momentary burning sensation and her eyes fluttered open in surprise. Gently he prodded her legs apart and, searching out her womanhood, breathed in her scent. Small reddish-brown hairs tickled his nose and he buried his face even deeper.

"Oh! Oh, Connor, what are you…?"

"Hush, my love. It's fine. Just relax with me."

"Oh, ooohhh."

Jolyn had never experienced such pleasures before. His tongue was rough and sensually delicious at the same time. Her hips had a mind of their own as they pressed up and up. Her head tingled, and her breasts ached with a new longing. She grabbed his hair and pulled him closer to her. Chills bolted down her spine all the way to her toes, causing them to feel as though she were being tickled with a feather. Connor was taking her higher and higher until she no longer felt in control of her physical being, when suddenly he maneuvered himself and thrust his hardened manhood deep within her.

Jolyn gasped from the suddenness of it and encircled her arms around his massively muscular body, undulating with him. They were one and she closed her eyes tight against the world.

Connor longed for Jolyn to reach ecstasy with him. Boldly he grabbed her hair in both his hands, and, staring into her eyes, kissed her hard and long. Exploring deep into one another's eyes, they climbed their peak explosion of love together.

Spent, they collapsed against the bed, drenched in their sweat and their love.

Connor had never felt this way about any woman in the world. He turned toward Jolyn and, piercing her glazed blue eyes, he softly whispered, "Jolyn Montgomery. I…you mean everything to me. And as soon as I finish with this something that I have to do, then I want us to be together, always."

Jolyn stared at this man. She had loved him from the very start, but could she believe him? Could she trust the love he seemed to have for her?

"Connor," she answered cautiously, "I want to be with you always."

Entwined in each other's arms they slept, although Jolyn did not fall asleep for a long time. Instead, she lay breathing in his musky scent, all the while thinking, wondering, and doubting.

Chapter 18

Jolyn sighed as she leaned back against the cushioned seat on the train with Arliss by her side. Chris and Annabel had finally returned and life there was business as usual. It had taken the combined efforts of Hawk, Connor, and herself to fight through the crowds. Hawk had secured her ticket at the boxcar that served as a ticket office, and both Connor and Hawk, using their best persuasive powers, had managed to ensure her a seat so she wouldn't have to wait in the overcrowded, oppressive canvas tent that functioned as a temporary waiting area.

The Creede depot had been, as usual, a madhouse. New arrivals swarmed the narrow planks that ran parallel to the rails. Boxes, barrels, and bags jammed the walkways. A few mothers with their children sagged wearily against their family possessions as they waited for their husbands to find housing where there was none. Boilers and horse-drawn carts filled the neighboring streets, where interested Creede citizens stood observing and gossiping. On the sidings spare pullmans held signs offering temporary accommodations for homeless passengers. Amidst the shifting disorder of man and merchandise, a blast of steam arose, signaling the Rio Grande's departure. Departing passengers scrambled to the platforms, a shrill whistle rent the air, and No. 5342 clattered out of the station to its destination three hours away, Alamosa.

Jolyn settled back and gazed at the passing countryside. She had spoken to Emmaline briefly, who had let her know that her patient was recovering very well and Jolyn did not need to follow up with him at all. Jolyn was uncomfortable with that decision, but she let it be, knowing that whomever she had treated for his gunshot wound had left her with such a nagging feeling of gloom that she was more than willing to let him continue his recuperation without her. She was returning to Alamosa alone once again. Someone was needed to manage the Alamosa store, and after a brief but stormy deliberation, Connor had agreed. Arliss was handy to have around and he gladly stepped up, stating he was certainly man enough to work the store alongside Jolyn. Besides, Connor could not possibly leave with Creede's population growing at a staggering rate and demanding more and more necessities. Since the wedding, he had spent every waking minute selling, ordering, and delivering at the Richardson Trading Post. Hawk was forced to delay his departure another week because Lucinda, struggling with her new condition, had finally agreed to share the news with Hawk. Jolyn insisted that Hawk, ecstatic at the thought of becoming a father, should remain at Lucinda's side for now. Jo convinced them all that she was quite capable of handling any problems that might arise at the store, and Hawk and Connor agreed somewhat unhappily.

Vaguely, she was aware that the seats around her had become filled, but she remained lost in thought. It was already near the end of September and while the nights were chilly, the days were still warm and she felt clammy and overheated with the rush of people and the tight spaces. She was returning to Alamosa, perhaps for the last time, and she was looking forward to seeing her familiar customers. They were becoming more than just customers as she shared in the stories of their lives and had grown fond of all their special quirks and qualities. In Alamosa, people had time to stop and chat and sometimes buy different items. Oftentimes, miners and farmers alike would gather around the potbelly stove, whether lit or not, and gossip about the affairs of the state. She would miss the tea parties, the socials, the fractious freighters, and Arliss. Most of all she would miss Arliss. It would be time for her to move on to parts unknown, but somewhere where she could settle down for good and build roots. Hawk and Lucinda would be busy getting married, having a baby, while Chris and Annabel were still in their honeymoon state of mind and living their dream. And Connor? What of Connor? She felt a deep love for him but knew that he was so focused on finding and killing Luke that he had no time for her, let alone a future together, even though he'd spoken of such things with her. Finding Luke could take months, years even.

In the more settled city of Alamosa, the ebb and flow of humanity had drifted in and out of the Alamosa Trading Post in unrushed waves, but in Creede, a mélange of customers crashed and tumbled in twenty-foot waves through the store, leaving only their silver in their wake. From seven a.m. to ten p.m. Richardson's was jam-packed with life—vibrant, energetic, and hopeful. The mining tramps spun a thousand tales that told the worst and best of men as they drifted through, picking up their grubstake, then heading for Campbell Mountain and Bachelor Hill to stake a claim. New arrivals poured through the doors, wave upon wave, with every new arrival of the Rio Grande. Life in Creede was hectic, exhausting, and exciting.

The train's whistle shrieked across her consciousness. The train jolted, and she, with Arliss on her side, and the other passengers tumbled forward as the train clamored to a halt.

She murmured an apology as she pulled herself back to a sitting position. She had collided with the two men who occupied the seat across from her, but whom she had scarcely noticed until now. They were rough men of indeterminate age and were obviously travelling together. They both wore fur hats, animal skins, and high-rising leather moccasins. Long-barrel rifles were propped against the seat next to her, which also held two well-used knapsacks. Arliss had tried to ask these strangers questions about their guns, their moccasins, and the animal furs, but they would have none of it. There was no conversation no matter how hard Arliss tried, so he finally gave up and eventually gave in to a long nap until the sudden halting of the train jolted him out of his dreams.

A hubbub rose from the disgruntled passengers. A few of the more curious had already abandoned their seats and were charging toward the nearest platform exits.

A brief glimpse from the window revealed no signs of bandits, Indians, or herds of buffalo that might have caused so abrupt a halt. Only the Rio Grande River flashed and fluttered quietly by, a deep blue against the dull green lowlands of the Rio Grande Valley. Curious but reassured, Jolyn and Arliss both settled back into their seats to await news.

She nodded politely to the two grizzled men, and the younger of the two eagerly leaned forward in response.

"How d'ya do, miss? Name's Jebediah. This here's my pa, Joshua." The older grunted his hello.

"Miss Jolyn Montgomery, and this here is young Arliss." She offered a slim gloved hand, which he took in his great paw and shook vigorously. Arliss, following Jolyn's protocol, shook hands with the huge man, and after shaking with the oversized hands, Arliss gingerly massaged his now pulped hand.

"Nice to meet ya both." The stranger flushed at his forwardness and ducked back into his seat.

"Would you be stopping off at Alamosa?" Jolyn asked curiously.

"Yes, miss. We're about trapped out." He glanced nervously at the older man, but his pa stared disinterestedly out the window.

"You see, Pa aint feelin'…"

Before he could finish his sentence, she saw both men stiffen in alarm. The buzz of the passengers ceased abruptly. She started to turn to see what had caused such unease, but a slight warning shake from the younger of the two men stopped her. Silently, she watched as the handful of curious passengers slowly backed away from exiting the cars and slipped into the nearest available seats.

A tall, lean man dressed in black and wearing a wide-rimmed black hat pulled low over his eyes stepped forward. His lower face was covered by a dark, thick, closely trimmed beard. Sharp and sinister, his narrow eyes flickered down the aisle. He carried a Colt menacingly in his gloved hand, as if it were an extension of the man himself. His voice crackled through the air like whiplashes.

"This is a holdup. Everyone will put their hands on top of their heads and hold them there until my partner arrives. If you move, yer dead."

A short, officious man in a tight suit stood up and blustered, "This is an outrage. If you think that you can march in here and rob innoc—"

The roar of the gun blasted the air and the man toppled to the floor. A spreading red stain spilled into the aisle and Jolyn could not take her eyes from it. Horrified, she instinctively reached for her medical bag. Gripping the bag, she walked unsteadily toward the fallen man, her eyes locked on the dark man, silently praying that he would do her no harm. He made no sign that he even noticed her approaching. She wobbled the few remaining feet to the injured man and sank gratefully to her knees. Once there, she tore strips from her petticoat and pressed them firmly onto the gaping hole in the man's chest.

Out of the corner of her eye, she caught a slight movement in the doorway, and the robber lunged backward like a striking snake. Fearfully, she huddled against the prostrate man.

"Easy, for Chrissakes," came a voice from outside. "It's me. I heard the gunshots. Who are you shooting?" The voice cracked with nervousness; it sounded uncomfortably familiar to Jolyn.

Jolyn relaxed slightly. They were only men, after all, and they had come to rob them, not to kill them, although why did the outlaw cruelly shoot this outspoken man? She sat up and concentrated on the growing stain, which was quickly soaking the wad of her makeshift gauze.

"Shut up. Get back to your post or you'll regret questioning me."

As the thug issued his terse order, he moved forward once again, halting before he reached the first set of seats. Ruthless, penetrating eyes slowly encompassed them all.

Ignoring his gaze as best she could, Jolyn formed another wad with more torn strips. She pressed it firmly against the oozing wound. Fine beads of perspiration formed on her forehead in the stifling car. The man lay still beneath her ministrations. The man was dying and she could do little to save him. She heard the clump of boots at the rear platform and the coach tipped slightly as the band of robbers mounted the car filled with the smell of sweat, blood, and death and joined the leader.

They seemed to be swarming into their coach. The leader was moving throughout while one of his gang cackled, "Well, folks, this is a holdup. Now, unless you want to end up like that man lying bleeding on the floor, you just remain quiet and seated until we are all through. We all have very itchy trigger fingers and we don't mind scratching them a bit." The steely voice ricocheted like a bullet throughout the coach. No one spoke. No one breathed. Fear and hopelessness careened down upon the passengers like an avalanche that sliced their souls in two.

Jolyn froze. It was the voice. Not the leader. No, his voice. The voice that had stalked her memory ever since that fateful night on the trail with James. All the anger and horror that tormented her in her dreams ruptured through her and she huddled over the bleeding man lest he see her.

What was she to do? she wondered. Certainly he would recognize her. She trembled at the thought. She would not allow herself to be captured by this murderer, Connor's brother—Luke. Oh, if only Connor had joined her on this train, then he would have found him. Connor would have killed him right here. But Connor was not with her and she remembered Arliss was still back in his seat. She prayed he would not move and come look for her. Stay, Arliss, she pleaded silently.

From the muffled sounds and breathless grunts, she could tell that Luke had started searching the passengers. What was he looking for? Money? Silver? Gold? Guns? She heard a low murmured plea that was cut short by a sharp thud and then more shuffling. Luke lumbered slowly, the hard snap of his boots warning everyone to obey, sending shivers of dread and terror through each person. Was that Arliss she heard call out? She was afraid to stand up and look. Each footstep brought him inexorably closer and closer until he was only a seat behind her. Every nerve ending in her body screamed from the tension.

She heard a scuffling of feet from the rear exit and shut her eyes, expecting another blast from the leader's gun. Or maybe it would be from another one of the men. Now she realized that was the voice of one of the other men from that horrible night. No more gunshots. Nothing. She slowly opened her eyes and stared into Luke's scarred face. He seemed to be glaring directly at her, and she held her breath.

"We've finished the other cars, thought I might be able to speed things along here," a high-pitched voice squealed nervously behind her. The shrill voice whined like a persistent mosquito in her mind. It was the rat. She prayed he would finish robbing the passengers. She would have a better chance of his not recognizing her. It had been dark, and he had never gotten a close look at her.

Abruptly Luke hissed, "Get out!"

She heard the scrambling of retreating feet. Her only chance now was that they would leave the rest of the car untouched.

"Finish quickly. We're out of time."

She felt the jouncing from the seats beside her. She kept her bonneted head down, and her eyes remained glued on the bleeding man, who she numbly realized was no longer breathing.

Then the outlaw was reaching over her, deftly searching the pockets of the passengers seated above her. He extracted everything from tobacco to jewelry and dropped them into two nearly filled bags.

Luke was reaching over her! That same brutal body. From the corner of her eye, she could see the tip of the scar on his left cheek, which extended above the bandanna, masking his lower face. That was where she had sliced him. Jolyn quickly lowered her eyes.

Slowly, almost deliberately, he twisted toward her. She felt his cold, impersonal hands slide over her fingers and wrists and then along her neckline. She felt the quick snap of the chain as he snatched her cameo from around her neck, a gift from Chris. Then he moved on.

Jolyn's heart throbbed with relief. She could breathe again. Patiently, she kept her head lowered and counted the seconds as Luke finished with the handful of remaining passengers. With each passenger he robbed he laughed and guffawed at their misfortune. Jolyn heard the thud of retreating boots and counted thirty seconds more. Slowly, she raised her head and looked down the aisle. They were gone. Softly, tenderly, she attempted to move the dead man to an opening underneath a shelf on the side of the train where there were no seats. A young mountaineer rushed to her side, and together they managed to position the portly man so that he lay somewhat dignified, as he appeared to be sleeping rather than to have suffered death by gunshot. The mountaineer, breathing heavily, reached shyly over and helped Jolyn to her feet.

"You all right, miss?"

"Yes." She offered him a shaky smile. "I—I'm fine. Thank you."

Suddenly a woman's scream radiated throughout the coach and Jolyn heard the terror in her voice. "Get off me! Take my jewels! Don't touch…!" But her voice was drowned as a hand covered the woman's mouth. Jolyn instinctively sprinted toward the woman in the connecting coach, passing a puzzled Arliss, who was seated paralyzed with horror. She beheld the evil killer, Luke, unbuckling his pants with one bandaged arm while the other hand smashed the poor women's lips flat. The other gang members stood gawking, their mouths open with lust, hoping they would be next. Jolyn halted a few feet from Luke and glared at his scarred and sweating face. She had lost all her fear, her intense hatred of him boiling up into a newfound courage. She would not allow him to rape this woman. She would beat him with everything she had in her. But just as he lifted the woman's dress and spread her legs, Jolyn's sudden presence interrupted his plan. With a fierce snarl on his face, his one hand still on the woman's mouth and his pants slipping down his legs, he turned to see who in hell had caused him to stop taking what was rightfully his. Icy-gray eyes bore into hers. He let go of the woman, who fell back onto her seat and immediately pushed her gown down. She raced to the other side of the coach into the arms of her friend. In one swift motion, Luke stood up, pulled his pants up, tightened his buckle, pulled out his Bowie knife, and faced Jolyn. His face contorted at the pain from his arm, but he refused to let that get in his way. His men took a step back and the other passengers cowered in their seats.

"You!" he rasped. "It is you!"

Luke advanced threateningly toward her.

"Do you have any idea how long I've waited for this moment? How I've dreamed of finding you? How I plotted what I would do to you once I found you again?" His venomous spittle flew as he spat menacingly at her. His boots smacked mockingly on the hard wooden floor as he approached her, his anger all-consuming.

The young trapper, seeing what was about to happen to this beautiful, brave young woman, stepped forward, shielding Jolyn with his massive frame.

Laughing cruelly at the unarmed man, Luke lunged forward, the knife's blade flashing. Stunned, almost blacking out, Jolyn found herself back again under the seats, writhing beneath Luke's powerful body, twisting desperately away, watching the knife flicker dully before it tore through flesh and bone.

"No!" she screamed. But it was too late. Jebediah, the sweet mountain man, staggered back, his hands clutching his belly.

Luke whirled about and stared half-crazed at the wild-eyed beauty before him.

How many times had he pictured finding her? How many times, when the scar she gave him became a raw ache, or when a woman twisted away in disgust at that mutilated pale slice, had he dreamed of punishing her? And here she was, his for the taking. To think that she had almost slipped through his hands once again.

Triumphantly, Luke pushed the man he had just stabbed aside. The stupid fool was going to die because he had wanted to save this whore! Luke reached for Jolyn. Blind with rage, she stumbled, turned, and scrambled down the aisle. Behind her in a blur she saw the whir of the hoary mountain man swinging his rifle to his shoulder and aiming at Luke. She heard a deafening explosion and screams from the other passengers. As she reached the platform, she glanced desperately behind her. The older man jolted backward, his rugged face ravaged with blood. Luke careened after Jolyn, leaving wounded men behind him. She tumbled down the steps and landed roughly on the pebbly ground. She clambered to her feet and raced desperately for the team of horses she saw tethered to the trees ahead. She dimly heard the crunch of booted feet behind her. Jolyn pulled up short. She would never have time to mount a horse. She could feel the heat of Luke's body closing in behind her. Her only chance now was to race beyond the horses to the other side where the tree line rose only fifty yards beyond the track.

Climbing and crawling up the side of the mountain, Jolyn was losing ground. She could hear his grunts and curses as he tripped and scraped his legs. She was winded. Her throat burned, as the thin cold air didn't hold enough oxygen and her lungs screamed for more. Suddenly her toe snagged a low tree root and she was catapulted to the ground. She felt a rough hand grip and twist her lower leg. Desperately she kicked out with her other leg, but that leg was snatched tightly. She felt herself hauled back, her head and shoulders dragging along rocks and tree roots and thorny bushes. Unceremoniously, Luke plucked her up, head bruised, shoulders scraped and bleeding. Jolyn wrenched her torn skirt down. Bravely, she turned and faced Luke.

Luke's marauders, having taken their stolen goods with them, raced off the train and now sat waiting on their horses, their eyes glued curiously to Luke and the beautiful young woman he had just grappled off the mountainside.

Luke yanked his kerchief down from his face and revealed the jagged purplish scar that nearly covered the left side of his face.

"This is the one." None of the men had to ask what Luke meant by that.

"Kill her and let's go." One of the men who Jolyn did not recognize had already turned his horse toward the river.

"She's coming with us." Luke's gravelly voice shook with suppressed rage.

"No! We already got one holed up because a you! And now you want another one? What do you think you're doing, Luke? This ain't no collection party. We got goods we need to take and move on out!"

"I tell you, I haven't waited all this time just to kill the bitch quickly," Luke railed.

The tall outlaw with his bronzed face and hardened eyes glanced with hatred at the rest of the motley gang. He was their leader and he knew it wouldn't take long before the other passengers came out blasting. He and these men had already wasted too much time. Luke, and one of his men, were new to this gang of bandits and Luke wasn't sure he could trust the leader. He squinted once more at Luke's acquisition and spat a long stream of hot tobacco on the ground.

"All right. She slows us down, I'll kill her myself."

Jolyn was lugged forward, her hands now tied roughly with frayed rope. One of the men hauled her up like a sack of grain and threw her onto Luke's saddle. Luke hoisted himself up behind Jolyn and yanked her painfully against him, smirking as his groin pressed hard against her buttocks.

The gang turned away from the train and galloped northwest. Behind them, they could hear a few rifle shots and then the hiss of steam as the train started up.

They rode fiercely for two hours, exchanging no words between them. When they reached the fork in the trail that would take them toward Telluride, the men dismounted and led their horses behind a large outcropping.

"We split the money and goods as agreed. If we are separated, each man will have his share. For now, it's better that no one but me and Jed know where we're heading. Any problems with that?" The man who was the leader shot each man a measuring look, stared menacingly at Luke, and then relaxed slightly.

"Jed, stay on lookout. I'll make sure you get your share."

"Right, Henry." Without hesitation, the young man with the large eyes and thin lips scampered up the rocks to stand guard.

Each man hunkered down in a circle and dumped his bag into the center. Luke shoved Jolyn down beside him and with gloating eyes devoured her.

Jolyn collapsed beside him. She was exhausted and frightened, but she was determined not to show it. She felt Luke's evil, malevolent eyes upon her and stared defiantly back.

Luke frowned, then looked away.

"I'll divide up the money first." Henry swiftly counted out eighty-four hundred dollars for each man. "Take ten items of jewelry each and we'll see what remains."

The men poked through the pile, picking out what they considered to be the most expensive items. When they had finished, Henry pushed the remaining items into one satchel.

"We'll look through the papers and purses later. Agreed?" He glanced up questioningly. All nodded in unison, then quickly began stuffing their saddlebags with their newly acquired goods.

"I'd like her purse now," Luke stated boldly.

"Curious?" Henry snickered. "Sure. Why not?"

Henry rummaged through the bag and tossed Luke the blue-and-black-trimmed cloth. Luke eagerly dumped its contents on the ground. A few curious bottles and pouches of herbs. Two silver dollars. Ticket stub. Comb. Mirror case. A needle, scalpel, and a pair of tweezers. And a letter, a letter addressed to a Miss Jolyn Montgomery from Miss Annabel Richardson.

"Jed. We're ready. All clear?"

"All clear."

"Okay, boys, let's ride."

Luke gawked, amazed, at the letter he held in his hand. Annabel. This woman knew his sister, Bel. His half-sister. He stared curiously at Jolyn. Jolyn. Could this be Connor's woman? Excitedly, he seized Jolyn by her short jacket and pulled her against him.

"Is this yours? Are you Jolyn Montgomery?" His words were filled with malice and hatred.

Jolyn focused her blazing eyes at him and said nothing.

"I said let's go, Luke," Henry ordered impatiently.

The men were all mounted and waiting.

Luke backhanded Jolyn across her cheek and dragged her to her feet. "I asked you if your name is Jolyn Montgomery?

Jolyn pushed ineffectually against him.

"Yes," she spat as she carefully touched her cheek, now cut and bleeding from his knuckles.

A fanatical gleam lit Luke's face. He scooped up his take and heaved her with him to his horse. After shoving the cash and jewelry into his saddlebags, Luke once again lifted Jolyn onto the saddle and joined her there. Deliberately, he pulled her familiarly against him. This time letting his hands roam freely across her breasts and rest possessively between her thighs. She stiffened in protest but his grip stayed strong. He waited for Henry's signal, and together the robbers took the left fork and continued at a gallop toward the pass.

"Well, Miss Jolyn Montgomery," Luke shouted in her ear, his tongue licking the outside edges with lust. "Maybe I won't kill you after all. Not yet, anyway. In fact, you just might be the break I've been looking for."

Jolyn stopped struggling and sagged wearily in the saddle. She must reserve her strength. There had to be a way out of this. There just had to be.

Chapter 19

"Where do you think you're taking me?" demanded Jolyn. She was sore and her wrists hurt where Luke had kept them tied together all day long.

"Shut up, woman. I'm sorry I didn't have the chance to kill you back near Cripple Creek. No woman ever scarred me before and no woman will ever do that to me again." He looked straight at her, then twisted the ropes on her wrists. Jolyn would not scream in pain. She would not give him the satisfaction.

But Luke knew he hurt her. There was a slight wince in her face and it made him feel good to see her tremble. Unconsciously his good arm felt the bandaged one. It was still sore but he knew it was healing.

Jolyn watched as Luke rubbed his dirty bandage. The realization suddenly hit her as solidly as if Luke smacked her again. "If only I had known that it was you under my knife, Luke Richardson, you wouldn't be here today."

"Oh, but, sweetheart," he returned coolly, "you'll get your chance to have me under you again, only this time without a knife." Luke threw his head back and laughed, his coldblooded cry echoing off the distant mountains sending an eerie noise throughout the valley.

"Hey, Luke, you wanna keep it down, man?" Slim brought his black mare up close to Luke's horse. He stared hungrily at Jolyn, wishing he had caught her that night. Damned if he knew how she'd slipped away from him. His wicked mind was already thinking how he could mount her if Luke was sleeping. If only. Mebbe later, Slim hoped, mebbe later.

"We still got quite a ways to go before we make it into Telluride, much less pass it, and we got to ride on by before we can camp for the night."

Slim had worked with Luke for a long time and knew the temper this man possessed. Luke seemed to stare right through Slim's beady eyes as he talked and for a brief minute Slim tasted fear in his mouth.

Luke spoke slowly and deliberately. "We'll make it past Telluride, Slim, and then some. I got a score to settle with this bitch and I'm gonna do it."

"Look, Luke, I got no call to argue with you about the woman. You wanted to bring her along with us to Robber's Roost, that's fine with me. I don't care what the other men say, but Luke, if she slows us down, well, hell, the others will probably give us the gate, and without our share of the catch." Luke contemplated this idea for a while. The other men were a new group he and Slim had joined up with only recently. The only old friend he had here was Slim. These new guys might not take to him the way his other men had done.

"No problem, Slim. I'll make sure she don't take off our time any. I'll tell you what. You ride up ahead and tell the others that I'll be glad to share my goods with them as soon as we hit the Roost."

"Sounds fair to me, boss," said Slim, prodding his horse into a faster trot to catch up with the others.

"I know Connor will find me and kill you for what you have done," proclaimed Jolyn.

Luke looked at the beautiful woman, her auburn hair thick and full, her soft face flushed from anger. He could smell her perfumed body as she shared his saddle, and for some reason he felt himself growing more desirous of her. He enjoyed watching Jolyn's hips undulate naturally on top of the horse, her long body swaying to and fro, and for a few minutes his own body radiated with heat and lust. His good hand reached up to rub his face, a habit he had developed ever since…ever since…

"I look forward to the day when I meet my half-brother again face to face, slut. I will show him what I have done to you and how much I have enjoyed it. Then I will let him watch you die, nice and slow. And then, once and for all, I will kill that bastard that my mother should never have had!"

Jolyn shivered. This man was mad. He was crazy. She needed to bide her time until Connor would be able to find her. So many unanswered questions. Jolyn was thinking and plotting an escape, oblivious of the lust and lechery in Luke's loins, but right now Jolyn knew she could not escape, not now anyway. Luke had her wrists tied together, and she was riding with him. She knew they were heading west of Creede somewhere, but it was all foreign territory. Dear God, she prayed, how was Connor supposed to find her out here in this mess? Where were they going? Robber's Roost? She had only heard about this hideout somewhere in Utah. Was it for real? How much farther are they taking me before they…? She did not want to think the unthinkable. Jolyn lurched forward when Luke's spurs dug deep into his horse as he urged his steed onward.

All afternoon the group journeyed on. There were five men and her. Despite the relaxed atmosphere of the riders, there was very little talking. Jolyn was glad about that. She did not want to be part of any conversation. She was hungry and tired and very scared of what would really happen to her. Connor had managed to save her once before, but would he be able to do it again?

The sun dipped below the San Juan Mountains and a faint reddish glow lingered on the quaking aspens. Her father had once told her a tale of an Indian legend and the shaking trees, but try as hard as she could, Jolyn could not remember the story. It helped her to pass the time though. She worried about Arliss. Poor little man. What was he doing now?

As if on cue, the men circled together, talking quickly in monosyllabic phrases. Jolyn could not discern one man from another. All of them had their hats pulled down over their bearded or stubbled faces and never bothered to look at one another during their entire conversation.

"Here."

"Good enough with me, Henry."

"It's quiet."

"We can rest the horses."

"How far'd we go, Henry?"

"About fifty miles or so."

"And tomorrow?"

"The same."

"And then?"

"Bout three more."

"Where we meeting Butch?"

"Down by the bend."

"From Brown's?"

"Yeah."

"Do you think the Kid's with 'em?"

"I dunno. Probably."

Jolyn shifted uncomfortably. She was not sure what these men had in mind. They had just robbed a train, kidnapped her, and were on their way to what seemed to be a meeting with Butch Cassidy. This can't be real, she thought.

The leader spoke. His voice was quiet but held a definite sense of authority.

"You!" he commanded. "Do you know how to cook?"

Quietly she answered, "Yes."

"Good," said Henry. "We'll camp here for the night and you can get the grub together."

Jolyn glanced over at Luke. He looked tense. So, Jolyn thought, he's afraid to go against the boss.

"Henry."

Henry turned and faced Luke. He was not pleased with Luke. The robbery had gone as planned until Luke had decided to add this woman. He didn't like unexpected things.

"What, Luke?"

"I can't untie the rope on her wrists. If I do, she'll run."

Henry shrugged. "So what if she does? It ain't no skin offa us. We don't need her anyways. You oughtta know Butch don't like strangers coming to the Roost and I ain't gonna back you up on this one."

Luke was defeated, but he couldn't let it show. Especially to Jolyn. "Fine, forget it," was all he could reply dryly.

Jolyn slid off her horse and leaned heavily against the saddle. Her thighs were sore from so much riding and her back hurt. Silently she rubbed at her chafed wrists.

Luke strolled up to her. His large legs were spread wide and his hands were to his sides. Strapped to one thigh was his Bowie knife in a leather sheath. He whipped out the blade and raised it high in the air. It caught the reflection of the setting sun, which burnt an image of blood red on the silver knife. Jolyn caught her breath. Then Luke sliced the blade downward, splitting Jolyn's wrist straps in two.

"You're free to tend to dinner," he growled, "but," he threatened, "try to escape me and I'll follow you just to see you ripped apart piece by purty piece."

Jolyn inhaled a shaky breath and nodded, her frightened blue eyes never leaving Luke's face. He shoved her hard and she went sprawling to the ground. The other men glanced over but never moved to help her.

Jolyn seized this opportunity to get away from Luke as fast as she could. Grabbing the large canteen off the pack from the horse, Jolyn raced up a path.

The sound of rushing water tickled Jolyn's ears as she tilted her head toward the vibrations. It was getting dark rapidly and Jolyn urged herself to move as quickly as she could. Following the gurgling sounds, Jolyn climbed higher and higher. There must be a falls of some sort up here, she speculated. A few hundred yards more and Jolyn found herself staring at the most beautiful sight she had ever seen.

"Oh," she sighed aloud. She had never witnessed anything as breathtaking as this. She had overheard Henry mention to Jed that they were near Bridal Veil Falls.

The wind blew the water down in an almost sideways fashion, and the sun, almost on the same level as the water, burst through the falls, splaying out every color of the rainbow. The roar of the water smashing upon the rocks was deafening. Jolyn smiled.

A fine mist of the frosty water gently stroked her face. Her tired, hot feet raced over the slippery rocks to an icy pool of water. Jolyn cupped her hands into the frigid liquid and splashed her face with the refreshing water. Then, like a doe in the woods, she dipped her face into the pool and delicately sipped.

Suddenly a twig snapped and Jolyn's head shot up. Twisting around, she found Luke looming dark and malicious above her.

"I just want you to know, purty woman," he snarled, "that I am always around, always near, and that I will never let you go."

Jolyn's face was dripping with water as she stood up. She said nothing. Turning her back on him, she filled the canteen with fresh water. Once it was full, she tightened the cap and stepped past Luke, who followed her as she descended the mountain.

Down below she smelled the smoke from the fire before she was able to locate the men. They were seated in a small circle. Each man had his heavy woolen cape over him, his hat pulled down low and his thoughts to himself. She knew they would want coffee, and in a hurry, so Jolyn set about completing her tasks. Making dinner for a bunch of men was easy for Jolyn, a normal chore.

Luke wandered into the camp as quietly as he could and took his place on the ground near Slim.

Henry lifted his head, his puffy cheeks pale against his full, dark beard. His black eyes seemed hidden underneath his thick eyebrows as he stared at Luke.

"You tell anyone about our plans?" he inquired. "You mention Robber's Roost to that piece you been seeing?"

Luke responded a bit too quickly. "No, Henry."

Henry eyed Luke carefully. He knew about Luke's temper. He'd heard about the bar scene and did not want him in on this last plan. Slim had spoken up for him, though, and he had agreed.

"Nothing at all, Luke? Not even a little 'I'll see you after things calm down?'"

Luke squirmed, his spurs clinking against each other on the ground.

The other men stared at the fire or watched Jolyn prepare their grub. They did not want to get involved. No one liked going against Henry.

"I swear, Henry, on my mother's grave, I didn't tell that whore anything at all. She was just something to amuse me for a time."

"Fuck your mother and her grave, Luke. If I ever hear tell that you wronged me, well, I don't forget, and I don't forgive."

Luke nodded, his long scar on his face burning a ghostly white in the dusk of the camp.

Jolyn felt the prickles run up and down her spine. She spooned out her stew slowly, the steam rising rapidly in the dark. A slight flurry of snowflakes filtered through the air and the men grumbled about an oncoming storm.

Dinner was eaten quickly and quietly. Laughter was sparse and dinner conversation even more so. She passed her coffee around and decided the lack of compliments was probably the compliment itself. She settled back against a nearby tree to eat of her own makings.

Surprisingly, it was Henry who got up, ambled to his horse, and came back with a hand-woven woolen blanket in his hands.

He stood in front of Jolyn. "Here, cover yerself up. It's gonna get a lot colder before it gets any warmer. The food was good. Thanks."

While eating, Jolyn overheard the men discussing something about Butch and Brown's Park. It seemed they were going to meet Butch and his men so Butch could lead them to another hideout, Robber's Roost.

"Are you sure Butch knows where he's going, Henry?" questioned Jed, the youngest of the outlaws.

"Butch told me he grew up near them parts, around Circleville. He's no stranger to the Roost."

"I heerd a man could get lost in the valley looking for the hideout and jest never come out again." Slim spoke nervously, his slight face pinched with fear and his high stubbled cheeks quivering in the flamelight.

"Once I heard about two lawmen who rode into the Roost looking for three rustlers," Luke added. "About a week later their bodies were found swinging from the Post Office Tree, naked and stiff."

Jed nodded his head in agreement. He pulled at his thin lips, a nervous habit he had, and blurted, "Uh-huh, I heerd that one too, Luke, only it was three lawmen looking for two rustlers and alls they found hanging from the Post Office Tree was their clothes."

"Don't matter," said Slim. "We got us the best guide in the world, and him and Henry ain't gonna lead us wrong."

Henry just grunted and sipped his hot coffee. He looked over at Jolyn, who had wrapped herself tightly in his blanket. All that poked out was a mass of red curls and two bright eyes.

Gazing past Jolyn, Henry searched out Luke, who was watching Henry watch Jolyn.

"I don't know why you got yerself tangled up with this woman, Luke," Henry said, "but if what you promised before is true, then I'm calling first grabs."

Luke never planned on anyone having Jolyn but himself, but now was not the time to argue. He grunted in return and went on watching Henry.

The rest of the men, having finished their dinner, laid the tin plates next to the fire and began unfolding their bedrolls. A few men wandered off into the woods, grumbling, and the rest crawled into their makeshift beds and promptly fell asleep.

Luke was not going to take any chances. Roughly he pulled Jolyn from the tree where she had been resting. Taking some rope, Luke tied Jolyn around her waist and then tied the rope to him. Lying down in his bag with her warm breath at his neck, Luke forced himself to only think about what he was going to do when he next met Connor. He wanted to teach Jolyn a lesson, he wanted revenge, but he did not want to tangle with Henry. Luke knew his time would come and when it did his revenge would be sweet.

Morning came bright and cold and clear. Henry had gotten up first and already had his horse packed and ready to go. Henry snarled at the men as he stepped among them, kicking those in the ribs who didn't move fast enough.

"Let's go, men. Butch sure as hell ain't gonna wait on us. Now, let's move out. We can catch some grub later."

Jolyn was too frozen to leave her blanket. There would be no fire this morning, no hot coffee, and no warm biscuits. On top of everything else she had to relieve herself. The men ignored her, but she couldn't go off by herself still attached to Luke.

Luke grumbled and twitched and then sat up, pulling Jolyn with him.

"My arm needs some tending," he muttered.

"Luke, I need to clean it with warm water and some soap," she said knowingly. "It's beginning to get some pus on it and that could mean trouble."

"You ain't gonna cut my arm off," he threatened, "or I'll kill you before the knife draws first blood."

"I wouldn't do that, but I do have to clean it. Now, untie me and let me tend to your arm."

Henry was watching the two of them the entire time. He didn't trust Luke and he didn't like the notion of having a woman along with them. Women were bad luck on the trail. There was always something going wrong. And when things went wrong on the trail, someone got hurt. Someone might die.

The men were ready to depart. The horses were a little jumpy from all the snow around them and the men were tending to their animals in an attempt to comfort them. Jolyn shook the blanket she'd worn last night. Folding it up, she headed over to Henry with it.

"Here," she said, handing him the blanket, "I thank you for your kindness and your consideration."

Henry stared at the stunning woman. If the men weren't all surrounding me right now, he thought, I'd take her here. Right here in the fallen leaves. I'd lay that beautiful rust-colored hair against these golden aspens and I'd make this woman forget there were any other men in the world.

"You go on ahead and keep the blanket for now. The wind's gonna pick up once we leave the woods and you're gonna need the extra warmth."

"Thank you, Henry," she forced out calmly. "I think you're right about the cold." As quickly as she could, Jolyn gathered the blanket in her arms and headed toward her horse.

Henry watched her go and after she had mounted, checked out Luke's reactions to the small conversation. Henry had never liked Luke, never trusted the man, and was almost sorry he had let him join his group. Henry ignored the icy look from Luke and got back on his horse.

"Let's head out, men. Next stop, the border."

Jolyn trotted along with the rest of the men. The winter would be upon them in another month or so, but out here Mother Nature liked to get a head start. It looked like it might snow, early for this time of year, but up in the mountains anything could happen. An early snow would be slippery for the horses and treacherous for the men riding the animals. Added to the rough terrain, the snow would hinder their travel time a bit and Jolyn overheard Henry several times discussing this matter with the other men.

"Hey, Henry," perked up Slim, "How far is it to the border anyways?"

"Well, boys." Henry chewed on his thoughts for a while. "I guess about fifty miles as the crow flies."

"Say, Henry, what if we don't meet up with Butch?" asked Jed, his large eyes darting back and forth.

"Yeah," agreed R.J. "How familiar are you with the Outlaw Trail?"

"Well," confided Henry, "I only been there a few times, but once I'm by the Henry Mountains, why, it won't be no trouble at all."

The men grunted, satisfied with their leader, and rode onward.

The day slowly dragged on. Jolyn was famished from hunger when the men finally decided to stop. Jolyn quickly volunteered to find water.

Henry spied Luke following her and stopped him.

"Luke, leave the woman alone. She ain't gonna take off and go anywhere. We're too far for her to make it alone. Now, give her some peace from you sniffing around her like a dog in heat."

Luke growled under his breath. He wanted to tell this bastard what he could do with his group of men, but he held himself in check. This was not the time or the place to confront the leader. There'd be plenty of time later.

Luke cursed to himself and turned away.

Alone, Jolyn found a small stream meandering along the path. She quickly found a private place for her ablutions. After finally relieving herself, Jolyn plodded on to the water. She was tired from riding, tired from a restless night strapped to Luke. But she swore she would find a way to escape. Not right now. It was too cold and she was not prepared. Instead, she rinsed out all the canteens and refilled them. She had to break a thin film of ice that had formed over the stream overnight. The water was frigid but refreshing and Jolyn splashed her face. For a few brief seconds, she forgot where she was and, most importantly, how dangerous Luke could be.

There was a time, she mused, when I never thought I'd find a man to love and for him to love me. Well, I finally found him, and it seems I just can't have him. Every time I get close something manages to drive us apart. What if he doesn't come for me? What if he doesn't even know? What if Luke…?"

"Hey, lady, you in there?"

It was Slim. Jolyn quickly retrieved all the canteens from the stream and tightened the lids.

"Uh, yes, I'm in here. I'm coming now."

Jolyn emerged from behind the brush.

"The boss is ready for some grub and he don't take kindly to having to wait."

Slim was a sad human being in Jolyn's eyes. He could be kind, but she doubted he ever had the opportunity to be his own person. He'd hooked his life to a killer, and maybe that was exciting and fulfilling, but one look at Slim and she could tell that was not the life he would have imagined for himself. Jolyn smiled. She would do what she could to befriend Slim because she might need his help at some point.

The two of them approached the circular clearing where the men had set up a small fire. Without being asked this time, Jolyn immediately set herself to getting the food prepared.

There was very little talking again. The men ate quickly, gulped the hot coffee, and doused the fire. They scrubbed their plates with some twigs and packed up. They were in a hurry. They wanted to get across into Utah before dark and there were many miles to cover.

On the trail again, the men rode hard and fast. The sky overhead was a rich deep blue and the snow crystals on the ground glittered in a multitude of bright red, orange, blue, and green. Coyote footprints graced the ground now and then and the lone sound of a wolf in the distance resounded hollowly in the thin air.

Jolyn concentrated on her riding. She had to keep up with the men. It seemed like hours passed by when suddenly there was whooping and shouting and cheering from all the men.

Jolyn looked at the men. They had taken off their hats and were whipping them through the air as they shouted with joy.

Slim rode by Jolyn. "We just crossed into Utah," he explained, wearing a goofy grin. "That makes it even harder for the law to follow us now."

After a few miles even Jolyn noticed something was different. The terrain had changed. Where Colorado was mountains filled with blues and greens and aquas, Utah was flat with red and orange rocks that shot right out of the earth and penetrated the deep-blue sky. They were heading toward the Colorado River and closer to their destination. Jolyn glanced over her shoulder, back toward Colorado.

"He ain't coming." Luke's voice was low and threatening in her ear. "He can't find us. He never has been able to find me before and he ain't gonna do it now."

Jolyn glared back at Luke. "He'll come. And he will kill you when he does." And she prayed silently.

"You're my woman now, bitch, and you'll do what I tell you to do and when I tell you to do it. Mebbe I need to give you a scar on your face to show you that you belong to me now." With that he took his cold finger and slowly pressed it against her cheek and downward to her chin as though a knife was slicing through her.

Jolyn froze in her saddle. This man scared her, and she wasn't sure how much the others would protect her. Luke might not be their friend, but they were a gang and she was their captive. She wasn't sure even Slim would stop Luke from completing his vulgar act.

Luke threw her a sinister smile. Jolyn turned back to face the path ahead. She was silent and Luke mistook her quiet for submission.

The sun was setting as they approached the Grand River. They headed straight for the wooden bridge, Dewey Bridge, one of the men called it. The cold orange sun reflected strips of apricot and yellow and pink against the cool running waters. The sand imitated the colors and it was hard to tell where the ground met the looming buttes around them.

They crossed the narrow bridge and then made camp.

Henry once again bellowed out orders and commands. In a matter of minutes, the horses were fed, a fire was built, and Jolyn was once again in charge of generating a dinner on very little food.

Sitting around the fire as the last rays of the sun scratched the dusty earth underneath them, Henry told his men his final plans for the trip.

"Well, my mangy group of thieves," he began, "we are supposed to meet Butch at Green River above Horsethief Canyon at sunrise tomorrow. If he's not there, then we're going to find the Roost ourselves. We've got two, mebbe three days' ride to go yet and I'm hoping to settle in the Roost before any big storms come our way. Any questions?" His deep-black eyes scanned the faces surrounding him.

A few mumbled "no's" could be heard round the fire. "Say, Henry," Luke started slowly and then raced on, "why don't we confuse everyone and head north up to Brown's Park? No one would think we'd gone so far up. Then we could be closer to Hole-in-the-Wall after our next holdup."

Henry looked curiously at Luke's smug expression.

"Who are we trying to confuse, Luke? Someone in particular? Someone from back home that mebbe knows where we're heading? We're confusing the hell out of everyone now by not going down to Santa Fe where it's nice and warm. You got a problem with that you let me know. And if for some reason you got a feeling someone is hot on our trail, why, I guess mebbe we oughtta leave you behind to wait up fer 'em and deal with them yourself. Otherwise, we're heading for the Roost. Besides, I hear you already got someone there you best deal with right quick now, right?"

Luke grumbled in agreement. He knew he had lost again. It was hard losing face in front of Jolyn so many times. There were so many enemies he was going to put in their places. And soon.

Jolyn remained still and calm as the conversation continued about the Roost and Butch Cassidy and who else might be at the hideout at the time. She wanted no part of their scheming and no part of the wrath of Luke. She saw how his body had shrunk every time Henry put him down. He didn't take well to that kind of talk and if she didn't watch out he would take it all out on her.

Sliding down into her blankets, Jolyn stared up at the sky dotted with stars that blazed far, far away. I wonder if Connor is looking at the same stars I am, she pondered, as a tiny warm tear glided down her cheek. In three more days I'll be stuck in a hideout that most lawmen can't find their way in or out. Oh, God, I must find a way to escape. Luke will see that I am destroyed piece by piece if I don't get away. I must be strong, but this is not going to be easy. Oh, Connor, my love, please hurry and find me. I don't know how much longer Luke will allow me to live. I don't know how much longer these men will let Luke live. Connor, if you can hear my thoughts, then please know how much I love you and wish you would come save me!

Chapter 20

HAWK BURST INTO CONNOR'S OFFICE with Lucinda close behind him.

Connor looked up, surprised. "What the hell…?"

"Ain't got time to explain, Connor. Old Number 4692's been hit. Early this afternoon. It had just passed Wason and was on its way to Wagon Wheel Gap."

"Jolyn?" Connor vaulted up. "Jolyn and Arliss were on that train."

Hawk scrunched up his forehead. "Damn it, Connor, I know that! I'm the one who put them both on the train! Jolyn was going to take care of things for me and Arliss was going to help her till I got back."

Suddenly Annabel flew in. "What is all the ruckus going on down below the Cliff? The whole town's gone down there! People are shouting all over the place!"

Connor marched around his desk toward the door, putting on his gun belt and heavy denim jacket as he went.

"Annabel, Lucinda," Connor called over his shoulder, "you two watch the office. Hawk, we'd better check out the situation."

"Connor, do you think it was the Wild Bunch that hit the train?" Hawk talked quickly as the two men flew out the door. "They've been around the area, or so I've heard from the men down at the Exchange Club."

Hawk and Connor headed toward the Cliff, the depot at the edge of town. Groups of men were running out of stores, saloons, and shacks down the dusty road toward the great throng that had built up numbering over three hundred strong.

Connor and Hawk exchanged glances. This was very serious. Their pace became a trot as the storefront windows flew by them. The noise from the crowd grew louder and louder.

"Look, Connor." Hawk nudged Connor with his elbow as they continued down the road. "There's Soapy. I guess his gang wasn't involved or else he wouldn't be here."

"I still wouldn't put it past him," grunted Connor. "That man's liable to do anything."

"I agree, but he wouldn't be standing around here. That's like asking to be lynched. Look at the women around him. There's Lilly, and Sandy, and the big one is Rose. And that one next to him is Lulu. They call her the Mormon Queen."

Connor stared at Hawk. "Since when do you know all the madams in this town? You're supposed to be from Alamosa and you're supposed to be getting married. If I were you I'd start forgetting their names right away!"

"And I suppose you want to meet them? You haven't been with another woman since you met Jolyn. And don't think I hadn't noticed. It just seems as if you're the only one who won't accept it. At least Lucinda knows my past and my love for women. And that of course is all in the past. I'm settled now."

Connor laughed and slowed down his pace. "And what do you mean I won't accept it? I told Jolyn how much I love her."

"Oh, you have, have you? Then tell me, Mr. Richardson, why was the woman of your life on the train to Alamosa? Answer me that one, bud."

"She had things to do, I guess." Connor fumbled for words. Finally he blurted out, "And I'm thinking she's worried I got Luke too much on my mind."

"Now why the hell do you have to keep reminding her about Luke for? Jolyn is the most agreeable person I know. She's thoughtful, considerate, downright smart too if you ask me and..."

Connor interrupted. "And she wants to get married."

"Married? So? What's wrong with that? Looks like I'm gonna be walking down that aisle of happiness real soon. I just didn't give Lucinda a real date. But at least she thinks it's going to happen, and for now that's important. What is wrong, my friend?"

"I told her I had to deal with Luke first. I want to catch that bastard and kill him before I can do anything else. I can't let that man roam free knowing he killed my father, let alone her uncle and brother. And who else has he killed besides them? And Jolyn's friend, James. I sure can't forget about him since Jolyn brings it up every chance she gets. James was with her when Luke and his gang ransacked their camp that night. Jolyn, lucky for me, managed to run and hide, but James, well, no one has heard from James since that fateful night. Don't know if he is dead or alive, but I'm aiming to find that out for Jolyn. Hawk, Luke doesn't deserve to live, and if I don't get him then nobody else will."

"And what about the law? Don't they have a right to him too?"

"Sure they do. And that's why Butch Cassidy is in jail and the Kid along with him and Harvey Logan and Pike Landusky and Bill Carver. And the list goes on and on. Luke Richardson is a two-bit no-good outlaw. The marshals in this area got bigger fish to catch and fry and Luke is just a small tadpole to them. But to me he's the whole pond and I've got to get him. I swore an oath and I'll never give up."

The two men had finally reached the train depot and the crowd was buzzing with rumors and stories. Calamity Jane, smoking her big cigar with her cards still in her hands, was talking the loudest as Connor and Hawk approached.

"I knew it, I just knew it was gonna happen one of these days!" she exclaimed. "Henry's been talking about hitting one of these runs for some time now. Blast that man!"

Connor looked over at Hawk, who just shrugged his shoulders in complete amazement.

The sheriff climbed onto the platform. The crowd threw shushes to each other until the worried mob finally calmed down.

"Okay, group, we got ourselves a problem right here. We understand that the train was hit a couple of hours ago. According to the wire we received it seems they were just after the bank money the train was carrying. As you know, the First Savings and Loan had a large shipment that was headed for Denver."

"Was anyone hurt?" a big burly man in the back shouted out.

"Did they take all the money?" another blurted out.

"Have they been captured yet?" a large woman barked.

"Sheriff Light," shouted Connor. The crowd hushed as they anxiously awaited Connor's question. Connor continued, this time not quite so loud. "John, what exactly did you hear?"

"Well, sir," Sheriff John Light answered, his voice wavering a bit, "the wire did mention that a woman was taken."

Connor's throat went dry. He swallowed slowly, looked over at Hawk, and then at the sheriff. "Any description on the woman, John?" Gentle gray eyes waited impatiently for the answer.

The sheriff knew about Connor and Jolyn. News like that wasn't kept quiet in a small town like Creede for very long.

"I'm sorry, Connor," John returned, "the wire specifically stated that a young woman with auburn hair was grabbed by a man with black hair and gray eyes and a long scar on his face."

Connor stopped breathing. His face paled and his eyes went blank. Automatically Connor's large hands balled into two huge fists. Like a cornered animal about to attack, Connor whipped around to Hawk and blasted, "God damn him, Hawk. God damn him for all he has done to me. This time he will not escape me. I will find that bastard. And when I do, he will rue the day that he ever came out West."

Hawk grabbed Connor by the shoulders. "Wait up, Connor, we can't go rushing after this man like this. Let's find out which way his gang was heading. Plus, we need more men. We can't go after Jolyn alone. He's too smart. There must be at least five men in that gang. He's slipped through your fingers too many times already." Hawk paused a minute. Still holding on to Connor's shoulders, Hawk turned toward the sheriff and yelled, “Hey, Sheriff Light, any word on which way the gang was heading?”

The sheriff was already gathering men to form into a posse.

“Well, Hawk,” Sheriff Light said, “with the snow and cold weather on us it’s more‘n likely they headed toward Sante Fe. From there they’ll probably aim for Mexico till the winter’s over with.”

The crowd was buzzing with the news. Arguments flew back and forth as to where the men were heading. Some argued for Mexico while some shouted about the Hole-in-the-Wall and still others thought the gang might just try to make it all the way to California and fool everyone.

Hawk turned to Connor, brown eyes piercing dazed gray ones.

“What do you think, Connor? Where do you think they were heading? If you got anything on your brother’s thinking, this is the time to use it. How does he react?”

Connor slumped his shoulders. “That’s just it, Hawk. Every time I get close to him, he always seems to be another step ahead of me. It’s almost as if he can smell me behind him.”

Hawk thought for a moment. “Connor. Luke’s not with his old group. I heard down at Kirmeavey’s he was hanging out with Henry Rathman Clayburn and his men. That means Luke won’t be making the decisions. He may put in his thoughts, but it’ll be H.R. that does the deciding.”

As Connor and Hawk stood talking next to the platform the rest of the crowd was slowly dispersing. The sheriff had organized a small posse of twelve men, and they were going to head out first thing in the morning.

“No sense starting out now, boys,” he explained, “it’ll be dark in a couple of hours. Might as well get a good night’s sleep and some hot food in our bellies before we head out tomorrow.”

“Connor?“ the sheriff called out, his heavy Texas drawl giving Connor’s name a sorrowful twang. “Are you going to come with us tomorrow, son?”

Connor clenched his jaw and squinted his eyes. His handsome face turned ugly with hate and contempt as he replied, "Yes, Sheriff, Hawk and I will be alongside you first thing in the morning. One thing, though, sir."

"Yes, Connor?"

"When we get them. I want Luke to myself."

"Understood, Connor. Now go get some rest, son."

Hawk and Connor found Chris in the crowd after talking with the sheriff. Chris wanted to go with them in the morning, but Connor wouldn't hear of it. Connor was too worried about Annabel. She had been through this horror once before and Connor was afraid she would have a breakdown.

"But Jolyn is my sister, Connor," he pleaded. "She's the only family I got left except for Annabel. I can't let you go without me."

Connor was adamant. "No, Chris. You have to stay here. I don't want the women alone. They need you. Annabel needs you. If something were to happen to you I don't know what Annabel would do. Trust me on this one, brother."

Chris could not win the argument. There was no changing Connor's decision. Hawk and Chris left to find the girls and explain what was going to happen. Lucinda and Annabel were both devastated. Lucinda was worried about Arliss, too. Hawk calmed her down, telling her he had received word from Alamosa that Arliss had arrived safely. Arliss was such a good boy. Arliss sent a telegram to Hawk telling Hawk that he would take care of the store and not to worry about him, just go and find Jolyn.

Knowing Lucinda and Annabel were in good hands, Connor headed right to his store. Inside he collected all the supplies he would need for at least two weeks. After that he would have to live off the land, but he wasn't worried. He had survived in the mountains before and he would do it again. He put his filled saddlebags by the front of the store and went to the back to lock up.

When the front door opened, Connor immediately figured Chris had come back to argue with him… He was still working on the back door while he shouted, "Forget it, Chris, I ain't gonna change my mind."

A very soft female voice replied sweetly, "Well, honey, do you think you could change your mind for me? Whatever needs changing, that is."

Connor's head shot up. Who the hell was that familiar voice? With rapid strides Connor flew into the main room to see Emmaline standing in front of him. Her pungent fragrance almost knocked him over. The makeup on her face was overdone and the neckline on her gaudy red dress plunged deeply. Her hair had been teased to a frazzle and as she smoothed her frizzy tresses with blood-red-painted fingernails, Connor's questioning expression quickly changed into a scowl.

"What do you want?" he growled.

"Why, sugar," Emmaline cooed gracefully, "I just thought that perhaps you might be wanting some company since your other lady friend decided to depart rather abruptly."

"Go home, Emmaline," Connor ordered. "I haven't got time for you."

"I guess you have been spending all your time with that sweet young thing. I guess that's why she left. You must've been giving her so much of yer loving she had to leave to get some fresh air."

Connor's jaw twitched, but he ignored her comments. "I'm getting ready to go on a trip, Emmaline. I have things to take care of right now. Would you please leave—now?" Connor's tired voice seemed to echo in the darkened room. He was worn out and needed rest.

"Well," teased Emmaline, "I reckon you and your brother don't see eye to eye on a whole lot of things. Especially your taste in women."

Connor's head shot up like a snapped twig. He looked hard and straight into Emmaline's eyes and said, "What did you say?"

Emmaline had him. She had him right where she wanted him and she wasn't going to let go.

Connor marched to Emmaline and grabbed her roughly by her shoulders. He squeezed hard until Emmaline moaned a little. She'd expected shock from Connor, but not violence.

"Emmaline, what do you know of my brother? Tell me now before I lose control."

Emmaline wasn't afraid. Luke was rougher and nastier than Connor and Luke only scared her a little. Still, it made her blood rush and she liked that feeling. It always gave her a thrill.

But Emmaline had miscalculated Connor's wrath.

"I don't want to hurt you, Emmaline," Connor hissed. "I really don't want to, but you are giving me no choice. If I have to threaten you with my gun I will. Now, what do you know of my brother? Was he here in town? Did he leave? Where was he heading? What did he tell you? What? WHAT?"

Emmaline threw her head back and laughed long and hard.

"Was he here? Was he here? Good God, Connor! Who do you think I've been with? Who do you think I've been working for? Did you think I was going to wait around for you? Especially after seeing you with that no-good red-headed bitch. I wanted you, Connor. I always wanted you. Luke was only second best. I didn't even know you two were brothers, but now it all makes sense.

"I could have let it go at that. All the spying around for him and asking questions. I didn't mind that. I didn't mind half the things he made me do. And I would have gone with him had he let me, but no. He told me it was too dangerous right now. He told me he would be back to get me as soon as he could. And I believed him. I really believed him. Until. Until I heard that he kidnapped that bitch of yours from the train. Now, that was the worst thing he could have done to me. And that's why I'm here, Connor Richardson. To tell you where to find that low-lying snake in the grass. Because I'm coming with you to get him. I want to be the one who puts the bullet right between his eyes. I don't care what you do with your woman, if she's still alive. I just want to get my sharp nails on Luke Richardson and let him know that he can't mess with Emmaline Burdette."

Slowly Connor pulled away and tenderly released her arm. Softly he asked, "Where are they heading, Emmaline? Do you know?"

"Yes," she whispered, "they're going to meet Butch Cassidy at Green River and head on down to Robber's Roost."

"Robber's Roost!" Connor gasped. "No one would ever have thought they'd ride that way this time of year."

Emmaline nodded her head in agreement. "I know. That's why he said it was such a perfect place to go. The leader of their group is good friends with Cassidy and said they'd be welcome at the Roost anytime."

"Emmaline, listen to me. I know you want to get Luke. We could use you out there on the trail. You go back and get your things together and we'll round up at daybreak and head on out. Do you understand, Emmaline?"

Emmaline looked deep into Connor's gentle gray eyes. She wasn't sure what was he was thinking. She wanted to believe him, wanted someone to believe in her, so she replied, "Fine, Connor. I'll be ready." Slowly she turned around, wrapped her shawl over her head, and left.

Connor watched her go. He stood at the door and followed her as she made her way back to the saloon. As soon as she was inside the building Connor grabbed all his heavy bags, then raced out the door and down to Chris's. He found Chris and Hawk and Annabel and Lucinda there.

Connor burst in the door and yelled, "Chris, Hawk, get your things. I know where Luke is hiding!"

Chris looked at Connor, puzzled. "Wha… I'm coming?"

But Hawk knew that look, knew Connor was dead serious about something. "Move it, Chris. I'm sure Connor will explain later."

The two women never had a chance to question. The three men were loaded up in a matter of minutes and the sound of the hooves beating the dirt road was their goodbye.

***

The determined men rode hard and fast. Fortunately for the three riders they followed a trail left in the snow on the ground that seemed to be an open invitation.

Finally Hawk spoke first. "Connor. Do you want to fill us in on this now? It's almost dark and we can barely see the tracks any more."

"Yea," Chris agreed, "What's going on, Connor? I thought you two were going with Sheriff Light in the morning. And," he added cautiously, "I thought you didn't want me around."

Connor sighed. The trio rode side by side along the valley between the two mountain ranges. The air was thin and cold and the aspens strained in the wind.

"Emmaline came to see me," he began. "She told me Luke was with Henry's gang and that they were heading out to Robber's Roost."

"In Utah?" Hawk exclaimed. "Why, everybody else is heading on down to Sante Fe. Why didn't you go get the sheriff?"

Connor knew he'd have to come up with a good reason why he didn't want anyone else with them. The woman he loved more than anything else in the world had been kidnapped by his half-brother. He was worried about her safety, and he just didn't want anyone else in on his revenge. He needed Hawk, and he felt Chris was one more strong man to have with them. His conscience nipped at him when he thought about leaving the women without any of their menfolk to watch them, but they would have to be strong. He had to believe that for now.

"There are lots of reasons, but for now, well, just stay with me on this one."

Hawk and Chris scrutinized Connor. They had never seen him act this way before. They knew there had to be more of an explanation, but for now they would follow his lead.

They made it up to Telluride, riding the horses hard. They found the campsite that Henry and his men had left. Connor stared at the footprint marks and swore he could identify Jolyn's. With night falling rapidly the men made camp there.

Early the next morning the men were up and gone. It would take them all day just to reach the Grand River at a point where they could cross it. Hawk had taken over as guide now. He had ridden with several men years ago all over this part of the country and knew the terrain well.

"We've got to head up north a bit, Connor," he advised. "I know you don't want to go out of your way, but the Dewey Bridge is going to be the only place to cross the river. It's that or head up into Wyoming or down to Arizona."

Connor nodded his head. "Whatever you say, Hawk."

The men rode their horses hard. The scenery flew by them. An occasional coyote's cry or the flight of a golden eagle broke the constant thud of horse's hoofbeats.

By the end of the second day they were well into Utah and close to the Grand River.

Just as Jolyn was being hauled into the structure that Cassidy had helped build, her three rescuers were crossing the river, hot on the trail.

The sun was strong, the sky a brilliant blue, and the snow was melting rapidly. At first Connor was afraid they would lose the trail, but Hawk had assured them that he knew where they were going.

"This is the Outlaw's Trail, Connor, and like it or not I've had to travel it a few times in my life. There are a few landmarks that make it clear where you're heading, so don't worry. We don't need their footprints. We should be there in two days, three at the most."

The journey to Utah was new to Connor, even though he had traveled quite a bit. The rugged terrain was awe-inspiring. The reds and golds and oranges of the rocks as they jutted up into the sky were in deep contrast to the soft blue-green mountains of Colorado. Here and there jackrabbits and kangaroo rats raced in front of them, and since the men were all good shots with their guns, they ate well.

As they approached Green River, Hawk pushed his steed harder and harder, knowing how close they were. Darkness fell upon them and it was finally Connor who stopped the group for dinner and sleep.

The morning burst upon them bright and clear. Red sandstone glittered in the light and gnarled juniper trees and pinyon pines lay scattered around them. They would make it to Horseshoe Canyon today and they were anxious. Even the horses stomped the ground, rested, fed, and ready to move on.

Massive crimson buttes rose majestically upward alongside slender ochre monoliths while the cold racing rivers sliced the earth's core at the bottom of these canyons. Chris was struck silent by its beauty.

They rode all day and camped that night outside Horseshoe Canyon. After dinner the men discussed their strategy.

"How in hell are we three supposed to go on in and say, 'excuse me, but we'd like Jolyn back'?" Hawk asked.

"I was hoping to sneak in and take her while everyone was sleeping," Connor retorted.

"Hmmmph," grunted Hawk.

The men sat around the small fire, each buried in his own thoughts as a lone coyote sang in the distance.

The morning welcomed them with a light coating of fresh snow on the ground, but nothing would discourage this band of brothers from their mission. Without a word, the men shook off the snow, gathered their meager belongings, checked their horses, and headed out, knowing that by the end of the day their search would be ended—but then what?

A herd of wild horses roamed the countryside, almost as if they were escorting Connor's group. The lead stallion, a dark, deep black-blue, snorted loud and strong, his steamy grunt more of a welcome than a challenge. The wild group followed the men for quite some time before they turned and galloped north.

Hawk was in the lead. He had led them down a switchback trail that dropped deep into the canyons. The threesome had to search for a low point in the river. Fortunately for them it was early winter, and the Green River was low enough for them to cross. Around midday Hawk spied something he was looking for. He spurred his horse on while the other two companions followed. He headed for something sticking up in the ground, a post of some sort. As they all approached it something flapping in the breeze gained their attention. Hawk rode up to the post and gently pulled off the notice. It was a letter. It was addressed to Butch and read:

der butch
codent wait fer ya at the river no more. we got a serprize fer ya.
henry

Hawk let Chris and Connor read it. Then he explained, "These guys have a system. A mail of some type to let them know anything before they get in. Looks like Luke is here all right, and I'll guess the surprise is Jolyn. They said Butch was in jail. Who knows for sure. Anyways, if he isn't here, then it should be easier for us. Let's hope that we don't meet him on the way out."

Tired, cold, and hungry, the men rode their horses even harder. Jolyn was in reach; Luke's outcome would be known soon enough. Brittle bodies pushed thoughts of a warm fire and a good hot meal out of their heads and rode on.

The Roost was a five-mile circular flat. In the northern part of the Roost the grassy plains turned into a labyrinth of canyons. Down below in these walls the outlaws hid. Only a few men really knew the route and Hawk was a bit apprehensive. The Henry Mountains loomed in the distance, and Jolyn was out there somewhere in between.

It was a good ten miles until Hawk suddenly veered the horses into a small cut. Connor and Chris both coughed out snow as the lead horse kicked up the small cold flakes. Carefully they guided their horses down another switchback trail and then finally down a steep embankment.

And then they saw it. There, snuggled against the pale-red rock that emerged high into the cloudless sky, was the campsite. The corral was filled with half a dozen horses and as the sun slipped quietly behind the Henry Mountains the men slid off their horses and let them graze quietly, away from the smell of the other horses.

Connor wasn't sure how many men were inside the small cabin. He heard voices and laughter. This will be a surprise attack at least, he thought.

Then, suddenly, as if fate was watching from somewhere in the canyons nearby, Jolyn appeared. A voice boomed out the door behind her but was indistinguishable.

Connor froze. Jolyn, with a shawl wrapped around her delicate shoulders, was carrying a pail and heading toward a small storage area. Seeing her again he realized all that he almost lost. His heart ached, and his throat burned dry with anguish and despair that he had not let himself feel these past days. He wanted to grab her, to touch her, to smell her sweet scent, and to love her forever, but first, he had better act quickly before he lost her again.

Connor looked at Hawk. Hawk looked at Chris. They would stalk near Jolyn, grab her, and leave. They would be a good half hour's ride before those men realized she had gone.

"But first," Connor whispered, "first, I kill Luke."

"NO!" Hawk shouted softly. "Things didn't work out the way you thought. We have a great opportunity to take Jolyn and go. We can always deal with Luke later."

Connor knew Hawk was right, but he didn't want to give up on Luke yet. Every time I'm near that bastard he manages to escape, he screamed inside his head. But Hawk was right. Ever since he had learned of Luke's murderous acts, Connor had thought of nothing else—until now. Now he realized that saving Jolyn was much more important than killing Luke. He would get to Luke…and soon.

Chris headed over to the corral, sneaked in, and took four fresh horses.

Hawk slithered by the front door of the cabin in case of any disturbance while Connor quietly crouched, waiting for Jolyn to cross his path. Suddenly she screamed. A lone kangaroo rat had jumped in her path. Someone inside heard her scream and stuck his head out the door. Hawk, rifle ready, aimed.

"Anything wrong out there?" a scratchy voice roared.

"Yes…no, it's just an animal. Thanks, Henry."

Jolyn moved on. Connor held his breath. Just a little bit more. Just a few steps. He could see her face bathed in moonlight, her long hair swaying back and forth as she tried not to stumble on the slippery rocks and juniper roots. Her brow was in a knot from concentrating and Connor wanted to gently erase her problems. He had traveled many miles to find his woman and he would never lose her again. In a few seconds he would have her and…

"Jolyn?" a voice thundered from the warm cabin. "Make sure you bring some of that extra whiskey in the back. You hear me, woman?"

That was Luke's voice. Hawk almost stood up and raced in the room himself to kill that murdering son of a… But then, suddenly they heard Jolyn call out, "Do you mind if James comes with me? It's getting too dark out here and I don't like the sound of coyotes out there."

Connor's body froze. James? The James she kept talking about? He was there? Connor turned to Chris and Hawk and explained, "There's another person in there who is a friend of Jolyn's from way back. She lost him the night Luke destroyed her campsite. She was afraid he was dead, but it looks like they kept him at this hideout. I don't know why they did that."

Hawk looked at Chris and Connor and very slowly and deliberately stated, "Those men are plain ruthless. If they didn't kill this young man right off then they may have been using him for, well, I'd rather not say right now. All I can tell you is he's probably pretty traumatized from these men."

Now it was Chris who spoke up. "We can't leave him, then. We have to grab them both. If we only saved Jolyn right now they probably would hurt this kid pretty bad. We have to take him. We don't have a choice. He'll never be able to escape on his own. Between the canyons and the ravines, the kid will die before any coyote even finds him."

Hawk looked at these men with whom he had bonded as close as three men could. "I agree," he said flatly. "You're right, Chris. We don't have a choice. We have to save them both. And if we can kill Luke, so much the better. If not, his time'll come. I promise you that on my mother's grave." Hawk spat on the ground to seal his promise. And the three men, in their convictions, quietly stalked toward Jolyn and James. Hawk crept over to the hideout to wait in case anyone should try to thwart their furtive heist.

Several of the horses neighed and Jolyn and James both stopped to look for where the sound was coming from. She tilted her head. The horses were not in the corral. She grabbed James's hand for protection. Something was happening! And then Connor snatched her in his arms, away from James, while covering her mouth tightly so she couldn't scream.

At that precise moment Chris swooped by with the horses. Connor heaved Jolyn up on one of the horses and quickly mounted right behind her. At the same instant, Chris leaned over and extended his arm toward James who, while somewhat shocked at the action taking place so swiftly, immediately acknowledged he was being saved. He grabbed onto the blessed arm and swung up behind Chris. A sharp whistle toward Hawk from Chris alerted Hawk the mission was complete. Hawk's boots scraped the gravel outside the doorway and suddenly there was a loud, powerful commotion from inside the wooden structure. Hawk turned and had taken two steps from the cabin when the thundering sound of a rifle exploded in the night.

"They shot Hawk!" cried Chris. Quickly Chris smacked his horse with the reins, shouted to James to hold on tight, and, grabbing the one free horse, raced back to save Hawk.

"Head out, Connor, we'll meet you back at the canyon," Chris bellowed over his shoulder. Chris had suddenly taken charge and Connor had no time to argue. Grabbing the reins with one hand and the holding on to Jolyn with the other, Connor yelled, "Heeyaaaaah!" and took off.

Jolyn turned her head and looked at her savior. He had come, just like she said he would. He had come for her and had taken James, too. Hot tears raced down her cheeks. She had been strong. She had held up her end and now she could relax. Connor glimpsed Jolyn and in the light of the stars he saw her tear-streaked face, and his heart melted.

The two raced over the snow-covered ground toward safety.

Chapter 21

Chris heard the gunfire and acted quickly. He untied the corral gate and the remaining horses raced out. Chris, with James seated behind him on top of a great black-and-white stallion, rode over to where he thought Hawk might be hiding, holding on to the reins of another large horse.

"Hawk," he whispered, "Hawk? Where are you?"

"Over here, Chris. In the small tree. Hurry, man, I'm hurt."

Chris could barely discern Hawk's form as he edged quietly toward him. In the distance he could hear the men cursing in their search for Hawk. Chris dismounted, looked up at James, and uttered in a hushed tone, "Look, kid, I don't nothing about you, but right now I gotta trust you with our lives. Hold on to this other horse while I go save my friend, and be quiet! Got that?" James nodded quickly and held tightly to both horses.

Chris got on the ground and crept forward, his stomach scraping the rocks and roots beneath him. He could barely make out the form of a body huddled underneath some skunkbrush. Chris crawled next to the curled-up form and grabbed him.

"I got you, Hawk. Are you hurt bad?" Concern filled Chris's whispered voice.

"I'll be okay. Let's get the hell out of here."

Chris was worried. "Can you ride, Hawk?"

Hawk nodded. "I'll make it. Let's go!"

Chris put his arm around Hawk as he helped him stand. Together they staggered over to the horses. Hawk saw a young man on top of Chris's steed and realized they must have saved James, too. Chris nodded and muttered softly, "Later, man. Later." Chris helped Hawk hoist his body onto the saddle. Hawk moaned as his injured leg pressed painfully against the leather. Chris secretly prayed that the outlaws would not hear them.

Stealthily, Chris guided both his and Hawk's steed around the back end of the corral. Chris could discern Luke's booming voice over the other men, cursing and shouting. If only they would stay over on the other side of the cabin, Chris thought to himself, then we'll make it. It was a dark night and if they were quiet, they could make it. Chris glanced over his shoulder at Hawk. Hawk was in pain. He sat hunched over his saddle and Chris hoped he wouldn't fall off. A dark wet stain was quickly spreading down his thigh. For a second Chris thought he should ride with Hawk, but he was afraid the weight of both men on the horse would be too dangerous.

The dusty ground was hard beneath the horses' hooves. Chris guided both horses as carefully as possible along a narrow path riddled with juniper roots. The animals halted abruptly, unwilling to move on. For a brief moment Chris panicked. Then he took a slow breath and dug his spurs deep into the flanks of his horse, and the animal edged forward. Fortunately for Hawk, his horse followed.

The shouting soon became a small tremble in the night breeze. Chris and Hawk, who was holding on as best he could, were heading east toward the canyon. They were riding free and safe with only the lonely sound of a coyote in the distance to remind them of their danger.

* * *

Jolyn moaned. She was galloping hard with Connor and she was exhausted. Connor gently pulled her back so she could lean on him. The woman had been kidnapped and on the road for almost a week and now he had kidnapped her back. Jolyn had lost her shawl in the shuffling and he knew she was cold.

Jolyn tilted her head as she gave a quick glance behind her. Connor's squared-off chin seemed to embrace the cold and any other enemies who would dare step in front of his path. He had come. Just like she'd known he would. She'd dreamed of this moment when he would rescue her from that evil monster. Thank God Butch Cassidy and his men had not met Luke and the other men at the river. What would they have done then? She didn't know. She only knew that she was the coldest she had ever been in her life, but she would not let Connor know. He had come all this way for her and she would not let anything stop the rescue. And James! She wanted to tell Connor everything that James had suffered. And she would when they were settled. She would have James tell his story of being kidnapped, hurt, and threatened with his life. It was almost too much to believe that she had found James and now Connor was taking her home. Home! What home? Where did she belong? Jolyn shook her head as if to stop herself from thinking. Not now, she mused, there will be a time. Or so she prayed.

The two seemed to ride on forever in the moonlight. Finally Connor slowed the horses to an easy trot as if he were searching for some familiar sign.

"Connor?" Jolyn shivered. "Is there something in that saddlebag I can put on?"

Expertly Connor halted his horse. He slid off his saddle and unbuttoned his flannel-lined denim jacket.

"Oh, no, I don't want your jacket," Jolyn argued.

"Jo, put it on." It was a command, not a request. Jolyn took the jacket and slipped it on.

"Thank you, Connor," Jolyn said gratefully.

Connor gazed up at Jolyn. She was still shivering even with his warm coat. He looked back over his shoulder, expectantly. He thought for a moment and then he made his decision.

"Jo." Connor reached his arms upward. "Come on down. We can walk from here. Besides, I think the walking might warm you up a bit."

Jolyn leaned over and relinquished the reins from his horse as Connor's two large hands gripped her securely about the waist. He pulled her down and she almost stumbled on the ground. Quickly Connor circled his arms around her, steadying her.

Jolyn stared into his soft, gentle eyes.

"What's wrong, Connor?"

Connor hesitated. He loosened his grip on Jolyn and turned around and seized the reins of his horse. With his other hand he tenderly pulled Jolyn close to him, keeping her warm with his body as they carefully hiked over the canyon floor.

Jolyn knew Connor was troubled. She would give him the opportunity to talk when he was ready. As for now, she enjoyed their close contact and his warmth. They were heading toward a large rock wall. As they got closer and closer, Jolyn saw a small opening in the rocky facade.

Connor dropped his arm from Jolyn's shoulder and reached for her hand.

"It's a mite tricky here," he explained as they began climbing up a small hill. "Hawk told me about this place near the San Rafael River. I thought we could hide out here for the night without Luke and those men finding us."

Connor tied the horse to a tall Fremont cottonwood near the opening of the overhang. He had wanted to hide out in the canyons but that would have been too treacherous with the horse at night.

Connor gathered some wood quickly and in a few minutes he had a fire blazing. He sat down next to Jolyn, who was warming her hands in the glowing flames. Her cheeks were flushed and the reflection of the rising sparks flickered in her tired eyes. She sighed and tilted her head toward Connor.

"Jolyn, I—I'm sorry you had to go through all of this. I never wanted you to leave me. I never wanted you to go back to Alamosa. Ever."

Jolyn's shoulders shuddered as if the weight of many things had finally fallen off.

She looked at Connor, her strong blue eyes piercingly searching for answers. "Then why do you make me doubt you? Doubt your feelings for me? Why do you always make me feel like I'm in the way of something else more important?"

Connor took a deep breath. This wasn't easy for him, but he owed it to Jolyn. She deserved to know the whole story. "Jo, all my life I had dreams. Big dreams. I saw myself owning a dozen stores, working side by side with my father. There was no room for a wife and a family. Or so I thought.

"Then my dream was shattered. My own brother. Yeah, I know he was my half-brother. But there were times I felt like we treated each other as true brothers. Maybe I was just dreaming that because I wanted it so bad. I always forgave him for the things he did to me. Somewhere along the road Luke drifted to the wrong side. I don't know why, and I guess I never will. He's hated me for a long time. I know that now. I don't know if he thought he was always second best to me or if maybe my father didn't show him equal love. Maybe he thought he should have been in charge of the stores because he was older. I don't know. Eventually I thought we would just go our separate ways and that would be the end of it. I never thought I would have to deal with him again.

"I was wrong. For some crazy reason he decided to shatter my dream into a million pieces. Not only did he kill your uncle and your brother and my father, but he killed my hopes along with the dream. I couldn't do it alone. Not even with Hawk at my side helping me all the time."

Connor lowered his eyes and leaned his head on his hands. He sighed as if he could not continue. Jolyn waited. She would not interfere now.

Connor cleared his throat and his feelings finally spilled out. "And then there was you. Dear Lord, I fell in love with you the minute I saw you out there on the ledge. Lying there, huddled and cold and lifeless. I wanted to bundle you up and save you from whatever disaster had happened to you. But I said to myself that you didn't fit in with my plans. There was no room for you. I didn't have time for you. Not then.

I had it all figured out, but now, there you were, and I was confused. I thought I would just drop you off with Hawk, who would know what to do. He would help you and I could continue with my pursuit of Luke. Most importantly, I had sworn I would get even with Luke. I swore to Annabel and the spirit of my father that Luke would pay for what he had done.

"And then," Connor whispered tenderly, "there was the night under the stars with you." Jolyn listened with all her heart, but she would not look at Connor. She stared blankly at the fire, her eyes filled with burning tears that dropped one by one on the earthen floor.

"I even remember when I thought you were Luke coming in the cabin," Connor continued. "I wanted you then. I always wanted you. But I was afraid. Afraid that if I gave in to my emotions I would forget my purpose. I could never let myself forget that mission. It hurt me more than I ever knew possible. I didn't know walking away from you could make my chest hurt so much."

Jolyn sniffed back tears. She had never forgotten the cabin. The memories scorched her, and she pulled her knees up close to her chin, hugging them for comfort.

Finally Jolyn held her head up to Connor and murmured, "But you let me go to Alamosa. You were willing to let me walk out of your life. Why?"

Connor shrugged. "I... You walked out of the store. I was too embarrassed to follow you. I was too prideful to come after you. I figured that if you loved me you would come back anyway."

"You figured! You figured! Connor Richardson! You figure too much! That's your real problem. After all, it was you who dumped me in Alamosa and said good luck honey and I hope you do well and so long. What was I supposed to think? The man I was falling in love with, or I thought I was falling in love with, had just said see you later like who knows when? What was I supposed to do?"

Jolyn let her tired body sag. She looked up at Connor. "Oh, Connor," Jolyn sighed adoringly. "I know now that I loved you the second I saw you. There I was enclosed in grief—my parents, James, the miners—and then those horrid men. My whole life blown up in front of me, and who walks into my life but you! Yes, I loved you.

"And, yes, I had dreams, too. I saw myself married to a man I could look up to. A man who treated me as his equal. We would own a house with a farm and we would raise our children together. But after my parents died, I didn't know what to do or where to go. James was guiding me to Creede when Luke and his motley gang of thugs raided our camp. And James"—Jolyn hiccupped as she caught her breath to stop from bursting into tears—"I thought for sure Luke had killed him, but I couldn't find him, just his jacket. Where was he? Had they kidnapped him? Why him? What would they want with James? He was barely a man. Would they hurt him? Use him for something? I didn't know. I was stricken with heartache. My whole life was falling apart in front of me and I wasn't sure what would happen to me."

Connor stood up, walked to the back of the shelter, and grabbed more wood. He put a few of the large pieces on the fire. He sat down beside Jolyn. He wrapped his arms around her and pulled her against his warmth.

"So there we were," he soothed, "each of us surrounded with our own problems. And then it was too late. When I heard you had been kidnapped I went crazy. It was then that I realized it, Jolyn."

Jolyn gazed up at him, snug in his arms. "Realized what, Connor?"

"That you meant everything to me. More than the death of Luke, more than any store, more than my whole life, because if you weren't a part of my life, well, then it just wasn't worth living."

Jolyn's tears flowed freely. Small, burning droplets fell softly onto Connor's hands. He held her face in his hands and turned her head toward his.

"Jolyn Montgomery, I never want to leave you again. Do you hear me? Do you understand me? Do you believe me?"

Jolyn inhaled, wiped her running nose, and cried, "Yes, my love."

For the first time in a long while Connor surrendered all control of his feelings. He gently laid Jolyn on the ground on top of the blanket. His hot lips caressed her flushed face and traveled the length of her smooth cheeks, leaving a searing trace wherever he kissed her. He descended to the soft curve of her throat, nuzzling her hungrily while Jolyn moaned softly. Lovingly he tugged at her thick, rich hair, spreading it over the blanket and tying his fingers in the long auburn tresses. A faint scent of lavender still clung to her body and Connor breathed it in deeply.

Jolyn responded to his every touch while he slowly, languidly disrobed her. Her skin, her breasts, tingled beneath his pressing body. Her nipples grew taut, hard with desire. Connor buried his face in her breasts, tenderly massaging them. He slipped a hardened nipple in his burning mouth and tasted her sweetness.

Jolyn's long graceful fingers traced his back, kneading his hard muscles, pulling him closer to her as she tugged at his shirt. She arched her back wantonly. His musky odor excited her, and she leaned her head against the top of his.

Connor was caressing and fondling her everywhere, memorizing every detail of her body. His hands traced up her legs and he gently parted her soft, satiny thighs, searching. Warm fingers found her cushioned mound and he touched her silky womanhood. It blazed with desire and throbbed from his touch.

Jolyn gasped and writhed with pleasure. She reached for his pants and unbuckled them. She reached for Connor's swollen manhood. Lovingly, she placed her delicate hands on his throbbing tumescence and massaged the ever-growing velvety life in her hands. Still lying side by side, she pressed his hardness against her satiny thighs and Connor groaned. He buried his hands in her hair and murmured, "Oh, my love, my Jo."

Suddenly the heavy sound of several hoofbeats split the night air. Jolyn sat up quickly and covered herself. Fear spread through her body. "No!" she hissed. "They couldn't have found us! Please, dear God!"

Connor jumped up, hiking his pants on as he ran to the opening of the cave. He reached for his gun, steadied it, and started to cock the trigger.

"We made it!" screamed Chris. "We're here, Connor!"

"Jesus Christ!" shouted Connor. "At least give a man a warning signal. I almost blew your God damn head off!"

Chris was too busy smiling to realize he'd almost lost his life. He stood there grinning like a small kid who'd just won a race. He surmised what was happening between his sister and Connor and he wanted to yell out with joy for them. James, still on the horse, was staring with his eyes wide open at Connor.

Connor looked past Chris and James. "Where's Hawk?" he demanded seriously, already forgetting his promises of love. "Is he okay?"

Just then Hawk's horse trotted in with Hawk barely sitting up. Chris ran over to help him dismount. Once Hawk was off his horse, he stubbornly refused more aid as he ignored Chris's help and stumbled into the cave. He did not know how much blood he had lost. He took a few more steps, staggered, and then crumpled to the floor.

"Oh my God, he's been shot!" screamed Jolyn.

"Leave me be," cried Hawk. "I can get up by myself. Good God, don't you dare lift me like that!"

It was too late. Chris and Connor had both hoisted up the rather large, hulking shape and carried him over to the blanket near the fire. They laid him down carefully, afraid to injure him anymore.

Quietly, without anyone asking, James took the reins of the two steeds and walked them over to where Connor's horse was tethered. He left the three animals munching on some much-needed feed. James sauntered to the fire where Hawk was stretched out, squatted down, and sucked in his breath as he saw the extent of Hawk's injury. With his eyes cast furtively downward, he spied Jolyn hurriedly redressing herself. He surmised what must have just happened with her and Connor and hoped for Jolyn's sake that this interlude gratified her. She deserved to be happy. For an aching moment he thought of Nattie and his plans to settle down with her in Utah on the farm. How ironic that he was so close to being with his Nattie and yet so far from being able to escape to her. The canyons and the coyotes were always surrounding him and without a weapon or a horse for safety he'd known he had no choice but to stay with those outlaws. They were going to use him in their next heist and he feared he would have been shot, but truthfully, after being holed up for so long at Robber's Roost he was apprehensive about seeing Nattie again. What would she think about him when he told her what the men wanted him to do? Or the suffering they had imposed upon him? Or the fact that maybe he hadn't been brave enough to escape to be with her? He brushed those thoughts aside as he saw Jolyn commence her doctoring with Hawk.

Jolyn was immediately at Hawk's side. She saw the crusted blood on his pant legs and quickly launched into action by first tearing his pants.

"How bad is the pain, Hawk?" Jolyn asked tenderly. Her eyes softened as she looked upon this man. He was her father and her brother all rolled into one.

Hawk, delirious from the pain and almost losing consciousness, smiled weakly at her. "Jo," he whispered. "Oh, Jo, it fucking hurts! Don't tell Lucinda I said that!"

Jolyn gave him a quick grin, expertly ripped a strip of her undergarments, and soaked it in some of the water from Connor's canteen. Gently, skillfully, she cleansed the wound even though her soft pressure had reopened the dried clot, causing more blood to flow.

She looked straight into Hawk's eyes, which were squinting from the pain. "Hawk, explain to me exactly what happened. Can you recall it for me?"

Hawk closed his eyes and tried to remember.

"I was waiting at the entrance to the hideout. Chris was to give me the signal." He stuttered slowly from the pain. "And then I heard a scream."

"Go on, Hawk," Jolyn urged, "that was me you heard screaming when an animal jumped in front of me."

"Well, then I reckon someone on the inside heard your scream and came running out, gun in tow. He musta heard me move in the bushes and shot blindly out the doorway. Then he raced inside to get the others. I took off and ran around alongside the canyon wall and hid under some bushes. I was jest about to pass out from the pain when good ole Chris come a trotting by with the horses and off we flew."

It was Chris's turn now. "Yes, Jo. Except it wasn't Luke who came out the door, though. Some other guy, kinda stocky in shape with black hair and a beard."

"That would have been Henry," Jolyn said softly.

Chris continued, "And then as soon as that guy, Henry you say, as soon as he turned around I grabbed Hawk and we made for the cave just like you said to Connor."

As the men were talking, Jolyn was busy working. Crouching on her haunches, Jolyn was totally absorbed in her task and completely blocked out everyone else around her. Taking the small bag she kept wrapped around her waist, she untied the leather pouch and selected a few special herbs that helped to coagulate the blood to prevent infections.

Jolyn ripped another section of her slip and tore it into several strips.

"I'm going to need fresh water," Jolyn declared. "Go out to the river and bring me as much as you can."

Connor nodded. "I'll see if there is a small creek nearby. James," he added, "why don't you come with me and we can talk some." Jolyn leaned over Hawk, who was now slipping in and out of consciousness, and carefully picked more debris from around his wound.

Chris watched his sister quietly as he sat next to the fire. He had shared many things with her in the past, but not until tonight had he felt a closeness like he felt now. He spoke softly, for her ears only.

"You know, sis, when you're treating Hawk like Mama used to do for people, well, in the firelight and all, you look just like her."

Jolyn lifted her head. Soft blue eyes looked lovingly into Chris's gentle hazel eyes and she smiled. "Thanks, Chris."

Just then Connor and James returned with their mission accomplished.

Jolyn's and Connor's eyes locked for a brief moment. Then he asked, "How is he, Jo? Is it bad?"

"No," replied Jolyn, "he really is lucky. The bullet passed right through the fleshy part of his thigh. All I have to do is clean him up, apply a small poultice, and he'll be fine. He just needs to rest a bit."

"Well," said Connor, "that is good news, because we are going to be out of here before the first ray of sunlight creeps up behind this hideout."

Chris and James followed Connor's lead and headed over to the corner to join him. All three men were asleep within a few minutes.

The night crawled along, the cry of a lone coyote in the distance Jolyn's only company as she kept her all-night vigil with Hawk. Right before dawn his fever broke and only then did she allow herself the pleasure of rest.

But it wasn't to last for very long. Connor was up shortly after that and quickly woke Chris. The two men made preparations for the ride and James helped in whatever chores needed doing. They woke Hawk up carefully. He seemed rested and in good spirits, if not a little sore. The last thing they did was wake Jolyn, hoping to give her as much rest as their time would allow.

"Come on now, Jo, we've got to go." Connor prodded her gently. "They'll be on our tails soon as sun's up. Come on." He gave up and, hoisting her over his shoulders, carried her to his horse.

"Chris, Jolyn can ride with me. I'll let her sleep as we ride. James, you ride with Hawk to make sure he is okay."

The day was crystal clear and the five weary travelers, with one sound asleep, rode their horses out of Robber's Roost, they hoped for the last time. The riding was relaxed; the land was one large flat rolling pasture and so far there was no sign of the men following them. Mule deer grazed silently, and rabbits were everywhere.

Jolyn woke up before midday, embarrassed at having slept so long. The men teased her unmercifully, for the group was in good spirits. They rode all day, not stopping for a break at all until near sunset. They wanted to put as many miles behind them as they could before they would rest.

As evening approached the group reached the Grand River. They followed it northeast toward Colorado. Connor pushed his group to keep riding. An hour or two later Connor was ready to stop. "All right, group, what do you say we stop here for the night? I don't think Luke's group of bandits followed us out here at all. But in case they did, I say we don't head back to Creede the same way we left it."

Hawk, having regained quite a bit of his strength, piped in, "Well, which way do you suggest, Connor?"

"Hmm. Hawk, remember the time when we had a bad shipment of wood from that wiry old man in Grand Junction? He tried to stiff us with that rotten batch?"

"Yes, I do. And you and I both went up there to give him back every piece of his shipment till he begged us to take a new load, free of charge."

"Yep, that's the one. Well, we made it up to Grand Junction in the middle of winter with a bit of snow on the ground then, too. Well sir, I was thinking…instead of going south by Moab, let's keep heading up north past the Grand and right into Colorado all the way to Grand Junction. There is no way that Luke would ever think we headed up that far. What do you say, Hawk?"

"I say let's do it, Connor. Providing one thing."

"What's that, Hawk?"

"That tonight you let Jolyn do the cooking. I seen a whole lot of rabbits today and I'm a hankering for one over a spit fire. I say, you boys see what you can do about shooting a couple? I sure am looking for some good grub to ease my pain a bit. Hahaha."

Connor laughed. It was good to see Hawk back to his old self, enjoying their time together. It was cold out, they were all hungry, but they were together. They were on their way home, albeit by a somewhat circuitous route.

The next few days brought them closer and closer to Grand Junction and farther and farther away from Jolyn's nightmare. Finally, the Grand River meandered back into Colorado and the five companions cheered and clapped as they stood on genuine Colorado soil.

"Grand Junction," shouted Connor, "here we come!"

"I give it a whoop whoop!" they agreed in unison.

Chapter 22

JUST OUTSIDE OF GRAND JUNCTION, nestled in the mountains, next to some prehistoric Indian ruins, stood an old white church. Connor steered his horse to the church as the group followed along silently. Connor dismounted his horse and asked Chris to join him. The two men stepped inside the white wooden structure.

After a few moments Connor and Chris returned. Connor looked up at Jolyn and said, "Excuse me, Jolyn, could I speak with you?"

Jolyn was confused. She did not know what to say. Chris and James just looked over at her and both shrugged their shoulders in unison. Hawk was nonplussed and just stared.

"Yes, Connor. Is anything wrong?" Perhaps he wanted to pray over her, she thought, and followed him in the building.

Inside, the stained glass and tiles reflected the Ute culture. Connor guided Jolyn down the aisle, turned to her, and dropped down onto one knee. "Jolyn Montgomery, would you do me the honor of marrying me and becoming my wife?"

Jolyn gazed down at the man she had loved for so long. She did not hesitate. "Oh, yes, oh, yes, Connor, I will!"

Connor rose slowly. He tenderly pulled her into his arms and as they embraced, the church bells rang out in glorious song. Connor and Jolyn looked at each other and smiled, and hand in hand walked out into the bright sunlight.

The other men were waiting outside, patiently. Chris had shared with them that once inside the church Connor had asked Chris for permission to marry Jolyn. And now, as the happy couple exited the church doors, and seeing Connor's wide grin and goofy expression on his face, the men knew something tremendous was about to transpire. They threw their hats up into the air, jumped off their horses and whooped in jubilation for Connor and Jolyn. Everybody was hugging until Connor finally stopped and said, "Hey, I think we'd better get back in the church. There just might be someone in there waiting for us."

The five close companions entered the church solemnly. Jolyn dropped to one knee and said a prayer. Both Connor and Chris were at her side to help her up. Connor looked over at Hawk and Chris as the three of them nodded in tacit agreement. James felt a bit left out until Connor grabbed him by his bicep and pulled him in with the group. James smiled at all of them, feeling a camaraderie he had not felt in a long time. The men, as if this had been rehearsed, shuffled around until Chris stood next to Jolyn while Connor, Hawk, and James waited patiently in front.

An elderly preacher was waiting good-naturedly for the group to march forward. With one crooked arm the aged preacher beckoned them. Connor, with James and Hawk supporting him on each side, proceeded down the aisle. Chris, his arm holding tightly to Jolyn's, walked his sister proudly to where Connor now stood, tall and handsome. The preacher, with cracked lips and a severely wrinkled face, smiled warmly at this odd group and commenced the ceremony.

Jolyn and Connor faced one another. The preacher spoke softly as the bride and groom held hands and loved each other with their eyes. As they were pronounced man and wife, Connor placed his hand under Jolyn's chin and lifted her tear-stained face. His other hand tenderly wiped away the warm liquid as he vowed to his new wife, "I love you, Jolyn Montgomery, and together we will conquer all."

Jolyn, her face flushed with tears and happiness, gazed up into silver pools that brimmed with adoration and warmth. "And I love you, Connor Richardson. And together we shall fulfill our dreams."

The next morning the five left the towering monoliths and rugged rock formations of Grand Junction and headed south to home. A soft snow was falling rapidly but this time the weather did not bother the group. While in town, they had stocked up on supplies, proper clothing, and extra supplies in the event that their journey was delayed.

The snow crunched under the horses' shoes. Every now and then a fleet of pronghorns would race by them as if laughing at the strange creatures on horses. James proved very handy with a shotgun, and he shot several wild grouse during the day, which resulted in a delicious dinner. By midday the light snow had stopped, and the group rested. Jolyn cooked the best wild grouse they had ever eaten. Leaning back on an old tree stump the five basked in the glow of full stomachs and happy hearts. A sudden crashing in the nearby trees brought out an old elk on the run and white-tailed deer scampered by the cold bubbling creek.

Hawk was the first to break the silence.

"Sometimes I just wish it could always be like this," he sighed.

"Well, now, don't that beat all," piped in Chris. "That's not the life you been telling me about, you old washed-out dog."

"I agree," laughed Connor, "just give me a pipe and a good fire and a hot woman and I'll think heaven is at my doorstep! Now isn't that what you always told me was your creed?"

Jolyn giggled, and Hawk winked at her.

"You know, Jo, it's all a lie. These men here are just a wee bit jealous because I'm still a single man."

"Excuse me," interrupted Jolyn, "but by the looks of someone's condition I know back home, well, it would seem only fitting and proper, Mr. Hawk, sir, that a wedding is in order, and soon!"

Hawk blushed and muttered, "Well, mebbe that does seem to be the right thing to do. You know, I certainly have learned a few things on this trip. I wasn't really sure if I wanted to marry Lucinda and settle down. I guess I had some growing up to do myself." Hawk looked directly at Jolyn and she smiled.

"Yes, my friend," agreed Jolyn, "I think we have all grown some."

Hawk smacked his hands. "By God, I'll do it. I'll do it, I say! That is, if all of you would be there to help me go through with it."

Connor smiled, his gray eyes twinkling in the waning sun. "You bet, old boy. We wouldn't miss this for the world!"

James cleared his throat as if he had something to say. Everyone turned to him and waited.

"You know," he began slowly, "I wouldn't be here with all of you right now if you hadn't come and saved me, too. I'm mighty grateful to all of you. I guess I haven't had the opportunity to officially thank each of you, but I do thank you!"

Connor studied the young man whom Jolyn had spoken of so dearly and with such grief these past few months. He grabbed a stick from the pile of firewood and brushed some dry tumbleweed around while thinking before he uttered, "James, we are very proud to have saved you from those thieving murderers. Jolyn has been inconsolable this whole time praying that you weren't killed by those sick bastards. We are just happy as a pig in the mud that you are with us. I noticed you've been a mite quiet since we left Grand Junction and, well, we are all just sitting here talking, and I was thinking mebbe you want to tell us what happened to you since the night you were kidnapped."

James dropped his chin on his chest, took a deep breath, and swallowed hard. He forced his shoulders back, lifted his head, and looked at everyone slowly, as if memorizing their faces. "I've wanted to tell you," he stuttered, his throat tightening as he tried to continue, "but I am very ashamed at myself."

Jolyn gasped. "Why, James? Why would you be ashamed for being held prisoner?"

James was shaking, but he forced himself to continue. "That night when Luke and his men came into our campsite, we were overpowered by them. I thought Luke was trying to hurt…" James took another deep breath. "I knew Luke was getting ready to rape Jolyn. I knew I couldn't stop him. I—I ran. I ran until two of the men, Slim was one, grabbed me from behind and hit me on the head with the butt of their rifle. That's the last thing I remember until the next day when I come to slung over a horse.

"Luke was cursing and holding a bandage over his bleeding face. I didn't know till much later that Jolyn had cut him and run away. I was confused as to why they didn't kill me, but I overheard the men talking about how they were going to use me in their robberies. They had some plan but first they had to go to their hideout for a while. It took a few days to get there. I didn't realize I was in Utah. So close to my girl, Nattie. So close." James held back a sob.

James picked up his canteen and took a long swallow. Holding on to the canteen as security, he muttered, "They hardly gave me food or drink and if I said anything, they beat me with sticks or just kicked me to shut me up. When we got to the hideout there was nobody there except one old man. They dumped me in the back of the shack and threatened to kill me if I tried to escape. They had big plans for me and I better not mess with them. A few of the men tried to hurt me real bad, but the old man threatened them. I'm not sure who he was, but they obeyed him and left me alone for the most part. Luke took Slim and they headed to Creede. Luke said he was looking for someone there and would maybe pick up a few more men for his next heist. I was told I would go into the bank in Denver and demand they turn over all the money. Luke and his men would be outside waiting and if I got shot doing it, well, they were going to shoot me if I didn't.

"I tried to escape a few times, but the coyotes got real close and I fell into a ravine one night and almost broke my ankle. So I stayed put. I figured I was going to die from the lawmen in the bank or from Luke. Either way I was a dead man. I was never going to see my Nattie and marry her." At this point, James, exhausted and spent with his story, closed his eyes as if to shut out the world.

Jolyn got up and went over to James and pulled him into her arms. James could not be strong any longer. He had released the shameful past, his body shaking from tears and humiliation.

"Shhhh," consoled Jolyn. "We are all here with you, James. What happened to you was not your fault. You're with us now. Let's get to Alamosa where you can rest your body, get some strength, and then we will help you get to Nattie." She looked at the group watching this interaction unfold. "Isn't that right, men? We will help James find his beloved, so he can start his life anew!"

In unison, the three men uttered cries of agreement.

Connor spoke first. "You know, James, you can stay with us in Alamosa or Creede for as long as you like. We'd be glad to set you up in the trading post 'cause we could use another hand. You could bring your girl Nattie with you and the two of you could start building roots there."

James wiped his eyes with his sleeve and said gratefully, "I can't thank you enough, Connor. All of you. I will send word to Nattie when we can. I was supposed to work on the farm with her and her daddy, but I'm not so sure of those plans anymore. I'm mighty beholden to you. And I thank you."

"And now," concluded Connor, "let's get some shut-eye and hope the snow has ended for a while. We still have some traveling to do tomorrow!"

Jolyn walked over to Connor, snuggled down next to him, and smiled. She loved leaning against him and inhaling his masculine scent laced with sweat, leather, and animal.

"The first thing I want to do when we get back home, husband, is to give you the best scrubbing of your life!"

"Only on one condition, wife," Connor countered, "and that is you will be in the tub with me!"

His deep, hearty laugh echoed through the small valley and Jolyn clung to him, whispering, "I love you, Connor Richardson."

"So," he whispered in her ear, "it's love you're wanting from me now, is it? Before it was save me and free me from those animals and now it's love me. Argh, my lady, you are too much for one man to handle."

Jolyn giggled. "It's a good thing for you we are on the trail surrounded by three of the nosiest men I know, else I'd teach you a thing or two, sir."

Connor might have been in close proximity with his male friends, but being pressed against Jolyn under the blankets out under the stars was too much for any healthy man. He quietly pulled Jolyn even closer, spreading her thighs with his hands.

"It's time, my love. I cannot wait for a proper celebration or a more private chamber. I need you, my Jo."

Jolyn, surprised her teasing had aroused her husband so quickly, was embarrassed.

"Shhh, Connor, they'll hear us."

"No, they won't." But then Connor glanced over to where Hawk, Chris, and James were busy snoring. Connor stood up and pulled Jolyn up with him. "Come on."

Carrying a couple of blankets, Jolyn and Connor quietly slipped away from camp. They headed toward a small creek that was hidden behind a thick group of golden aspens. They laid one blanket down and quickly snuggled together under the other one for warmth.

Beneath the quivering aspens, the two touched and explored each other. Their bodies were sore and tired from so much riding, but the gentle massaging and caressing soothed their exhausted forms.

Jolyn quivered and Connor was concerned. "Are you still cold, my wife?"

Smiling, Jolyn shook her head. "No, my husband. It is just that your touch sends ripples of delicious chills down my back."

"Well," responded Connor, "let me see if I can remedy the problem." And with that he turned Jolyn onto her back and covered her body with his.

With a warm kiss Connor sealed their marriage vows once again as he entered his wife. Jolyn's eyes opened wide as she felt his blazing penetration. Her breasts were crushed against his soft downy chest as his hands tenderly kneaded her buttocks, pulling her in closer and closer.

In the distance the steady hum of Cottonwood Creek's icy water raced over ancient rocks as the two lovers undulated under the clearing skies. Connor's kisses left torrid burning marks on Jolyn's silky skin. Every time his lips moved to blaze a new trail, a rush of cold night air slipped in under the blankets and with frigid fingers chilled her scorching body.

The ground below them seemed to melt away under their lovemaking. Connor squeezed her harder and harder and yet she could not get enough. Sparks of torrid liquid poured through her veins and her mouth fell open, breathing deeply. Her hands traveled over his body, leaving nothing untouched.

A mountain wolf bayed in the distance, but the two never heard anything except their own thundering heartbeats. Connor bent down, his burning tongue devouring Jolyn's ripe nipples, breathing in her female essence, savoring her salty skin now perspiring with desire. Jolyn arched her back, pulling Connor deeper and deeper within her. Jolyn's creamy white throat strained as she extended her head backward and stared up into the black sky.

Connor's hips moved faster and faster and Jolyn matched his every move. Their bodies were meshed as one and swayed rhythmically.

"Jolyn, I love you," Connor said breathlessly, but Jolyn was unable to answer, as at that precise moment the two lovers reached their peak of fiery passion and soared. Spent, they collapsed, and, still united, closed their eyes and rested.

Later they crept back to their campsite, and by the sound of the snoring realized nobody had ever missed them.

The next day Jolyn rose, her cheeks redder than the canyons they had left, her lips swollen and bruised. She limped a bit at first until Chris laughed so hard she threw a pot at him. Connor jokingly punched him in the shoulder and the jubilant group set off again.

The majestic snow-covered mountains to the west fed the many rivers that they passed on their way. Later that day they traveled through the Ute Indian area and were grateful no one stopped them. The Uncompahgre mountain ranges were ahead to the east and that meant they were getting close to Creede, which was beyond that mountain range in the San Juans. The group hoped to reach Ouray before nightfall.

Just outside of Ouray, a traveler crossed their path and, after sharing some small talk, the group was told a bunch of outlaws had ridden through Ouray that morning.

"It can't be," said Hawk after the wanderer had left, "there's no way Luke could have beaten us over here."

"I'm not taking any chances this time," claimed Connor. "I want Luke, but when I'm ready for him, not when he's ready for me. Let's camp near here for tonight and tomorrow we'll pass by Ouray and make it safely to Creede."

The horses neighed softly as the weary travelers picked their way through the towering pines at the foot of Uncompahgre Peak. Protected on the north side by the sheer cliff of this peak, the men set up camp and Jolyn set off to find water.

This time their nighttime activity was uneventful, as both were too exhausted and too wary about intruders to relax in a nuptial interlude. The evening rotated into night and night crept slowly into dawn. Waking, the bone-weary bunch was grateful for no surprise visitors, and with only the steam from their noses for conversation, they headed on the last leg of their journey.

There was no fanfare for the fatigued five as they crept into Creede in the darkness of night. As usual, Kirmeavy's was lit up, as was Ford's and several of the other saloons. Creede Avenue was quiet and still, as if the looming mountains kept a hush over the boomtown.

They headed straight over to Hoover's Livery. They felt bad that they had to wake the young boy who was apprenticed there, but they had no choice. Finally they could head home. Each of the party was deep in thoughts and mumbled their goodnights to each other as they separated. Hawk slung his arm around James. "You're coming with me, son. You stay with me here tonight and we'll figure out what you want to do tomorrow. For now, a good night's rest in a real bed is in order!"

For a second Jolyn was confused and didn't know where she was going until Connor grabbed her gently.

"Jolyn, remember, honey, you're with me."

Jolyn tried as hard as she could to smile. Her lips seemed to move, but nothing happened.

"Okay, pardner, take it easy," said Connor as he bent down and lifted Jolyn in his arms. "You've had quite a busy two weeks, wife, and I'm sorry, but I can't promise you I can keep up this kind of lifestyle."

Jolyn lifted her shoulders as if she was trying to answer him, but only succeeded in dropping her head onto his shoulders and closing her eyes.

"So this is what evenings at home are going to be like," he teased, trying to spark his wife. "Well, thank goodness there's always Kirmeavy's Saloon or I'd be a lonely man."

Jolyn managed to whisper in his ear, "I'll get you for that one, Connor Richardson, but it'll have to wait until…" and then Jolyn slipped into a long-awaited deep sleep.

Early the next morning Connor left Jolyn still sleeping in bed and crept out in search of the sheriff. He found him slumped over his desk with a bottle of whiskey nestled in his short, chubby fingers.

Connor was not a patient man and he kicked the desk three times with his boots before the sheriff stirred.

"Sheriff. Sheriff. God damn it, John, wake up!" shouted Connor. He had many things to do today and he did not like wasting his time.

"Hmmm. What? What? What's going on here? Who got out last night? Who got killed? Confound it, tell me!"

"John, it's only me, Connor Richardson. I'm back."

"Back? Where the hell did you go, God damn it? We waited nearly an hour for you before we just took off. Where in blazes did you go?"

"We got a tip that Jolyn might be out in Robber's Roost with Luke and his new gang. We followed them there, captured her and her missing friend James, and came home. Rode in late last night. Just wanted to tell you."

Even in his very heavy Texas drawl John was quite irritated. "Well, thanks for nothing. Nobody tells me a darn blasted thing around here. Where did you get a tip? Who told you?"

"I'm sorry," Connor explained, "I can't tell you who told me, but one thing, Sheriff, we didn't get Luke. He was there all right, with the new gang he's been hanging out with, but the odds were against us, so we just took Jolyn and James and got the hell out of there."

"Robber's Roost, you say? Now, why would they head all the way over to them parts?"

"Probably because they gambled that we would go south. I'm sorry I couldn't tell you."

"It's no problem, Richardson. Besides, while we were there we did find Claymon Lewis, who we'd been hunting on and off for some time now. Got him locked up in the cell right now or else I'd be home sleeping in my own bed."

"Sheriff, I do want you to know, I'm still looking for Luke, so if you hear anything, anything at all, well, I sure would appreciate you keeping me informed."

"Uh-huh, sure, fine."

"Later, John." And Connor left. He had many errands to complete this morning and he wanted to make sure he got to them all.

His next stop was Kirmeavy's. The saloon had a sour smell to it early in the morning. It was funny how you never noticed it at night, especially after a few beers.

The place was deserted. A few stragglers had crashed on the floor and were still sleeping off their night's drinking. The bartender was nowhere in sight. Connor, knowing the place well, raced up the stairs two at a time. Once upstairs, he walked slowly down the hall, seeing it as if for the first time. The cheap red wallpaper with the tacky flowers and trees on it, the dusty gas lamps on the wall and the thin ragged carpeting beneath him. When had he changed? When did he suddenly see things so differently?

Room number 54. He knocked softly. A voice from inside mumbled and a hard thud banged on the floor. A quick conversation was exchanged, and he heard someone's heavy boots run to the other side of the bedroom.

A soft patter of stockinged feet approached the door. A low, nasally voice called out, "Who's there?"

Connor answered in a monotone. "It's me, Emmaline. Connor."

"Ohhh, just a minute, Connor, sweetie. I'll be right with you, honey." Again a quick pounding of boots on the floor and then another door was opened and slammed shut. Must be the side door, he smiled to himself. These ladies always kept an escape route. One never knew who might be coming to get someone.

Emmaline opened the door hesitantly. The stench of beer and cheap perfume rushed out, leaving Connor gagging for air.

"Can we talk?" Connor gasped.

"Why, sure, sugar, come right on in. Ain't nobody here but you and me and you do look like you might need me for a quick pick-me-up."

Connor's stomach turned sour and he sucked in a few more short breaths so as not to become ill.

"No, Emmaline, I can't come in. I just came by to thank you for what you did." He hesitated and thought before he spoke again. "And to tell you to be on guard."

"Fer what, honey? Your little woman gonna come around here?"

"I don't mean Jolyn. Luke isn't dead. Not yet, anyway, and I fear he may head back this way soon. We found him where you told us to look, but I wasn't able to kill him."

"Why you no-good two-bit piece of coal," Emmaline shrieked, suddenly remembering that Connor had left her behind. "I came back to your store so as I could go with you and you was gone. Why didn't you wait for me, you low-life?"

Connor had been afraid things might develop this way. Still, he kept calm, even though several doors had opened and a few heads had quickly popped out and then swooped back in again.

"I have to be going, Emmaline, only I wanted to tell you one important thing."

"I don't have to listen to you, Connor Richardson. The last time I listened to you, you lied. Get out of my life, you bastard, and I hope that red-headed bitch you wound up with poisons you with her cooking." Emmaline had had enough. She slammed the door in Connor's face.

Connor, too quick at losing his composure, shouted through the door.

"I just thought you might want to know, you blonde hussy, to be careful." And he stomped down the hallway and bolted out of the saloon.

Emmaline reopened her door, and, leaning against the doorjamb, chewing on a toothpick, she ran her broken red nails through her teased hair. She whispered softly to herself, "Thanks for nothing, Connor Richardson. Thanks for nothing."

Connor's next stop was the jeweler down the street. The owner of the store had been a steady customer of Connor's for a long time. Unfortunately, there was never anything Connor had wanted to purchase from him, until now. He strolled into the store and up to the counter.

"Travis," he called toward the back. "Good morning back there," he boomed. "You got a paying customer out here looking for some goods. Hey, Travis, wake up back there."

Two seconds later a small, peevish-looking man with a thick handlebar mustache came scampering out the back-room door. His hazel eyes darted back and forth, and he had a nervous twitch in his right cheek. He was drying his hands on an old worn-out checkered cloth and he was twisting and turning the rag so hard Connor coughed to suppress the laughter he was holding inside.

"Yes, Mr. Richardson. Why, good morning to you, sir. What can I do for you, sir? Why, this is an honor to have you come in. I'm not delinquent on my bills with you, am I, sir?"

This time Connor let go with a belly laugh so strong it rattled the glass counters on which Travis Clarkson was leaning.

"No, no, Mr. Clarkson. Why, I've just come to purchase something. Actually, I was interested in this nice little purple stone here." Connor pointed to the ring and Travis quickly brought it out for him.

"It's a beautiful amethyst, Mr. Richardson. In fact, an old miner by the name of Doc just brought it in to me a few days ago. I only set it in the ring yesterday. Why, if you touch it you can still feel the warmth it brung out from the cave walls."

"It looks fine to me," praised Connor. "I'll take it." After paying for his purchase Connor was out the door and on to complete another errand.

In the meantime, Jolyn had finally awakened to find Connor gone. She decided to make herself at home in her new place. Jolyn busied herself with cooking, cleaning, and then finally treating herself to a deliciously warm bath.

Her eyes were closed and she was on the edge of dreaming when she heard someone bounding up the stairs. Connor burst into the room. It had happened so quickly Jolyn screamed. She sat up abruptly in the wooden tub, the hot, steamy water sloshing over the sides.

"Connor, what?"

Connor had efficiently accomplished his errands. Standing there ogling his new wife was the pinnacle of his morning. Discovering her wet body glistening in the tub, Connor saw an opportunity he was not going to let pass him by. Before Jolyn could shriek another yelp he stripped naked and plunged into the tub with her.

"Aaaah, this does feel so good," he sighed.

"Connor, I really had intended on this being a party for one," admonished Jolyn. "After all, you leave me alone this morning, without telling me your whereabouts. I have to fend for myself for breakfast. I didn't even open the store yet, hoping to at least clean myself before presenting my tired, dirty body to the people of Creede for the first time as Mrs. Connor Richardson."

"Oh, oh, my wet, gorgeous wife," crooned Connor as he picked up her soapy arms and raised them in the air. "If you are telling me that you are indeed married to that wonderful man who owns so many stores in these parts, then please tell me, madame, where might I see a ring on your finger that tells the world that you belong to one such man?"

Jolyn blushed to the roots of her auburn tresses. She lowered her eyes and stared into the cooling sudsy water. "I am married to the most handsome man in the world, sir, however, due to a matter of inconvenience and other areas of a personal nature, this young admirable husband has not yet had the opportunity perchance to obtain the traditional wedding ring."

"So he's a cheap bastard! Is that what you're trying to tell me, my lady?" Connor's eyes twinkled.

"No, he is not cheap, I mean, he does have the financial security to purchase such a gift. I'm sure when the gentleman sees fit and as the occasion arises, I will receive such a present."

Connor could hold back no longer.

"Well, little lady, then you are in luck." Connor leaned over the tub for his pants and pulled out a small box. In all his nakedness Connor now presented his gift formally to Jolyn.

"Mrs. Connor Richardson, may I present you with this ring, which is but a small token of my love, my devotion…and my great desire to make wet, clean love with you in exactly thirty seconds."

Jolyn gasped as she opened the box, which contained the most beautiful amethyst ring she had ever seen.

"Oh, Connor, oh…it's beautiful…it's absolutely magnificent! Oh, how can I thank you?"

Connor did not reply. He did not have to use any words. He had already picked Jolyn up out of the tub and before the ring slid over her knuckle, the two young lovers were warming their clean, soaking bodies with the heat and passion of their love.

Chapter 23

TIME PASSED QUICKLY FOR THE newly married couple. Jolyn was busy helping Connor in the store and Connor was busy building his strong empire. A short while later, Chris and a very pregnant Annabel were waving goodbye to Connor and Jolyn at the train station.

It might have been February, but the Richardsons had decided to take a trip to Alamosa to see Hawk and his new wife, Lucinda, who was due to give birth at any time. After Alamosa the two were going to take a small trip down to Conejos to the cabin next to the Conejos River. Connor and Jolyn wanted to spend some time alone, without the pressures of the store and the townsfolk around them.

Jolyn was happy. She was going to see how Arliss was doing. She wanted to check on Lucinda and see how her pregnancy was coming along. Jolyn liked Creede, but the rowdy miners and the fighting men were a hard lot to deal with every day. In addition to the rough inhabitants, Emmaline kept coming to see Jolyn under the guise of buying something from the store. Before she would leave she always made some nasty comment about Connor or gave a fake compliment to Jolyn or said how she'd enjoyed seeing Connor the previous night. Jolyn knew it was all a pack of lies, but the constant stress of dealing with the woman had worn Jolyn down.

The sheriff visited Connor every two days or so without any news about Luke's whereabouts, leaving Connor in a sullen and depressed mood. Just when he was lifting himself out of his haze, John Light would make another surprise visit. Luke was seen in Wyoming near Hole-in-the-Wall. Then there was a bank robbery near Denver that supposedly included Luke. The Denver heist was the one James had told them about, where he was going to be forced to enter the bank and announce the holdup. A train was robbed on its way to Leadville and once again Luke's name was brought up. One day a miner from California came through and said he brought a message to a Mr. Richardson from another Mr. Richardson stating he'd be dropping by soon. So it was a great thrill and a huge relief for Jolyn when Connor suggested the two take this trip, even if it was in the dead of winter.

When Jolyn got on the train she seemed somewhat jittery. Connor tried joking, teasing, and even singing, but nothing worked. Instead they sat close together, holding hands while watching the scenery pass.

Arriving later that afternoon in Alamosa, Connor and Jolyn immediately went to the store, but found it closed.

"Something's wrong," cursed Connor. "Hawk would never close up like that."

"It must be Lucinda," said Jolyn. "Hurry, let's go to their new house. They must be there."

Twenty minutes later all four of them were laughing and crying at the same time. Connor and Jolyn had rushed over to the house only to find that Lucinda had indeed had the baby only late the night before. Hawk had been the one to help deliver the baby, but now that Jolyn was there, Lucinda was more than grateful for her help.

"You did a good job there, Hawk," joked Connor.

Hawk took it all in stride as he held little Mary Catherine in his arms. "Ain't she just the cutest little thing? She's got Lucinda's eyes and hair and nose and…"

"Aww, but now let's pray she doesn't grow your beard," piped in Jolyn. Hawk tossed her a heartwarming glance with his deep brown eyes. The burly man cradled the small baby sleeping snugly in his large hairy arms.

Connor and Jolyn enjoyed their stay with Hawk and Lucinda. After several days Lucinda cornered Jolyn alone.

"Jolyn, I really do want to thank you."

"Oh, Lucinda. For what? For helping you with the baby? I love doing that sort of thing."

"No, Jo. For something a lot more important. For Hawk."

"What do you mean, 'for Hawk'?"

"Jo," began Lucinda, "I know I wasn't the brightest girl. And there were times when I thought I would use Hawk and then move on and get me another man who would take me away from all this."

"Away from Alamosa?" laughed Jolyn. "I love this town!"

"Yes, you love it, but you've traveled. The furthest place I've been is to Creede and back. Why, you're going down to Conejos to the old hunting cabin and he's never even taken me there. Yet!"

"Hawk is a great guy, Luce. I really do love that man. From the first day he took me in and trained me in the store, why, there's been nothing but love in my heart for that big bear."

"That's just the point I'm trying to make, Jolyn. You see, while Hawk and I were seeing each other, why, even after I knew I was pregnant with Mary Catherine, I wasn't sure I should stay. I had these crazy thoughts of just picking up and going out West! I wanted to go to San Francisco. I wanted to build a life for me out there!"

Jolyn lowered her eyes. "Lucinda, I'm sorry you felt that way."

Lucinda sighed. "I know that now, Jolyn. For a while I was filled with so much anger and hatred for what could have been…well, it's not nice what I thought of most of the time. But anyways, it seemed that after Hawk went with Connor and Chris to find you and bring you home, why, I thought that might be the last time I would see Hawk. It was then that I realized how much I loved him and how badly I wanted to settle down wherever he was in this world. Whether it was Alamosa or San Francisco or anywhere else, it really didn't matter to me anymore. As long as I was with Hawk, my dream had come true. And now with our baby girl, why, I'm so happy I could just burst. I love that man, big as he is, and with a heart twice the size of his chest. And the way he is with our baby, why, it makes me cry just to think I almost missed out on all of this."

Jolyn was already in tears. Lucinda reached over and hugged Jolyn.

"Thanks, Jolyn. For listening to me, for being there for me, why, just everything!"

Just then the two men came back in the room, looked at each other in wonder, and said simultaneously, "Women!"

Early the next morning Connor and Jolyn left for Conejos. They said their goodbyes and left with promises to visit soon.

They had taken a carriage and two horses so they could travel comfortably this time. This trip held a different purpose for the couple; it was filled with love and joy for each. Snuggled underneath the heavy blankets, breathing in the cold, crisp mountain air, the two lovers embraced their journey.

Conejos was beautiful in the winter. The river cut through the mountains, slicing the snow-covered ground like a knife cutting butter. They set up all their belongings in the cabin and Connor immediately had a glowing fire dancing in the huge fireplace.

"This cabin has so many memories, but what is more important is that together we will build new memories filled with our love." The fireplace was made out of huge rocks brought in from the river and it reached from the floor to the ceiling. The hardwood floors shone with a brilliance that was only surpassed by the deep mahogany furniture on top of it. The bearskins and the elk heads lined the walls.

Jolyn loved everything about the cabin. Suddenly she said, "I think I'd better go down to the river and get some water."

"I'll go with you."

Together, arm in arm, they walked down to the river. The sun was a brilliant ball of fire in the sky and even though there was snow on the ground, the two did not need jackets. The air was so thin that the warm rays of the sun kept them warm and happy.

The river water was icy cold. There was a small wooden bridge that crossed the river to the other side. Jolyn could see a cave even from that distance.

"What's in the cave over there?"

"Oh, that's an old silver mine. It's been mined out and they closed it down a few years ago. It belongs to Hawk. We can go there tomorrow and scout around. Sometimes you can still pick up a few things."

Jolyn and Connor filled several pails of water. They returned to the cabin, ready to cook, eat, settle, and rest.

After dinner the two sat and talked for what seemed like hours. It was a time of peace and respite from their hard work at the store. Jolyn liked to talk about James. She was so thrilled that he and Nattie had finally married and James was going to be a father! Connor had agreed that come warm weather the two of them would travel up to northern Utah to see James, Nattie, and the new baby! Jolyn couldn't be happier. Sometimes she wished she could share her bliss with her parents, but in her heart, she knew they were watching her and smiling in joy.

The cabin chilled a bit as evening wore on and Connor finally said, "Come, let's lie down on the bearskin by the fireplace."

"And who caught that bear?" asked Jolyn.

"Well, actually it was me and Hawk, but that's a story for another night. Right now I think I'd like to see how that bear takes to having you lie on top of him."

"Well, Mr. Richardson, since we share so many of the chores and the responsibilities around here, I will only honor that request if you are there beside me."

"No sooner said than done, wife. I am only here to please you, my lady."

Lying naked on the bear with the glow of the fire on their bodies, Jolyn looked over at Connor lovingly and cooed, "You know, there was a time when I dreamed about this day, but never thought… I love you, Connor Richardson. Like the rushing river outside our doorstep that flows with eternal strength, so too will my love flow for you."

Connor gazed into her eyes, those beautiful, brilliant blue eyes, and whispered softly, "Jolyn, waking up with you at my side creates such an energy in me that I feel I can do anything in the world. My love for you is as strong as the mountains that surround us, my wife, and the day that these mountains should ever crumble will be the day that this earth falls apart."

And with that he sought her lips, ever ready and sweet for him. Jolyn returned his kiss with a fervor that would never be satiated. His tongue traveled down her neck, lingering on a pulsating throb in her neck. Warmed by the fire, his hands lingered on her breasts, kneading and stroking until Jolyn moaned with pleasure.

"Oh, yes, Connor, yes, my husband."

This time there was no one near them, in the next room or a few feet away. It was only them and the mountains and a desire that only their lovemaking could quench.

Jolyn rolled onto her back as Connor continued kissing and tasting her. Gently he prodded her knees and they fell apart, eager for his touch. Connor swooped up one long graceful leg and massaged her firm thigh. Tenderly he kissed the inside of her leg again and again until he reached her soft, satiny womanhood. Breathing in the lavender scent that belonged only to Jolyn, he tasted her silky inner being. She quivered beneath his kisses. Jolyn could no longer bear this sweet pleasure and grabbed Connor's hair with both her hands. Softly she cried out. An aching need burned through her. Sensing this, Connor sat up and placed his throbbing manhood next to her thigh. The burning organ seared Jolyn's satiny skin as she pulled him closer to her. Jolyn grasped Connor on the buttocks, massaging and squeezing him until his bulging manhood dove deep within her. Their rhythm was constant motion, fluid and graceful and hot as the burning flames next to them. Jolyn dug her nails into Connor's back as she moaned and writhed beneath his pulsating body.

They saw only each other. They needed only each other. Time was not important; they did not rush. Each moment was savored and slowly, languidly, the two touched and explored and tasted of each other. And finally, when they reached their highest peak together, they called out their names as their lips sought each other and sealed their love together, forever.

The week was spent to the fullest. The days were filled with discovering the countryside. They hiked over La Manga Pass and on another exploration discovered a beautiful falls on the other side of the Conejos River. Jolyn discovered a large chunk of silver deeply embedded in a piece of rock and Connor finally comprehended how much fun he had been missing in the past few years.

Their nights were filled with lovemaking and exploring each other's wants and desires. But after ten days they knew it was time to go home. They had shared a special time, but there were chores that had to be done, responsibilities that needed fulfilling. Life went on, and regretfully Connor and Jolyn headed home. They chose to ride the carriage all the way to Creede, to spend more time with each other before going back to the grind of their business.

At home, Jolyn and Connor were happy. Jolyn had fixed up the room above the store as their temporary home. Connor had purchased some land in Upper Creede, and they hoped to build a large home that summer.

In May, Annabel, with the help of Jolyn, delivered a healthy baby boy. They named him Samuel Henry in honor of the two deceased grandfathers. Chris and Annabel were the happiest parents she had ever seen.

Creede was still a boomtown, with hundreds of people pouring in daily. Connor's store grew and grew, and his business flourished throughout Colorado.

One night, in Tortoni's, Connor waited impatiently for Jolyn. She was supposed to meet him there for dinner and she was late. It was a special treat to eat out and it wasn't like Jolyn to be late, but Connor, hungry and irritable, was not in a forgiving mood.

Finally Jolyn arrived, looking pale and weak. She had been acting funny lately, Connor thought. Throwing up in the morning, giving up certain foods, and the other night he could have sworn she swooned while cooking dinner. Maybe I'll have her see a doctor in town, he mused. She can't always be her own doctor.

Jolyn sat down next to him. She knew he was angry with her. She kissed him quickly on the cheek and put her hands in her lap meekly.

"What's wrong?" he asked. Maybe she really was sick. Concern covered his face.

"Well, Connor. I think there's a problem with the design for the house."

"What?" he shouted. "We've gone all through that, Jolyn. What could possibly be wrong now?"

Jolyn smiled. She could not hold back any longer. She picked up his hands and held them. Lovingly she gazed into his eyes and whispered, "Connor, I think we're going to need another bedroom in the house. For a baby. Our baby. I'm with child."

Connor's mouth dropped. It couldn't be true. It was something he longed for and was too afraid to question her about, for fear he might upset her.

"Are you sure?" he asked delicately. Jolyn nodded. "Oh, Jolyn. Oh, Jo, that is absolutely the most fantastic, most wonderful news I've ever heard! I…I… "

Just then Sheriff John Light erupted into the restaurant. Connor looked up, his face radiant with pure joy.

"Excuse me, Connor," the sheriff said grimly. "We just found Emmaline dead over at Kirmeavy's. Stabbed to death. I'm sorry to inform you, sir, but you're under arrest for the murder of Emmaline."

Chapter 24

"EMMALINE? MURDERED?" CONNOR SHOOK HIS head in disbelief. "Granted, Sheriff Light, that does come as a shock, but why are you telling me and my wife?"

"Beggin' your pardon, ma'am, but rumors have it, Connor, that you and Miss Emmaline were purty close. I have eyewitnesses that say they've seen you visitin' with Miss Emmaline over at Kirmeavy's."

"Dammit, John, you know those rumors are a pack of lies. I....I.... once a very long time ago I was with her, but nothing....nothing. And besides, that was before and now, well, hell, how could anyone in his right mind think I would be interested in a two-bit whore like that when I have a woman like Jolyn?" Connor said angrily.

"I realize that, Connor," the sheriff agreed in his thick Texas drawl. "I find it hard to believe myself. But there's more. I've got witnesses that say you was over at Kirmeavy's last evenin' at the 'proxmate time that Emmaline was stabbed."

"You must be mistaken, Sheriff Light," said Jolyn matter-of-factly. "Connor was with me the entire evening. We both worked the store until ten, had a late-night dinner, and went to bed. And I assure you that Connor was with me all night."

Ex-gunman sheriff of police John Light, a tough, resourceful man, flushed beneath her perusal.

"I don't doubt that at all, ma'am. May me and mah assistant sit down for a moment?" John Light helped himself to a seat at the table and waved his assistant into the place next to him.

"Yes, go right ahead." Jolyn nodded ironically.

"Not a'tall, ma'am, not a'tall. Now, where was I? Oh, yeah. From what we can figure, Emmaline was killed sometime yesterday afternoon.

No one saw her after four p.m. Now, the bartender swears that he saw you, Connor, at the bar at near and about that time."

"Yes, that's true. I received a message saying someone could give me information on the whereabouts of my half-brother, Luke. I'm sure you're aware of this, Sheriff, but Luke was responsible for that recent train holdup in which my wife was kidnapped and nearly killed. I've been trying to track him down for some time now. Naturally I followed up on this most recent lead. I arrived at Kirmeavy's at about four, waited around for a half hour, and when nobody showed up, I left. If you talked to the bartender, certainly he told you the same thing."

"Yes and no. He remembers you all right, but he can't swear that you remained at the bar the whole time, or that when you left, you didn't go upstairs first."

"But certainly there were other witnesses. Lilly was running a poker game with Poker Alice the whole time I was there. I'm sure one of them saw me."

"Look, Sheriff Light, my husband is no murderer!" Jolyn clasped Connor's hand with hers. "Unless you have better proof than this for your accusations…"

"I'm getting to that, Mrs. Richardson. Now, before I move on, is there anyone else who might be able to back your story?

Connor thought hard for a moment. "I'm not sure. What about the boy who delivered the message to me? He shouldn't be too hard to find. He was about twelve years old. Brown hair. Brown eyes. Medium height. He was wearing an old Union jacket."

"I'm sorry, Connor. Do you realize how many boys in Creede fit that description? Pouring into Creede every day, roaming the streets, living in those shacks on Willow Creek. It'd be nigh impossible to track down a boy like that."

"That's your job, isn't it?" Jolyn remarked rather caustically.

"Easy, Jo. The man's only doing his job," Connor soothed.

Jo locked eyes with Connor. How could he remain so calm? Didn't he realize the seriousness of the sheriff's accusation?

"Well, Sheriff Light, if that's all, I think Connor and I will be leaving. I'm afraid I've lost my appetite."

"No, ma'am, that isn't quite all. The facts are that Connor was seen by several witnesses arguing with the deceased right outside her door. He was also seen at the saloon at the same time Emmaline was kilt. They also found a knife with the Richardson mark on the hilt lying next to the body. I'm real sorry, Connor, but until I find evidence to the contrary, I'm going to have to place you under arrest."

Connor glared threateningly at the two law officers who were slinking behind Light. He watched John Light slip his gun from its holster and cradle it in his palm. Connor glanced over at Jolyn's worried face and squeezed her fingers reassuringly.

"John, I really don't think that's necessary. Do you? If I promise not to leave town and agree to make myself available to you at any time, couldn't you place me under some form of house arrest? You know my word is good. And I'm worried about Jolyn's safety. I suspect that Luke is behind this, and if you lock me up, that'll make my wife little more than a sitting duck."

"I'm sorry, Connor, I can't do that. There's just too much evidence against you. Now, if you'll agree to come along quietly, no one will get hurt."

"Can you give me a few moments alone with my wife?"

Sheriff Light nodded, and with a signal to one of his assistants, he rose and moved toward the door.

"Jolyn, you've got to promise me that you'll go directly to Chris's. Under no circumstances are you to return home alone. Agreed?"

"But Connor, I'll need to pick up some clothes and an overnight bag."

"No!" Frustrated, Connor looked at Jolyn's stubborn jaw. "Listen, Jo. Luke is dangerous. I can't risk losing you. Please promise me that you won't return to the store."

Jolyn stared into Connor's concerned eyes and touched his cheek with her palm. "All right, Connor. I promise."

Connor rose and turned to where the two law officers were waiting with the sheriff. He whirled about and hesitated for a moment, as though he wished to tell her something. Instead, he bent forward and swiftly kissed Jolyn on the cheek. "Don't worry. Things have a way of working themselves out. Just be sure to go directly to Chris's when you leave here."

Jolyn watched as Sheriff Light and the two assistants escorted her husband from the dining room. Connor walked straight and tall among them, dwarfing the three men like a mountain spruce among three scrub pines. Jolyn stared at the door long after the men had passed through it. She was worried. The fact that John Light had so readily arrested a leading citizen like Connor meant that the sheriff must have found some very convincing evidence against him, and in Creede, the law acted first and listened later. She had to act quickly if she was going to save Connor, but what could she possibly do to help?

"Mrs. Richardson, you havva a leettle glass of wine before you go, yes?" Mrs. Galbardi, warm and matronly, patted Jolyn's cheek as she would a small child's. She poured a generous portion of Chianti into a glass and set it before Jolyn. "You drinka dis all up and den my boy, Guiseppe, he taka you where you wanta go."

"Yes, thank you," Jo murmured politely to the woman.

Mrs. Galbardi continued to hover over her table until Jolyn obediently took a sip of the red wine. Nodding approvingly, the warm-hearted woman scurried away to assist her other guests.

As customers bustled in and out, Jolyn sat numbly, her fingers curled loosely around the glass stem. Struggling against the waves of despair, she desperately sought a solution to the problem. There had to be one. There was the boy, of course, but that would take time, maybe weeks, and they didn't have weeks. Then there was the possibility of a witness who could swear that Connor had never left the bar, but the sheriff could probably find just as many drunks who could say that Connor did. There was the knife, but the sheriff would have only Connor's word that the knife was not his.

Jolyn sighed. She might as well head for Chris's. She motioned toward Mrs. Galbardi, who immediately hurried forward. "What do I owe you for the wine?"

"Owe? No, no. You no pay me nothing. You havva great heart and big problems. You no pay me nothing. Should I call for Guiseppe, now, yes?"

"Yes, Mrs. Galbardi, you may call for Guiseppe now." Jolyn smiled faintly. "And thank you so much for your kindness."

Mrs. Galbardi flushed with pleasure and then disappeared into the kitchen.

As Jolyn stared after her departing figure, her mind still churned. If Connor hadn't killed Emmaline, then someone else had. A vision of a broad, ugly knife worn on Luke's belt flickered through Jolyn's memory. Luke. If she could find one scrap of evidence that could prove that it was Luke's knife, that Luke had been in the saloon at the time of Emmaline's murder, then Connor would go free.

Excitedly, she snatched up her shawl and rushed from the restaurant. She had promised Connor not to return home; she had not sworn that she wouldn't stop anywhere else. Kirmeavy's was only three blocks away. She could sneak in by the back steps, then hopefully she could find Emmaline's room.

Jolyn was grabbed roughly from behind.

"Hey, honey, what's yer hurry. Ain't ya got time fer a rich miner?"

Jolyn fought wildly with elbows and feet. Using an old trick she'd learned from Hawk, she slammed her heel into her attacker's instep. The miner released her with a yowl. Without delay, Jolyn raced the length of the street, dodging through a few of the small groups that huddled in front of the more popular houses. When she reached the end, she glanced nervously behind her, but saw no sign of anyone following her.

Swiftly, she whirled onto Creede Avenue and headed briskly toward Willow Bridge.

Jolyn breathed a sigh of relief when she reached the backyard of Kirmeavy's. Stealthily, she climbed the steps to the second floor. She had just slipped through the door on the landing when she heard the warning click of a door opening to her left. She fumbled for the latch behind her, but it was too late. She stared into the surprised face of a woman of her own build and stature. Her hair was darker, though, her outfit flimsy, and her eyes speculative.

"You lookin' for someone, sugar?"

"Why, yes, that is, not someone, exactly." Jolyn wasn't sure how much she should reveal to the woman.

The woman shut the door and impatiently stepped into the light of the hallway. She looked much older than she'd first appeared. Makeup hung on her well-lined face like gaudy wallpaper.

"Husband? Boyfriend? Look, honey, my advice to you is to go home. He'll be back. They always go back."

When Jolyn still lingered in the hallway, the prostitute shrugged and turned away. She swayed toward the sounds of laughter and drunken shouts, the young woman at the door already forgotten.

"Wait. Please." Jolyn spoke desperately.

The woman wiped her running nose with her hands and paused without turning.

"I was a friend of Emmaline's," Jolyn continued, less urgently now, "and I'd like to see her effects. Could you tell me which room was hers?"

The woman turned then and narrowed her eyes suspiciously at Jolyn. "Emmaline had no friends. If you've come to steal…"

"Oh, no. It's nothing like that. I swear it. Look, I need to take a look around her room. It's important. If it's money you want…"

The prostitute gave one last measuring look, then shrugged. As she turned and continued down the carpeted hallway, she called back over her shoulder, "It's the second door on your left." And she disappeared down the staircase.

Jolyn hurried down the hall and darted into the room. She was immediately assailed by the sour odors of cheap perfume and old sweat. Leaning against the door with her shawl pressed against her nose, she waited for her eyes to adjust to the darkness. Soon she was able to discern shapes—bureau, screen, bed, and bedside stand. Cautiously stepping over the little mounds of shoes and clothes that were scattered across the floor, Jolyn made her way to the dresser, where she had spotted the dull gleam of an oil lamp's glass cover.

Out of the corner of her eye, she thought she caught some furtive movement to her left. Frightened, she froze and peered anxiously into the shadows around her. Nothing. Relieved, she crept once again toward the dresser. She would light the lamp, search the room for clues, and get out of there. As she reached for a match, she heard a low scraping sound. Alarmed, she whirled about, her hand reaching for a solid hand mirror that rested on the bureau top.

"Who's there?" she whispered, her voice hissing eerily in the room.

Nervously, she scanned the room. She could see nothing unusual in the dim light; nothing appeared different from when she had first entered Emmaline's chamber, and yet, something wasn't quite right. Maybe she should leave, get out while she still could. Nerves. She scolded herself. Just nerves. Jolyn took a deep breath and let it out slowly. She had come to help Connor, and help him she would.

Determinedly, Jolyn turned back to the dresser, set the mirror back down, and fumbled for a match. She had just grasped one with her fingertips when she heard a loud crash behind her. Before she could move, she felt a heavy weight land against her, crashing her forward into the dresser. She was pressed mercilessly against the brass handles, which dug into her flesh. One of her attacker's arms was wrapped tightly about her shoulders, trapping her arms to her sides. With his other hand he pressed a cloth that reeked with a sweet, cloying scent. Chloroform.

Jolyn twisted furiously in his arms, trying frantically to break free so that she could take in some air. Her attacker effortlessly tightened his hold, and Jolyn felt herself slipping helplessly into unconsciousness. With one last effort, Jolyn threw herself backward, praying that her weight would throw him off balance. Nothing. He was as unmovable as a rock face. Jolyn's world spun dizzily about her. She was caught in a whirlpool of liquid coal, her leadened body plunging downward, her head sinking after. She was drowning, drowning in darkness. Then she knew no more.

When Jolyn awoke, she was lying on the soiled, musty mattress of Emmaline's bed. Her hands were painfully bound behind her back, and she was gagged with a foul-tasting cloth. Surprisingly, her legs had been left free. Slowly, her head pounding and her stomach queasy, Jolyn rolled to her side. Curling her back and sliding her arms down behind her body, Jolyn managed to slip her arms in front of her. Clumsily, she tore off the gag with fingers made nearly useless by the constraining knots at her wrists. Gradually, Jolyn slipped her legs over the side of the bed and sat up.

In the early morning's first light, the curtainless room was stained red. Bits of lace and satin dotted the floor and hung from opened drawers. The bedside stand and dresser tops were layered with empty whiskey glasses, cheap baubles, and cigar stubs. Tacked onto a painted wooden screen, which stood in the far corner, was a poster of a younger Emmaline posing in a dance-hall dress. Jolyn stumbled to the screen and cautiously peered behind it. Only a flimsy robe and a cracked chamber pot sat behind it. In the corner lay a small pearl-handled gun, which must have been kicked there in some earlier scuffle.

Excitedly, Jolyn grasped it and checked the cylinder. It was empty. Discouraged, she dropped it to the floor.

After availing herself of the commode, Jolyn awkwardly tried the door. It was locked. She considered shouting for help, but she was uncertain of her captor's whereabouts. She couldn't run the risk of his hearing her. If it was Luke, having eluded him twice, she stood little chance of surviving another encounter. She hobbled stiffly to the window, but it was tightly jammed. No matter how hard she pressed against the jamb with her shoulder the window wouldn't budge. Her head had now begun to throb steadily, and her wrists ached painfully. She pressed her forehead against the cool glass and gazed despairingly into the empty yard below. She mustn't give up hope. She needed to find something sharp-edged; she would have a better chance with her hands free.

She eyed the liquor bottle lying beside the stand and eagerly reached over and picked it up. Using a towel, she wrapped the bottle to muffle the sound and knocked it with a resounding whack against the bedpost. The glass shattered a few inches below the lip. With great care, Jolyn rubbed the rope along the jagged edge of the bottle's base, pulling her hands back as far as possible. The glass kept slipping from under the rope, and Jolyn was constantly nicking her wrists and forearms, causing tiny rivulets of blood to trickle onto the glass. Determined, she squatted down and held the base between her feet. Again, she sawed the rope against the knifelike edge. This time the bottle remained still, and Jolyn grew excited as she saw the frayed edges give way. Only a few more seconds and she would be completely free from the rope.

She heard a rattle at the door. Panic-stricken, she worked her arms so that they were once again behind her back and scurried for the bed. Just as the door opened, she managed to curl up in the position in which she had awakened. She prayed that he would not notice the glass and could only hope that Luke would assume she had managed to slip off the gag without the use of her hands. Her head turned away from the door, Jolyn lay listening for her captor's approach. The room remained silent. Yet, even though she had not heard the door click shut, she could have sworn that someone had entered the room. She waited, counting slowly to a hundred. Still she heard no sound. Cautiously, she turned her head toward the door.

At the foot of the bed stood a creature that barely resembled a man. His clothes hung in shambles upon his scarecrow frame. A Colt dangled from his raw, bony hands. His greasy hair hung in uneven strands and framed his hollow-cheeked features. His face was pale and shadowed—a death mask. A ghastly purple gash, like raw meat, clung to the left side of his face. Only his eyes showed any sign of life. They glowed fiercely from some inner maniacal light. It was Luke, quite deadly, quite mad.

He grinned crazily. Then, reaching forward, he gripped her ankle and dragged her toward him. Kicking and screaming, Jolyn struggled wildly in his grasp, but Luke seemed oblivious to her blows. Inch by inch, he drew her forward until he was able to seize her about the neck and lift her up toward him. Coughing and choking, Jolyn strained against the knots that still held her wrists. If only she could get her hands free, she might stand a chance. Unexpectedly, Luke loosened his hold. Jolyn became dimly aware of shouting and banging on the bedroom door. Connor. It was Connor's voice.

"Connor!" Jolyn screamed joyfully. "I'm in here."

Luke seized Jolyn, lifted her off the bed, and held her in front of him. Facing the door, he brutally placed the barrel of his .45 against her forehead and drew back the hammer.

"Jolyn, you bitch," he spat dispassionately, "if you do not remain still, I will shoot you right now."

Jolyn immediately fell silent, and he grunted approvingly. Easing the hammer down, he pulled her back toward the window, where they stood starkly against the morning light that poured into the room.

With a thundering crash, Connor burst into the room, but drew up short when he spied Luke holding Jolyn like a shield before him. Although in the light Connor could see no more than her silhouette enshrouded in Luke's, Jolyn appeared to be unharmed.

"Let her go, Luke," Connor commanded quietly, his one hand holding his gun by his side.

Luke snickered crazily.

"I said let her go!"

"Oh, no," Luke hissed, "I give the orders now. Not Mother, not Father, not you. Me. Just me." Luke swung his gun wildly in the air.

Connor took a threatening step forward but was halted as Luke pressed the barrel of the gun harder against Jolyn's temple.

"Now, Connor, it's my turn to give the demands. Drop your gun," Luke hissed gloatingly.

Both Luke's and Jolyn's faces were obscured by the light behind them, and it was impossible to tell what either was thinking. With a feeling of helplessness, Connor dropped his gun.

"I'm going to kill you now, just like I killed our father. But before I do, I want you to know what I plan to do with your whore after you're dead. I plan to keep her with me for a very long time. She'll cook for me, clean for me, and whore for me just like her little boyfriend did when I took him that night!" Luke was so caught up in his bragging that he did not notice as Connor shifted dangerously close to him.

Luke's head snapped up in attention. His crazed eyes stared like two cold balls of iron. His yellow teeth dripped with spittle when he spewed out, "Don't try it, Connor! I'd just as soon kill her as take her with me. As a matter of fact, I'd love to see your face as she lies bleeding at your feet."

For one insane moment, Connor thought Luke would shoot Jolyn right then. Connor stepped back hastily, and his movement seemed to electrify Luke back to reality.

Glaring triumphantly at Connor, Luke openly fondled Jolyn with his free hand. "When I'm through with her, when she's all used up, I'll sell her in some saloon to the highest bidder. Oh yeah, she's gonna be real sorry she crossed me."

Jolyn gave no sign that she had heard Luke's words. Connor tried to discern Jolyn's expression, but she was still a dark shadow against the growing bright light. Could she see him clearly? Did she see how much he loved her? Did she understand that he was willing to die as long as she and their unborn child would go on living? If only he had explained to her that he and Sheriff Light had faked the whole arrest as a scheme to trap Luke. Maybe she wouldn't be here now.

"Jolyn, I…"

"No more talk. From now on, the only voice she'll be hearing is mine."

Luke smiled mockingly at Connor. Connor's anguished expression was everything Luke had hoped for in this confrontation. This was how he had envisioned his final encounter with his half-brother. Slowly, he aimed the Colt toward Connor's chest. The gun felt heavy and swollen in his feverish hand. Luke gripped the gun, but his sweating hands betrayed him. As he slowly pulled the trigger, a tremendous surge of power pulsed through him, and for a split second he reveled in its force. It rushed through him, swelling to an insurmountable height. This was Luke's shining moment.

Until, at the precise instant that Luke pulled the trigger, Jolyn flung her body against Luke's raised arm, and the bullet aimed for Connor's heart struck harmlessly into the wall. As Luke had bragged incessantly, he had been oblivious to Jolyn's writhing body in front of him. She had managed to work her hands free and now she clung recklessly onto Luke's gun arm as he thrashed her from side to side in an attempt to shake her off.

"Jo," Connor shouted, "Let go. Run!"

Jolyn did not move swiftly enough. With one mighty blow of his left fist, Luke knocked her senseless across the room.

Enraged, Connor launched himself into Luke and the two of them crashed onto the floor. The floorboards cracked under the impact of the two men's weight. Kicking and flailing, the two men rolled across the floor, each fighting for possession of Luke's gun. With a violent twist, Connor managed to lock Luke's body beneath his own. He gripped Luke's hand, which still clutched the .45, and smashed it repeatedly against the leg of the bed. Luke dropped the gun. With his forearm, Connor placed a stranglehold on Luke's neck, but Luke snapped his wrist. With a brutal jab to Connor's face and a knee-jam to his groin, he freed himself. He sprang upward and raced out the doorway.

Connor tore after him and charged full-force into Luke's retreating back. Connor's powerful frame slammed Luke against the wall, shattering the hanging oil lamp. Grunting noisily, the two men grappled for dominance. Neither noticed the flames that burst into a hundred tiny fountains sending rivulets of fire in every direction. Luke plowed an elbow into Connor's chest, and Connor stumbled backward. Once again Luke tried to escape. He scrambled toward the stairwell, and Connor dove after him. Connor tackled him around the knees. Caught off balance at the top of the stairs, both men tumbled in a welter of arms and legs to the bottom of the steps.

They lay momentarily still. Luke attempted to push himself up, but with a groan he slumped back down to the floor in an exhausted heap. Connor, who had rolled several feet into the room, staggered to his feet. Ignoring the surprised stares of the few die-hard gamblers still playing poker at six in the morning, Connor stumbled over to the bar, where he knew Andy kept his rifle. Andy was already there, passively handing him the butt of the Winchester.

"There are two shots in the chamber," Andy stated flatly.

Connor nodded and, gasping for air, turned back toward Luke, who now lay half-propped on the bottom stair. Connor stopped a few feet short of Luke, cocked the rifle, and took careful aim. Connor regarded his half-brother with loathing and fury. This was the man who had cold-bloodedly killed Connor's father, Jolyn's other brother, and her uncle, let alone countless others. He'd wounded his sister to the point that she almost died. This was the man who'd kidnapped Jolyn's friend. Luke had brutally stabbed his Emmaline for snitching and framed Connor for the murder. This was the monster who had kidnapped, abused, and nearly killed his wife, who meant more to him than life itself. Rage ripped through him, and he fingered the trigger idly. Unkempt, sweating profusely, and bleeding, Luke glared dazedly back. Connor lifted the rifle and aimed for his heart. Luke was vermin, and he deserved to die. This diabolical murderer had to pay for his sins.

Suddenly, an explosion of sparks rained down upon them. A scorching wave of heat whooshed down the stairs and hit them like a blast of steam. Connor, his arm upraised to protect his face from the searing heat, looked up to the witness the entire second floor in roaring flames. He could hear the screams of the women caught in the blaze. No one could possibly survive such an inferno.

"Jolyn!" Connor screamed. He dropped the rifle. Without thinking, he made a dash for the steps. As he leaped over Luke's body, his heel was caught, and he was thrown off balance. He tried to catch himself but missed the balustrade and tumbled back onto the floor. He felt a booted foot planted against his chest, and he was shoved onto his back.

Shocked, Connor looked up into the barrel of the rifle. Luke's deformed face, twisted by his hellish grin, rose ghoulishly behind it.

A gun roared. Connor's body was jolted back from the power of the blast. Stupefied, Connor watched the bright red stain as it spread across Luke's chest. Luke toppled forward, the rifle slipping uselessly from his lifeless hands. He was dead.

Epilogue

While the world is filled with sorrow,
And hearts must break and bleed,
It's day all day in the day-time
And there is no night in Creede.
Cy Wyman

SHROUDED IN FLAME, JOLYN STOOD frozen at the top of the stairs, Luke's .45 slipping from her nerveless fingers. Connor watched with growing fear as the fiery rafters fell about her.

"Run to me!" he screamed.

Horrified, Connor saw the flames licking a path toward her feet. Hungry sparks exploded from the dry wood and showered all about her.

Connor vaulted up the stairs and seized her in his arms. Holding her tightly against him, he leaped wildly down the steps and careened toward the door, ducking the falling timbers that crashed in his wake. Gratefully, he burst through the door, the cool, moist air soothing his aching lungs.

Jolyn slipped from his arms, her hands still gripping his neck, and hugged him to her.

"You're here. You're alive." She stroked his face wonderingly.

"Jo, Jo, I almost lost you."

Slowly, they became aware of the noise and confusion around them. They looked back at Kirmeavy's saloon, stunned to find that the building was now little more than a pile of smoldering rubble.

Shocked, Connor and Jolyn stared at the frail wooden shacks that lined Willow Creek ablaze before them. Fanned by the warm canyon breeze, the fire was spreading rapidly toward the business district, consuming everything in its path. Women screamed as they wrenched their children from their burning homes and plunged into the shallow creek waters. Men dashed about firing warning shots into the early morning sky. Bob Ford's canvas tent and those like it were already little more than cinders. A few blocks away, the whistle of the train pierced a warning cry, and bells clanged in alarm.

Jolyn suddenly broke free from Connor's embrace and mindlessly dashed along the street, fighting the hysterical crowd in an attempt to reach Richardson's. She raced against the blaze as it swept like a red monster, devouring building upon building along Creede Avenue.

"Jolyn," he cried, "no!" But his voice was lost amidst the frantic cries of the chaotic citizens.

Connor rushed into the throng, desperately shoving people out of his way. Jolyn was heading for the Big Bridge, which Connor could see was already a sheet of fire. To his left the Orleans Club belched forth scores of half-dressed inhabitants and showered the mob with flying sparks and crackling timber.

Jolyn was caught in a sudden surge of fleeing bodies and was borne helplessly back, unable to reach the bridge before it collapsed into Willow Creek.

Chris. Annabel. There was no way to reach them. She sobbed hopelessly.

"Jo!" Connor shouted. "Jo!" This time Jolyn miraculously heard him and turned in the direction of his voice.

"Here! Here!" she wept breathlessly. Connor searched the crowd. Smoke-ravaged, feverish faces flashed by him. The shifting horde parted slightly, and he spotted a small mass of crimson hair burnished by the flames around them.

He squeezed through the crowd once more. He lunged forward and seized her arm. Jo whirled about, her face racked with tears. Connor clutched her to him.

"Chris! Annabel! Little Sam!" Against Connor's shoulder, her muffled voice cracked. "Oh, Connor, I couldn't reach them. How could they possibly have survived?"

"Shhh, Jo, we'll find them," he soothed. "We'll find them."

"But how? The bridge is gone, and the whole block has caught fire. Our store. Everything. Gone." Her body shook with uncontrollable sobs.

Connor led her away from the crowded street. Without looking back, he sidestepped the debris that littered the street and headed for the Brainard and Beebe Hotel, the only building on the east bank left unscathed from the fire.

"Connor!" Chris's voice rang out from the hotel boardwalk. "Thank God you're both safe. Bel has been frantic with worry."

As if in a dream, Jolyn lifted her head. She brushed back a mass of tendrils from her soot-stained face and stared into Chris's welcoming one. Annabel stood by his side, cradling their son in her arms. Jolyn rushed into Chris's arms.

"How did you ever manage to get away in time?"

Annabel glanced sheepishly at Connor and then at her husband.

"I'll let the men explain."

Chris handed Jo back to Connor and shuffled his feet nervously.

"Remember, Jo, we had your welfare in mind. You see, Annabel and me had orders to wait for you back at the house. When you arrived from the restaurant, we were to hide you there. Connor suspected that Luke was close. He didn't want to take any chances with you or Annabel getting hurt. When Connor found out that you had never showed up at our place, he told us to get over here anyway. He said when he'd found you, he'd carry you here himself."

"Connor?" Jolyn asked, surprised. "But Connor was arrested?"

"Oh, that." Chris shrugged. "That was just a plot to lure Luke out into the open."

Connor's arm tightened affectionately around Jo's shoulders.

"I didn't count on your going off on your own," he murmured against her hair.

"Well, what did you expect me to do? Sit idly by while my husband was hung for a murder he didn't commit? And why didn't you tell me what you were planning?"

"As honest and as straightforward as you are? I wasn't sure you would be able to give a convincing enough performance."

Jolyn wasn't sure whether or not she should hit her beloved or thank him.

"Connor's not the only one guilty of keeping secrets. What about you, Jo?" Annabel smiled conspiratorially. "Have you told him yet?"

Jolyn's hand smoothed her small growing mound.

"Oh, yes, he knows." She nearly burst with laughter at her brother's shocked expression and her husband's foolish grin.

Now that the explanations were over, the two couples turned toward the business district, which had been razed to the ground. It had taken a little over two hours for the conflagration to burn an area a half mile long and an eighth of a mile wide. Now, only the delineation between dirt road and ashes marked where the buildings had once been. Incredibly, a few canvas tents had already sprung up on the blackened, not-yet-cool earth. Hundreds of mining men, speculators, gamblers, dance-hall girls, and businessmen stood, mounted like statues on a wasteland of dreams. Beyond, the Mammoth Mountains loomed.

Awestruck, the four gazed at their dreams now turned to ashes. They saw before them man's vulnerability against the backdrop of nature's impregnability.

Little Sam stirred, then released a wail that split the suspended silence.

Annabel hushed the infant, crooning softly as she gently stroked his chubby cheeks.

"Excuse us," she said shyly. "It's time for his feeding. Chris, are you coming?"

Chris nodded, and the two strolled quietly into the hotel.

Hand in hand, Connor and Jolyn left the hotel's porch and walked the few blocks toward the remains of Richardson's Trading Post.

As they stared at the ashes and twisted timber that had once been their home, they felt ravaged.

"It's gone," Connor whispered desolately. "All gone."

Jolyn grasped Connor's hand and held it against her swollen belly. He felt a soft kick tickle his hand.

No. He gazed lovingly into Jo's wise face. Not all gone.

"Wood, sir?" asked a youth passing by. "Rio Grande freighter just arrived with a new shipment, but there ain't no lumber yard to store it in. Mr. Rakestraw is donatin' lumber to anyone willin' to carry it away. You interested?"

"You bet," said Connor. "I'll need all you can carry. And, boy!" Connor called after him.

"Yes, sir?"

"See if you can find a few friends," Connor called after the boy's retreating figure. "I'll pay a dollar per head for every load. I've got a store to build!"

Jolyn curled her head happily against Connor's shoulder. She looked at the destruction that surrounded them and for a moment sobbed with despair. But then she turned and lifted her head toward the mountains that rose majestically to the heavens. Their love was like the mountains, she believed. Powerful, unyielding, and sustaining. Out of the ashes, there would be new growth, and Jolyn and Connor would build a new life, together.